This is a collection of superlative stories—comic and tragic, exciting and thoughtful, passionate and reflective — from five countries: the United States, Russia, Ireland, Italy and Spain.

Some of the authors are world-famous, others nationally praised, still others relatively unknown. No single thread connects their stories, but they have two qualities in common: their feeling about life is serious and profound, and as they reveal us to ourselves, they also entertain us.

These are, in short, great stories.

FELIPE ALFAU

SAUL BELLOW

LUIGI PIRANDELLO

WALTER VAN TILBURG CLARK

KATHERINE ANNE PORTER

F. SCOTT FITZGERALD

JAMES JOYCE

WILLIAM GOYEN

JOAQUIN ARDERIUS

PEGGY BENNETT

ISAAK BABEL

J. F. POWERS

JAMES AGEE

13

great
stories

EDITED BY DANIEL TALBOT

a dell first edition

Published by DELL PUBLISHING COMPANY, INC.

261 Fifth Avenue, New York 16, New York

© 1955, by Daniel Talbot

Designed and Produced by Western Printing & Lithographing Company

Printed in U.S.A.

ACKNOWLEDGMENTS: The following selections in this anthology are reproduced by permission of the authors, their publishers or their agents:

"The Beggar from LOCOS": A Comedy of Gestures, by Felipe Alfau; © 1936, by Felipe Alfau. By permission of Rinehart & Company, Inc.

"Looking for Mr. Green" by Saul Bellow, © 1951, by Commentary Magazine. By permission of Russell & Volkening, Inc.

"The Jar" by Luigi Pirandello, from BETTER THINK TWICE ABOUT IT, © 1934, by Luigi Pirandello. Published by E. P. Dutton & Co., Inc.

"Hook" by Walter Van Tilburg Clark, from THE WATCHFUL GODS AND OTHER STORIES, © 1940, by Walter Van Tilburg Clark. By permission of Random House, Inc., New York.

"The Downward Path to Wisdom" by Katherine Anne Porter, © 1939, by Katherine Anne Porter. From THE LEANING TOWER AND OTHER STORIES, by permission of Harcourt, Brace and Company, Inc.

"The World's Fair" by F. Scott Fitzgerald, originally published in Kenyon Review; © 1948, by Frances Scott Fitzgerald Lanahan. By permission of Harold Ober Associates.

"The White Rooster" by William Goyen, © 1947, by William Goyen. From GHOST AND FLESH, by permission of Random House, Inc., New York.

"Two Gallants" by James Joyce, from DUBLINERS, included in THE PORTABLE JAMES JOYCE, © 1946, 1947, by the Viking Press, Inc. By permission of The Viking Press, Inc., New York.

"The Bath of Death" by Joaquin Arderius © 1955, by Angel Flores. By permission of the copyright holder.

"And I am Black, but O! my soul is White" by Peggy Bennett, from THE VARMINTS, © 1946, by Alfred A. Knopf, Inc.

"Benya Krik, the Gangster" by Isaak Babel from BENYA KRIK, THE GANGSTER AND OTHER STORIES, edited by Avrahn Yarmolinsky, © 1948, by Schocken Books, Inc., New York.

"The Eye" from PRINCE OF DARKNESS AND OTHER STORIES by J. F. Powers, © 1947, by J. F. Powers. By permission of Doubleday & Company, Inc.

"The Morning Watch" by James Agee, © 1950, by James Agee. By permission of Houghton, Mifflin Company.

contents

The Beggar

FELIPE ALFAU

Felipe Alfau was born in Spain, and came to this country at the age of fourteen. His ambition was to become a music conductor and composer; achieving neither, he wrote music criticism for a brief period for La Prensa, the Spanish newspaper in New York. He decided to write in English because he felt that he could not reach a Spanish audience. His first book of fiction, LOCOS: A Comedy of Gestures, written in 1928 when he was under twenty, was published eight years later by Farrar and Rinehart. In 1929 Doubleday published a children's book of his. He stopped writing for over twenty years and has been working in a bank in New York City as a translator. Alfau has recently completed a novel, as yet unpublished.

IT IS LONG SINCE begging took alarming proportions in Spain. This situation is now definitely established upon a safe, sure basis, having taken deep root in the Spanish soil. It is now a broad, solid organization which grows steadily. Begging in Spain is, besides a respectable occupation, a profitable business and an enviable profession.

Much has been said about the corrupted ways of beggary in Spain, such a topic being one of the general themes of conversation and dispute which resound in all social classes except those composed of the cream of this type. Much has been said about the sincere ways of beggary in Spain, especially since the law forbade the exercise of this profession in its purest sense openly, that is, without the aid of some small merchandise as, for instance, pencils or shoestrings. I know not whether such a law still obtains.

During the days following the promulgation of this law, which applied to the beggar as well as the beggee, a certain individual by the name of Garcia was walking in no particular direction, carefully scrutinizing the face of every passer-by with the intention of discovering some friend or acquaintance, no matter how remote, or even a faint family likeness to someone he knew, that he might accost the person in order to borrow some money to pay his room and board.

Garcia was not a beggar. He did not wear the uniform. In other words, he was well dressed. Garcia belonged to another profession which, although having many fundamental points in common with it, is not precisely begging. The profession to which Garcia belonged may appear at first sight more brilliant than begging, since in a single stroke and with a bit of good luck it can net as much as a whole week's earnings from hard, honest labor at straight begging, but under a closer examination it proves to be less profitable in the long run, and begging is a much better one in principle as the field is not so restricted.

Garcia belonged to a profession just as popular as that of begging and which counted on just as skillful performers. Garcia boasted of being one of the best exponents, but now he was disappointed and tired of it. It required too much subtlety and brain work, too much being on one's guard. Garcia was willing to give up. This fact, considering that Garcia was one of the high lights of his class, proves that it was not as sound as that of begging, as I never heard of a beggar willing to give up.

Yes, Garcia had decided to give up. As a matter of fact, a friend of his, a certain Don Gil Bejarano, had offered him a position in the office of the Prefect of Police, his brother-in-law, as a fingerprint expert. Fingerprints were Don Gil's mania and he had taught Garcia all he knew about them, perhaps more. Don Gil had offered Garcia the position provided Garcia were willing to let Don Gil have part of his pay, and Garcia had accepted. This was, of course, a secret pact of which Garcia expected to rid himself as soon as he could devise a plan to do so.

But, the position did not begin until next month and Garcia knew that he would not get his pay until the end of that month. Like most people of his profession and caliber, Garcia exercised a tremendous amount of delicacy concerning money that he might earn through such a conventional profession as the one he was about to embrace. When Don Gil made him the offer he did not want to show any hurry or eagerness for fear of losing the position; quite the contrary, he had acted nonchalant and carefully avoided asking to begin earlier. Garcia did not want Don Gil to suspect that he was pressed for money, lest Don Gil might make the terms worse.

The dialogue ran something like this:

Garcia—"Oh, any old time."

Don Gil—"Will next month do?"

Garcia—"Certainly, whenever you want; there is no hurry."

Don Gil—"All right, next month, then."

Garcia—"By the way, can you let me have five?"

And Don Gil had refused.

Garcia had decided to give up his profession in view of this last blow to it, and definitely accept what Don Gil offered. The thing had been arranged for next month and it would be six weeks before Garcia could get his pay. This was the reason why at the present moment he was looking for some victim upon whom to deliver the last stroke of the profession he was forsaking.

However, luck was not with Garcia and so far he had not discovered a single face offering the slightest excuse for an approach. Garcia was rather despondent. He had not eaten since the night before, he had in his pocket exactly a five centimes copper piece and a twenty-five pesetas gold piece. This latter, of course, did not count, for Garcia based upon it much of his social effect.

It is quite fashionable in Spain to have a sentimental story to display at café tables, or at a bench in El Prado, late at night, or at the moment of exchanging confidences. The sentimentalism about *The Mother* is a question that carries weight in Spain to exculpate an inexculpable individual. One often hears people say:

"He may be a crook or a criminal, but he loves his mother," and that settles it.

Well, Garcia, once in a time of buoyancy, decided to make an investment. He bought a twenty-five pesetas gold piece which he always carried about with him, and whenever anyone remarked about it, he would say:

"Yes—" here an effective sigh—"my mother gave it to me on the day of my first communion"—a skeptical smile—"I shall always keep it with me. No matter how hard up I may have been at times, I never dreamed of changing it. Some people may think it silly, but what the devil! A mother is a mother, you know we only have one mother"—(profound silence and a dreamy expression). Garcia had always considered it a great drawback to his profession not to be able to produce tears at will.

And now Garcia was facing the problem of having to change the twenty-five pesetas gold piece and dispense with his sentimental tale, since now he had a job and would probably need it no more.

It was while thus occupied that he was accosted in his turn by a beggar.

Garcia's first impulse was to laugh long and loud, but knowing that a gentleman should never take such liberties with a beggar, he repressed his desire. Besides, should he refuse, he feared his financial condition would be suspected. Even an unknown beggar's opinion counts under certain circumstances. Therefore, Garcia took the man into a doorway (for it was forbidden to give alms in public) and gave him the five centimes piece.

Immediately after, he went to a café across the street in order to change the twenty-five pesetas gold piece.

With a heroic and resolute gesture that was to put an end to his past life, Garcia slammed the coin on the counter:

"Change, please."

The man on the other side of the counter looked at the coin and at Garcia.

"Change for what?" He shouted loudly, brutally, cruelly. . . .

Garcia looked at the coin and then realized that he had given the beggar the gold piece.[1] Without regarding the other

---

[1] *Garcia had other plans for this story, but by substituting one coin for the other and creating an unexpected situation for him, I have him at my mercy. He has now no time to formulate a new plan of battle and I can make him do as I please and have the story follow along the lines I choose.*

man's leer, Garcia picked up the coin and ran out of the café like a madman.

"Better use more sand on that *perro chico* next time!" shouted the man at his back.

In two leaps Garcia was back on the spot of the accident, but the beggar was gone. He inquired from other beggars the whereabouts of a man of such and such a description.

"He always closes at six," prompted a fellow without legs, from the floor. "He has this post during the day and I have it at night."

Another beggar told him the name and address, explaining how to get there, with his only hand.

"Una limosnita por amor de Dios," said the fellow without legs.

"Perdone, hermano," answered Garcia, rushing away. He did not want to part with his only coin.

Garcia walked in the direction he had been given, his heart sinking at every step. He felt surprised after a while at finding himself in a prosperous part of the town, by far more prosperous than the one in which he lived. He found the address in a modern building.

Before the doorman, Garcia hesitated, and if the doorman had not noticed him, Garcia would have turned on his heels.

However, the doorman had seen him and the doorman had asked:

"Que desea, caballero?"

It was too late. Garcia inquired purely in a formal way, feeling quite sure of the answer:

"El Señor Don Laureano Baez?"

"Principal derecha," was the laconic answer.

Garcia was nonplused. He ascended two flights of stairs making different conjectures at each step. He rang the bell on the right-hand side door and before he had time to think what he could say if this Laureano Baez was not the Laureano Baez, a girl opened the door.

"El Señor Don Laureano Baez?"

"Si, señor, pase usted."

Garcia advanced over the carpeted corridor feeling like an intruder, feeling his false position when he should annoy the respectable and important citizen Don Laureano Baez with his stupid inquiry.

"Will you please come into the dining room? He is having his dinner and will see you there."

Garcia saw an opening:

"Oh, I wouldn't think of interrupting him now. I will come back some other time. I did not know I was intruding. If I had only known . . ."

But the girl would not have him depart. He insisted, but she persisted in almost a diabolical manner, Garcia thought.

And then he was ushered into the dining room and there was his man.

Accustomed as Garcia was to remembering people's faces, he could not connect the two individuals for the first few seconds, so startling was the difference in appearance. He was facing a respectable and venerable gentleman of advanced age, dressed in quiet good taste, sitting at a copious dinner in which Garcia's quick eye discovered a bottle of excellent Rioja wine, another bottle of Ojen and part of a chicken roasted just so.

The least that can be said is that Garcia was flabbergasted. He felt sure that he was in the presence of no less a personage than the Minister of Finance.

And the man also recognized him and rose in the best style:

"Well, how are you? Sit down, sit down; won't you have a bite? A customer," he explained to the girl.

"Oh, yes?" said she with a solicitous air.

All this should have banished the last doubts in Garcia's mind but now he felt small, shrinking, like a poor man who has come to ask a favor or recommendation instead of a reimbursement. He did not know how to begin and fell on the chair which the girl pushed against the back of his legs. Since he gave the coin to that man sitting in front of him, every move he had taken had been forced. He felt in front of a superior character that for the past hour or so had been playing with him.[1] Following a confusion of ideas, very natural in his condi-

---

[1] *That is what Garcia felt, but although he does not know it, I am the one who is forcing his actions. Since I had the inspiration of substituting the coins I have had him in my power and now can confidently leave him in the expert hands of the reliable veteran Don Laureano Baez.*

tion, Garcia attributed the results of mere coincidences to the powerful will which emanated from the strong personality into whose lair he had been trapped. The man was now regarding him without reserve, with a gay smile. But Garcia did not cough or swallow, he just began:

"I trust that you will not consider me impertinent if I . . ."

"Of course not!" exclaimed the beggar without waiting to hear what the impertinence might be, and he filled a small glass with Ojen and offered it to Garcia, and also pushed toward him a golden cigarette case.

Garcia swallowed the Ojen and declined the cigarettes. After the past incidents he needed some restorative and something to give him courage to go on. The Ojen must have been powerful because Garcia hesitated no more and laid his soul bare:

"I am glad to see that you remember me. This afternoon I gave you a coin."

The beggar nodded his head in an affirmative way. Garcia poured some Ojen in the beggar's glass and then filled his own.

"I am sorry to have been compelled to take this step, but this afternoon I gave you a twenty-five pesetas gold piece by mistake."

The beggar raised his brows and opened his mouth, but Garcia did not let him speak.

"Of course, it is not the money. I could never dream of taking back what I give, even through an error." Garcia emptied his glass and the beggar imitated him, dissolving his action in a gesture which meant that he did not doubt his guest in the least.

"Excellent Ojen!" exclaimed Garcia.

"Ojen Morales," was the indorsing answer.

"As I was saying, it is not the money; of course, you know that. But that coin is not like all other coins. . . ."

The beggar rose:

"My dear man, you do not have to explain. An error, that is more than enough. We all make mistakes." He turned to the girl. "Lunarito, get me my begging suit." He addressed Garcia. "I have not emptied the pockets yet. Your coin must be there still. . . ."

Garcia also rose.

"Of course, it is not the money, Don Laureano,"—he felt friendly toward his host—"and I could not dream of taking it back without explaining to you. That coin means a lot to me."

"I do not doubt that," said the beggar uncompromisingly, and he filled Garcia's glass again and then his own.

Lunarito entered carrying with difficulty a bunch of rags of unsuspected weight, undoubtedly the begging suit, and laid it on the beggar's half-outstretched arms as an acolyte would lay a cassock on his priest's hands. The beggar cleared part of the table and emptied his pockets one by one.

Soon there was a pile of coins upon the table, a pile of such dimensions that it was difficult to understand how it could come from those rags which now hung limp.

Garcia spotted his coin among the abundant copper but he was too delicate to reach for it. He drank his third glass of Ojen instead, eying the coin surreptitiously.

The beggar also saw it.

"Aha, there you are, sir. As you see, we nearly always get copper." He handed the coin to Garcia. "I am sorry you had to come all the way here, although it is a pleasure to have you with us."

Such graciousness from his host overcame Garcia. He felt that the coin was decreasing in importance. He felt for the man in front of him the utmost admiration. He was conscious of remarkable changes inside of him, he was aware that there was a revolution going on in his brain and suddenly felt sentimental. He now considered that the most important find that day had not been that of his golden coin, but that of this great character whose existence he did not suspect in the world. The broad, frank figure of the beggar was standing before him, leaning on the table flooded with coins. Garcia had never seen so much money at once. He sank back into his chair and regarded the beggar with open mouth, shaking his head with a seraphic smile.

"Lunarito, take that money and throw it in the drawer."

"I would have never taken it back from you . . . but that coin . . ."

"We will speak of something else, if you please." The beggar sat down again.

Garcia turned the coin in his hands and insisted:

"No, I must tell you. . . . Yes, your generosity . . ." He felt eloquent, but somehow the thoughts seemed to escape his mind, they seemed to be thoughts that had a will and words of themselves, that threatened to pour out of his mouth, disregarding his critical ability which appeared to be weak. The beggar was looking at him with an indulgent smile. Garcia made an effort. He filled his glass and emptied it.

"Yes . . . my mother—" Garcia attempted a sigh. His throat closed and quenched it. . . . "My mother gave it to me on the day of my first communion . . ." he attempted the skeptical smile, but he knew that it was only a grimace—"I shall always keep it. . . ." He could not remember the speech he had so often delivered. There was something else that he wanted to say. "Some people think it silly . . . yes, there is only one mother, you know . . . there is only one mother. . . . Oh! There is only . . ." He felt choking, for once tears were coming to his aid. No, to spoil his acting, to give him away. He did not suspect himself capable of producing tears and now he wished. . . .

The beggar was watching him from the other side of the table with that profound, wise smile of his, and there was greatness in his countenance. Garcia felt small and mean before that man. He knew that the beggar could read through him, that he was laughing at him, at his efforts and failing attempts at hypocrisy; resenting having his intelligence offended so grossly. Garcia knew that he was a poor amateur before a great master in a profession greater than his, in a great profession; a man who had grown white hair playing on human sympathy and sentiments; a man who understood, with whom all this farce was unnecessary and useless.

And the beggar was watching him and smiling indulgently, almost like a father to a son, seeing through him, looking through him and recognizing beyond this miserable Garcia infinite other Garcias whom he had encountered in his long, intense life, disappointed at finding that people are always false and weak, that they lack the courage to be direct, that a man would lower himself to try and deceive a master for a small golden coin. And Garcia could no longer meet the smiling eyes of the beggar and felt the blood mounting to his cheeks; he felt ashamed, another new feeling he owed to this extraordinary man, and an overwhelming desire to be sincere, to confess to this understanding soul; he felt repentant and that tears were pushing their way out mightily. . . . And then Garcia burst out crying and reached across the table and pressed the beggar's hand.

"That story I told you about my mother giving me the coin is not true . . . it is not true. . . . I am just a dirty liar. . . . I have repaid your generosity with a lie. . . . My mother never gave me such a coin, I bought it myself." Garcia's expression was now quite comical, his staring eyes trying to assume an appealing look and the saliva dripping from the corner of his mouth. "My mother never gave it to me. I only said that for effect and everything I said was nothing but a lie . . . forgive me; you are a great man and can forgive, you understand. . . . I admire you, Don Laureano, I am proud to be your friend . . . I . . ."

The beggar assumed an expression as much like what he thought Garcia expected as possible. With his free hand he patted Garcia's hand:

"You need not explain, my boy." Garcia just loved this *boy*. "I told you that there was no necessity to explain. Of course, I understand, but don't worry. After all, it is all the same to me. Really, all this is none of my business. The coin is yours, you gave it to me by mistake . . . all this is . . . unnecessary. . . ." He filled his glass and drank it.

"I never would have taken it back from you . . but I will be frank with you now. It is all I have. I am broke. I have not eaten since last night because, in my stupidity, I thought that the coin was more profitable in my pocket than in my stomach. As a matter of fact, I only had that coin and a five centimes piece, which I intended to give to you." Garcia produced the copper coin. "Here it is . . . have it, it was intended for you."

The beggar pushed back the coin.

"You need it more than I. I could not accept it after what you say."

"But it is your profession, this is a business question; you cannot refuse me that pleasure, at least let me feel . . ."

"Impossible, it would be a crime; it makes me realize how often men who need money more than we do, come to our aid and keep our business going. . . . Impossible, impossible, you keep it; it would be a crime."

The Ojen was taking effect on both men alike. The beggar felt now for this stranger before him a sympathy he had never given to anyone before. He felt friendly toward this young

man who had come to him with the intention of deceit and then
had broken down and cried in bitter sincerity before his obvious superiority. A tremendous affection for this honest youth
who recognized his indubitable greatness; an infinite sorrow for
this poor being who had not eaten since the night before, who
had offered him alms at a moment in which it meant that he
was giving his last negotiable piece of money away for charity.
He was sorry for this man who, impelled by necessity, was now
on the verge of changing a coin upon which he had based all
the past transactions of his life. . . . And he also felt admiration
for this young man who, on an empty stomach, showed enough
character to admit his hypocrisy, to give himself away, because
with an amazing intuition he had recognized in him a great man.
And the tears rolled from the beggar's eyes.

"You say you have not eaten since last night?"

"Yes. . . . You see, I have accepted a position, but I do not
begin working until next month. I have no money now and I
did not want to change this coin because I depended on the
sentimental tale attached to it for borrowing money from my
friends. But your great example has enlightened me. I will
change the coin now, I shall never borrow again. I have accepted a position and will work honestly for my money. . . .
You have saved me . . . !"

"Yes, my friend, you are right; you must work honestly; follow my example; it is hard, I know it. I usually work from six
in the morning until six in the evening, but there is a satisfaction in knowing that you have earned a modest living, that you
owe nothing to anyone. . . ."

Both men looked at each other and again cried abundantly in
silence. At last the beggar repeated stupidly:

"You say you have not eaten since last night?"

Garcia shook his head.

"Lunarito!" cried the beggar suddenly with a broken voice.

Lunarito appeared at the door and regarded both men with
the utmost perplexity. They were holding each other's hands,
their cheeks wet with tears.

"Lunarito, set another dish. This gentleman will do me the
honor of dining with me. And bring another bottle of Ojen."

Lunarito brought the dish and the bottle and Garcia began to
eat in silence. He felt terribly hungry; the Ojen had awakened

his appetite, which had long since gone to sleep for lack of
attention. The beggar watched him eat with a tender expression.
Every time Garcia lifted his eyes from the dish, the beggar met
them with a maternal smile and filled both glasses with Ojen. At
last he cried again:

"Lunarito, Lunarito, bring another glass."

Lunarito appeared with a glass in her hand and a blank expression on her face. Garcia looked up from his dish. The beggar smiled:

"A toast, a toast. . . . At last the hour of acknowledgment between two social classes has arrived." He addressed Garcia, who
staggered to his feet and filled the three glasses.

"To you, my friend, my brother . . . !" They all drank, Lunarito obediently.

Garcia felt a necessity to refer to politics as he always did
when he heard the word classes mentioned:

"If the government only knew . . . !"

The beggar circled around the table and approached Garcia
confidentially. Lunarito disappeared again.

"Never mind the government, my boy . . . you say that you
are broke?" he whispered.

"What did you say?"

"That you have no money," the beggar explained.

"Oh, yes, I am broke, but now I am going to change this
coin and that will carry me through. . . ."

"Change that coin? No, my boy, don't even think of such a
thing. You said your father gave it to you on your birthday?"

"Yes, but as I have told you . . . I don't begin work until . . ."

"Don't worry about that, young man; after all, we only have
one father. . . ."

Garcia made a doubting noise.

"Whether we have any certainty about the particular circumstances, my boy, we only have one real father. . . . You must
keep the coin." The beggar produced a wallet. "When do you
say you begin work?"

"Next month . . . but . . ."

The beggar took a handful of bills and offered them to Garcia without counting them:

"Here, my boy, this will help you along, and if you need
anything. . . ."

If there has ever been a grateful look in this world, it was the one which Garcia gave the beggar. He reeled on his feet, his mouth quivered and he fell, embracing his benefactor, covering his shoulder with fresh tears. He was sobbing aloud, crying words of thanks. At last he fell on his knees and insisted on kissing the beggar's hand.

Again Lunarito appeared in the door and her eyes registered the most comical surprise. Then Garcia rose and she saw both men reeling down the corridor, heard the door open and their voices:

"I would have never taken it from you. . . ."

"If you ever need anything come to me as if I were your father."

"You are the greatest man I have ever met."

"The hour of acknowledgment has arrived."

"If the government only knew . . . !"

"Never mind the government, my boy; after all, we only have one father."

And then Lunarito heard the door close.

Looking for Mr. Green

SAUL BELLOW

Born in Lachine, Canada in 1915, Saul Bellow has spent most of his life in Chicago. He studied at Chicago University, at Northwestern and Wisconsin, and he has taught anthropology. He was connected with the editorial department of the Encyclopedia Britannica for three years. While working there, his first novel, Dangling Man, *was published. This was followed in 1947 by another novel,* The Victim, *a work that deals with a persecuted Jew. He has taught at a number of leading American universities and he has been a Guggenheim Fellow. For his third novel,* The Adventures of Augie March, *Mr. Bellow won The National Book Award of 1953.*

Whatsoever thy hand findeth to do, do it with thy might. . . .

HARD WORK? No, it wasn't really so hard. He wasn't used to walking and stair-climbing, but the physical difficulty of his new job was not what George Grebe felt most. He was delivering Relief checks in the Negro district, and although he was a native Chicagoan this was not a part of the city he knew much about—it needed a depression to introduce him to it. No, it wasn't literally hard work, not as reckoned in foot-pounds, but yet he was beginning to feel the strain of it, to grow aware of its peculiar difficulty. He could find the streets and numbers, but the clients were not where they were supposed to be, and he felt like a hunter inexperienced in the camouflage of his game. It was an unfavorable day, too—fall and cold, dark weather, windy. But, anyway, instead of shells in his deep trench coat pocket he had the cardboard of checks, punctured for the spindles of the file, the holes reminding him of the holes in player-piano paper. And he didn't look much like a hunter, either; his was a city figure entirely, belted up in this Irish conspirator's coat. He was slender without being tall, stiff in the back, his legs looking shabby in a pair of old tweed pants, gone through and fringy at the cuffs. With this stiffness, he kept his head forward, so that his face was red from the sharpness of the weather; and it was an indoors sort of face with gray eyes that persisted in some kind of thought and yet seemed to avoid definiteness of conclusion. He wore sideburns that surprised you somewhat by the tough curl of the blond hair and the effect of assertion in their length. He was not so mild as he looked, nor so youthful; and nevertheless there was no effort on his part to seem what he was not. He was an educated man; he was a bachelor; he was in some ways simple; without lushing, he liked a drink; his luck had not been good. Nothing was deliberately hidden.

He felt that his luck was better than usual today. When he had reported for work that morning, he had expected to be shut up in the Relief office at a clerk's job, for he had been hired downtown as a clerk, and he was glad to have, instead, the freedom of the streets and welcomed, at least at first, the vigor of the cold and even the blowing of the hard wind. But on the other hand he was not getting on with the distribution of the checks. It was true that it was a city job; nobody expected you to push too hard at a city job. His supervisor, that young Mr. Raynor, had practically told him that. Still, he wanted to do well at it. For one thing, when he knew how quickly he could deliver a batch of checks, he would know also how much time he could expect to clip for himself. And then, too, the clients would be waiting for their money. That was not the most important consideration, though it certainly mattered to him. No, but he wanted to do well, simply for doing-well's sake, to acquit himself decently of a job because he so rarely had a job to do that required just this sort of energy. Of this peculiar energy he now had a superabundance; once it had started to flow, it flowed all too heavily. And, for the time being anyway, he was balked. He could not find Mr. Green.

So he stood in his big-skirted trench coat with a large envelope in his hand and papers showing from his pocket, wondering why people should be so hard to locate who were too feeble or sick to come to the station to collect their own checks. But Raynor had told him that tracking them down was not easy at first and had offered him some advice on how to proceed. "If you can see the postman, he's your first man to ask, and your best bet. If you can't connect with him, try the stores and tradespeople around. Then the janitor and the neighbors. But you'll find the closer you come to your man the less people will tell you. They don't want to tell you anything."

"Because I'm a stranger."

"Because you're white. We ought to have a Negro doing this, but we don't at the moment, and of course you've got to eat, too, and this is public employment. Jobs have to be made. Oh, that holds for me too. Mind you, I'm not letting myself out. I've got three years of seniority on you, that's all. And a law degree. Otherwise, you might be back of the desk and I might be going out into the field this cold day. The same dough pays us both and for the same, exact, identical reason. What's my law degree got to do with it? But you have to pass out these checks, Mr. Grebe, and it'll help if you're stubborn, so I hope you are."

"Yes, I'm fairly stubborn."

Raynor sketched hard with an eraser in the old dirt of his desk, left-handed, and said, "Sure, what else can you answer to such a question. Anyhow, the trouble you're going to have is that they don't like to give information about anybody. They think you're a plain-clothes dick or an installment collector, or summons-server or something like that. Till you've been seen around the neighborhood for a few months and people know you're only from the Relief."

It was dark, ground-freezing, pre-Thanksgiving weather, the wind played hob with the smoke, rushing it down, and Grebe missed his gloves, which he had left in Raynor's office. And no one would admit knowing Green. It was past three o'clock and the postman had made his last delivery. The nearest grocer, himself a Negro, had never heard the name Tulliver Green, or said he hadn't. Grebe was inclined to think that it was true, that he had in the end convinced the man that he only wanted to deliver a check. But he wasn't sure. He needed experience in interpreting looks and signs and, even more, the will not to be put off or denied and even the force to bully, if need be. If the grocer did know, he had got rid of him easily. But since most of his trade was with reliefers, why should he prevent the delivery of a check? Maybe Green, or Mrs. Green, if there was a Mrs. Green, patronized another grocer. And was there a Mrs. Green? It was one of Grebe's great handicaps that he hadn't looked at any of the case records. Raynor should have let him read files for a few hours. But he apparently saw no need for that, probably considering the job unimportant. Why prepare systematically to deliver a few checks?

But now it was time to look for the janitor. Grebe took in the building in the wind and gloom of the late November day —trampled, frost-hardened lots on one side; on the other, an automobile junk yard and then the infinite work of Elevated frames, weak-looking, gaping with rubbish fires; two sets of leaning brick porches three stories high and a flight of cement stairs to the cellar. Descending, he entered the underground passage where he tried the doors until one opened and he found himself in the furnace room. There someone rose toward him and approached, scraping on the coal grit and bending under the canvas-jacketed pipes.

"Are you the janitor?"

"What do you want?"

"I'm looking for a man who's supposed to be living here. Green."

"What Green?"

"Oh, you maybe have more than one Green?" said Grebe with new, pleasant hope. "This is Tulliver Green."

"I don't think I c'n help you, mister. I don't know any."

"A crippled man."

The janitor stood bent before him. Could it be that he was crippled? Oh, God! what if he was. Grebe's gray eyes sought with excited difficulty to see. But no, he was only very short and stooped. A head awakened from meditation, a strong-haired beard, low, wide shoulders. A staleness of sweat and coal rose from his black shirt and the burlap sack he wore as an apron.

"Crippled how?"

Grebe thought and then answered with the light voice of unmixed candor, "I don't know. I've never seen him." This was damaging, but his only other choice was to make a lying guess, and he was not up to it. "I'm delivering checks for the Relief to shut-in cases. If he weren't crippled he'd come to collect himself. That's why I said crippled. Bedridden, chair-ridden . . . is there anybody like that?"

This sort of frankness was one of Grebe's oldest talents, going back to childhood. But it gained him nothing here.

"No suh. I've got four buildin's same as this that I take care of. I don' know all the tenants, leave alone the tenants' tenants. The rooms turn over so fast, people movin' in and out every day. I can't tell you."

"Then where should I ask?"

The janitor opened his grimy lips but Grebe did not hear him in the piping of the valves and the consuming pull of air to flame in the body of the furnace. He knew, however, what he had said.

"Well, all the same, thanks. Sorry I bothered you, I'll prowl around upstairs again and see if I can turn up someone who knows him."

Once more in the cold air and early darkness, he made the short circle from the cellarway to the entrance crowded be-

tween the brickwork pillars and began to climb to the third
floor. Pieces of plaster ground under his feet; strips of brass
tape from which the carpeting had been torn away marked old
boundaries at the sides. In the passage, and cold reached him
worse than in the street; it touched him to the bone. The hall
toilets ran like springs. He thought grimly as he heard the wind
burning around the building with a sound like that of the furnace, that this was a great piece of constructed shelter. Then
he struck a match in the gloom and searched for names and
numbers among the writings and scribbles on the walls. He saw
"WHOODY-DOODY GO TO JESUS," and zigzags, caricatures, sexual
scrawls, and curses. So the sealed rooms of pyramids were also
decorated, and the caves of human dawn.

The information on his card was, TULLIVER GREEN—APT
3D. There were no names, however, and no numbers. His
shoulders drawn up, tears of cold in his eyes, breathing vapor,
he went the length of the corridor and told himself that if he
had been lucky enough to have the temperament for it he
would bang on one of the doors and bawl out "Tulliver Green!"
until he got results. But it wasn't in him to make an uproar and
he continued to burn matches, passing the light over the walls.
At the rear, in a corner off the hall, he discovered a door he
had not seen before and he thought it best to investigate. It
sounded empty, when he knocked, but a young Negress answered, hardly more than a girl. She opened only a bit, to
protect the warmth of the room.

"Yes suh?"

"I'm from the district Relief station on Prairie Avenue. I'm
looking for a man named Tulliver Green to give him his
check. Do you know him?"

No, she didn't; but he thought she had not understood anything of what he had said. She had a dream-bound, dream-blind
face, very soft and black, shut off. She wore a man's jacket
and pulled the ends together at her throat. Her hair was parted
in three directions, at the sides and transversely, standing up
at the front in a dull puff.

"Is there somebody around here who might know?"

"I jus' taken this room las' week."

He observed that she shivered, but even her shiver was som-
nambulistic and there was no sharp consciousness of cold in the

big smooth eyes of her handsome face.

"All right, miss, thank you. Thanks," he said, and went to try another place.

Here he was admitted. He was grateful, for the room was warm. It was full of people, and they were silent as he entered— ten people, or a dozen, perhaps more, sitting on benches like a parliament. There was no light, properly speaking, but a tempered darkness that the window gave, and everyone seemed to him enormous, the men padded out in heavy work clothes and winter coats, and the women huge, too, in their sweaters, hats and old furs. And, besides, bed and bedding, a black cooking range, a piano piled towering to the ceiling with paper, a dining-room table of the old style of prosperous Chicago. Among these people Grebe, with his cold-heightened fresh color and his smaller stature, entered like a school lad. Even though he was met with smiles and good will, he felt that all the currents ran against him and that he would make no headway. Without having spoken a single word he knew that he was already outweighed and overborne. Nevertheless he began: "Does anybody here know how I can deliver a check to Mr. Tulliver Green?"

"Green?" It was the man that had let him in who answered. He was in shirt sleeves, in a checkered shirt, and had a queer, high head, profusely overgrown, long as a shako; the veins entered it strongly from his forehead. "I never heard mention of him. Is this where he live?"

"This is the address they gave me at the station. He's a sick man, and he'll need his check. Can't anybody tell me where to find him?"

He stood his ground and waited for a reply, his crimson wool scarf wound about his neck and drooping outside his trench coat, pockets weighted with the block of checks and official forms. They must have realized that he was not a college boy employed afternoons by a bill collector, trying foxily to pass for a Relief clerk, recognized that he was an older man who knew himself what need was, who had had more than an average seasoning in hardship. It was evident enough if you looked at the marks under his eyes and at the sides of his mouth.

"Anybody know this sick man?"

"No suh." On all sides he saw heads shaken and smiles of

denial. No one knew. And maybe it was true, he considered, standing silent in the earthen, musky human gloom of the place as the rumble continued. But he could never really be sure.

"What's the matter with this man?" said shako-head.

"I've never seen him. All I can tell you is that he can't come in person for his money. It's my first day in this district."

"Maybe they given you the wrong number?"

"I don't believe so. But where else can I ask about him?" He felt that his persistence amused them deeply, and in a way he shared their amusement that he should stand up so tenaciously to them. Though smaller, though slight, he was his own man, he retracted nothing about himself, and he looked back at them, gray-eyed, with amusement and also with a sort of effrontery. On the bench, some man spoke in his throat, the words impossible to catch, and a woman answered with a wild, shrieking laugh, quickly cut off.

"Well, so nobody will tell me?"

"Ain't nobody who knows."

"At least, if he lives here, he pays rent to someone. Who manages the building?"

"Greatham Company. That's on 39th Street."

Grebe wrote it in his pad. But, in the street again, a sheet of wind-driven paper clinging to his leg while he deliberated what direction to take next, it seemed a feeble lead to follow. Probably this Green didn't rent a flat, but a room. Sometimes there were as many as twenty people living in an apartment; the real estate agent would know only the lessee. And not even the latter could tell you who the renters were. In some places the beds were even used in shifts, watchmen, or jitney drivers or short-order cooks in night joints turning out after a day's sleep and surrendering their beds to a sister, a nephew, or perhaps a stranger, a transient who paid something for it. There were large numbers of these transients in this terrific, blight-bitten portion of the city between Cottage Grove and Ashland, wandering from house to house and room to room. When you saw them wander, how would you know? They didn't carry bundles on their backs or look picturesque. You simply saw a man, a Negro, walking in the street or riding in the car, like everyone else, with his thumb closed on a transfer. And therefore how were you supposed to tell? Grebe fancied the

Greatham agent would only laugh at his question.

But how much it would simplify his task to be able to say that Green was old, or blind, or consumptive. An hour in the files, taking a few notes, and he need not have been at such a disadvantage. When Raynor gave him the block of checks, he had asked, "How much should I know about these people?" Then Raynor had looked as though he were preparing to accuse him of trying to make the job more important than it was. He smiled, because by then they were on fine terms, but nevertheless he had been getting ready to say something like that when the confusion began in the station over Staika and her children.

Grebe had waited a long time for this job. It came to him through the pull of an old schoolmate in the Corporation Counsel's Office, never a close friend, but suddenly sympathetic and interested—pleased to show, moreover, how well he had done, how strongly he was coming through these miserable times. Well, he was coming through strongly, as strongly as the Democratic administration itself. Grebe had gone to see him in City Hall, and they had had a counter lunch or beers at least once a month for a year, and finally it had been possible to swing the job. He didn't mind being assigned the lowest clerical grade, nor even being a messenger, though Raynor thought he did.

This Raynor was an original sort. Grebe had immediately taken to him. As was proper on the first day, Grebe had come early, but he waited long, for Raynor was late. At last he darted into his cubicle of an office as though he had just jumped from one of those hurtling huge red Indiana Avenue cars. His thin, rough face was wind-stung and he was grinning and saying something breathlessly to himself. In his hat, a small fedora, and his coat, the velvet collar a neat fit about his neck, and his silk muffler that set off the nervous twist of his chin—he swayed and turned himself in his swivel chair, feet leaving the ground; so that he pranced a little as he sat. Meanwhile he took Grebe's measure out of his eyes, eyes of an unusual vertical length, a trace sardonic. So the two men sat for a while, saying nothing, while the supervisor raised his hat from his miscombed hair and put it in his lap. His cold-darkened hands were not clean. A steel beam passed through the little makeshift room from which machine belts once had hung. The building was an old factory.

"I'm younger than you; I hope you won't find it hard taking orders from me," said Raynor. "But I don't make them up, either. You're how old, about?"

"Thirty-five."

"And you thought you'd be inside doing paper-work. But it so happens I have to send you out."

"I don't mind."

"And it's mostly a Negro load we have in this district."

"So I thought it would be."

"Fine. You'll get along. *C'est un bon boulot.* Do you know French?"

"Some."

"I thought you'd be a university man."

"Have you been in France?" said Grebe.

"No, that's the French of the Berlitz School. I've been at it for more than a year, just as I'm sure people have been, all over the world, office boys in China and braves in Tanganyika. In fact, I damn well know it. Such is the attractive power of civilization. It's overrated, but what do you want? *Que voulez vous?* I get *Le Rire* and all the spicy papers, just like in Tanganyika. It must be mystifying, out there. But my reason is that I'm aiming at the diplomatic service. I have a cousin who's a courier, and the way he describes it is awfully attractive. He rides in the *wagons-lits* and reads books. While we . . . What did you do before?"

"I sold."

"Where?"

"Canned meat at Stop and Shop. In the basement."

"And before that?"

"Window shades, at Goldblatt's."

"Steady work?"

"No, Thursdays and Saturdays. I also sold shoes."

"You've been a shoe-dog, too. Well. And prior to that? Here it is in your folder." He opened the record. "St. Olaf's College, instructor in classical languages. Fellow, University of Chicago, 1926-27, I've had Latin, too. Let's trade quotations—*Dum spiro spero.*"

"*Da dextram misero.*"

"Alea jacta est."

"Excelsior."

Raynor shouted with laughter, and other workers came to look at him over the partition. Grebe also laughed, feeling pleased and easy. The luxury of fun on a nervous morning.

When they were done and no one was watching or listening, Raynor said rather seriously, "What made you study Latin in the first place. Was it for the priesthood?"

"No."

"Just for the hell of it? As a luxury? Oh, the things people think they can pull!" He made his cry hilarious and tragic. "I ran my pants off so I could study for the bar, and I've passed the bar, so I get twelve dollars a week more than you as a bonus for having seen life straight and whole. I'll tell you, as a man of culture, that even though nothing looks to be real, and everything stands for something else. and that thing for another thing, and that thing for a still further one—there ain't any comparison between twenty-five and thirty-seven dollars a week, regardless of the last reality. Don't you think that was clear to your Greeks? They were a thoughtful people, but they didn't part with their slaves."

This was a great deal more than Grebe had looked for in his first interview with his supervisor. He was too shy to show all the astonishment he felt. He laughed a little, aroused, and brushed at the sunbeam that covered his head with its dust. "Do you think my mistake was so terrible?"

"Damn right it was terrible, and you know it now that you've had the whip of hard times laid on your back. You should have been preparing yourself for trouble. Your people must have been well off to send you to the university. Stop me, if I'm stepping on your toes. Did your mother pamper you? Did your father give in to you? Were you brought up tenderly, with permission to go out and find out what were the last things that everything else stands for while everybody else labored in the fallen world of appearances?"

"Well, no, it wasn't exactly like that." Grebe smiled. *The fallen world of appearances!* no less. But now it was his turn to deliver a surprise. "We weren't rich. My father was the last genuine English butler in Chicago. . . ."

"Are you kidding?"

"Why should I be?"

"In a livery."

"In livery. Up on the Gold Coast."

"And he wanted you to be educated like a gentleman?"

"He did not. He sent me to the Armour Institute to study chemical engineering. But when he died I changed schools."

He stopped himself, and considered how quickly Raynor had reached him. In no time he had your valise on the table and your things unpacked. And afterwards, in the streets, he was still reviewing how far he might have gone, and how much he might have been led to tell if they had not been interrupted by Mrs. Staika's great noise.

But just then a young woman, one of Raynor's workers, ran into the cubicle exclaiming, "Haven't you heard all the fuss?"

"We haven't heard anything."

"It's Staika, giving out with all her might. Reporters are coming. She said she phoned the papers, and you know she did."

"But what is she up to?" said Raynor.

"She brought her wash and she's ironing it here, with our current, because the Relief won't pay her electric bill. She has her ironing board set up by the admitting desk, and her kids are with her, all six. They never are in school more than once a week. She's always dragging them around with her because of her reputation."

"I don't want to miss any of this," said Raynor jumping up. Grebe, as he followed with the secretary, said, "Who is this Staika?"

"They call her the 'Blood Mother of Federal Street.' She's a professional donor at the hospitals. I think they pay ten dollars a pint. Of course it's no joke, but she makes a very big thing out of it and she and the kids are in the papers all the time."

Scores of people, staff and clients divided by a plywood barrier, stood in the narrow space of the entrance, and Staika was shouting in a gruff, mannish voice, plunging the iron on the board and slamming it on the metal rest.

"My father and mother came in a steerage, and I was born in our own house, Robey by Huron. I'm no dirty immigrant. I'm a US citizen. My husband is a gassed veteran from France with lungs weaker'n paper, that hardly can he go to the toilet by himself. These six children of mine, I have to buy the shoes for their feet with my own blood. Even a lousy little white communion necktie, that's a couple of drops of blood; a little piece of mosquito veil for my Vadja so she won't be ashamed in church for the other girls, they take my blood for it by Goldblatt. That's how I keep goin'. A fine thing if I had to depend on the Relief. And there's plenty of people on the rolls— fakes! There's nothin' *they* can't get, that can go and wrap bacon at Swift and Armour any time. They're lookin' for them by the Yards. They never have to be out of work. Only they rather lay in their lousy beds and eat the taxpayers' money." She was not afraid, in a predominantly Negro station, to shout this way about Negroes.

Grebe pressed himself forward to get a nearer view of the woman. She was flaming with anger and with pleasure at herself, broad and huge, a golden-headed woman who wore a cotton cap laced with pink ribbon. She was barelegged and had on black gym-shoes, her hoover apron was open and her great breasts, not much restrained by a man's undershirt, hampered her arms as she worked at the kid's dress on the ironing board. And the children, silent and white, with a kind of locked obstinacy, in sheepskins and lumberjackets, stood behind her. She had captured the station, and the pleasure it gave her was enormous. Yet her grievances were true grievances, if wrongly aimed, and she put the whole force of her spirit into them. But she attacked with her voice. Her small eyes she kept averted, and her look was hidden, so that she seemed to be spinning and planning as she raged.

"They send me out college case-workers in silk panties to talk me out of what I got comin'. Are they better'n me? Who told them? Fire them. Let 'em go and get married, and then you won't have to cut electric from folks' budget."

The chief supervisor, Mr. Ewing, could not silence her and he stood with folded arms at the head of his staff, bald, trying to appear mocking, saying to his subordinates like the ex-school principal he was, "Pretty soon she'll be tired and go."

"Nothing doing," said Raynor to Grebe. "She'll get what she wants. She knows more about the Relief even than Ewing. She's been on the rolls for years, and she always gets what she wants because she puts on a noisy show. Ewing knows it. He'll give in soon. He's only saving face. If he gets bad publicity, the Commissioner'll have him on the carpet, downtown. She's got him submerged; she'll submerge everybody in time, and that includes nations and governments." Grebe replied with his characteristic smile, disagreeing completely. Who would ever take Staika's orders, and what changes could her yelling bring about?

No, what Grebe saw in her, the power that made her a real center of attention, and made obedient and attracted people listen, was that her cry expressed the war of flesh and blood, made a little crazy and intensely ugly, on place and condition. And at first, when he went out, she somehow presided over the whole district for him, and it took color from her; literally her color, in the spotty curb-fires, and the fires under the El, the straight alley of flamey gloom. Later too, when he went into a tavern for a shot of rye, the sweat of beer, by way of West Side Polish streets, led him to think of her again.

He wiped the corners of his mouth with his muffler, his handkerchief being too deep in his pocket to reach for, and went out again to get on with the delivery of his checks. The air bit cold and hard and a few flakes of snow formed near him. A train struck by and left a quiver in the frames and a bristling icy hiss over the rails.

Crossing the street, he descended a flight of board steps into a basement grocery, setting off a little bell. It was a dark, long store and it caught you with its stinks of smoked meat, soap, dried peaches, and fish. There was a fire wrinkling and flapping in the little stove, and the proprietor was waiting, an Italian with a long, hollow face and stubborn bristles. He kept his hands warm under his apron.

No, he didn't know Green. You knew people, but not names. The same man might not have the same name twice. The police didn't know, either, and mostly didn't care. When somebody was shot or knifed they took the body away and didn't look for the murderer. In the first place, nobody would tell them anything. So they made up a name for the coroner and called it quits. And in the second place, they didn't give a goddam anyhow. But they couldn't get to the bottom of a thing even if they wanted to. Nobody would get to know even a tenth of what went on among these people. They stabbed and stole, they did every corrupt thing you ever heard of, men and men, women and women, parents and children, worse than the animals. They carried on their own way, and the crimes passed off like a smoke. There was never anything like it in the history of the world.

It was a long speech, deepening with every word in its fantasy and passion and becoming increasingly senseless and terrible: a swarm amassed by suggestion and by steady invention, a huge, hugging, despairing knot, a human wheel rolling through his shop.

Grebe felt that he must interrupt him. He said, sharply, "What are you talking about! All I asked was whether you knew this man."

"That isn't even the half if it. I been here six years. You probably don't want to believe this. But suppose it's true?"

"All the same," said Grebe, "there must be a way to find a person."

The Italian's close-spaced eyes had been queerly concentrated, as were his muscles, while he leaned across the counter trying to convince Grebe. Now he gave up the effort and sat down on his stool. "Oh . . . I suppose. Once in a while. But I been telling you, even the cops don't get anywhere."

"They're always after somebody. It's not the same thing."

"Well, keep trying if you want. I can't help you."

But he didn't keep trying. He had no more time to spend on Green. He slipped Green's check to the back of the block. The next name on the list was FIELD, WINSTON.

He found the back-yard bungalow without the least trouble; it shared a lot with another house, a few feet of yard between. Grebe knew these two-shack arrangements. They had been built in vast numbers in the days before the swamps were filled and the streets raised, and they were all the same—a boardwalk along the fence, well under street level, three or four ball-headed posts for clotheslines, greening wood, dead shingles, and a long, long flight of stairs to the rear door.

A twelve-year-old boy let him into the kitchen, and there the old man was sitting by the table in a wheel chair.

"Oh, it's d' government man," he said to the boy when Grebe drew out his checks. "Go bring me my box of papers." He cleared a space on the table.

"Oh, you don't have to go to all that trouble," said Grebe.

But Field laid out his papers: Social Security card, Relief certification, letters from the state hospital in Manteno and a naval discharge dated San Diego, 1920.

"That's plenty," Grebe said. "Just sign."

"You got to know who I am," the old man said. "You're from the government. It's not your check, it's a government check and you got no business to hand it over till everything is proved."

He loved the ceremony of it, and Grebe made no more objections. Field emptied his box and finished out the circle of cards and letters.

"There's everything I done and been. Just the death certificate and they can close book on me." He said this with a certain happy pride and magnificence. Still he did not sign; he merely held the little pen upright on the golden green corduroy of his thigh. Grebe did not hurry him. He felt the old man's hunger for conversation.

"I got to get better coal," he said. "I send my little gran'son to the yard with my order and they fill his wagon with screening. The stove ain't made for it. It fall through the grate. The order says Franklin County egg-size coal."

"I'll report it and see what can be done."

"Nothing can be done, I expect. You know and I know. There ain't no little ways to make things better, and the only big thing is money. That's the only sunbeams, money. Nothing is black where it shines, and the only place you see black is where it ain't shining. What we colored have to have is our own rich. There ain't no other way."

Grebe sat, his reddened forehead bridged levelly by his closer-cut hair and his cheeks lowered in the wings of his collar—the caked fire shone hard within the isinglass and iron frames but the room was not comfortable—sat and listened while the old man unfolded his scheme. This was to create one Negro millionaire a month by subscription. One clever, good-hearted young fellow elected every month would sign a contract to use the money to start a business employing Negroes. This would be advertised by chain-letters and word of mouth, and every Negro wage-earner would contribute a dollar a month. Within five years there would be sixty millionaires.

"That'll fetch respect," he said with a throat-stopped sound

that came out like a foreign syllable. "You got to take and or-
ganize all the money that gets thrown away on the policy wheel
and horse race. As long as they can take it away from you, they
got no respect for you. Money, that's d' sun of human kind!"
Field was a Negro of mixed blood, perhaps Cherokee, or
Natchez; his skin was reddish. And he sounded, speaking about
a golden sun in this dark room, and looked, shaggy and slab-
headed, with the mingled blood of his face and broad lips, the
little pen still upright in his hand, like one of the underground
kings of mythology, the old judging Minos himself.

And now he accepted the check and signed. Not to soil the
slip, he held it down with his knuckles. The table budged and
creaked, the center of the gloomy, heathen midden of the
kitchen covered with bread, meat, and cans, and the scramble
of papers.

"Don't you think my scheme'd work?"

"It's worth thinking about. Something ought to be done, I
agree."

"It'll work if people will do it. That's all. That's the only
thing, anytime. When they understand it in the same way, all
of them."

"That's true," said Grebe, rising. His glance met the old
man's.

"I know you got to go," he said. "Well, God bless you, boy,
you ain't been sly with me. I can tell it in a minute."

He went back through the buried yard. Someone nursed a
candle in a shed, where a man unloaded kindling wood from
a sprawl-wheeled baby buggy and two voices carried on a high
conversation. As he came up the sheltered passage he heard
the hard boost of the wind in the branches and against the house
fronts, and then, reaching the sidewalk, he saw the needle-eye-
red of cable towers in the open icy height hundreds of feet above
the river and the factories: those keen points. From here, his
view was unobstructed all the way to the South Branch and
its timber banks, and the cranes beside the water. Rebuilt after
the Great Fire, this part of the city was, not fifty years later, in
ruins again, factories boarded up, buildings deserted or fallen,
gaps of prairie between. But it wasn't desolation that this made
you feel, but rather a faltering of organization that set free a
huge energy, an escaped, unattached, unregulated power from

the giant raw place. Not only must people feel it but, it seemed to Grebe, they were compelled to match it. In their very bodies. He no less than others, he realized. Say that his parents had been servants in their time, whereas he was not supposed to be one. He thought that they had never owed any service like this, which no one visible asked and probably flesh and blood could not even perform. Nor could anyone show why it should be performed; or see what the performance would lead to. That did not mean that he wanted to be released from it, he realized with a grimly pensive face. On the contrary. He had something to do. To be compelled to feel this energy and yet have nothing to do—that was horrible; that was suffering; he knew what that was. It was now quitting time. Six o'clock. He could go home if he liked, to his room, that is, to wash in hot water, to pour a drink, lie down on his quilt, read the paper, eat some liver paste on crackers before going out to dinner. But to think of this actually made him feel a little sick, as though he had swallowed hard air. He had six checks left, and he was determined to deliver at least one of these: Mr. Green's check.

So he started. He had four or five dark blocks to go, past open lots, condemned houses, old foundations, closed schools, black churches, mounds, and he reflected that there must be many people alive who had once seen the neighborhood rebuilt and new. Now there was a second layer of ruins; centuries of history accomplished through human massing. Numbers had given the place forced growth; enormous numbers had also broken it down. Objects once so new, so concrete that it could never have occurred to anyone they stood for other things, had crumbled. Therefore, reflected Grebe, the secret of them was out. It was that they stood for themselves by agreement, and were natural and not unnatural by agreement, and when the things themselves collapsed the agreement became visible. What was it, otherwise, that kept cities from looking peculiar? Rome, that was almost permanent, did not give rise to thoughts like these. And was it abidingly real? But in Chicago, where the cycles were so fast and the familiar died, and rose changed, and died again in thirty years, you saw the common agreement or covenant, and you were forced to think about appearances and realities.—He remembered Raynor and he smiled; that was a clever boy—. Once you saw that a great many things became intelligible. For instance, why Mr. Field should conceive such a scheme. Of course, if people were to agree to create a millionaire, a real millionaire would come into existence. And if you wanted to know how Mr. Field was inspired to think of this, why, he had within sight of his kitchen window the chart, the very bones of a successful scheme—the El with its blue and green confetti of signals. People consenting to pay dimes and ride the crash-box cars, it was a success. Yet how absurd it looked; how little real to start with. And yet Yerkes, the great financier who built it, had known that he could get people to agree to its reality. Viewed as itself, what a scheme of a scheme it seemed, how close to an appearance. Then why wonder at Mr. Field's idea? He had grasped a principle. And then Grebe remembered, too, that Mr. Yerkes had established the Yerkes Observatory and endowed it with millions. Now why did the notion reach him in his New York museum of a palace or his Aegean-bound yacht to give money to astronomers? Was he awed perhaps by the success of his bizarre enterprise and therefore ready to spend money to find out where in the universe being and seeming were identical? Yes, he wanted to know what abides; and is flesh Bible-grass; and offered money to be burned in the fire of suns. Okay, then, Grebe thought further, these things exist because people consent to exist with them—we have got so far—and also there is a reality which doesn't depend on consent but within which consent is a game. But what about need, the need that keeps so many vast thousands in position? You tell me that, you private little gentleman and *decent* soul—he used these words against himself scornfully. Why is the consent given to misery? And why so painfully ugly? Because there *is something* that is dismal and permanently ugly? Here he sighed and gave it up, and thought it was enough for the present moment that he had a real check in his pocket for a Mr. Green who could be real beyond question. If only his neighbors didn't think they had to conceal him.

This time he stopped at the second floor. He struck a match and found a door. Presently a man answered his knock and Grebe had the check ready and showed it even before he began. "Does Tulliver Green live here? I'm from the Relief."

The man narrowed the opening and spoke to someone at his back.

"Does he live here?"

"Uh-unh. No."

"Or anywhere in this building? He's a sick man and he can't come for his dough." He held the check up into the light, which was smoky and smelled of charred lard, and the man held off the brim of his cap to study it.

"Uh-unh. Never seen the name."

"There's nobody around here that uses crutches?"

He seemed to think, but it was Grebe's impression that he was simply waiting for a decent interval to pass.

"No, suh. Nobody I ever see."

"I've been looking for this man all afternoon," Grebe spoke out with sudden force, "and I'm going to have to carry this check back to the station. It seems strange not to be able to find a person to *give* him something when you're looking for him for a good reason. I suppose if I had bad news for him I'd find him quick enough."

There was a responsive motion in the other man's face. "That's right, I reckon."

"It almost doesn't do any good to have a name if you can't be found by it. It doesn't stand for anything. He might as well not have any," he went on, smiling. It was as much of a concession as he could make to his great desire to laugh.

"Well, now, there's a little old knot-back man I see once in a while. He might be the one you lookin' for. Downstairs."

"Where? Right side or left? Which door?"

"I don't know which. Thin face little knot-back with a stick."

But no one answered at any of the doors on the first floor. He went to the end of the corridor, searching by matchlight, and found only a stairless exit to the yard, a drop of about six feet. But there was a bungalow near the alley, an old house like Mr. Field's. To jump was unsafe. He ran from the front door, through the underground passage and into the yard. The place was occupied. There was a light through the curtains, upstairs. The name on the ticket under the broken, scoop-shaped mailbox was Green! He exultantly rang the bell and pressed against the locked door. Then the lock clicked faintly and a long staircase opened before him. Someone was slowly coming down—a woman. He had the impression in the weak light that she was shaping her hair as she came, making herself present-

able, for he saw her arms raised. But it was for support that
they were raised; she was feeling her way downward, down the
walls, stumbling. Next he wondered about the pressure of her
feet on the treads; she did not seem to be wearing shoes. And
it was a freezing stairway. His ring had got her out of bed, perhaps, and she had forgotten to put them on. And then he saw
that she was not only shoeless but naked; she was entirely
naked, blundering down and talking to herself, a heavy woman,
naked and drunk. The contact of her breasts on his coat made
him go back against the door with a blind, rousing shock. See
what he had tracked down, in his hunting game! He hadn't
reckoned with such prey. The woman was saying to herself,
furious with insult, "So I caint——, huh? I'll show that —— —
kin' I, cain't I."

What should he do now? Why, he should go. He should turn
and go. He could not talk to this woman. He could not keep her
standing naked in the cold. However, he could not go. He could
not acknowledge that what he had found was too much for him.

He said, "Is this where Mr. Green lives?"

But she was still talking to herself and did not hear him.

"Is this Mr. Green's house?"

At last she turned her furious drunken glance on him. "What
do you want?"

Again her eyes wandered from him, a dark wink of blood
in their enraged brilliance. He wondered that she didn't feel
the cold.

"I'm from the Relief."

"Awright, what?"

"I've got a check for Tulliver Green."

This time she heard him and put out her hand.

"No, no, for *Mister* Green. He's got to sign," he said ridicu-
lously. How was he going to get Green's signature tonight!

"I'll take it."

He desperately shook his head, thinking of Mr. Field's pre-
cautions about identification. "I can't let you have it. It's for
him. Is he upstairs?"

"Awright. Take it up yourself, you goddam fool."

Yes, he was a goddamned fool. Of course he could not go
up. Green would be drunk and naked, too. And perhaps he
would appear on the landing soon. He looked eagerly up to the

narrow height of the green wall. Empty! It remained empty!

"Hell with you, then!" he heard her cry and suddenly saw, with burning self-ridicule, how far his desire had carried him. Then why didn't he leave? He made ready to go.

"I'll come tomorrow, tell him."

"Ah, hell with you. Don' never come. What you doin' here in the night-time. Don' come back." She yelled so that he saw the breadth of her tongue. She stood astride in the long cold box of the hall and held on to the bannister and the wall. The bungalow itself was shaped something like a box, an immense sentry box pointing into the freezing air and sharp, wintry lights.

"If you are Mrs. Green, I'll give you the check," he said, changing his mind.

"Give here, then." She took it, took the pen offered with it in her left hand, and tried to write on the wall. He looked around, almost as though to see whether his madness was being observed, and came near believing that someone was standing on a mountain of used tires in the auto-junking shop next door.

"But are you Mrs. Green?" he now thought to ask. But she was already climbing the stairs with the check, and it was too late, if he had made an error, if he was now in trouble, to undo the thing. However, a moment came, illuminated from the greatest height, when you could not refuse to yield a check, a municipal check, and therefore his worry stung him only superficially. Besides, though she might not be Mrs. Green, he was convinced that Mr. Green was upstairs. Whoever she was, the woman stood for Green whom this time he was not to see. "Well, you silly bastard," he said to himself, "so you found him. So what?" But it was important that there was a real Mr. Green whom they could not keep him from reaching because he seemed to come as an emissary from hostile appearances. And though the self-ridicule was slow to diminish, and his face, throat and chest, arms, his whole body blazed with it, he had, nevertheless, a reason for elation, too. "For after all," he said, "I *did* get to him."

The Jar

LUIGI PIRANDELLO

The son of a wealthy sulphur mine owner who fought the Mafia, Luigi Pirandello was born in Sicily in 1867. He studied at the University of Rome, where he came under the influence of an eminent philologist. After receiving a doctor's degree in philological studies in Germany, he returned to Rome. A few years later he married the daughter of his father's business partner. For ten contented years he wrote and published numerous short stories, and then his father's mines were flooded. Pirandello had to take a job teaching Italian literature at a teacher's college in Rome. Worry and anxiety over money drove his wife to hysteria and fits of jealousy. A few years before her death, Pirandello began writing plays, among them his widely acclaimed masterpiece, Six Characters in Search of An Author. *After he won the Nobel Prize for Literature in 1934, he divided his royalties among his three children, and traveled from country to country, an aimless wanderer, leaving no forwarding address, without any attachments or property. He died in 1936.*

THE OLIVE CROP was a bumper one that year: the trees had flowered luxuriantly the year before, and, though there had been a long spell of misty weather at the time, the fruit had set well. Lollo Zirafa had a fine plantation on his farm at Primosole. Reckoning that the five old jars of glazed earthenware which he had in his wine-cellar would not suffice to hold all the oil of that harvest, he had placed an order well beforehand at Santo Stefano Di Camastra, where they are made. His new jar was to be of greater capacity—breast-high and pot-bellied; it would be the mother-superior to the little community of five other jars.

I need scarcely say that Don Lollo Zirafa had had a dispute with the potter concerning this jar. It would indeed be hard to name anyone with whom he had not picked a quarrel: for every trifle—be it merely a stone that had fallen from his boundary wall, or a handful of straw—he would shout out to the servants to saddle his mule, so that he could hurry to the town and file a suit. He had half-ruined himself, because of the large sums he had had to spend on court fees and lawyers' bills, bringing actions against one person after another, which always ended in his having to pay the costs of both sides. People said that his legal adviser grew so tired of seeing him appear two or three times a week that he tried to reduce the frequency of his visits by making him a present of a volume which looked like a prayer-book: it contained the judicial code—the idea being that he should take the trouble to see for himself what the rights and wrongs of the case were before hurrying to bring a suit.

Previously, when anyone had a difference with him, they would try to make him lose his temper by shouting out: "Saddle the mule!" but now they changed it to "Go and look up your pocket-code!" Don Lollo would reply: "That I will and I'll break the lot of you, you sons of bitches!"

In course of time, the new jar, for which he had paid the goodly sum of four florins, duly arrived; until room could be found for it in the wine-cellar, it was lodged in the crushing-shed for a few days. Never had there been a finer jar. It was quite distressing to see it lodged in that foul den, which reeked of stale grape-juice and had that musty smell of places deprived of light and air.

It was now two days since the harvesting of the olives had begun, and Don Lollo was almost beside himself, having to supervise not only the men who were beating down the fruit from the trees, but also a number of others who had come with mule-loads of manure to be deposited in heaps on the hillside, where he had a field in which he was going to sow beans for the next crop. He felt that it was really more than one man could manage, he was at his wits' ends whom to attend to: cursing like a trooper, he vowed he would exterminate, first this man and then that, if an olive—one single olive—was missing: he almost talked as if he had counted them, one by one, on his trees; then he would turn to the muleteers and utter the direst threats as to what would happen, if any one heap of manure were not exactly the same size as the others. A little white cap on his head, his sleeves rolled up and his shirt open at the front, he rushed here, there and everywhere; his face was a bright red and poured with sweat, his eyes glared about him wolfishly, while his hands rubbed angrily at his shaven chin, where a fresh growth of beard always sprouted the moment the razor had left it.

At the close of the third day's work, three of the farm-hands —rough fellows with dirty, brutish faces—went to the crushing-shed; they had been beating the olive trees and went to replace their ladders and poles in the shed. They stood aghast at the sight of the fine new jar in two pieces, looking for all the world as if some one had caught hold of the bulging front and cut it off with a sharp sweep of the knife.

"Oh, my God! look! look!"

"How on earth has that happened?"

"My holy aunt! When Don Lollo hears of it! The new jar! What a pity, though!"

The first of the three, more frightened than his companions, proposed to shut the door again at once and to sneak away very quietly, leaving their ladders and poles outside leaning up against the wall; but the second took him up sharply.

"That's a stupid idea! You can't try that on Don Lollo. As like as not he'd believe we broke it ourselves. No, we all stay here!"

He went out of the shed and, using his hands as a trumpet, called out:—

"Don Lollo! Oh! Don LOLLOOOOO!"

When the farmer came up and saw the damage, he fell into a towering passion. First he vented his fury on the three men. He seized one of them by the throat, pinned him against the wall, and shouted:—

"By the Virgin's blood, you'll pay for that!"

The other two sprang forward in wild excitement, fell upon Don Lollo and pulled him away. Then his mad rage turned against himself: he stamped his feet, flung his cap on the ground, and slapped his cheeks, bewailing his loss with screams suited only for the death of a relation.

"The new jar! A four-florin jar! Brand new!"

Who could have broken it? Could it possibly have broken of itself? Certainly some one must have broken it, out of malice or from envy at his possession of such a beauty. But when? How? There was no sign of violence. Could it conceivably have come in a broken condition from the pottery? No, it rang like a bell on its arrival.

As soon as the farm-hands saw that their master's first outburst of rage was spent, they began to console him, saying that he should not take it so to heart, as the jar could be mended. After all, the break was not a bad one, for the front had come away all in one piece; a clever rivetter could repair it and make it as good as new. Zi' Dima Licasi[1] was just the man for the job: he had invented a marvellous cement made of some composition which he kept a strict secret—miraculous stuff! Once it had set, you couldn't loosen it, even with a hammer. So they suggested that, if Don Lollo agreed, Zi' Dima Licasi should turn up at day-break and—as sure as eggs were eggs—the jar would be repaired and be even better than a new one.

For a long time Don Lollo turned a deaf ear to their advice—it was quite useless, there was no making good the damage—but in the end he allowed himself to be persuaded and punctually at day-break Zi' Dima Licasi arrived at Primosole, with his outfit in a basket slung on his back. He turned out to be a misshapen old man with swollen, crooked joints, like the stem of an ancient Saracen olive tree. To extract a word from him, it looked as if you would have to use a pair of forceps on his mouth.

His ungraceful figure seemed to radiate discontent or gloom, due perhaps to his disappointment that no one had so far been found willing to do justice to his merits as an inventor. For Zi' Dima Licasi had not yet patented his discovery; he wanted to make a name for it first by its successful applica-

---

[1] 'Zi' (uncle) is used as a familiar prefix.

tion. Meanwhile he felt it necessary to keep a sharp lookout, for fear lest some one steal the secret of his process.

"Let me see that cement of yours," began Don Lollo in a distrustful tone, after examining him from head to foot for several minutes.

Zi' Dima declined, with a dignified shake of the head.

"You'll see its results."

"But, will it hold?"

Zi' Dima put his basket on the ground and took out from it a red bundle composed of a large cotton handkerchief, much the worse for wear, wrapped round and round something. He began to unroll it very carefully, while they all stood round watching him with close attention. When at last, however, nothing came to light save a pair of spectacles with bridge and sides broken and tied up with string, there was a general laugh. Zi' Dima took no notice, but wiped his fingers before handling the spectacles, then put them on and, with much solemnity, began his examination of the jar, which had been brought outside on to the threshing-floor. Finally he said:

"It'll hold."

"But I can't trust cement alone," Don Lollo stipulated, "I must have rivets as well."

"I'm off," Zi' Dima promptly replied, standing up and replacing his basket on his back.

Don Lollo caught hold of his arm:—

"Off? Where to? You've got no more manners than a pig! . . . Just look at this pauper putting on an air of royalty! . . . Why! you wretched fool, I've got to put oil in that jar, and don't you know that oil oozes? Yards and yards to join together, and you talk of using cement alone! I want rivets—cement and rivets. It's for me to decide."

Zi' Dima shut his eyes, closed his lips tightly and shook his head. People were all like that—they refused to give him the satisfaction of turning out a neat bit of work, performed with artistic thoroughness and proving the wonderful virtues of his cement.

"If," he said, "the jar doesn't ring as true as a bell once more . . ."

"I won't listen to a word," Don Lollo broke in. "I want rivets! I'll pay you for cement and rivets. How much will it come to?"

"If I use cement only . . ."

"My God! what an obstinate fellow! What did I say? I told you I wanted rivets. We'll settle the terms after the work is done. I've no more time to waste on you."

And he went off to look after his men.

In a state of great indignation Zi' Dima started on the job and his temper continued to rise as he bored hole after hole in the jar and in its broken section—holes for his iron rivets. Along with the squeaking of his tool went a running accompaniment of grunts which grew steadily louder and more frequent; his fury made his eyes more piercing and bloodshot and his face became green with bile. When he had finished that first operation, he flung his borer angrily into the basket and held the detached portion up against the jar to satisfy himself that the holes were at equal distances and fitted one another; next he took his pliers and cut a length of iron wire into as many pieces as he needed rivets, and then called to one of the men who were beating the olive trees to come and help him.

"Cheer up, Zi' Dima!" said the labourer, seeing how upset the old man looked.

Zi' Dima raised his hand with a savage gesture. He opened the tin which contained the cement and held it up towards heaven, as if offering it to God, seeing that men refused to recognise its value. Then he began to spread it with his finger all round the detached portion and along the broken edge of the jar. Taking his pliers and the iron rivets he had prepared, he crept inside the open belly of the jar and instructed the farmhand to hold the piece up, fitting it closely to the jar as he had himself done a short time previously. Before starting to put in the rivets, he spoke from inside the jar:—

"Pull! Pull! Tug at it with all your might! . . . You see it doesn't come loose. Curses on people who won't believe me! Knock it! Yes, knock it! . . . Doesn't it ring like a bell, even with me inside it? Go and tell your master that!"

"It's for the top-dog to give orders, Zi' Dima," said the man with a sigh, "and it's for the under-dog to carry them out. Put the rivets in. Put'em in."

Zi' Dima began to pass the bits of iron through the adjacent holes, one on each side of the crack, twisting up the ends with his pliers. It took him an hour to put them all in, and he poured with sweat inside the jar. As he worked, he complained of his misfortune and the farm-hand stayed near, trying to console him.

"Now help me to get out," said Zi' Dima, when all was finished.

But large though its belly was, the jar had a distinctly narrow neck—a fact which Zi' Dima had overlooked, being so absorbed in his grievance. Now, try as he would, he could not manage to squeeze his way out. Instead of helping him, the farm-hand stood idly by, convulsed with laughter. So there was poor Zi' Dima, imprisoned in the jar which he had mended and—there was no use in blinking at the fact—in a jar which would have to be broken to let him out, and this time broken for good.

Hearing the laughter and shouts, Don Lollo came rushing up. Inside the jar Zi' Dima was spitting like an angry cat.

"Let me out," he screamed, "for God's sake! I want to get out! Be quick! Help!"

Don Lollo was quite taken aback and unable to believe his own ears.

"What? Inside there? He's rivetted himself up inside?"

Then he went up to the jar and shouted out to Zi' Dima:—

"Help you? What help do you think I can give you? You stupid old dodderer, what d'you mean by it? Why couldn't you measure it first? Come, have a try! Put an arm out . . . that's it! Now the head! Up you come! . . . No, no, gently! . . . Down again. . . . Wait a bit! . . . Not that way. . . . Down, get down. . . . How on earth could you do such a thing? . . . What about my jar now? . . .

"Keep calm! Keep calm!" he recommended to all the onlookers, as if it was they who were becoming excited and not himself. . . . "My head's going round! Keep calm! This is quite a new point! Get me my mule!"

He rapped the jar with his knuckles. Yes, it really rang like a bell once again.

"Fine! Repaired as good as new. . . . You wait a bit!" he said to the prisoner; then instructed his man to be off and saddle the mule. He rubbed his forehead vigorously with his fingers, and continued:—

"I wonder what's the best course. That's not a jar, it's a con-

trivance of the devil himself. . . . Keep still! Keep still!" he exclaimed, rushing up to steady the jar, in which Zi' Dima, now
in a towering passion, was struggling like a wild animal in a
trap.

"It's a new point, my good man, which the lawyer must
settle. I can't rely on my own judgment. . . . Where's that mule?
Hurry up with the mule! . . . I'll go straight there and back.
You must wait patiently: it's in your own interest. . . . Meanwhile, keep quiet, be calm! I must look after my own rights.
And, first of all, to put myself in the right, I fulfill my obliga-
tion. Here you are! I am paying you for your work, for a
whole day's work. Here are your five lire. Is that enough?"

"I don't want anything," shouted Zi' Dima. "I want to get
out!"

"You shall get out, but meanwhile I, for my part, am paying
you. There they are—five lire."

He took the money out of his waistcoat pocket and tossed
it into the jar, then enquired in a tone of great concern:—

"Have you had any lunch? . . . Bread and something to eat
with it, at once! . . . What! You don't want it? Well, then,
throw it to the dogs! I shall have done my duty when I've given
it to you."

Having ordered the food, he mounted and set out for the
town. His wild gesticulations made those who saw him gallop-
ing past think that he might well be hastening to shut himself
up in a lunatic asylum.

As luck would have it, he did not have to spend much time
in the ante-room before being admitted to the lawyer's study;
he had, however, to wait a long while before the lawyer could
finish laughing, after the matter had been related to him. An-
noyed at the amusement he caused, Don Lollo said irritably:—

"Excuse me, but I don't see anything to laugh at. It's all
very well for your Honour, who is not the sufferer, but the jar
is my property."

The lawyer, however, continued to laugh and then made
him tell the story all over again, just as it had happened, so
that he could raise another laugh out of it.

"Inside, eh? So he'd rivetted himself inside?" And what did
Don Lollo want to do? . . . "To ke . . . to ke . . . keep him there
inside—ha! ha! ha! . . . keep him there inside, so as not to lose

the jar?"

"Why should I lose it?" cried Don Lollo, clenching his fists. "Why should I put up with the loss of my money, and have people laughing at me?"

"But don't you know what that's called?" said the lawyer at last. "It's called 'wrongful confinement'."

"Confinement? Well, who's confined him? He's confined himself! What fault is that of mine?"

The lawyer then explained to him that the matter gave rise to two cases: on the one hand he, Don Lollo, must straightway liberate the prisoner, if he wished to escape from being prosecuted for wrongful confinement; while, on the other hand, the rivetter would be responsible for making good the loss resulting from his lack of skill or his stupidity.

"Ah!" said Don Lollo, with a sigh of relief. "So he'll have to pay me for my jar?" .

"Wait a bit," remarked the lawyer. "Not as if it were a new jar, remember!"

"Why not?"

"Because it was a broken one, badly broken, too."

"Broken! No, Sir. Not broken. It's perfectly sound now and better than ever it was—he says so himself. And if I have to break it again, I shall not be able to have it mended. The jar will be ruined, Sir!"

The lawyer assured him that that point would be taken into account and that the rivetter would have to pay the value which the jar had in its present condition.

"Therefore," he counselled, "get the man himself to give you an estimate of its value first."

"I kiss your hands," Don Lollo murmured, and hurried away.

On his return home towards evening, he found all his labourers engaged in a celebration around the inhabited jar. The watch-dogs joined in the festivities with joyous barks and capers. Zi' Dima had not only calmed down, but had even come to enjoy his curious adventure and was able to laugh at it, with the melancholy humour of the unfortunate.

Don Lollo drove them all aside and bent down to look into the jar.

"Hallo! Getting along well?"

"Splendid! An open-air life for me!" replied the man. "It's

better than in my own house."

"I'm glad to hear it. Meanwhile I'd just like you to know that that jar cost me four florins when it was new. How much do you think it is worth now?"

"With me inside it?" asked Zi' Dima.

The rustics laughed.

"Silence!" shouted Don Lollo. "Either your cement is of some use or it is of no use. There is no third possibility. If it is of no use, you are a fraud. If it is of some use, the jar, in its present condition, must have a value. What is that value? I ask for your estimate."

After a space for reflection, Zi' Dima said:—

"Here is my answer: if you had let me mend it with cement only—as I wanted to do—first of all I should not have been shut up inside it and the jar would have had its original value, without any doubt. But spoilt by these rivets, which had to be done from inside, it has lost most of its value. It's worth a third of its former price, more or less."

"One-third? That's one florin, thirty-three cents."

"Maybe less, but not more than that."

"Well," said Don Lollo. "Promise me that you'll pay me one florin thirty-three cents."

"What?" asked Zi' Dima, as if he did not grasp the point.

"I will break the jar to let you out," replied Don Lollo. "And —the lawyer tells me—you are to pay me its value according to your own estimate—one florin thirty-three."

"I? Pay?" laughed Zi' Dima, "I'd sooner stay here till I rot!"

With some difficulty he managed to extract from his pocket a short and peculiarly foul pipe and lighted it, puffing out the smoke through the neck of the jar.

Don Lollo stood there scowling: the possibility that Zi' Dima would no longer be willing to leave the jar, had not been foreseen either by himself or by the lawyer. What step should he take now? He was on the point of ordering them to saddle the mule, but reflected that it was already evening.

"Oh ho!" he said. "So you want to take up your abode in my jar! I call upon all you men as witnesses to his statement. He refuses to come out, in order to escape from paying. I am quite prepared to break it. Well, as you insist on staying there, I shall take proceedings against you tomorrow for unlawful occupancy of the jar and for preventing me from my rightful use of it."

Zi' Dima blew out another puff of smoke and answered calmly:—

"No, your Honour. I don't want to prevent you at all. Do you think I am here because I like it? Let me out and I'll go away gladly enough. But as for paying, I wouldn't dream of it, your Honour."

In a sudden access of fury Don Lollo made to give a kick at the jar but stopped in time. Instead he seized it with both hands and shook it violently, uttering a hoarse growl.

"You see what fine cement it is," Zi' Dima remarked from inside.

"You rascal!" roared Don Lollo. "Whose fault is it, yours or mine? You expect me to pay for it, do you? You can starve to death inside first. We'll see who'll win."

He went away, forgetting all about the five lire which he had tossed into the jar that morning. But the first thing Zi' Dima thought of doing was to spend that money in having a festive evening, in company with the farm-hands, who had been delayed in their work by that strange accident, and had decided to spend the night at the farm, in the open air, sleeping on the threshing-floor. One of them went to a neighbouring tavern to make the necessary purchases. The moon was so bright that it seemed almost day—a splendid night for their carousal.

Many hours later Don Lollo was awakened by an infernal din. Looking out from the farm-house balcony, he could see in the moonlight what looked like a gang of devils on his threshing-floor: his men, all roaring drunk, were holding hands and performing a dance round the jar, while Zi' Dima, inside it, was singing at the top of his voice.

This time Don Lollo could not restrain himself, but rushed down like a mad bull and, before they could stop him, gave the jar a push which started it rolling down the slope. It continued on its course, to the delight of the intoxicated company, until it hit an olive tree and cracked in pieces, leaving Zi' Dima the winner in the dispute.

Hook

WALTER VAN TILBURG CLARK

Born in 1909 in Maine, Walter Van Tilburg Clark went to high school in Reno, Nevada, then attended the University of Nevada. Later he taught English for ten years in a small town high school in New York. For a good number of years now he has been living on an old ranch in Washoe Valley, Nevada, writing full time, with occasional lecturing stints at university writing centers. Among his books are The Ox-Bow Incident *(1940; the basis of a brilliant movie made in the early forties);* The City of Trembling Leaves *(1945);* The Track of the Cat *(1949); and* The Watchful Gods, And Other Stories *(1950), from which the story "Hook" has been chosen.*

1

HOOK, THE HAWKS' CHILD, was hatched in a dry spring among the oaks beside the seasonal river, and was struck from the nest early. In the drouth his single-willed parents had to extend their hunting ground by more than twice, for the ground creatures upon which they fed died and dried by the hundreds. The range became too great for them to wish to return and feed Hook, and when they had lost interest in each other they drove Hook down into the sand and brush and went back to solitary courses over the bleaching hills.

Unable to fly yet, Hook crept over the ground, challenging all large movements with recoiled head, erected, rudimentary wings, and the small rasp of his clattering beak. It was during this time of abysmal ignorance and continual fear that his eyes took on the first quality of a hawk, that of being wide, alert and challenging. He dwelt, because of his helplessness, among the rattling brush which grew between the oaks and the river. Even in his thickets and near the water, the white sun was the

dominant presence. Except in the dawn, when the land wind
stirred, or in the late afternoon, when the sea wind became
strong enough to penetrate the half-mile inland to this turn in
the river, the sun was the major force, and everything was dry
and motionless under it. The brush, small plants and trees
alike husbanded the little moisture at their hearts; the moving
creatures waited for dark, when sometimes the sea fog came
over and made a fine, soundless rain which relieved them.

The two spacious sounds of his life environed Hook at this
time. One was the great rustle of the slopes of yellowed wild
wheat, with over it the chattering rustle of the leaves of the
California oaks, already as harsh and individually tremulous
as in autumn. The other was the distant whisper of the foaming edge of the Pacific, punctuated by the hollow shoring of the
waves. But these Hook did not yet hear, for he was attuned by
fear and hunger to the small, spasmodic rustlings of live things.
Dry, shrunken, and nearly starved, and with his plumage delayed, he snatched at beetles, dragging in the sand to catch
them. When swifter and stronger birds and animals did not
reach them first, which was seldom, he ate the small, silver
fish left in the mud by the failing river. He watched, with nearly
chattering beak, the quick, thin lizards pause, very alert, and
raise and lower themselves, but could not catch them because
he had to raise his wings to move rapidly, which startled them.

Only one sight and sound not of his world of microscopic
necessity was forced upon Hook. That was the flight of the big
gulls from the beaches, which sometimes, in quealing play,
came spinning back over the foothills and the river bed. For
some inherited reason, the big, ship-bodied birds did not frighten
Hook, but angered him. Small and chewed-looking, with his
wide, already yellowing eyes glaring up at them, he would
stand in an open place on the sand in the sun and spread his
shaping wings and clatter his bill like shaken dice. Hook was
furious about the swift, easy passage of gulls.

His first opportunity to leave off living like a ground owl
came accidentally. He was standing in the late afternoon in the
red light under the thicket, his eyes half-filmed with drowse
and the stupefaction of starvation, when suddenly something
beside him moved, and he struck, and killed a field mouse driven
out of the wheat by thirst. It was a poor mouse, shriveled and

lice ridden, but in striking, Hook had tasted blood, which raised nest memories and restored his nature. With started neck plumage and shining eyes, he tore and fed. When the mouse was devoured, Hook had entered hoarse adolescence. He began to seek with a conscious appetite, and to move more readily out-of shelter. Impelled by the blood appetite, so glorious after his long preservation upon the flaky and bitter stuff of bugs, he ventured even into the wheat in the open sun beyond the oaks, and discovered the small trails and holes among the roots. With his belly often partially filled with flesh, he grew rapidly in strength and will. His eyes were taking on their final change, their yellow growing deeper and more opaque, their stare more constant, their challenge less desperate. Once during this transformation, he surprised a ground squirrel, and although he was ripped and wing-bitten and could not hold his prey, he was not dismayed by the conflict, but exalted. Even while the wing was still drooping and the pinions not grown back, he was excited by other ground squirrels and pursued them futilely, and was angered by their dusty escapes. He realized that his world was a great arena for killing, and felt the magnificence of it.

The two major events of Hook's young life occurred in the same day. A little after dawn he made the customary essay and succeeded in flight. A little before sunset, he made his first sustained flight of over two hundred yards, and at its termination struck and slew a great buck squirrel whose thrashing and terrified gnawing and squealing gave him a wild delight. When he had gorged on the strong meat, Hook stood upright, and in his eyes was the stare of the hawk, never flagging in intensity but never swelling beyond containment. After that the stare had only to grow more deeply challenging and more sternly controlled as his range and deadliness increased. There was no change in kind. Hook had mastered the first of the three hungers which are fused into the single, flaming will of a hawk, and he had experienced the second.

The third and consummating hunger did not awaken in Hook until the following spring, when the exultation of space had grown slow and steady in him, so that he swept freely with the wind over the miles of coastal foothills, circling, and ever in sight of the sea, and used without struggle the warm currents lifting from the slopes, and no longer desired to scream at the range of his vision, but intently sailed above his shadow swiftly climbing to meet him on the hillsides, sinking away and rippling across the brush-grown canyons.

That spring the rains were long, and Hook sat for hours, hunched and angry under their pelting, glaring into the fogs of the river valley, and killed only small, drenched things flooded up from their tunnels. But when the rains had dissipated, and there were sun and sea wind again, the game ran plentiful, the hills were thick and shining green, and the new river flooded about the boulders where battered turtles climbed up to shrink and sleep. Hook then was scorched by the third hunger. Ranging farther, often forgetting to kill and eat, he sailed for days with growing rage, and woke at night clattering on his dead tree limb, and struck and struck and struck at the porous wood of the trunk, tearing it away. After days, in the draft of a coastal canyon miles below his own hills, he came upon the acrid taint he did not know but had expected, and sailing down it, felt his neck plumes rise and his wings quiver so that he swerved unsteadily. He saw the unmated female perched upon the tall and jagged stump of a tree that had been shorn by storm, and he stooped, as if upon game. But she was older than he, and wary of the gripe of his importunity, and banked off screaming, and he screamed also at the intolerable delay.

At the head of the canyon, the screaming pursuit was crossed by another male with a great wing-spread, and the light golden in the fringe of his plumage. But his more skillful opening played him false against the ferocity of the twice-balked Hook. His rising maneuver for position was cut short by Hook's wild, upward swoop, and at the blow he raked desperately and tumbled off to the side. Dropping, Hook struck him again, struggled to clutch, but only raked and could not hold, and, diving, struck once more in passage, and then beat up, yelling triumph, and saw the crippled antagonist side-slip away, half-tumble once, as the ripped wing failed to balance, then steady and glide obliquely into the cover of brush on the canyon side. Beating hard and stationary in the wind above the bush that covered his competitor, Hook waited an instant, but when the bush was still, screamed again, and let himself go off with the current, reseeking, infuriated by the burn of his own wounds, the thin choke-thread of the acrid taint.

On a hilltop projection of stone two miles inland, he struck her down, gripping her rustling body with his talons, beating her wings down with his wings, belting her head when she whimpered or thrashed, and at last clutching her neck with his hook and, when her coy struggles had given way to stillness, succeeded.

In the early summer, Hook drove the three young ones from their nest, and went back to lone circling above his own range. He was complete.

2

Throughout that summer and the cool, growthless weather of the winter, when the gales blew in the river canyon and the ocean piled upon the shore, Hook was master of the sky and the hills of his range. His flight became a lovely and certain thing, so that he played with the treacherous currents of the air with a delicate ease surpassing that of the gulls. He could sail for hours, searching the blanched grasses below him with telescopic eyes, gaining height against the wind, descending in mile-long, gently declining swoops when he curved and rode back, and never beating either wing. At the swift passage of his shadow within their vision, gophers, ground squirrels and rabbits froze, or plunged gibbering into their tunnels beneath matted turf. Now, when he struck, he killed easily in one hard-knuckled blow. Occasionally, in sport, he soared up over the river and drove the heavy and weaponless gulls downstream again, until they would no longer venture inland.

There was nothing which Hook feared now, and his spirit was wholly belligerent, swift and sharp, like his gaze. Only the mixed smells and incomprehensible activities of the people at the Japanese farmer's home, inland of the coastwise highway and south of the bridge across Hook's river, troubled him. The smells were strong, unsatisfactory and never clear, and the people, though they behaved foolishly, constantly running in and out of their built-up holes, were large, and appeared capable, with fearless eyes looking up at him, so that he instinctively swerved aside from them. He cruised over their yard, their gardens, and their bean fields, but he would not alight close to their buildings.

But this one area of doubt did not interfere with his life. He ignored it, save to look upon it curiously as he crossed, his afternoon shadow sliding in an instant over the chicken-and-crate-cluttered yard, up the side of the unpainted barn, and then out again smoothly, just faintly, liquidly rippling over the furrows and then over the stubble of the grazing slopes. When the season was dry, and the dead earth blew on the fields, he extended his range to satisfy his great hunger, and again narrowed it when the fields were once more alive with the minute movements he could not only see but anticipate.

Four times that year he was challenged by other hawks blowing up from behind the coastal hills to scud down his slopes, but two of these he slew in mid-air, and saw hurtle down to thump on the ground and lie still while he circled, and a third, whose wing he tore, he followed closely to earth and beat to death in the grass, making the crimson jet out from its breast and neck into the pale wheat. The fourth was a strong flier and experienced fighter, and theirs was a long, running battle, with brief, rising flurries of striking and screaming, from which down and plumage soared off.

Here, for the first time, Hook felt doubts, and at moments wanted to drop away from the scoring, burning talons and the twisted hammer strokes of the strong beak, drop away shrieking, and take cover and be still. In the end, when Hook, having outmaneuvered his enemy and come above him, wholly in control, and going with the wind, tilted and plunged for the death rap, the other, in desperation, threw over on his back and struck up. Talons locked, beaks raking, they dived earthward. The earth grew and spread under them amazingly, and they were not fifty feet above it when Hook, feeling himself turning toward the underside, tore free and beat up again on heavy, wrenched wings. The other, stroking swiftly, and so close to down that he lost wing plumes to a bush, righted himself and planed up, but flew on lumberingly between the hills and did not return. Hook screamed the triumph, and made a brief pretense of pursuit, but was glad to return, slow and victorious, to his dead tree.

In all these encounters Hook was injured, but experienced only the fighter's pride and exultation from the sting of wounds received in successful combat. And in each of them he learned new skill. Each time the wounds healed quickly, and left him a more dangerous bird.

In the next spring, when the rains and the night chants of the little frogs were past, the third hunger returned upon Hook with a new violence. In this quest, he came into the taint of a young hen. Others too were drawn by the unnerving perfume, but only one of them, the same with which Hook had fought his great battle, was a worthy competitor. This hunter drove off two, while two others, game but neophytes, were glad enough that Hook's impatience would not permit him to follow and kill. Then the battle between the two champions fled inland, and was a tactical marvel, but Hook lodged the neck-breaking blow, and struck again as they dropped past the treetops. The blood had already begun to pool on the gray, fallen foliage as Hook flapped up between branches, too spent to cry his victory. Yet his hunger would not let him rest until, late in the second day, he drove the female to ground among the laurels of a strange river canyon.

When the two fledglings of this second brood had been driven from the nest, and Hook had returned to his own range, he was not only complete, but supreme. He slept without concealment on his bare limb, and did not open his eyes when, in the night, the heavy-billed cranes coughed in the shallows below him.

•

3

The turning point of Hook's career came that autumn, when the brush in the canyons rustled dryly and the hills, mowed close by the cattle, smoked under the wind as if burning. One midafternoon, when the black clouds were torn on the rim of the sea and the surf flowered white and high on the rocks, raining in over the low cliffs, Hook rode the wind diagonally across the river mouth. His great eyes, focused for small things, stirring in the dust and leaves, overlooked so large and slow a movement as that of the Japanese farmer rising from the brush and lifting the two black eyes of his shotgun. Too late Hook saw and, startled, swerved, but wrongly. The surf muffled the reports, and nearly without sound, Hook felt the minute whips of the first shot, and the astounding, breath-taking blow of the second.

Beating his good wing, tasting the blood that quickly swelled into his beak, he tumbled off with the wind and struck into the thickets on the far side of the river mouth. The branches tore him. Wild with rage, he thrust up and clattered his beak, challenging, but when he had fallen over twice, he knew that the trailing wing would not carry, and then heard the boots of the hunter among the stones in the river bed and, seeing him loom at the edge of the bushes, crept back among the thickest brush and was still. When he saw the boots stand before him, he reared back, lifting his good wing and cocking his head for the serpent-like blow, his beak open but soundless, his great eyes hard and very shining. The boots passed on. The Japanese farmer, who believed that he had lost chickens, and who had cunningly observed Hook's flight for many afternoons, until he could plot it, did not greatly want a dead hawk.

When Hook could hear nothing but the surf and the wind in the thicket, he let the sickness and shock overcome him. The fine film of the inner lid dropped over his big eyes. His heart beat frantically, so that it made the plumage of his shot-aching breast throb. His own blood throttled his breathing. But these things were nothing compared to the lightning of pain in his left shoulder, where the shot had bunched, shattering the airy bones so the pinions trailed on the ground and could not be lifted. Yet, when a sparrow lit in the bush over him, Hook's eyes flew open again, hard and challenging, his good wing was lifted and his beak strained open. The startled sparrow darted piping out over the river.

Throughout that night, while the long clouds blew across the stars and the wind shook the bushes about him, and throughout the next day, while the clouds still blew and massed until there was no gleam of sunlight on the sand bar, Hook remained stationary, enduring his sickness. In the second evening, the rains began. First there was a long, running patter of drops upon the beach and over the dry trees and bushes. At dusk there came a heavier squall, which did not die entirely, but slacked off to a continual, spaced splashing of big drops, and then returned with the front of the storm. In long, misty curtains, gust by gust, the rain swept over the sea, beating down its heaving, and coursed up the beach. The little jets of dust ceased to rise about the drops in the fields, and the mud began to gleam. Among the boulders of the river bed, darkling pools grew slowly.

Still Hook stood behind his tree from the wind, only gentle drops reaching him, falling from the upper branches and then again from the brush. His eyes remained closed, and he could still taste his own blood in his mouth, though it had ceased to come up freshly. Out beyond him, he heard the storm changing. As rain conquered the sea, the heave of the surf became a hushed sound, often lost in the crying of the wind. Then gradually, as the night turned toward morning, the wind also was broken by the rain. The crying became fainter, the rain settled toward steadiness, and the creep of the waves could be heard again, quiet and regular upon the beach.

At dawn there was no wind and no sun, but everywhere the roaring of the vertical, relentless rain. Hook then crept among the rapid drippings of the bushes, dragging his torn sail, seeking better shelter. He stopped often and stood with the shutters of film drawn over his eyes. At midmorning he found a little cave under a ledge at the base of the sea cliff. Here, lost without branches and leaves about him, he settled to await improvement.

When, at midday of the third day, the rain stopped altogether, and the sky opened before a small, fresh wind, letting light through to glitter upon a tremulous sea, Hook was so weak that his good wing trailed also to prop him upright, and his open eyes were lusterless. But his wounds were hardened, and he felt the return of hunger. Beyond his shelter, he heard the gulls flying in great numbers and crying their joy at the cleared air. He could even hear, from the fringe of the river, the ecstatic and unstinted bubblings and chirpings of the small birds. The grassland, he felt, would be full of the stirring anew of the close-bound life, the undrowned insects clicking as they dried out, the snakes slithering down, heads half erect, into the grasses where the mice, gophers and ground squirrels ran and stopped and chewed and licked themselves smoother and drier.

With the aid of this hunger, and on the crutches of his wings, Hook came down to stand in the sun beside his cave, whence he could watch the beach. Before him, in ellipses on tilting planes, the gulls flew. The surf was rearing again, and beginning to shelve and hiss on the sand. Through the white foam-writing it left, the long-billed pipers twinkled in bevies, escaping each wave, then racing down after it to plunge their fine drills into the minute double holes where the sand crabs bubbled. In the third row of breakers two seals lifted sleek, streaming heads and barked, and over them, trailing his spider legs, a great crane flew south. Among the stones at the foot of the cliff, small red and green crabs made a little, continuous rattling and knocking. The cliff swallows glittered and twanged on aerial forays.

The afternoon began auspiciously for Hook also. One of the two gulls which came squabbling above him dropped a freshly caught fish to the sand. Quickly Hook was upon it. Gripping it, he raised his good wing and cocked his head with open beak at the many gulls which had circled and come down at once toward the fall of the fish. The gulls sheered off, cursing raucously. Left alone on the sand, Hook devoured the fish and, after resting in the sun, withdrew again to his shelter.

4

In the succeeding days, between rains, he foraged on the beach. He learned to kill and crack the small green crabs. Along the edge of the river mouth, he found the drowned bodies of mice and squirrels and even sparrows. Twice he managed to drive feeding gulls from their catch, charging upon them with buffeting wing and clattering beak. He grew stronger slowly, but the shot sail continued to drag. Often, at the choking thought of soaring and striking and the good, hot-blood kill, he strove to take off, but only the one wing came up, winnowing with a hiss, and drove him over onto his side in the sand. After these futile trials, he would rage and clatter. But gradually he learned to believe that he could not fly, that his life must now be that of the discharged nestling again. Denied the joy of space, without which the joy of loneliness was lost, the joy of battle and killing, the blood lust, became his whole concentration. It was his hope, as he charged feeding gulls, that they would turn and offer battle, but they never did. The sandpipers, at his approach, fled peeping, or, like a quiver of arrows shot together, streamed out over the surf in a long curve. Once, pent beyond bearing, he disgraced himself by shrieking challenge at the businesslike heron which flew south every evening at the same time. The heron did not even turn his head, but flapped and glided on.

Hook's shame and anger became such that he stood awake at night. Hunger kept him awake also, for these little leavings of the gulls could not sustain his great body in its renewed violence. He became aware that the gulls slept at night in flocks on the sand, each with one leg tucked under him. He discovered also that the curlews and the pipers, often mingling, likewise slept, on the higher remnant of the bar. A sensation of evil delight filled him in the consideration of protracted striking among them.

There was only half of a sick moon in a sky of running but far-separated clouds on the night when he managed to stalk into the center of the sleeping gulls. This was light enough, but so great was his vengeful pleasure that there broke from him a shrill scream of challenge as he first struck. Without the power of flight behind it, the blow was not murderous, and this newly discovered impotence made Hook crazy, so that he screamed again and again as he struck and tore at the felled gull. He slew the one, but was twice knocked over by its heavy flounderings, and all the others rose above him, weaving and screaming, protesting in the thin moonlight. Wakened by their clamor, the wading birds also took wing, startled and plaintive. When the beach was quiet again, the flocks had settled elsewhere, beyond his pitiful range, and he was left alone beside the single kill. It was a disappointing victory. He fed with lowering spirit.

Thereafter, he stalked silently. At sunset he would watch where the gulls settled along the miles of beach, and after dark he would come like a sharp shadow among them, and drive with his hook on all sides of him, till the beatings of a poorly struck victim sent the flock up. Then he would turn vindictively upon the fallen and finish them. In his best night, he killed five from one flock. But he ate only a little from one, for the vigor resulting from occasional repletion strengthened only his ire, which became so great at such a time that food revolted him. It was not the joyous, swift, controlled hunting anger of a sane hawk, but something quite different, which made him dizzy if it continued too long, and left him unsatisfied with any kill.

Then one day, when he had very nearly struck a gull while driving it from a gasping yellowfin, the gull's wing rapped against him as it broke for its running start, and, the trailing wing failing to support him, he was knocked over. He flurried awkwardly in the sand to regain his feet, but his mastery of the beach was ended. Seeing him, in clear sunlight, struggling after the chance blow, the gulls returned about him in a flashing cloud, circling and pecking on the wing. Hook's plumage showed quick little jets of irregularity here and there. He reared back, clattering and erecting the good wing, spreading the great, rusty tail for balance. His eyes shone with a little of the old pleasure. But it died, for he could reach none of them. He was forced to turn and dance awkwardly on the sand, trying to clash bills with each tormentor. They banked up quealing and returned, weaving about him in concentric and overlapping circles. His scream was lost in their clamor, and he appeared merely to be hopping clumsily with his mouth open. Again he fell sideways. Before he could right himself, he was bowled over, and a second time, and lay on his side, twisting his neck to reach them and clappering in blind fury, and was struck three times by three successive gulls, shrieking their flock triumph.

Finally he managed to roll to his breast, and to crouch with his good wing spread wide and the other stretched nearly as far, so that he extended like a gigantic moth, only his snake head, with its now silent scimitar, erect. One great eye blazed under its level brow, but where the other had been was a shallow hole from which thin blood trickled to his russet gap.

In this crouch, by short stages, stopping repeatedly to turn and drive the gulls up, Hook dragged into the river canyon and under the stiff cover of the bitter-leafed laurel. There the gulls left him, soaring up with great clatter of their valor. Till nearly sunset Hook, broken spirited and enduring his hardening eye socket, heard them celebrating over the waves.

When his will was somewhat replenished, and his empty eye socket had stopped the twiching and vague aching which had forced him often to roll ignominiously to rub it in the dust, Hook ventured from the protective lacings of his thicket. He knew fear again, and the challenge of his remaining eye was once more strident, as in adolescence. He dared not return to the beaches, and with a new, weak hunger, the home hunger, enticing him, made his way by short hunting journeys back to the wild wheat slopes and the crisp oaks. There was in Hook an unwonted sensation now, that of the ever-neighboring possi-

bility of death. This sensation was beginning, after his period
as a mad bird on the beach, to solidify him into his last stage of
life. When, during his slow homeward passage, the gulls wafted
inland over him, watching the earth with curious, miserish eyes,
he did not cower, but neither did he challenge, either by opened
beak or by raised shoulder. He merely watched carefully, learning his first lessons in observing the world with one eye.

At first the familiar surroundings of the bend in the river and
the tree with the dead limb to which he could not ascend, aggra-
vated his humiliation, but in time, forced to live cunningly and
half-starved, he lost much of his savage pride. At the first flight
of a strange hawk over his realm, he was wild at his helplessness,
and kept twisting his head like an owl, or spinning in the grass
like a small and feathered dervish, to keep the hateful beauty of
the wind-rider in sight. But in the succeeding weeks, as one
after another coasted his beat, his resentment declined, and
when one of the raiders, a haughty yearling, sighted his up-
staring eye, and plunged and struck him dreadfully, and failed
to kill him only because he dragged under a thicket in time, the
second of his great hungers was gone. He had no longer the
true lust to kill, no joy of battle, but only the poor desire to fill
his belly.

Then truly he lived in the wheat and the brush like a ground
owl, ridden with ground lice, dusty or muddy, ever half-starved,
forced to sit for hours by small holes for petty and unsatisfying
kills. Only once during the final months before his end did he
make a kill where the breath of danger recalled his valor, and
then the danger was such as a hawk with wings and eyes would
scorn. Waiting beside a gopher hole, surrounded by the high,
yellow grass, he saw the head emerge, and struck, and was
amazed that there writhed in his clutch the neck and dusty
coffin-skull of a rattlesnake. Holding his grip, Hook saw the
great, thick body slither up after, the tip an erect, strident blur,
and writhe on the dirt of the gopher's mound. The weight of
the snake pushed Hook about, and once threw him down, and
the rising and falling whine of the rattles made the moment terrible, but the vaulted mouth, gaping from the closeness of
Hook's grip, so that the pale, envenomed sabers stood out free,
could not reach him. When Hook replaced the grip of his beak
with the grip of his talons, and was free to strike again and again

at the base of the head, the struggle was over. Hook tore and
fed on the fine, watery flesh, and left the tattered armor and
the long, jointed bone for the marching ants.

When the heavy rains returned, he ate well during the period
of the first escapes from flooded burrows, and then well enough,
in a vulture's way, on the drowned creatures. But as the rains
lingered, and the burrows hung full of water, and there were no
insects in the grass and no small birds sleeping in the thickets, he
was constantly hungry, and finally unbearably hungry. His sod-
den and ground-broken plumage stood out raggedly about him,
so that he looked fat, even bloated, but underneath it his skin
clung to his bones. Save for his great talons and clappers, and
the rain in his down, he would have been like a handful of air.
He often stood for a long time under some bush or ledge, heedless of the drip, his one eye filmed over, his mind neither asleep
or awake, but between. The gurgle and swirl of the brimming
river, and the sound of chunks of the bank cut away to splash
and dissolve in the already muddy flood, became familiar to
him, and yet a torment, as if that great, ceaselessly working
power of water ridiculed his frailty, within which only the faint-
est spark of valor still glimmered. The last two nights before the
rain ended, he huddled under the floor of the bridge on the
coastal highway, and heard the palpitant thunder of motors
swell and roar over him. The trucks shook the bridge so that
Hook, even in his famished lassitude, would sometimes open his
one great eye wide and startled.

5

After the rains, when things became full again, bursting with
growth and sound, the trees swelling, the thickets full of song
and chatter, the fields, turning green in the sun, alive with rustling passages, and the moonlit nights strained with the song of
the peepers all up and down the river and in the pools in the
fields, Hook had to bear the return of the one hunger left him.
At times this made him so wild that he forgot himself and
screamed challenge from the open ground. The fretfulness of it
spoiled his hunting, which was not entirely a matter of patience.
Once he was in despair, and lashed himself through the grass

and thickets, trying to rise when that virgin scent drifted for a
few moments above the current of his own river. Then, breathless, his beak agape, he saw the strong suitor ride swiftly down
on the wind over him, and heard afar the screaming fuss of the
harsh wooing in the alders. For that moment even the battle
heart beat in him again. The rim of his good eye was scarlet, and
a little bead of new blood stood in the socket of the other. With
beak and talon, he ripped at a fallen log, and made loam and
leaves fly from about it.

But the season of love passed over to the nesting season, and
Hook's love hunger, unused, shriveled in him with the others,
and there remained in him only one stern quality befitting a
hawk, and that the negative one, the remnant, the will to endure. He resumed his patient, plotted hunting, now along a
field of the Japanese farmer, but ever within reach of the river
thickets.

Growing tough and dry again as the summer advanced, in-
ured to the family of the farmer, whom he saw daily, stooping
and scraping with sticks in the ugly, open rows of their fields,
where no lovely grass rustled and no life stirred save the shame-
less gulls, which walked at the heels of the workers, gobbling
the worms and grubs they turned up, Hook became nearly content with his shard of life. The only longing or resentment to
pierce him was that which he suffered occasionally when forced
to hide at the edge of the mile-long bean field from the wafted
cruising and the restive, down-bent gaze of one of his own kind.
For the rest, he was without flame, a snappish, dust-colored
creature, fading into the grasses he trailed through, and suited
to his petty ways.

At the end of that summer, for the second time in his four
years, Hook underwent a drouth. The equinoctial period passed
without a rain. The laurel and the rabbit-brush dropped dry
leaves. The foliage of the oaks shriveled and curled. Even the
night fogs in the river canyon failed. The farmer's red cattle on
the hillside lowed constantly, and could not feed on the dusty
stubble. Grass fires broke out along the highways, and ate fast
in the wind, filling the hollows with the smell of smoke, and
died in the dirt of the shorn hills. The river made no sound.
Scum grew on its vestigal pools, and turtles died and stank
among the rocks. The dust rode before the wind, and ascended

and flowered to nothing between the hills, and every sunset was red with the dust in the air. The people in the farmer's house quarreled, and even struck one another. Birds were silent, and only the hawks flew much. The animals lay breathing hard for very long spells, and ran and crept jerkily. Their flanks were fallen in, and their eyes were red.

At first Hook gorged at the fringe of the grass fires on the multitudes of tiny things that came running and squeaking. But thereafter there were the blackened strips on the hills, and little more in the thin, crackling grass. He found mice and rats, gophers and ground-squirrels, and even rabbits, dead in the stubble and under the thickets, but so dry and fleshless that only a faint smell rose from them, even on the sunny days. He starved on them. By early December he had wearily stalked the length of the eastern foothills, hunting at night to escape the voracity of his own kind, resting often upon his wings. The queer trail of his short steps and great horned toes zigzagged in the dust and was erased by the wind at dawn. He was nearly dead, and could make no sound through the horn funnels of his clappers.

Then one night the dry wind brought him, with the familiar, lifeless dust, another familiar scent, troublesome, mingled and unclear. In his vision-dominated brain he remembered the swift circle of his flight a year past, crossing in one segment, his shadow beneath him, a yard cluttered with crates and chickens, a gray barn and then again the plowed land and the stubble. Traveling faster than he had for days, impatient of his shrunken sweep, Hook came down to the farm. In the dark wisps of cloud blown among the stars over him, but no moon, he stood outside the wire of the chicken run. The scent of fat and blooded birds reached him from the shelter, and also within the enclosure was water. At the breath of the water, Hook's gorge contracted, and his tongue quivered and clove in its groove of horn. But there was the wire. He stalked its perimeter and found no opening. He beat it with his good wing, and felt it cut but not give. He wrenched at it with his beak in many places, but could not tear it. Finally, in a fury which drove the thin blood through him, he leaped repeatedly against it, beating and clawing. He was thrown back from the last leap as from the first, but in it he had risen so high as to clutch with his beak at the top wire. While he lay on his breast on the ground, the significance of this came upon him.

Again he leapt, clawed up the wire, and, as he would have
fallen, made even the dead wing bear a little. He grasped the
top and tumbled within. There again he rested flat, searching the
dark with quick-turning head. There was no sound or motion
but the throb of his own body. First he drank at the chill metal
trough hung for the chickens. The water was cold, and loosened
his tongue and his tight throat, but it also made him drunk and
dizzy, so that he had to rest again, his claws spread wide to brace
him. Then he walked stiffly, to stalk down the scent. He trailed
it up the runway. Then there was the stuffy, body-warm air,
acrid with droppings, full of soft rustlings as his talons clicked
on the board floor. The thick, white shapes showed faintly in
the darkness. Hook struck quickly, driving a hen to the floor
with one blow, its neck broken and stretched out stringily. He
leaped the still pulsing body, and tore it. The rich, streaming
blood was overpowering to his dried senses, his starved, leathery body. After a few swallows, the flesh choked him. In his
rage, he struck down another hen. The urge to kill took him
again, as in those nights on the beach. He could let nothing
go. Balked of feeding, he was compelled to slaughter. Clattering,
he struck again and again. The henhouse was suddenly filled
with the squawking and helpless rushing and buffeting of the
terrified, brainless fowls.

Hook reveled in mastery. Here was game big enough to offer
weight against a strike, and yet unable to soar away from his
blows. Turning in the midst of the turmoil, cannily, his fury
caught at the perfect pitch, he struck unceasingly. When the
hens finally discovered the outlet, and streamed into the yard,
to run around the fence, beating and squawking, Hook followed
them, scraping down the incline, clumsy and joyous. In the
yard, the cock, a bird as large as he, and much heavier, found
him out and gave valiant battle. In the dark, and both earth-
bound, there was little skill, but blow upon blow, and only
chance parry. The still squawking hens pressed into one corner
of the yard. While the duel went on, a dog, excited by the
sustained scuffling, began to bark. He continued to bark, running back and forth along the fence on one side. A light flashed
on in an uncurtained widow of the farmhouse, and streamed
whitely over the crates littering the ground.

Enthralled by his old battle joy, Hook knew only the burly cock before him. Now, in the farthest reach of the window light, they could see each other dimly. The Japanese farmer, with his gun and lantern, was already at the gate when the finish came. The great cock leapt to jab with his spurs and, toppling forward with extended neck as he fell, was struck and extinguished. Blood had loosened Hook's throat. Shrilly he cried his triumph. It was a thin and exhausted cry, but within him as good as when he shrilled in mid-air over the plummeting descent of a fine foe in his best spring.

The light from the lantern partially blinded Hook. He first turned and ran directly from it, into the corner where the hens were huddled. They fled apart before his charge. He essayed the fence, and on the second try, in his desperation, was out. But in the open dust, the dog was on him, circling, dashing in, snapping. The farmer, who at first had not fired because of the chickens, now did not fire because of the dog, and, when he saw that the hawk was unable to fly, relinquished the sport to the dog, holding the lantern up in order to see better. The light showed his own flat, broad, dark face as sunken also, the cheekbones very prominent, and showed the torn-off sleeves of his shirt and the holes in the knees of his overalls. His wife, in a stained wrapper, and barefooted, heavy black hair hanging around a young, passionless face, joined him hesitantly, but watched, fascinated and a little horrified. His son joined them too, encouraging the dog, but quickly grew silent. Courageous and cruel death, however it may afterward sicken the one who has watched it, is impossible to look away from.

In the circle of the light, Hook turned to keep the dog in front of him. His one eye gleamed with malevolence. The dog was an Airedale, and large. Each time he pounced, Hook stood ground, raising his good wing, the pinions newly torn by the fence, opening his beak soundlessly, and, at the closest approach, hissed furiously, and at once struck. Hit and ripped twice by the whetted horn, the dog recoiled more quickly from several subsequent jumps and, infuriated by his own cowardice, began to bark wildly. Hook maneuvered to watch him, keeping his head turned to avoid losing the foe on the blind side. When the dog paused, safely away, Hook watched him quietly, wing partially lowered, beak closed, but at the first move again lifted the wing and gaped. The dog whined, and the man spoke to him encouragingly. The awful sound of his voice made Hook for an instant twist his head to stare up at the immense figures behind the light. The dog again sallied, barking, and Hook's head spun back. His wing was bitten this time, and with a furious side-blow, he caught the dog's nose. The dog dropped him with a yelp, and then, smarting, came on more warily, as Hook propped himself up from the ground again between his wings. Hook's artificial strength was waning, but his heart still stood to the battle, sustained by a fear of such dimension as he had never known before, but only anticipated when the arrogant young hawk had driven him to cover. The dog, unable to find any point at which the merciless, unwinking eye was not watching him, the parted beak waiting, paused and whimpered again.

"Oh, kill the poor thing," the woman begged.

The man, though, encouraged the dog again, saying, "Sick him; sick him."

The dog rushed bodily. Unable to avoid him, Hook was bowled down, snapping and raking. He left long slashes, as from the blade of a knife, on the dog's flank, but before he could right himself and assume guard again, was caught by the good wing and dragged, clattering, and seeking to make a good stroke from his back. The man followed them to keep the light on them, and the boy went with him, wetting his lips with his tongue and keeping his fists closed tightly. The woman remained behind, but could not help watching the diminished conclusion.

In the little, palely shining arena, the dog repeated his successful maneuver three times, growling but not barking, and when Hook thrashed up from the third blow, both wings were trailing, and dark, shining streams crept on his black-fretted breast from the shoulders. The great eye flashed more furiously than it ever had in victorious battle, and the beak still gaped, but there was no more clatter. He faltered when turning to keep front; the broken wings played him false even as props. He could not rise to use his talons.

The man had tired of holding the lantern up, and put it down to rub his arm. In the low, horizontal light, the dog charged again, this time throwing the weight of his forepaws against Hook's shoulder, so that Hook was crushed as he struck. With his talons up, Hook raked at the dog's belly, but the dog conceived the finish, and furiously worried the feathered bulk. Hook's neck went limp, and between his gaping clappers came only a faint chittering, as from some small kill of his own in the grasses.

In this last conflict, however, there had been some minutes of the supreme fire of the hawk whose three hungers are perfectly fused in the one will; enough to burn off a year of shame.

Between the great sails the light body lay caved and perfectly still. The dog, smarting from his cuts, came to the master and was praised. The woman, joining them slowly, looked at the great wingspread, her husband raising the lantern that she might see it better.

"Oh, the brave bird," she said.

The Downward Path to Wisdom

KATHERINE ANNE PORTER

Born in Indian Creek, Texas in 1894, Katherine Anne Porter has traveled widely in Europe and America. She began writing at a very early age but made no attempts to publish until she was in her thirties. In 1931 she won a Guggenheim Fellowship for study abroad. Miss Porter has written numerous book reviews, political articles, and short stories. She has published three well-known collections of short fiction, Flowering Judas, The Leaning Tower, *and* Pale Horse, Pale Rider; *and, most recently, a collection of essays and critical writings,* The Days Before.

IN THE SQUARE BEDROOM with the big window Mama and Papa were lolling back on their pillows handing each other things

from the wide black tray on the small table with crossed legs.
They were smiling and they smiled even more when the little
boy, with the feeling of sleep still in his skin and hair, came in
and walked up to the bed. Leaning against it, his bare toes
wriggling in the white fur rug, he went on eating peanuts which
he took from his pajama pocket. He was four years old.

"Here's my baby," said Mama. "Lift him up, will you?"

He went limp as a rag for Papa to take him under the arms
and swing him up over a broad, tough chest. He sank between
his parents like a bear cub in a warm litter, and lay there comfortably. He took another peanut between his teeth, cracked
the shell, picked out the nut whole and ate it.

"Running around without his slippers again," said Mama.
"His feet are like icicles."

"He crunches like a horse," said Papa. "Eating peanuts before breakfast will ruin his stomach. Where did he get them?"

"You brought them yesterday," said Mama, with exact memory, "in a grisly little cellophane sack. I have asked you dozens
of times not to bring him things to eat. Put him out, will you?
He's spilling shells all over me."

Almost at once the little boy found himself on the floor
again. He moved around to Mama's side of the bed and leaned
confidingly near her and began another peanut. As he chewed
he gazed solemnly in her eyes.

"Bright-looking specimen, isn't he?" asked Papa, stretching
his long legs and reaching for his bathrobe. "I suppose you'll
say it's my fault he's dumb as an ox."

"He's my little baby, my only baby," said Mama richly, hugging him, "and he's a dear lamb." His neck and shoulders were
quite boneless in her firm embrace. He stopped chewing long
enough to receive a kiss on his crumby chin. "He's sweet as
clover," said Mama. The baby went on chewing.

"Look at him staring like an owl," said Papa.

Mama said, "He's an angel and I'll never get used to having
him."

"We'd be better off if we never *had* had him," said Papa.
He was walking about the room and his back was turned when
he said that. There was silence for a moment. The little boy
stopped eating, and stared deeply at his Mama. She was looking
at the back of Papa's head, and her eyes were almost black.

"You're going to say that just once too often," she told him in a low voice. "I hate you when you say that."

Papa said, "You spoil him to death. You never correct him for anything. And you don't take care of him. You let him run around eating peanuts before breakfast."

"You gave him the peanuts, remember that," said Mama. She sat up and hugged her only baby once more. He nuzzled softly in the pit of her arm. "Run along, my darling," she told him in her gentlest voice, smiling at him straight in the eyes. "Run along," she said, her arms falling away from him. "Get your breakfast."

The little boy had to pass his father on the way to the door. He shrank into himself when he saw the big hand raised above him. "Yes, get out of here and stay out," said Papa, giving him a little shove toward the door. It was not a hard shove, but it hurt the little boy. He slunk out, and trotted down the hall trying not to look back. He was afraid something was coming after him, he could not imagine what. Something hurt him all over, he did not know why.

He did not want his breakfast; he would not have it. He sat and stirred it round in the yellow bowl, letting it stream off the spoon and spill on the table, on his front, on the chair. He liked seeing it spill. It was hateful stuff, but it looked funny running in white rivulets down his pajamas.

"Now look what you're doing, dirty boy," said Marjory. "You dirty little old boy."

The little boy opened his mouth to speak for the first time. "You're dirty yourself," he told her.

"That's right," said Marjory, leaning over him and speaking so her voice would not carry. "That's right, just like your papa. Mean," she whispered, "mean."

The little boy took up his yellow bowl full of cream and oatmeal and sugar with both hands and brought it down with a crash on the table. It burst and some of the wreck lay in chunks and some of it ran all over everything. He felt better.

"You see?" said Marjory, dragging him out of the chair and scrubbing him with a napkin. She scrubbed him as roughly as she dared until he cried out. "That's just what I said. That's exactly it." Through his tears he saw her face terribly near, red and frowning under a stiff white band, looking like the face of somebody who came at night and stood over him and scolded him when he could not move or get away. "Just like your papa, *mean.*"

The little boy went out into the garden and sat on a green bench dangling his legs. He was clean. His hair was wet and his blue woolly pull-over made his nose itch. His face felt stiff from the soap. He saw Marjory going past a window with the black tray. The curtains were still closed at the window he knew opened into Mama's room. Papa's room. Mommanpoppas-room, the word was pleasant, it made a mumbling snapping noise between his lips; it ran in his mind while his eyes wandered about looking for something to do, something to play with.

Mommanpoppas' voices kept attracting his attention. Mama was being cross with Papa again. He could tell by the sound. That was what Marjory always said when their voices rose and fell and shot up to a point and crashed and rolled like the two tomcats who fought at night. Papa was being cross, too, much crosser than Mama this time. He grew cold and disturbed and sat very still, wanting to go to the bathroom, but it was just next to Mommanpoppasroom; he didn't dare think of it. As the voices grew louder he could hardly hear them any more, he wanted so badly to go to the bathroom. The kitchen door opened suddenly and Marjory ran out, making the motion with her hand that meant he was to come to her. He didn't move. She came to him, her face still red and frowning, but she was not angry; she was scared just as he was. She said, "Come on, honey, we've got to go to your gran'ma's again." She took his hand and pulled him. "Come on quick, your gran'ma is waiting for you." He slid off the bench. His mother's voice rose in a terrible scream, screaming something he could not understand, but she was furious; he had seen her clenching her fists and stamping in one spot, screaming with her eyes shut; he knew how she looked. She was screaming in a tantrum, just as he remembered having heard himself. He stood still, doubled over, and all his body seemed to dissolve, sickly, from the pit of his stomach.

"Oh, my God," said Marjory. "Oh, my God. Now look at you. Oh, my God. I can't stop to clean you up."

He did not know how he got to his grandma's house, but he

was there at last, wet and soiled, being handled with disgust in the big bathtub. His grandma was there in long black skirts saying, "Maybe he's sick; maybe we should send for the doctor."

"I don't think so, m'am," said Marjory. "He hasn't et anything; he's just scared."

The little boy couldn't raise his eyes, he was so heavy with shame. "Take this note to his mother," said Grandma.

She sat in a wide chair and ran her hands over his head, combing his hair with her fingers; she lifted his chin and kissed him. "Poor little fellow," she said. "Never you mind. You always have a good time at your grandma's, don't you? You're going to have a nice little visit, just like the last time."

The little boy leaned against the stiff, dry-smelling clothes and felt horribly grieved about something. He began to whimper and said, "I'm hungry. I want something to eat." This reminded him. He began to bellow at the top of his voice; he threw himself upon the carpet and rubbed his nose in a dusty woolly bouquet of roses. "I want my peanuts," he howled. "Somebody took my peanuts."

His grandma knelt beside him and gathered him up so tightly he could hardly move. She called in a calm voice above his howls to Old Janet in the doorway, "Bring me some bread and butter with strawberry jam."

"I want peanuts," yelled the little boy desperately.

"No, you don't, darling," said his grandma. "You don't want horrid old peanuts to make you sick. You're going to have some of grandma's nice fresh bread with good strawberries on it. That's what you're going to have." He sat afterward very quietly and ate and ate. His grandma sat near him and Old Janet stood by, near a tray with a loaf and a glass bowl of jam upon the table at the window. Outside there was a trellis with tube-shaped red flowers clinging all over it, and brown bees singing.

"I hardly know what to do," said Grandma, "it's very . . ."

"Yes, m'am," said Old Janet, "it certainly is . . ."

Grandma said, "I can't possibly see the end of it. It's a terrible . . ."

"It certainly is bad," said Old Janet, "all this upset all the time and him such a baby."

Their voices ran on soothingly. The little boy ate and forgot to listen. He did not know these women, except by name. He could not understand what they were talking about; their hands and their clothes and their voices were dry and far away; they examined him with crinkled eyes without any expression that he could see. He sat there waiting for whatever they would do next with him. He hoped they would let him go out and play in the yard. The room was full of flowers and dark red curtains and big soft chairs, and the windows were open, but it was still dark in there somehow; dark, and a place he did not know, or trust.

"Now drink your milk," said Old Janet, holding out a silver cup.

"I don't want any milk," he said, turning his head away.

"Very well, Janet, he doesn't have to drink it," said Grandma quickly. "Now run out in the garden and play, darling. Janet, get his hoop."

A big strange man came home in the evenings who treated the little boy very confusingly. "Say 'please,' and 'thank you,' young man," he would roar, terrifyingly, when he gave any smallest object to the little boy. "Well, fellow, are you ready for a fight?" he would say, again, doubling up huge, hairy fists and making passes at him. "Come on now, you must learn to box." After the first few times this was fun.

"Don't teach him to be rough," said Grandma. "Time enough for all that."

"Now, Mother, we don't want him to be a sissy," said the big man. "He's got to toughen up early. Come on now, fellow, put up your mitts." The little boy liked this new word for hands. He learned to throw himself upon the strange big man, whose name was Uncle David, and hit him on the chest as hard as he could; the big man would laugh and hit him back with his huge, loose fists. Sometimes, but not often, Uncle David came home in the middle of the day. The little boy missed him on the other days, and would hang on the gate looking down the street for him. One evening he brought a large square package under his arm.

"Come over here, fellow, and see what I've got," he said, pulling off quantities of green paper and string from the box which was full of flat, folded colors. He put something in the little boy's hand. It was limp and silky and bright green with a tube on the end. "Thank you," said the little boy nicely, but not knowing what to do with it.

"Balloons," said Uncle David in triumph. "Now just put your mouth here and blow hard." The little boy blew hard and the green thing began to grow round and thin and silvery.

"Good for your chest," said Uncle David. "Blow some more." The little boy went on blowing and the balloon swelled steadily.

"Stop," said Uncle David, "that's enough." He twisted the tube to keep the air in. "That's the way," he said. "Now I'll blow one, and you blow one, and let's see who can blow up a big balloon the fastest."

They blew and blew, especially Uncle David. He puffed and panted and blew with all his might, but the little boy won. His balloon was perfectly round before Uncle David could even get started. The little boy was so proud he began to dance and shout, "I beat, I beat," and blew in his balloon again. It burst in his face and frightened him so he felt sick. "Ha ha, ho ho ho," whooped Uncle David. "That's the boy. I bet I can't do that. Now let's see." He blew until the beautiful bubble grew and wavered and burst into thin air, and there was only a small colored rag in his hand. This was a fine game. They went on with it until Grandma came in and said, "Time for supper now. No, you can't blow balloons at the table. Tomorrow maybe." And it was all over.

The next day, instead of being given balloons, he was hustled out of bed early, bathed in warm soapy water and given a big breakfast of soft-boiled eggs with toast and jam and milk. His grandma came in to kiss him good morning. "And I hope you'll be a good boy and obey your teacher," she told him.

"What's teacher?" asked the little boy.

"Teacher is at school," said Grandma. "She'll tell you all sorts of things and you must do as she says."

Mama and Papa had talked a great deal about School, and how they must send him there. They had told him it was a fine place with all kinds of toys and other children to play with. He felt he knew about School. "I didn't know it was time, Grandma," he said. "Is it today?"

"It's this very minute," said Grandma. "I told you a week ago."

Old Janet came in with her bonnet on. It was a prickly look-ing bundle held with a black rubber band under her back hair. "Come on," she said. "This is my busy day." She wore a dead cat slung around her neck, its sharp ears bent over under her baggy chin.

The little boy was excited and wanted to run ahead. "Hold to my hand like I told you," said old Janet. "Don't go running off like that and get yourself killed."

"I'm going to get killed, I'm going to get killed," sang the little boy, making a tune of his own.

"Don't say that, you give me the creeps," said old Janet. "Hold to my hand now." She bent over and looked at him, not at his face but at something on his clothes. His eyes followed hers.

"I declare," said Old Janet, "I did forget. I was going to sew it up. I might have known. I *told* your grandma it would be that way from now on."

"What?" asked the little boy.

"Just look at yourself," said Old Janet crossly. He looked at himself. There was a little end of him showing through the slit in his short blue flannel trousers. The trousers came halfway to his knees above, and his socks came halfway to his knees below, and all winter long his knees were cold. He remembered now how cold his knees were in cold weather. And how sometimes he would have to put the part of him that came through the slit back again, because he was cold there too. He saw at once what was wrong, and tried to arrange himself, but his mittens got in the way. Janet said, "Stop that, you bad boy," and with a firm thumb she set him in order, at the same time reaching under his belt to pull down and fold his knit undershirt over his front.

"There now," she said, "try not to disgrace yourself today." He felt guilty and red all over, because he had something that showed when he was dressed that was not supposed to show then. The different women who bathed him always wrapped him quickly in towels and hurried him into his clothes, because they saw something about him he could not see for himself. They hurried him so he never had a chance to see whatever

it was they saw, and though he looked at himself when his
clothes were off, he could not find out what was wrong with
him. Outside, in his clothes, he knew he looked like everybody
else, but inside his clothes there was something bad the matter
with him. It worried him and confused him and he wondered
about it. The only people who never seemed to notice there
was something wrong with him were Mommanpoppa. They
never called him a bad boy, and all summer long they had
taken all his clothes off and let him run in the sand beside a
big ocean.

"Look at him, isn't he a love?" Mamma would say and Papa
would look, and say, "He's got a back like a prize fighter."
Uncle David was a prize fighter when he doubled up his mitts
and said, "Come on, fellow."

Old Janet held him firmly and took long steps under her big
rustling skirts. He did not like Old Janet's smell. It made him
a little quivery in the stomach; it was just like wet chicken
feathers.

School was easy. Teacher was a square-shaped woman with
square short hair and short skirts. She got in the way sometimes, but not often. The people around him were his size;
he didn't have always to be stretching his neck up to faces bent
over him, and he could sit on the chairs without having to
climb. All the children had names, like Frances and Evelyn
and Agatha and Edward and Martin, and his own name was
Stephen. He was not Mama's "Baby," nor Papa's "Old Man";
he was not Uncle David's "Fellow" or Grandma's "Darling,"
or even Old Janet's "Bad Boy." He was Stephen. He was learning to read, and to sing a tune to some strange-looking letters
or marks written in chalk on a blackboard. You talked one
kind of lettering, and you sang another. All the children talked
and sang in turn, and then all together. Stephen thought it a fine
game. He felt awake and happy. They had soft clay and paper
and wires and squares of colors in tin boxes to play with; colored blocks to build houses with. Afterward they all danced in
a big ring, and then they danced in pairs, boys with girls. Stephen danced with Frances, and Frances kept saying, "Now you
just follow me." She was a little taller than he was, and her hair
stood up in short, shiny curls, the color of an ash tray on Papa's
desk. She would say, "You can't dance." "I can dance too,"

said Stephen, jumping around holding her hands, "I can, too, dance." He was certain of it. *"You* can't dance," he told Frances, "you can't dance at all."

Then they had to change partners, and when they came round again, Frances said, "I don't *like* the way you dance." This was different. He felt uneasy about it. He didn't jump quite so high when the phonograph record started going dumdiddy dumdiddy again. "Go ahead, Stephen, you're doing fine," said Teacher, waving her hands together very fast. The dance ended, and they all played "relaxing" for five minutes. They relaxed by swinging their arms back and forth, then rolling their heads round and round.

When Old Janet came for him he didn't want to go home. At lunch his grandma told him twice to keep his face out of his plate. "Is that what they teach you at school?" she asked. Uncle David was at home. "Here you are, fellow," he said and gave Stephen two balloons. "Thank you," said Stephen. He put the balloons in his pocket and forgot about them. "I told you that boy could learn something," said Uncle David to Grandma. "Hear him say 'thank you'?"

In the afternoon at school Teacher handed out big wads of clay and told the children to make something out of it. Anything they liked. Stephen decided to make a cat, like Mama's Meeow at home. He did not like Meeow, but he thought it would be easy to make a cat. He could not get the clay to work at all. It simply fell into one lump after another. So he stopped, wiped his hands on his pull-over, remembered his balloons and began blowing one.

"Look at Stephen's horse," said Frances. "Just look at it."

"It's not a horse, it's a cat," said Stephen. The other children gathered around. "It looks like a horse, a little," said Martin.

"It is a cat," said Stephen, stamping his foot, feeling his face turning hot. The other children all laughed and exclaimed over Stephen's cat that looked like a horse. Teacher came down among them. She sat usually at the top of the room before a big table covered with papers and playthings. She picked up Stephen's lump of clay and turned it round and examined it with her kind eyes. "Now, children," she said, "everybody has the right to make anything the way he pleases. If Stephen says this is a cat, it *is* a cat. Maybe you were thinking about a horse, Stephen?"

"It's a *cat*," said Stephen. He was aching all over. He knew then he should have said at first, "Yes, it's a horse." Then they would have let him alone. They would never have known he was trying to make a cat. "It's Meeow," he said in a trembling voice, "but I forgot how she looks."

His balloon was perfectly flat. He started blowing it up again, trying not to cry. Then it was time to go home, and Old Janet came looking for him. While Teacher was talking to other grown-up people who came to take other children home, Frances said, "Give me your balloon; I haven't got a balloon." Stephen handed it to her. He was happy to give it. He reached in his pocket and took out the other. Happily, he gave her that one too. Frances took it, then handed it back. "Now you blow up one and I'll blow up the other, and let's have a race," she said. When their balloons were only half filled Old Janet took Stephen by the arm and said, "Come on here, this is my busy day."

Frances ran after them, calling, "Stephen, you give me back my balloon," and snatched it away. Stephen did not know whether he was surprised to find himself going away with Frances' balloon, or whether he was surprised to see her snatching it as if it really belonged to her. He was badly mixed up in his mind, and Old Janet was hauling him along. One thing he knew, he liked Frances, he was going to see her again tomorrow, and he was going to bring her more balloons.

That evening Stephen boxed awhile with his uncle David, and Uncle David gave him a beautiful orange. "Eat that," he said, "it's good for your health."

"Uncle David, may I have some more balloons?" asked Stephen.

"Well, what do you say first?" asked Uncle David, reaching for the box on the top bookshelf.

"Please," said Stephen.

"That's the word," said Uncle David. He brought out two balloons, a red and a yellow one. Stephen noticed for the first time they had letters on them, very small letters that grew taller and wider as the balloon grew rounder. "Now that's all, fellow," said Uncle David. "Don't ask for any more because that's all." He put the box back on the bookshelf, but not before Stephen had seen that the box was almost full of balloons. He didn't say a word, but went on blowing, and Uncle David blew also. Stephen thought it was the nicest game he had ever known.

He had only one left, the next day, but he took it to school and gave it to Frances. "There are a lot," he said, feeling very proud and warm; "I'll bring you a lot of them."

Frances blew it up until it made a beautiful bubble, and said, "Look, I want to show you something." She took a sharp-pointed stick they used in working the clay; she poked the balloon, and it exploded. "Look at that," she said.

"That's nothing," said Stephen, "I'll bring you some more."

After school, before Uncle David came home, while Grandma was resting, when Old Janet had given him his milk and told him to run away and not bother her, Stephen dragged a chair to the bookshelf, stood upon it and reached into the box. He did not take three or four as he believed he intended; once his hands were upon them he seized what they could hold and jumped off the chair, hugging them to him. He stuffed them into his reefer pocket where they folded down and hardly made a lump.

He gave them all to Frances. There were so many, Frances gave most of them away to the other children. Stephen, flushed with his new joy, the lavish pleasure of giving presents, found almost at once still another happiness. Suddenly he was popular among the children; they invited him specially to join whatever games were up; they fell in at once with his own notions for play, and asked him what he would like to do next. They had festivals of blowing up the beautiful globes, fuller and rounder and thinner, changing as they went from deep color to lighter, paler tones, growing glassy thin, bubbly thin, then bursting with a thrilling loud noise like a toy pistol.

For the first time in his life Stephen had almost too much of something he wanted, and his head was so turned he forgot how this fullness came about, and no longer thought of it as a secret. The next day was Saturday, and Frances came to visit him with her nurse. The nurse and Old Janet sat in Old Janet's room drinking coffee and gossiping, and the children sat on the side porch blowing balloons. Stephen chose an apple-colored one and Frances a pale green one. Between them on the bench lay a tumbled heap of delights still to come.

"I once had a silver balloon," said Frances, "a beyootiful silver one, not round like these; it was a long one. But these are even nicer, I think," she added quickly, for she did want to be polite.

"When you get through with that one," said Stephen, gazing at her with the pure bliss of giving added to loving, "you can blow up a blue one and then a pink one and a yellow one and a purple one." He pushed the heap of limp objects toward her. Her clear-looking eyes, with fine little rays of brown in them like the spokes of a wheel, were full of approval for Stephen. "I wouldn't want to be greedy, though, and blow up all your balloons."

"There'll be plenty more left," said Stephen, and his heart rose under his thin ribs. He felt his ribs with his fingers and discovered with some surprise that they stopped somewhere in front, while Frances sat blowing balloons rather halfheartedly. The truth was, she was tired of balloons. After you blow six or seven your chest gets hollow and your lips feel puckery. She had been blowing balloons steadily for three days now. She had begun to hope they were giving out. "There's boxes and boxes more of them, Frances," said Stephen happily. "Millions more. I guess they'd last and last if we didn't blow too many every day."

Frances said somewhat timidly, "I tell you what. Let's rest awhile and fix some liquish water. Do you like liquish?"

"Yes, I do," said Stephen, "but I haven't got any."

"Couldn't we buy some?" asked Frances. "It's only a cent a stick, the nice rubbery, twisty kind. We can put it in a bottle with some water, and shake it and shake it, and it makes foam on top like soda pop and we can drink it. I'm kind of thirsty," she said in a small, weak voice. "Blowing balloons all the time makes you thirsty, I think."

Stephen, in silence, realized a dreadful truth and a numb feeling crept over him. He did not have a cent to buy licorice for Frances and she was tired of his balloons. This was the first real dismay of his whole life, and he aged at least a year in the next minute, huddled, with his deep, serious blue eyes focused down his nose in intense speculation. What could he do to please Frances that would not cost money? Only yesterday Uncle David had given him a nickel, and he had thrown it away on gumdrops. He regretted that nickel so bitterly his neck and forehead were damp. He was thirsty too.

"I tell you what," he said, brightening with a splendid idea, lamely trailing off on second thought, "I know something we can do, I'll—I . . ."

"I *am* thirsty," said Frances with gentle persistence. "I think I'm so thirsty maybe I'll have to go home." She did not leave the bench, though, but sat, turning her grieved mouth toward Stephen.

Stephen quivered with the terrors of the adventure before him, but he said boldly, "I'll make some lemonade. I'll get sugar and lemon and some ice and we'll have lemonade."

"Oh, I love lemonade," cried Frances. "I'd rather have lemonade than liquish."

"You stay right here," said Stephen, "and I'll get everything."

He ran around the house, and under Old Janet's window he heard the dry, chattering voices of the two old women whom he must outwit. He sneaked on tiptoe to the pantry, took a lemon lying there by itself, a handful of lump sugar and a china teapot, smooth, round, with flowers and leaves all over it. These he left on the kitchen table while he broke a piece of ice with a sharp metal pick he had been forbidden to touch. He put the ice in the pot, cut the lemon and squeezed it as well as he could—a lemon was tougher and more slippery than he had thought—and mixed sugar and water. He decided there was not enough sugar so he sneaked back and took another handful. He was back on the porch in an astonishingly short time, his face tight, his knees trembling, carrying iced lemonade to thirsty Frances with both his devoted hands.

A pace distant from her he stopped, literally stabbed through with a thought. Here he stood in broad daylight carrying a teapot with lemonade in it, and his grandma or Old Janet might walk through the door at any moment.

"Come on, Frances," he whispered loudly. "Let's go round to the back behind the rose bushes where it's shady." Frances leaped up and ran like a deer beside him, her face wise with knowledge of why they ran; Stephen ran stiffly, cherishing his teapot with clenched hands.

It was shady behind the rose bushes, and much safer. They

sat side by side on the dampish ground, legs doubled under,
drinking in turn from the slender spout. Stephen took his just
share in large, cool, delicious swallows. When Frances drank
she set her round pink mouth daintily to the spout and her
throat beat steadily as a heart. Stephen was thinking he had
really done something pretty nice for Frances. He did not know
where his own happiness was; it was mixed with the sweet-
sour taste in his mouth and a cool feeling in his bosom because
Frances was there drinking his lemonade which he had got for
her with great danger.

Frances said, "My, what big swallows you take," when his
turn came next.

"No bigger than yours," he told her downrightly. "You take
awfully big swallows."

"Well," said Frances, turning this criticism into an argument
for her rightness about things, "that's the way to drink lemonade anyway." She peered into the teapot. There was quite a
lot of lemonade left and she was beginning to feel she had
enough. "Let's make up a game and see who can take the biggest swallows."

This was such a wonderful notion they grew reckless, tip-
ping the spout into their opened mouths above their heads until
lemonade welled up and ran over their chins in rills down their
fronts. When they tired of this there was still lemonade left in
the pot. They played first at giving the rose bush a drink and
ended by baptizing it. "Name father son holygoat," shouted
Stephen, pouring. At this sound Old Janet's face appeared over
the low hedge, with the tan, disgusted-looking face of Frances'
nurse hanging over her shoulder.

"Well, just as I thought," said Old Janet. "Just as I expected."
The bag under her chin waggled.

"We were thirsty," he said; "we were awfully thirsty." Frances said nothing, but she gazed steadily at the toes of her shoes.

"Give me that teapot," said Old Janet, taking it with a rude
snatch. "Just because you're thirsty is no reason," said Old
Janet. "You can ask for things. You don't have to steal."

"We didn't steal," cried Frances suddenly. "We didn't. We
didn't!"

"That's enough from you, missy," said her nurse. "Come
straight out of there. You have nothing to do with this."

"Oh, I don't know," said Old Janet with a hard stare at Frances' nurse. "*He* never did such a thing before, by himself."

"Come on," said the nurse to Frances, "this is no place for you." She held Frances by the wrist and started walking away so fast Frances had to run to keep up. "Nobody can call *us* thieves and get away with it."

"You don't have to steal, even if others do," said Old Janet to Stephen, in a high carrying voice. "If you so much as pick up a lemon in somebody else's house you're a little thief." She lowered her voice then and said, "Now I'm going to tell your grandma and you'll see what you get."

"He went in the icebox and left it open," Janet told Grandma, "and he got into the lump sugar and spilt it all over the floor. Lumps everywhere underfoot. He dribbled water all over the clean kitchen floor, and he baptized the rose bush, blaspheming. And he took your Spode teapot."

"I didn't either," said Stephen loudly, trying to free his hand from Old Janet's big hard fist.

"Don't tell fibs," said Old Janet; "that's the last straw."

"Oh, dear," said Grandma. "He's not a baby any more." She shut the book she was reading and pulled the wet front of his pull-over toward her. "What's this sticky stuff on him?" she asked and straightened her glasses.

"Lemonade," said Old Janet. "He took the last lemon."

They were in the big dark room with the red curtains. Uncle David walked in from the room with the bookcases, holding a box in his uplifted hand. "Look here," he said to Stephen. "What's become of all my balloons?"

Stephen knew well that Uncle David was not really asking a question.

Stephen, sitting on a footstool at his grandma's knee, felt sleepy. He leaned heavily and wished he could put his head on her lap, but he might go to sleep, and it would be wrong to go to sleep while Uncle David was still talking. Uncle David walked about the room with his hands in his pockets, talking to Grandma. Now and then he would walk over to a lamp and, leaning, peer into the top of the shade, winking in the light, as if he expected to find something there.

"It's simply in the blood, I told her," said Uncle David. "I told her she would simply have to come and get him, and keep him. She asked me if I meant to call him a thief and I said if she could think of a more exact word I'd be glad to hear it."

"You shouldn't have said that," commented Grandma calmly.

"Why not? She might as well know the facts. . . . I suppose he can't help it," said Uncle David, stopping now in front of Stephen and dropping his chin into his collar, "I shouldn't expect too much of him, but you can't begin too early—"

"The trouble is," said Grandma, and while she spoke she took Stephen by the chin and held it up so that he had to meet her eye; she talked steadily in a mournful tone, but Stephen could not understand. She ended, "It's not just about the balloons, of course."

"It *is* about the balloons," said Uncle David angrily, "because balloons now mean something worse later. But what can you expect? His father—well, it's in the blood. He—"

"That's your sister's husband you're talking about," said Grandma, "and there is no use making things worse. Besides, you don't really *know*."

"I *do* know," said Uncle David. And he talked again very fast, walking up and down. Stephen tried to understand, but the sounds were strange and floating just over his head. They were talking about his father, and they did not like him. Uncle David came over and stood above Stephen and Grandma. He hunched over them with a frowning face, a long, crooked shadow from him falling across them to the wall. To Stephen he looked like his father, and he shrank against his grandma's skirts.

"The question is, what to do with him now?" asked Uncle David. "If we keep him here, he'd just be a—I won't be bothered with him. Why can't they take care of their own child? That house is crazy. Too far gone already, I'm afraid. No training. No example."

"You're right, they must take him and keep him," said Grandma. She ran her hands over Stephen's head; tenderly she pinched the nape of his neck between thumb and forefinger. "You're your Grandma's darling," she told him, "and you've had a nice long visit, and now you're going home. Mama is coming for you in a few minutes. Won't that be nice?"

"I want my mama," said Stephen, whimpering, for his grandma's face frightened him. There was something wrong with her smile.

Uncle David sat down. "Come over here, fellow," he said, wagging a forefinger at Stephen. Stephen went over slowly, and Uncle David drew him in between his wide knees in their loose, rough clothes. "You ought to be ashamed of yourself," he said, "stealing Uncle David's balloons when he had already given you so many."

"It wasn't that," said Grandma quickly. "Don't say that. It will make an impression——"

"I hope it does," said Uncle David in a louder voice; "I hope he remembers it all his life. If he belonged to me I'd give him a good thrashing."

Stephen felt his mouth, his chin, his whole face jerking. He opened his mouth to take a breath, and tears and noise burst from him. "Stop that, fellow, stop that," said Uncle David, shaking him gently by the shoulders, but Stephen could not stop. He drew his breath again and it came back in a howl. Old Janet came to the door.

"Bring me some cold water," called Grandma. There was a flurry, a commotion, a breath of cool air from the hall, the door slammed, and Stephen heard his mother's voice. His howl died away, his breath sobbed and fluttered, he turned his dimmed eyes and saw her standing there. His heart turned over within him and he bleated like a lamb, "Maaaaama," running toward her. Uncle David stood back as Mama swooped in and fell on her knees beside Stephen. She gathered him to her and stood up with him in her arms.

"What are you doing to my baby?" she asked Uncle David in a thickened voice. "I should never have let him come here. I should have known better——"

"You always should know better," said Uncle David, "and you never do. And you never will. You haven't got it here," he told her, tapping his forehead.

"David," said Grandma, "that's your——"

"Yes, I know, she's my sister," said Uncle David. "I know it. But if she must run away and marry a——"

"Shut up," said Mama.

"And bring more like him into the world, let her keep them at home. I say let her keep——"

Mama set Stephen on the floor and, holding him by the hand, she said to Grandma all in a rush as if she were reading something, "Good-by, Mother. This is the last time, really the last. I can't bear it any longer. Say good-by to Stephen; you'll never see him again. You let this happen. It's your fault. You know David was a coward and a bully and a self-righteous little beast all his life and you never crossed him in anything. You let him bully me all my life and you let him slander my husband and call my baby a thief, and now this is the end. . . . He calls my baby a thief over a few horrible little balloons because he doesn't like my husband. . . ."

She was panting and staring about from one to the other. They were all standing. Now Grandma said, "Go home, daughter. Go away, David. I'm sick of your quarreling. I've never had a day's peace or comfort from either of you. I'm sick of you both. Now let me alone and stop this noise. Go away," said Grandma in a wavering voice. She took out her handkerchief and wiped first one eye and then the other and said, "All this hate, hate—what is it for? . . . So this is the way it turns out. Well, let me alone."

"You and your little advertising balloons," said Mama to Uncle David. "The big honest businessman advertises with balloons and if he loses one he'll be ruined. And your beastly little moral notions . . ."

Grandma went to the door to meet Old Janet, who handed her a glass of water. Grandma drank it all, standing there.

"Is your husband coming for you, or are you going home by yourself?" she asked Mama.

"I'm driving myself," said Mama in a far-away voice as if her mind had wandered. "You know he wouldn't set foot in this house."

"I should think not," said Uncle David.

"Come on, Stephen darling," said Mama. "It's far past his bedtime," she said, to no one in particular. "Imagine keeping a baby up to torture him about a few miserable little bits of colored rubber." She smiled at Uncle David with both rows of teeth as she passed him on the way to the door, keeping between him and Stephen. "Ah, where would we be without high moral standards," she said, and then to Grandma, "Good night, Mother," in quite her usual voice. "I'll see you in a day or so."

"Yes, indeed," said Grandma cheerfully, coming out into the hall with Stephen and Mama. "Let me hear from you. Ring me up tomorrow. I hope you'll be feeling better."

"I feel very well now," said Mama brightly, laughing. She bent down and kissed Stephen. "Sleepy, darling? Papa's waiting to see you. Don't go to sleep until you've kissed your papa good night."

Stephen woke with a sharp jerk. He raised his head and put out his chin a little. "I don't want to go home," he said; "I want to go to school. I don't want to see Papa, I don't like him."

Mama laid her palm over his mouth softly. "Darling, don't."

Uncle David put his head out with a kind of snort. "There you are," he said. "There you've got a statement from head-quarters."

Mama opened the door and ran, almost carrying Stephen. She ran across the sidewalk, jerking open the car door and dragging Stephen in after her. She spun the car around and dashed forward so sharply Stephen was almost flung out of the seat. He sat braced then with all his might, hands digging into the cushions. The car speeded up and the trees and houses whizzed by all flattened out. Stephen began suddenly to sing to himself, a quiet, inside song so Mama would not hear. He sang his new secret; it was a comfortable, sleepy song: "I hate Papa, I hate Mama, I hate Grandma, I hate Uncle David, I hate Old Janet, I hate Marjory, I hate Papa, I hate Mama . . ."

His head bobbed, leaned, came to rest on Mama's knee, eyes closed. Mama drew him closer and slowed down, driving with one hand.

The World's Fair

F. SCOTT FITZGERALD

F. Scott Fitzgerald was born in St. Paul in 1896 and died forty-four years later in Hollywood. He attended Princeton

University, left in 1917 without a degree, and then served in the U.S. Army as a lieutenant until 1919. His first novel, This Side of Paradise, *was published in the next year. He is best known for two later novels,* The Great Gatsby *and* Tender Is The Night, *books which are among the best American fiction of our time. Fitzgerald wrote primarily about upper-class Americans—of their dissipated lives, and of their tendency to self-destruction. His point of view towards these people was basically sympathetic and he depicted their lives with an insight that perhaps only Henry James has otherwise given us. The self-contained selection below was written as part of a novel originally called* Our Type, *which was supposed to be about an intellectual murder on the Leopold-Loeb idea, and also about Fitzgerald's own hectic experiences in Paris. The book was never completed and Fitzgerald incorporated* The World's Fair, *in unrecognizable form, into* Tender Is The Night.

ALL THAT AFTERNOON Francis knew that part of Dinah wanted to be rid of him, to be swiftly busy with her own affairs. She was short in her speech when he went with her persistently to a milliner's shop and she made him wait outside; he spent the time gazing at a miniature of the battlefields in the window of a tourist office. There was dust gathered on the tangle of tiny tree trunks, wrecked toy tanks, broken caissons, and roofless doll houses marked Verdun, Côté 304, Cambrai, and the panorama seemed as old as the war itself; it depressed him as it lay baking and fading in the sun. He grew cross at waiting but as Dinah came out of the shop the middle phase of the day moved past, the sky deepened and they both relaxed a little feeling the better hours ahead. Still she insisted she had things to do but instinct told him that had she entirely wanted to be rid of him she could have easily done so and he took this as a concession.

He tried to get her to go to the Ritz but she wouldn't and they had tea at Sherry's.

"You'll both be tired of me soon," he said. "I hear you get tired of everybody."

"No. It's just that you have quarrels or you go to new places and then you like the people that you see most of—don't you think?"

"Please don't get tired of me."

"I like old friends."

"Am I an old friend?"

"You'll age," she laughed.

"Because you're the two most charming people I've ever met." He knew that neither of them ever got tired of that, and in addition he meant it. The sound of it and the tea excited him and he struck a more decided note. "I'm falling terribly in love with you and I know it's absurd—no, but really."

She drew on her gloves and suddenly time seemed to be getting short, night coming, the end coming. And as time grew shorter so her qualities grew larger inside the reduced dimension. She was kinder and sweeter; the bravery of all her words grew—those words of hers that it seemed brave for her to speak at all, as if she alone knew how presumptuous it was to speak. Her mouth which in youth had been hurt so much, frightened so persistently into silence by a mother or a series of governesses, became now for a moment something that could be hurt again, and when she stood up she was taller, very tall, flowering in a beautiful straight line from her perfect hat.

"I won't go yet," he said, and reluctantly she sat down again; he was not sure what he was going to say but unexpectedly he was saying it, "I know that being in love with you leads nowhere but I can't help it—those things happen. You belong to Seth and I like him better than any man I know, but there you are, I'm in love with you." He paused and then leaned forward, "I love you, Dinah. I love your dear face and your dear self."

"I suppose this was your line to every girl in Hollywood."

"No. There was only one there. And that was different. She was older."

"So am I."

"No, I mean really older—almost—faded. I was crazy about her and then when she liked me she seemed old. And then when I broke it off I was sorry and I used to have a queer painful feeling when I saw her, but I never wanted to go back."

She sat balanced on the edge of her chair, not restless but resistant. She sat that way for half an hour while they drank a port. He knew that she was entirely womanly, that she would not help him or encourage him by so much as a word and he knew that Seth was always with her, was with her now, but he knew too that in different degrees they were both in the grey gentle world of a hangover when the nerves relax in bunches like piano strings and crackle suddenly like wicker chairs. The nerves so raw and tender must surely join other nerves, lips to lips, breast to breast.

In the taxi they clung together and she kissed him really and they stayed close. They stopped thinking with an almost painful relief, stopped seeing; they only breathed and sought each other. Their lips became things interchangeably owned in common but twice she whispered don't in a cool little voice with no doubt in it whatever.

The lift in her apartment house was broken. As she started up the stairs he went beside her and at a touch of his hand she stopped at the first landing. By the dimming light of a window above they embraced breathlessly. Again he went with her— she was careful on the next landing, on the third more careful still. On the next—there were three more—she stopped halfway and kissed him fleetingly good-bye. At his urgency she walked down with him to the one below. Then it was good-bye with their arms stretching to touch hands along the diagonals of the bannister and then the fingers slipping apart. The next floor swallowed her, then the next diminishing; a door opened and closed above.

Across the street Francis lingered a moment, in love now and wildly jealous of her absence watching the last sunlight smoulder on the apartment's big front windows. Even as he watched a taxi drove up and Seth got out and went into the house. His step was quick and alert as if he had just come from some great doings and was hurrying on toward others, organizer of gaiety, master of a richly encrusted, esoteric happiness. His hat was a grand hat and he carried a heavy stick and thin yellow gloves. Francis thought what a good time everyone would have who was with him tonight, and the aura of Seth's good taste cooled his blood for a moment.

"Yes," he said to himself, "they're the most attractive people in the world. Absolutely perfect."

He hurried on for he was to meet that girl a little after eight.

When Francis reached the bar where he had arranged to meet Wanda Breasted he found her in company of three other girls. They were tall slender girls with rather small, well-carried heads, groomed to the preciseness of manikins' heads, and charming floating faces. They had evidently been in the bar a long time but none of them was tight and when Wanda presented Francis, their heads above their black tailored suits waved gracefully at him like cobras' hoods or long-stemmed flowers in the wind. Francis had an immediate feeling that he had met all three of them somewhere before. Wanda whispered to him that they were all having dinner together—she couldn't avoid it, but he was not to pay for anything for it was Miss Hart's party and there was another young man, now out telephoning, who would join them presently.

Wanda said to the others that he was a friend of Seth Piper's and at once the three women extended themselves toward him expressing surprise and interest that the Pipers were in Paris. The girl whose mouth twisted kindly under a hooked nose said:

"Not that I should be concerned—after their being so obviously fed up with me."

Then the tallest and handsomest girl said bitterly, "I must say I prefer people whose lives have more corrugated surfaces. Seth might be all right if she'd give him a chance."

Miss Hart, a boyish, jaunty girl who might have been anything between twenty-five and thirty-five, spoke in a hearty voice.

"After all, darling, what's so extraordinary about them. I've met them here and there and after expecting at least St. Louis and Joan of Arc I haven't been able to get really excited about them."

"Seth's the extraordinary one," said the girl the Pipers were fed up with. "Dinah's just a very loyal, frank person."

"A loyal frank person," repeated the other bitterly. "Yes—she's going to be that if she has to bitch everybody in the world to do it."

Francis was furious but he was somewhat intimidated by their height and sleekness and by the attentive and finely critical look they bent upon him whenever he opened his mouth to speak. Feeling himself slipping here and there among changing indignations he gave up and told himself how hard and super-

ficial everyone was after Seth and Dinah. They were in any
case not talking to him, but to each other. Again they reminded
him of something and again it slipped away.

"I don't really think she likes all this changing around of
friends," insisted Miss Taube. "Of course my private opinion
is that Seth made her up."

"But why the entirely liquid Mr. Grant?" asked Miss Hart.

"That's Mrs. Grant—Seth will stand a lot from anyone
capable of telling him in new ways how charming he is."

"My God!" muttered Francis—they all threw him a flinching glance and Miss Taube said conciliatingly:

"After all, I'm only sorry Seth doesn't like me any more—
and some day it might be his whim to honor me once again
with a moment or so of his attentions, and hand me my self-
respect, my justification on a platter as he has a way of doing."

The handsomest head swayed forward eagerly like a cobra's
hood.

"Once I tried to paint him. I know how his face goes but I
always had one eye left over. The answer was that his eyes are
too close together."

"My God," said Francis again.

"So are mine, dearest. Seth's great quality is in that politeness of his that seems to extend right out of the ordinary world
of courtesy. One advantage of politeness like that in a man is to
be able to deal with women on our own grounds—please or
torture them as it may prove necessary. And not fire random
shots from his own camp many miles away. Like Big Bertha
you know, accidentally slaying whole congregations."

"What struck me is their self-satisfaction, their positive admiration for their own things—"

"—Which you must admit are usually the best things."

"Oh, they give a good show—I'd be the last one to ever deny
that. I remember that famous houseboat party. And I'm willing
to admit that Seth is quite amusing—but so Irish—his face
begins to move before he says anything in that Irish way. And
those phrases he uses over and over: 'Oldest inhabitant gnawed
by rodents'—how many times have you heard him say that?
And that one way of imitating everything, whether it's an Eng-
lishman or a billy goat—he widens his nostrils, waves his head
from side to side and talks through his nose."

"Everybody has only one way of imitating that they use for everything."

Sometime during this conversation they were joined by the young man who had been telephoning. To Francis' disgust he was One of the Boys, and Francis searched vainly for any way he might extricate himself from the situation. He looked reproachfully at Wanda who smiled back encouragingly—and again his desire for her was renewed. She was a special red and white type that always aroused him and certainly the pressure of her hand the other day had been in a sense a promise, of how much he couldn't say.

Through dinner he felt his mind wandering off the company —things were so dead after the Pipers and he wondered what they were doing tonight. They had saved tonight for something, perhaps he thought with a sudden sense of being shut out— perhaps to be alone.

He drank a lot of champagne at dinner but was taciturn and had the feeling that the three girls didn't like him any more than he liked them. First he felt this only casually but later it deepened and dancing afterwards at the Boeuf sur le Toit he saw they were inclined to be cold with him.

"I'm getting tight and cross," he thought, "I'd better go home. What a rotten evening. What bum people." He asked Wanda if they couldn't go.

"Yes, but wait," she answered. "They'll be furious if I take you off."

"Well, who are they? Why should you care?"

"I don't, but wait."

They were dancing close together and suddenly he told her he wanted her. Surely her smile as she bent back and looked up at him was consent, yet she said:

"Isn't this enough?"

"Of course not."

"Don't you think this is enough?"

He got nothing more than that from her but his next glass of champagne made him genial at last; he even consented to move on to another place but Miss Carmichael was in the taxi with Wanda and himself and he could do no more than press her hand.

He knew they were girls of some distinction—he did not

make the mistake of lumping them as bluestockings or Lesbians. They were three tall rich American girls and that was the principal thing about them. To be a tall rich American girl is a form of hereditary achievement whether or not progress does eventually culminate in her insouciant promenade along the steel girder of our prosperity. Nevertheless, it was increasingly clear to him that Miss Taube had more immediate concerns—there was a flick of the lip somewhere, a bending of the smile toward some indirection, a momentary lifting and dropping of the curtain over a hidden passage. An hour later he came out of somewhere to a taxi whither they had preceded him and found Wanda limp and drunk in Miss Taube's arms.

"What's the idea?" he demanded furiously.

Miss Taube smiled at him. Wanda opened her eyes sleepily and said:

"Hello."

"What's all this business?" he repeated.

"I love Wanda," said Miss Taube.

"Vivian is a nice girl," said Wanda. "Come sit back here with us."

"Why can't you get out of the taxicab and go home with your friends," said Francis harshly to Miss Taube. "You know you have no business to do this. She's tight."

"I love Wanda," repeated Miss Taube good-naturedly.

"I don't care. Please get out."

In answer Wanda drew the girl close to her again, whereupon in a spasm of fury Francis opened the door, took her by the arm and before the girl understood his purpose deposited her in a sitting position on the curb.

"This is perfectly outrageous!" she cried.

"I should say it is!" he agreed, his voice trembling. A chasseur and several by-standers hurried up; Francis spoke to the driver and got into the cab quickly. The incident had wakened Wanda.

"Why did you do that?" she demanded. "I'll have to go back."

"Do you realize what she was doing?"

"Vivian's a nice girl."

"Vivian's a ——"

"I don't feel good."

"What's your address?"

She told him, and he sat back robbed and glowering. The sight of this almost legendary aberration in action had spoiled some great series of human facts for him, as it had when he had first become aware of its other face some years before. Better Hollywood's bizarre variations on the normal, with George Collins on the phone ordering twelve beautiful girls for dinner, none over nineteen. He wanted to go back and kill that girl.

The cab stopped in front of a cluster of murky brown doors so alike that to be identified it seemed that hers must be counted off from the abutting blackness of an alley.

"Can you get in alone?"

"Maybe." But getting from the cab she wobbled helplessly and he helped her to the door and up an ancient circular stairway to her apartment where he fumbled in her bag for the key.

It was one room in listless disorder, opening off a bathroom with a tin tub. The day bed was covered with a length of blue felt on which reversed letters of ravelled thread spelled out "Bryn Mawr—1924." Wanda went into the bathroom without speaking and Francis opened a window which looked on a narrow and tubular court, grey as rats, but echoing at the moment to a plaintive and peculiar music. It was two men chanting in an unfamiliar language full of K's and L's—he leaned out but he could not see them; there was obviously a religious significance in the sounds, and tired and emotionless he let them pray for him too, but what for, save that he should never lose himself in the darkness of his own mind, he did not know. He felt no passion, only a lowering of his faculties—but they tightened with a nervous wrench of his heart at the sound of a pistol shot from the bathroom.

"Ah, my!" he gasped.

In a second he opened the door of the bathroom. Wanda faced him weakly with a small pistol wobbling in her hand. It was an old pistol for as he took it away from her a slice of pearl came off the handle and fell on the floor.

"What do you want to do?" he asked imperatively.

"I don't know, I was just shooting it."

She sat down on the water closet with a coquettish smile. Her eyes, glazed a few minutes since, were full of an impish malice.

"What's the trouble? Are you in any trouble?"

"Nobody's in trouble. Nothing's trouble. Everybody is responsible for what they do."

"You're not, you're tight."

Any minute he expected a knocking at the door but perhaps from fear or indifference, nothing stirred in the house—even the singing in the areaway continued, sad as a flute, and moment by moment they were more alone in the flat.

"You'd better go to bed," he said.

She laughed scornfully.

"Go to bed and lie there? What for?"

"Well—" he said, after considering unsuccessfully, "I don't like to go away and leave you like this. Are you all right now?"

"Oh, get out!" she said unpleasantly. "Leave me my pistol."

He took out the little shells and handed the gun to her, but at the look of childish craftiness in her eyes he took it back quickly.

"You've got more shells. Look here, you're behaving like an idiot. What's the matter—are you broke?"

She shook her head.

"Just lousy with money."

"Is it something about that girl?"

Her eyes narrowed defiantly.

"She's a very nice girl. She's been very good to me."

"She wasn't behaving very well tonight."

"She's very nice." Suddenly she seemed to remember. "You were the one. You pulled her out of the cab into the public gutter. She'll never forgive that," she shook her head solemnly, "never—never. Got a cigarette?"

She leaned back comfortably against the waterpipe, as one enjoying the moment at leisure. Francis lit her a cigarette impatiently and waited. He was very tired but he was afraid to leave her alone, as much for himself as for her. At the moment he didn't give a damn whether she killed herself or not because he was so tired, but her friends knew that he had taken her home and there was a concierge below.

"I'm pretty tired," he said—unfortunately, because this gave her an advantage; she wasn't tired; although her mind moved in a tedious half time like a slow moving picture her nerves were crowded with feverish traffic. She tried to think of some mischief.

"You were after me," she said accusingly.

"What of it?"

She laughed sneeringly.

"I'll go home—if you'll tell me where the rest of the shells are and then hop into bed and get some sleep."

"Oh, s . . . !" she cried, "You'll tuck the baby in will you—you God damn old fool—you meig me sick to my stomach."

Half an hour passed. When he was silent she took her ease refusing to leave the bathroom. When he made a motion to go she woke like a watchdog, and held him there. He looked in the bureau for shells till she cried: "Let my things alone." He thought of calling the concierge but that would be to arouse the house surely; dawn was filtering into the bedroom now, the singing had long ago ceased.

He hated her for entangling him in this sordidness—it was unbelievable that he had ever desired her, a hysterical Lesbian, keeping him there as if she had any possible right. He would have liked to hit her—but at the thought of her bruised in all this trouble of hers a complete revulsion of feeling went over him; he went and knelt beside her and put his arm about her shoulder.

"Poor little girl—what is it? Tell me. Are you busted or something, or have you gotten mixed up with those Lesbians?"

She broke down suddenly.

"Oh, no," she cried, "I wanted to see if I could—sleep with you—I—"

Then as suddenly she was herself again.

"You can go now," she said after a moment coldly.

"What are you going to do?"

"Going to sleep, what do you think I'm going to do—set myself on fire? Take the pistol if you want."

She began taking off her dress.

Without looking at him she turned on the hot water in the wash basin, and looked at herself in the mirror.

"Good-bye."

"Bye."

Outside it was morning; he stopped at a workman's bistro for a cup of coffee. "Good God, this is getting to be a hell of a world," he thought. Now he remembered stories he had heard in California. It was all very depressing and it frightened him, as if someone he knew were being operated on. He wanted to see Seth and Dinah and he made up his mind on a savage impulse to tell the story to his mother. "God damn these women!" he thought.

Two Gallants

JAMES JOYCE

Now recognized as one of the great prose writers of modern times, James Joyce was born in a suburb of Dublin in 1882. After attending Jesuit schools there, he went to Paris at the age of twenty. He was married in 1904, lived in Zurich for a while, then got a job as a tutor in the Berlitz School in Trieste. He began writing Dubliners *that same year but it was not published until 1914. He finished his most popular work,* Ulysses, *in 1921. A long, turbulent battle for the book's American publication then took place; this fight resulted in the famous Judge Woolsey decision which allowed Random House to publish the book in 1934. Five years later, his even more difficult prose work,* Finnegans Wake, *was published—a book on which Joyce worked seventeen years. The great Irish writer died in Zurich in 1941, practically penniless.*

THE GREY WARM EVENING of August had descended upon the city and a mild warm air, a memory of summer, circulated in the streets. The streets, shuttered for the repose of Sunday, swarmed with a gaily coloured crowd. Like illumined pearls the lamps shone from the summits of their tall poles upon the living texture below which, changing shape and hue unceasingly, sent up into the warm grey evening air an unchanging, unceasing murmur.

Two young men came down the hill of Rutland Square. One of them was just bringing a long monologue to a close. The other, who walked on the verge of the path and was at times obliged to step on to the road, owing to his companion's rudeness, wore an amused listening face. He was squat and ruddy.

A yachting cap was shoved far back from his forehead and the narrative to which he listened made constant waves of expression break forth over his face from the corners of his nose and eyes and mouth. Little jets of wheezing laughter followed one another out of his convulsed body. His eyes, twinkling with cunning enjoyment, glanced at every moment towards his companion's face. Once or twice he rearranged the light waterproof which he had slung over one shoulder in toreador fashion. His breeches, his white rubber shoes and his jauntily slung waterproof expressed youth. But his figure fell into rotundity of the waist, his hair was scant and grey and his face, when the waves of expression had passed over it, had a ravaged look.

When he was quite sure that the narrative had ended he laughed noiselessly for fully half a minute. Then he said:

"Well! . . . That takes the biscuit!"

His voice seemed winnowed of vigour; and to enforce his words he added with humour:

"That takes the solitary, unique, and, if I may so call it, *recherché* biscuit!"

He became serious and silent when he had said this. His tongue was tired for he had been talking all the afternoon in a public-house in Dorset Street. Most people considered Lenehan a leech but, in spite of this reputation, his adroitness and eloquence had always prevented his friends from forming any general policy against him. He had a brave manner of coming up to a party of them in a bar and of holding himself nimbly at the borders of the company until he was included in a round. He was a sporting vagrant armed with a vast stock of stories, limericks and riddles. He was insensitive to all kinds of discourtesy. No one knew how he achieved the stern task of living, but his name was vaguely associated with racing tissues.

"And where did you pick her up, Corley?" he asked.

Corley ran his tongue swiftly along his upper lip.

"One night, man," he said, "I was going along Dame Street and I spotted a fine tart under Waterhouse's clock and said good-night, you know. So we went for a walk round by the canal and she told me she was a slavey in a house in Baggot Street. I put my arm round her and squeezed her a bit that night. Then next Sunday, man, I met her by appointment. We went out to Donnybrook and I brought her into a field there. She told me she used to go with a dairyman. . . . It was fine, man. Cigarettes every night she'd bring me and paying the tram out and back. And one night she brought me two bloody fine cigars —O, the real cheese, you know, that the old fellow used to smoke. . . . I was afraid, man, she'd get in the family way. But she's up to the dodge."

"Maybe she thinks you'll marry her," said Lenehan.

"I told her I was out of a job," said Corley. "I told her I was in Pim's. She doesn't know my name. I was too hairy to tell her that. But she thinks I'm a bit of class, you know."

Lenehan laughed again, noiselessly.

"Of all the good ones ever I heard," he said, "that emphatically takes the biscuit."

Corley's stride acknowledged the compliment. The swing of his burly body made his friend execute a few light skips from the path to the roadway and back again. Corley was the son of an inspector of police and he had inherited his father's frame and gait. He walked with his hands by his sides, holding himself erect and swaying his head from side to side. His head was large, globular and oily; it sweated in all weathers; and his large round hat, set upon it sideways, looked like a bulb which had grown out of another. He always stared straight before him as if he were on parade and, when he wished to gaze after someone in the street, it was necessary for him to move his body from the hips. At present he was about town. Whenever any job was vacant a friend was always ready to give him the hard word. He was often to be seen walking with policemen in plain clothes, talking earnestly. He knew the inner side of all affairs and was fond of delivering final judgments. He spoke without listening to the speech of his companions. His conversation was mainly about himself: what he had said to such a person and what such a person had said to him and what he had said to settle the matter. When he reported these dialogues he aspirated the first letter of his name after the manner of Florentines.

Lenehan offered his friend a cigarette. As the two young men walked on through the crowd Corley occasionally turned to smile at some of the passing girls but Lenehan's gaze was fixed on the large faint moon circled with a double halo. He watched earnestly the passing of the grey web of twilight across its face. At length he said:

"Well . . . tell me, Corley, I suppose you'll be able to pull it off all right, eh?"

Corley closed one eye expressively as an answer.

"Is she game for that?" asked Lenehan dubiously. "You can never know women."

"She's all right," said Corley. "I know the way to get around her, man. She's a bit gone on me."

"You're what I call a gay Lothario," said Lenehan. "And the proper kind of a Lothario, too!"

A shade of mockery relieved the servility of his manner. To save himself he had the habit of leaving his flattery open to the interpretation of railery. But Corley had not a subtle mind.

"There's nothing to touch a good slavey," he affirmed. "Take my tip for it."

"By one who has tried them all," said Lenehan.

"First I used to go with girls, you know," said Corley, unbosoming; "girls off the South Circular. I used to take them out, man, on the tram somewhere and pay the tram or take them to a band or a play at the theatre or buy them chocolate and sweets or something that way. I used to spend money on them right enough," he added, in a convincing tone, as if he was conscious of being disbelieved.

But Lenehan could well believe it; he nodded gravely.

"I know that game," he said, "and it's a mug's game."

"And damn the thing I ever got out of it," said Corley.

"Ditto here," said Lenehan.

"Only off of one of them," said Corley.

He moistened his upper lip by running his tongue along it. The recollection brightened his eyes. He too gazed at the pale disc of the moon, now nearly veiled, and seemed to meditate.

"She was . . . a bit of all right," he said regretfully.

He was silent again. Then he added:

"She's on the turf now. I saw her driving down Earl Street one night with two fellows with her on a car."

"I suppose that's your doing," said Lenehan.

"There was others at her before me," said Corley philosophically.

This time Lenehan was inclined to disbelieve. He shook his head to and fro and smiled.

"You know you can't kid me, Corley," he said.

"Honest to God!" said Corley. "Didn't she tell me herself?"

Lenehan made a tragic gesture.

"Base betrayer!" he said.

As they passed along the railings of Trinity College, Lenehan skipped out into the road and peered up at the clock.

"Twenty after," he said.

"Time enough," said Corley. "She'll be there all right. I always let her wait a bit."

Lenehan laughed quietly.

"Ecod! Corley, you know how to take them," he said.

"I'm up to all their little tricks," Corley confessed.

"But tell me," said Lenehan again, "are you sure you can bring it off all right? You know it's a ticklish job. They're damn close on that point. Eh? . . . What?"

His bright, small eyes searched his companion's face for reassurance. Corley swung his head to and fro as if to toss aside an insistent insect, and his brows gathered.

"I'll pull it off," he said. "Leave it to me, can't you?"

Lenehan said no more. He did not wish to ruffle his friend's temper, to be sent to the devil and told that his advice was not wanted. A little tact was necessary. But Corley's brow was soon smooth again. His thoughts were running another way.

"She's a fine decent tart," he said, with appreciation; "that's what she is."

They walked along Nassau Street and then turned into Kildare Street. Not far from the porch of the club a harpist stood in the roadway, playing to a little ring of listeners. He plucked at the wires heedlessly, glancing quickly from time to time at the face of each new-comer and from time to time, wearily also, at the sky. His harp, too, heedless that her coverings had fallen about her knees, seemed weary alike of the eyes of strangers and of her master's hands. One hand played in the bass the melody of *Silent, O Moyle,* while the other hand careered in the treble after each group of notes. The notes of the air sounded deep and full.

The two young men walked up the street without speaking, the mournful music following them. When they reached Stephen's Green they crossed the road. Here the noise of trams, the lights and the crowd released them from their silence.

"There she is!" said Corley.

At the corner of Hume Street a young woman was standing. She wore a blue dress and a white sailor hat. She stood on the curbstone, swinging a sunshade in one hand. Lenehan grew lively.

"Let's have a look at her, Corley," he said.

Corley glanced sideways at his friend and an unpleasant grin appeared on his face.

"Are you trying to get inside me?" he asked.

"Damn it!" said Lenehan boldly, "I don't want an introduction. All I want is to have a look at her. I'm not going to eat her."

"O . . . A look at her?" said Corley, more amiably. "Well . . . I'll tell you what. I'll go over and talk to her and you can pass by."

"Right!" said Lenehan.

Corley had already thrown one leg over the chains when Lenehan called out:

"And after? Where will we meet?"

"Half ten," answered Corley, bringing over his other leg.

"Where?"

"Corner of Merrion Street. We'll be coming back."

"Work it all right now," said Lenehan in farewell.

Corley did not answer. He sauntered across the road swaying his head from side to side. His bulk, his easy pace, and the solid sound of his boots had something of the conqueror in them. He approached the young woman and, without saluting, began at once to converse with her. She swung her umbrella more quickly and executed half turns on her heels. Once or twice when he spoke to her at close quarters she laughed and bent her head.

Lenehan observed them for a few minutes. Then he walked rapidly along beside the chains at some distance and crossed the road obliquely. As he approached Hume Street corner he found the air heavily scented and his eyes made a swift anxious scrutiny of the young woman's appearance. She had her Sunday finery on. Her blue serge skirt was held at the waist by a belt of black leather. The great silver buckle of her belt seemed to depress the centre of her body, catching the light stuff of her white blouse like a clip. She wore a short black jacket with mother-of-pearl buttons and a ragged black boa. The ends of

her tulle collarette had been carefully disordered and a big
bunch of red flowers was pinned in her bosom stems upwards.
Lenehan's eyes noted approvingly her stout short muscular
body. Frank rude health glowed in her face, on her fat red
cheeks and in her unabashed blue eyes. Her features were
blunt. She had broad nostrils, a straggling mouth which lay
open in a contented leer, and two projecting front teeth. As he
passed Lenehan took off his cap and, after about ten seconds,
Corley returned a salute to the air. This he did by raising his
hand vaguely and pensively changing the angle of position of
his hat.

Lenehan walked as far as the Shelbourne Hotel where he
halted and waited. After waiting for a little time he saw them
coming towards him and, when they turned to the right, he followed them, stepping lightly in his white shoes, down one side
of Merrion Square. As he walked on slowly, timing his pace to
theirs, he watched Corley's head which turned at every moment towards the young woman's face like a big ball revolving
on a pivot. He kept the pair in view until he had seen them
climbing the stairs of the Donnybrook tram; then he turned
about and went back the way he had come.

Now that he was alone his face looked older. His gaiety
seemed to forsake him and, as he came by the railings of the
Duke's Lawn, he allowed his hand to run along them. The
air which the harpist had played began to control his movements. His softly padded feet played the melody while his
fingers swept a scale of variations idly along the railings after
each group of notes.

He walked listlessly round Stephen's Green and then down
Grafton Street. Though his eyes took note of many elements of
the crowd through which he passed they did so morosely. He
found trivial all that was meant to charm him and did not answer the glances which invited him to be bold. He knew that
he would have to speak a great deal, to invent and to amuse, and
his brain and throat were too dry for such a task. The problem
of how he could pass the hours till he met Corley again troubled him a little. He could think of no way of passing them but
to keep on walking. He turned to the left when he came to the
corner of Rutland Square and felt more at ease in the dark
quiet street, the sombre look of which suited his mood. He

paused at last before the window of a poor-looking shop over which the words *Refreshment Bar* were printed in white letters. On the glass of the window were two flying inscriptions: *Ginger Beer* and *Ginger Ale*. A cut ham was exposed on a great blue dish while near it on a plate lay a segment of very light plum-pudding. He eyed this food earnestly for some time and then, after glancing warily up and down the street, went into the shop quickly.

He was hungry for, except some biscuits which he had asked two grudging curates to bring him, he had eaten nothing since breakfast-time. He sat down at an uncovered wooden table opposite two work-girls and a mechanic. A slatternly girl waited on him.

"How much is a plate of peas?" he asked.

"Three halfpence, sir," said the girl.

"Bring me a plate of peas," he said, "and a bottle of ginger beer."

He spoke roughly in order to belie his air of gentility for his entry had been followed by a pause of talk. His face was heated. To appear natural he pushed his cap back on his head and planted his elbows on the table. The mechanic and the two work-girls examined him point by point before resuming their conversation in a subdued voice. The girl brought him a plate of grocer's hot peas, seasoned with pepper and vinegar, a fork and his ginger beer. He ate his food greedily and found it so good that he made a note of the shop mentally. When he had eaten all the peas he sipped his ginger beer and sat for some time thinking of Corley's adventure. In his imagination he beheld the pair of lovers walking along some dark road; he heard Corley's voice in deep energetic gallantries and saw again the leer of the young woman's mouth. This vision made him feel keenly his own poverty of purse and spirit. He was tired of knocking about, of pulling the devil by the tail, of shifts and intrigues. He would be thirty-one in November. Would he never get a good job? Would he never have a home of his own? He thought how pleasant it would be to have a warm fire to sit by and a good dinner to sit down to. He had walked the streets long enough with friends and with girls. He knew what those friends were worth: he knew the girls too. Experience had embittered his heart against the world. But all hope had not left

him. He felt better after having eaten than he had felt before,
less weary of his life, less vanquished in spirit. He might yet be
able to settle down in some snug corner and live happily if he
could only come across some good simple-minded girl with a
little of the ready.

He paid twopence halfpenny to the slatternly girl and went
out of the shop to begin his wandering again. He went into
Chapel Street and walked along towards the City Hall. Then he
turned into Dame Street. At the corner of George's Street he
met two friends of his and stopped to converse with them. He
was glad that he could rest from all his walking. His friends
asked him had he seen Corley and what was the latest. He replied that he had spent the day with Corley. His friends talked
very little. They looked vacantly after some figures in the
crowd and sometimes made a critical remark. One said that he
had seen Mac an hour before in Westmoreland Street. At this
Lenehan said that he had been with Mac the night before in
Egan's. The young man who had seen Mac in Westmoreland
Street asked was it true that Mac had won a bit over a billiard
match. Lenehan did not know: he said that Holohan had stood
them drinks in Egan's.

He left his friends at a quarter to ten and went up George's
Street. He turned to the left at the City Markets and walked
on into Grafton Street. The crowd of girls and young men
had thinned and on his way up the street he heard many groups
and couples bidding one another good-night. He went as far
as the clock of the College of Surgeons: it was on the stroke
of ten. He set off briskly along the northern side of the Green
hurrying for fear Corley should return too soon. When he
reached the corner of Merrion Street he took his stand in the
shadow of a lamp and brought out one of the cigarettes which
he had reserved and lit it. He leaned against the lamp-post and
kept his gaze fixed on the part from which he expected to see
Corley and the young woman return.

His mind became active again. He wondered had Corley
managed it successfully. He wondered if he had asked her
yet or if he would leave it to the last. He suffered all the pangs
and thrills of his friend's situation as well as those of his own.
But the memory of Corley's slowly revolving head calmed him
somewhat: he was sure Corley would pull it off all right. All at

once the idea struck him that perhaps Corley had seen her
home by another way and given him the slip. His eyes searched
the street: there was no sign of them. Yet it was surely half-an-
hour since he had seen the clock of the College of Surgeons.
Would Corley do a thing like that? He lit his last cigarette and
began to smoke it nervously. He strained his eyes as each tram
stopped at the far corner of the square. They must have gone
home by another way. The paper of his cigarette broke and he
flung it into the road with a curse.

Suddenly he saw them coming towards him. He started with
delight and keeping close to his lamp-post tried to read the
result in their walk. They were walking quickly, the young
woman taking quick short steps, while Corley kept beside her
with his long stride. They did not seem to be speaking. An inti-
mation of the result pricked him like the point of a sharp instru-
ment. He knew Corley would fail; he knew it was no go.

They turned down Baggot Street and he followed them at
once, taking the other footpath. When they stopped he stopped
too. They talked for a few moments and then the young woman
went down the steps into the area of a house. Corley remained
standing at the edge of the path, a little distance from the front
steps. Some minutes passed. Then the hall-door was opened
slowly and cautiously. A woman came running down the front
steps and coughed. Corley turned and went towards her. His
broad figure hid hers from view for a few seconds and then she
reappeared running up the steps. The door closed on her and
Corley began to walk swiftly towards Stephen's Green.

Lenehan hurried on in the same direction. Some drops of
light rain fell. He took them as a warning and, glancing back
towards the house which the young woman had entered to see
that he was not observed, he ran eagerly across the road. Anxiety and his swift run made him pant. He called out:

"Hallo, Corley!"

Corley turned his head to see who had called him, and then
continued walking as before. Lenehan ran after him, settling the
waterproof on his shoulders with one hand.

"Hallo, Corley!" he cried again.

He came level with his friend and looked keenly in his face.
He could see nothing there.

"Well?" he said. "Did it come off?"

They had reached the corner of Ely Place. Still without answering, Corley swerved to the left and went up the side street. His features were composed in stern calm. Lenehan kept up with his friend, breathing uneasily. He was baffled and a note of menace pierced through his voice.

"Can't you tell us?" he said. "Did you try her?"

Corley halted at the first lamp and stared grimly before him. Then with a grave gesture he extended a hand towards the light and, smiling, opened it slowly to the gaze of his disciple. A small gold coin shone in the palm.

The White Rooster

WILLIAM GOYEN

Now in his middle thirties, William Goyen was born in East Texas and lived there as a child. He grew up in Houston and attended Rice Institute, then taught at the University of Houston. He served in the U.S. Navy during World War II as an officer on an aircraft carrier. Mr. Goyen has won two Guggenheim fellowships and a prize for his novel, The House of Breath, *from the Texas Institute of Arts and Letters. His short stories have appeared in* Horizon, Accent, Partisan Review, Southwest Review, *and* Harper's Bazaar. *"The White Rooster" was made into an experimental movie by a Princeton University film group.*

THERE WERE TWO disturbances in Mrs. Marcy Samuels' life that were worrying her nearly insane. First, it was, and had been for two years now, Grandpa Samuels, who should have long ago been dead but kept wheeling around her house in his wheel chair, alive as ever. The first year he came to live with them it was plain that he was in good health and would probably live long. But during the middle of the second year he fell thin and coughing and after that there were some weeks when Mrs. Samuels and her husband, Watson, were sure on Monday that he would die and relieve them of him before Saturday. Yet he wheeled on and on, not ever dying at all.

The second thing that was about to drive Marcy Samuels crazy was a recent disturbance which grew and grew until it became a terror. It was a stray white rooster that crowed at her window all day long and, worst of all, in the early mornings. No one knew where he came from, but there he was, crowing to all the other roosters far and near—and they answering back in a whole choir of crowings. His shrieking was bad enough, but then he had to outrage her further by digging in her pansy bed. Since he first appeared to harass her, Mrs. Samuels had spent most of her day chasing him out of the flowers or throwing objects at him where he was, under her window, his neck stretched and strained in a perfectly blatant crow. After a week of this, she was almost frantic, as she told her many friends on the telephone or in town or from her back yard.

It seemed that Mrs. Samuels had been cursed with problems all her life and everyone said she had the unluckiest time of it. That a woman sociable and busy as Marcy Samuels should have her father-in-law, helpless in a wheel chair, in her house to keep and take care of was just a shame. And Watson, her husband, was no help at all, even though it was his very father who was so much trouble. He was a slow, patient little man, not easily ruffled. Marcy Samuels was certain that he was not aware that her life was so hard and full of trouble.

She could not stand at her stove, for instance, but what Grandpa Samuels was there, asking what was in the pot and smelling of it. She could not even have several of the women over without him riding in and out among them, weak as he was, as they chatted in confidence about this or that town happening, and making bright or ugly remarks about women and what they said, their own affairs. Marcy, as she often told Watson, simply could not stop Grandpa's mouth, could not stop his wheels, could not get him out of her way. And she was busy. If she was hurrying across a room to get some washing in the sink or to get the broom, Grandpa Samuels would make a surprise run out at her from the hall or some door and streak across in front of her, laughing fiendishly or shouting boo! and

then she would leap as high as her bulbous ankles would lift her
and scream, for she was a nervous woman and had so many
things on her mind. Grandpa had a way of sneaking into
things Marcy did, as a weevil slips into a bin of meal and bores
around in it. He had a way of objecting to Marcy, which she
sensed everywhere. He haunted her, pestered her. If she would
be bending down to find a thing in her cupboard, she would
suddenly sense some shadow over her and then it would be
Grandpa Samuels, he would be there, touch her like a ghost in
the ribs and frighten her so that she would bounce up and let
out a scream. Then he would just sit and grin at her with an
owlish face. All these things he did, added to the trouble it was
for her to keep him, made Marcy Samuels sometimes want to
kill Grandpa Samuels. He was everywhere upon her, like an
evil spirit following her; and indeed there was a thing in him
which scared her often, as if he was losing his mind or trying
to kill her.

As for Grandpa, it was hard to tell whether he really had
a wicked face or was deliberately trying to look mean, to keep
Marcy troubled and to pay her back for the way she treated
him. It may have been that his days were dull and he wanted
something to happen, or that he remembered how he heard
her fight with her son, her husband, at night in their room because Watson would not put him in a Home and get the house
and Marcy free of him. "You work all day and you're not
here with him like I am," she would whine. "And you're not
man enough to put him where he belongs." He had been wicked
in his day, as men are wicked, had drunk always and in all
drinking places, had gambled and had got mixed up in some
scrapes. But that was because he had been young and ready.
He had never had a household, and the wife he finally got had
long since faded away so that she might have been only a
shadow from which this son, Watson, emerged, parentless. Then
Grandpa had become an old wanderer, lo here lo there, until
it all ended in this chair in which he was still a wanderer through
the rooms of this house. He had a face which, although mis-
chievous lines were scratched upon it and gave it a kind of
devilish look, showed that somewhere there was abundant untouched kindness in him, a life which his life had never been
able to use.

Marcy could not make her husband see that this house was cursed and tormented; and then to have a scarecrow rooster annoying her the length of the day and half the early morning was too much for Marcy Samuels. She had nuisances in her house and nuisances in her yard.

It was on a certain morning that Mrs. Samuels first looked out her kitchen window to see this gaunt rooster strutting white on the ground. It took her only a second to know that this was the rooster that crowed and scratched in her flowers and so the whole thing started. The first thing she did was to poke her blowsy head out her window and puff her lips into a ring and wheeze shooooooo! through it, fiercely. The white rooster simply did a pert leap, erected his flamboyantly combed head sharp into the air, chopped it about for a moment, and then started scratching vigorously in the lush bed of pansies, his comb slapping like a girl's pigtails.

Since her hands were wet in the morning sink full of dishes, Mrs. Samuels stopped to dry them imperfectly and then hurried out the back door, still drying her hands in her apron. Now she would get him, she would utterly destroy him if she could get her hands on him. She flounced out the door and down the steps and threw her great self wildly in the direction of the pansy bed, screaming shoo! shoo! go 'way! go 'way! and then cursed the rooster, Marcy Samuels must have been a terrible sight to any barnyard creature, her hair like a big bush and her terrible bosom heaving and falling, her hands thrashing the air. But the white rooster was not dismayed at all. Again he did a small quick hop, struck his beak into the air, and stood firmly on his ground, his yellow claw spread over the face of a purple pansy and holding it to the ground imprisoned as a cat holds down a mouse. And then a sound, a clear melodious measure, which Mrs. Samuels thought was the most awful noise in the world, burst from his straggly throat.

He was plainly a poorly rooster, thin as some sparrow, his white feathers drooping and without lustre, his comb of extravagant growth but pale and flaccid, hanging like a wrinkled glove over his eye. It was clear that he had been run from many a yard and that in fleeing he had torn his feathers and so tired himself that whatever he found to eat in random places was not enough to keep any flesh on his carcass. He would not be a good eating chicken, Mrs. Samuels thought, running at him, for he has no meat on him at all. Anyway, he was not like a chicken but like some nightmare rooster from Hades sent to trouble her. Yet he was most vividly alive in some courageous way.

She threw a stone at him and at this he leaped and screamed in fright and hurdled the shrubbery into a vacant lot. Mrs. Samuels dashed to her violated pansy bed and began throwing up loose dirt about the stems, making reparations. This was no ordinary rooster in her mind. Since she had a very good imagination and was, actually, a little afraid of roosters anyway, the white rooster took on a shape of terror in her mind. This was because he was so indestructible. Something seemed to protect him. He seemed to dare her to capture him, and if she threw a shoe out her window at him, he was not challenged, but just let out another startling crow at her. And in the early morning in a snug bed, such a crowing is like the cry of fire! or an explosion in the brain.

It was around noon of that day that Mrs. Samuels, at her clothesline, sighted Mrs. Doran across the hedge, at her line, her long fingers fluttering over the clothespins like butterflies trying to light there.

"That your rooster that's been in my pansy bed and crows all the time, Mrs. Doran?"

"Marcy, it must be. You know we had two of them intending to eat them for Christmas, but they both broke out of the coop and went running away into the neighborhood. My husband Carl just gave them up because he says he's not going to be chasing any chickens like some farmer."

"Well then I tell you we can't have him here disturbing us. If I catch him do you want him back?"

"Heavens no, honey. If you catch him, do what you want to with him, we don't want him any more. Lord knows where the other one is." And then she unfolded from her tub a long limp outing gown and pinned it to the line by its shoulders to let it hang down like an effigy of herself.

Mrs. Samuels noticed that Mrs. Doran was as casual about the whole affair as she was the day she brought back her water pitcher in several pieces, borrowed for a party and broken by the cat. It made her even madder with the white rooster. This simply means killing that white rooster, she told herself as she went from her line. It means wringing his neck until it is twisted clean from his breastbone—if we can catch him; and I'll try— catch him and throw him in the chickenyard and hold him there until Watson comes home from work and then Watson will do the wringing, not me. When she came in the back door she was already preparing herself in her mind for the killing of the white rooster, how she would catch him and then wait for Watson to wring his neck—if Watson actually could get up enough courage to do anything at all for her.

In the afternoon around two, just as she was resting, she heard a cawing and it was the rooster back again. Marcy bounded from her bed and raced to the window. "Now I will get him," she said severely.

She moved herself quietly to a bush and concealed herself behind it, her full-blown buttocks protruding like a monstrous flower in bud. Around the bush in a smiling innocent circle were the pansies, all purple and yellow faces, bright in the wind. When he comes scratching here, she told herself, and when he gets all interested in the dirt, I'll leap up on him and catch him sure.

Behind the bush she waited; her eyes watched the white rooster moving towards the pansy bed, pecking here and there in the grass at whatever was there and might be eaten. As she prepared herself to leap, Mrs. Samuels noticed the white hated face of Grandpa at the window. He had rolled his wheel chair there to watch the maneuvers in the yard. She knew at a glance that he was against her catching the white rooster. But because she hated him, she did not care what he thought. In fact she secretly suspected Grandpa and the rooster to be partners in a plot to worry her out of her mind, one in the house, the other in the yard, tantalizing her outside and inside; she wouldn't put it past them. And if she could destroy the rooster that was a terror in the yard she had a feeling that she would be in a way destroying a part of Grandpa that was a trouble in her house. She wished she were hiding behind a bush to leap out upon *him* to wring *his* neck. He would not die, only wheel through her house day after day, asking for this and that, meddling in everything she did.

The rooster came to the pansy bed so serene, even in rags

of feathers, like a beggar-saint, sure in his head of something,
something unalterable, although food was unsure, even life.
He came as if he knew suffering and terror, as if he were all
alone in the world of fowls, far away from his flock, alien and
far away from any golden grain thrown by caring hands, stealing a wretched worm or cricket from a foreign yard. What made
him so alive, what did he know? Perhaps as he thrust the horned
nails of his toes in the easy earth of the flower bed he dreamed
of the fields on a May morning, the jeweled dew upon their
grasses and the sun coming up like the yolk of an egg swimming
in an albuminous sky. And the roseate freshness of his mouth
when he was a tight-fleshed slender-thighed cockerel, alert on
his hill and the pristine morning breaking all around him. To
greet it with cascading trills of crowings, tremulous in his throat,
was to quiver his thin red tongue in trebles. What a joy he felt
to be of the world of wordless creatures, where crowing or
whirring of wings or the brush of legs together said everything,
said praise, we live. To be of the grassy world where things
blow and bend and rustle; of the insect world so close to it
that it was known when the most insignificant mite would turn
in its minute course or an ant haul an imperceptible grain of
sand from its tiny cave.

And to wonder at the world and to be able to articulate the
fowl-wonder in the sweetest song. He knew time as the seasons
know it, being of time. He was tuned to the mechanism of dusk
and dawn, it may have been in his mind as simple as the dropping of a curtain to close out the light or the lifting of it to let
light in upon a place. All he knew, perhaps, was that there is a
going round, and first light comes ever so tinily and speck-like,
as through the opening of a stalk, when it is time. Yet the thing
that is light breaking on the world is morning breaking open,
unfolding within him and he feels it and it makes him chime,
like a clock, at his hour. And this is daybreak for him and he
feels the daybreak in his throat, and tells of it, rhapsodically,
not knowing a single word to say.

And once he knew the delight of wearing red-blooded wattles hanging folded from his throat and a comb climbing up his
forehead all in crimson horns to rise from him as a star, pointed.
To be rooster was to have a beak hard and brittle as shell,
formed just as he would have chosen a thing for fowls to pick

grain or insect from their place. To be bird was to be of feathers and shuffle and preen them and to carry wings and arch and fold them, or float them on the wind, to be wafted, to be moved a space by them.

But Marcy Samuels was behind the bush, waiting, and while she waited her mind said over and over, "If he would die!" If he would die, by himself. How I could leap upon him, choke the life out of him. The rooster moved toward the pansies, tail feathers drooped and frayed. If he would die, she thought, clenching her fists. If I could leap upon him and twist his old wrinkled throat and keep out the breath.

At the window, Grandpa Samuels knew something terrible was about to happen. He watched silently. He saw the formidable figure of Mrs. Samuels crouching behind the bush, waiting to pounce upon the rooster.

In a great bounce-like movement, Mrs. Samuels suddenly fell upon the rooster, screaming, "If he would die!" And caught him. The rooster did not struggle, although he cawed out for a second and then meekly gave himself up to Mrs. Samuels. She ran with him to the chickenyard and stopped at the fence. But before throwing him over, she first tightened her strong hands around his neck and gritted her teeth, just to stop the breathing for a moment, to crush the crowing part of him, as if it were a little waxen whistle she could smash. Then she threw him over the fence. The white rooster lay over on his back, very tired and dazed, his yellow legs straight in the air, his claws clenched like fists and not moving, only trembling a little. The Samuels' own splendid golden cock approached the shape of feathers to see what this was, what had come over into his domain, and thought surely it was dead. He leaped upon the limp fuss of feathers and drove his fine spurs into the white rooster just to be sure he was dead. And all the fat pampered hens stood around gazing and casual in a kind of fowlish elegance, not really disturbed, only a bit curious, while the golden cock bristled his fine feathers and, feeling in himself what a thing of price and intrepidity he was, posed for a second like a statue imitating some splendid ancestor cock in his memory, to comment upon this intrusion and to show himself unquestionable master, his beady eyes all crimson as glass hat pins. It was apparent that his hens were proud of him and that in their eyes he had lost none of his prowess by not having himself captured the rooster, instead of Mrs. Samuels. And Marcy Samuels, so relieved, stood by the fence a minute showing something of the same thing in her that the hens showed, very viciously proud. Then she brushed her hands clean of the white rooster and marched victoriously to the house.

Grandpa Samuels was waiting for her at the door, a dare in his face, and said, "Did you get him?"

"He's in the yard waiting until Watson comes home to kill him. I mashed the breath out of the scoundrel and he may be dead the way he's lying on his back in the chickenyard. No more crowing at my window, no more scratching in my pansy bed, I'll tell you. I've got one thing off my mind."

"Marcy," Grandpa said calmly and with power, "that rooster's not dead that easily. Don't you know there's something in a rooster that won't be downed? Don't you know there's some creatures won't be dead easily?" And wheeled into the living room.

But Mrs. Samuels yelled back from the kitchen,

"All you have to do is wring their necks."

All afternoon the big wire wheels of Grandpa Samuels' chair whirled through room and room. Sometimes Mrs. Samuels thought she would pull out her mass of wiry hair, she got so nervous with the cracking of the floor under the wheels. The wheels whirled around in her head just as the crow of the rooster had burst in her brain all week. And then Grandpa's coughing: he would, in a siege of cough, dig away down in his throat for something troubling him there, and, finally, seizing it as if the cough were a little hand reaching for it, catch it and bring it up, the old man's phlegm, and spit it quivering into a can which rode around with him on the chair's footrest.

"This is as bad as the crowing of the white rooster," Mrs. Samuels said to herself as she tried to rest. "This is driving me crazy." And just when she was dozing off, she heard a horrid gurgling sound from the front bedroom where Grandpa was. She ran there and found him blue in his face and gasping.

"I'm choking to death with a cough, get me some water, quick!" he murmured hoarsely. As she ran to the kitchen faucet, Marcy had the picture of the white rooster in her mind, lying breathless on his back in the chickenyard, his thin yellow

legs in the air and his claws closed and drooped like a wilted
flower. "If he would die," she thought. "If he would strangle
to death."

When she poured the water down his throat, Marcy Samuels
put her fat hand there and pressed it quite desperately as if the
breath were a little bellows and she could perhaps stop it still
just for a moment. Grandpa was unconscious and breathing
laboriously. She heaved him out of his chair and to his bed,
where he lay crumpled and exhausted. Then was when she went
to the telephone and called Watson, her husband.

"Grandpa is very sick and unconscious and the stray rooster
is caught and in the chickenyard to be killed by you," she told
him. "Hurry home, for everything is just terrible."

When Marcy went back to Grandpa's room with her hopeful
heart already giving him extreme unction, she had the shock of
her life to find him not dying at all but sitting up in his bed with
a face like a caught rabbit, pitiful yet daredevilish.

"I'm all right now, Marcy, you don't have to worry about *me*.
You couldn't *kill* an old crippled man like *me*," he said firmly.

Marcy was absolutely spellbound and speechless, but when
she looked out Grandpa's window to see the white rooster
walking in the leaves, like a resurrection, she thought she would
faint with astonishment. Everything was suddenly like a haunted
house; there was death and then a bringing to life again all
around her and she felt so superstitious that she couldn't trust
anything or anybody. Just when she was sure she was going to
lose her breath in a fainting spell, Watson arrived home. Marcy
looked wild. Instead of asking about Grandpa, whether he was
dead, he said, "There's no stray rooster in my chickenyard like
you said, because I just looked." And when he looked to see
Grandpa all right and perfectly conscious he was in a quandary
and said they were playing a trick on a worried man.

"This place is haunted, I tell you," Marcy said, terrorized,
"and you've got to do something for once in your life." She
took him in the back room where she laid out the horror and
the strangeness of the day before him. Watson, who was always
calm and a little underspoken, said, "All right, pet, all right.
There's only one thing to do. That's lay a trap. Then kill him.
Leave it to me, and calm your nerves." And then he went to
Grandpa's room and sat and talked to him to find out if he

was all right.

For an hour, at dusk, Watson Samuels was scrambling in a lumber pile in the garage like a possum trying to dig out. Several times Mrs. Samuels inquired through the window by signs what he was about. She also warned him, by signs, of her fruit-jars stored on a shelf behind the lumber pile and to be careful. But at a certain time during the hour of building, as she was hectically frying supper, she heard a crash of glass and knew it was her Mason jars all over the ground, and cursed Watson.

When finally Mr. Samuels came in, with the air of having done something grand in the yard, they ate supper. There was the sense of having something special waiting afterwards, like a fancy dessert.

"I'll take you out in awhile and show you the good trap I built," Watson said. "That'll catch anything."

Grandpa, who had been silent and eating sadly as an old man eats (always as if remembering something heart-breaking), felt sure how glad they would be if they could catch *him* in the trap.

"Going to kill that white rooster, son?" he asked.

"It's the only thing to do to keep from making a crazy woman out of Marcy."

"Can't you put him in the yard with the rest of the chickens when you catch him?" He asked this mercifully. "That white rooster won't hurt anybody."

"You've seen we can't keep him in there, Papa. Anyway, he's probably sick or got some disease."

"His legs are scaly. I saw that," Mrs. Samuels put in.

"And then he'd give it to my good chickens," said Mr. Samuels. "Only thing for an old tramp like that is to wring his neck and throw him away for something useless and troublesome."

When supper was eaten, Watson and Marcy Samuels hurried out to look at the trap. Grandpa rolled to the window and watched through the curtain. He watched how the trap lay in the moonlight, a small dark object like a box with one end open for something to run in, something seeking a thing needed, like food or a cup of gold beyond a rainbow, and hoping to find it here within this corner space. "It's just a box with one side kicked out," he said to himself. "But it is a trap and built to snare and to hold." It looked lethal under the moon; it cast a shadow longer than itself and the open end was like a big mouth, open to swallow down. He saw his son and his son's wife—how they moved about the trap, his son making terrifying gestures to show how it would work, how the guillotine end would slide down fast when the cord was released from inside the house, and close in the white rooster, close him in and lock him there, to wait to have his neck wrung off. He was afraid, for Mrs. Samuels looked strong as a lion in the night, and how cunning his son seemed! He could not hear what they spoke, only see their gestures. But he heard when Mrs. Samuels pulled the string once, trying out the trap, and the top came sliding down with a swift clap when she let go. And then he knew how adroitly they could kill a thing and with what craftiness. He was sure he was no longer safe in this house, for after the rooster then certainly he would be trapped.

The next morning early the white rooster was there, crowing in a glittering scale. Grandpa heard Marcy screaming at him, threatening, throwing little objects through the window at him. His son Watson did not seem disturbed at all; always it was Marcy. But still the rooster crowed. Grandpa went cold and trembling in his bed. He had not slept.

It was a rainy day, ashen and cold. By eight o'clock it had settled down to a steady gray pour. Mrs. Samuels did not bother with the morning dishes. She told Grandpa to answer all phone calls and tell them she was out in town. She took her place at the window and held the cord in her hand.

Grandpa was so quiet. He rolled himself about ever so gently and tried not to cough, frozen in his throat with fear and a feeling of havoc. All through the house, in every room, there was darkness and doom, the air of horror, slaughter and utter finish. He was so full of terror he could not breathe, only gasp, and he sat leaden in his terror. He thought he heard footsteps creeping upon him to choke his life out, or a hand to release some cord that would close down a heavy door before him and lock him out of his life forever. But he would not keep his eyes off Marcy. He sat in the doorway, half obscured, and peeked at her; he watched her like a hawk.

Mrs. Samuels sat by the window in a kind of ecstatic readiness. Everywhere in her was the urge to release the cord—even before the time to let it go, she was so passionately anxious. Sometimes she thought she could not trust her wrist, her fingers, they were so ready to let go, and then she changed the cord to the other hand. But her hands were so charged with their mission that they could have easily thrust a blade into a heart to kill it, or brought down mightily a hammer upon a head to shatter the skull in. Her hands had well and wantonly learned slaughter from her heart, had been thoroughly taught by it, as the heart whispers to its agents—hands, tongue, eyes—to do their action in their turn.

Once Grandpa saw her body start and tighten. She was poised like a huge cat, watching. He looked, mortified, through the window. It was a bird on the ground in the slate rain. Another time, because a dog ran across the yard, Mrs. Samuels jerked herself straight and thought, something comes, it is time.

And then it seemed there was a soft ringing in Grandpa's ears, almost like a delicate little jingle of bells or of thin glasses struck, and some secret thing told him in his heart that it was time. He saw Mrs. Samuels sure and powerful as a great beast, making certain, making ready without flinching. The white rooster was coming upon the grass.

He strode upon the watered grass all dripping with the rain, a tinkling sound all about him, the rain twinkling upon his feathers, forlorn and tortured. Yet even now there was a blaze of courage about him. He was meager and bedraggled. But he had a splendor in him. For now his glory came by being alone and lustreless in a beggar's world, and there is a time for every species to know lacklustre and loneliness where there was brightness and a flocking together, since there is a change in the way creatures must go to find their ultimate station, whether they fall old and lose blitheness, ragged and lose elegance, lonely and lose love; and since there is a shifting in the levels of understanding. But there is something in each level for all creatures, pain or wisdom or despair, and never nothing. The white rooster was coming upon the grass.

Grandpa wheeled so slowly and so smoothly towards Mrs. Samuels that she could not tell he was moving, that not one board cracked in the floor. And the white rooster moved toward the trap, closer and closer he moved. When he saw the open door leading to a dry place strewn with grain, he went straight for it, a haven suddenly thrown up before his eye, a warm dry place with grain. When he got to the threshold of the trap and lifted his yellow claw to make the final step, Grandpa Samuels was so close to Mrs. Samuels that he could hear her passionate breath drawn in a kind of lust-panting. And when her heart must have said, "Let go!" to her fingers, and they tightened spasmodically so that the veins stood turgid blue in her arm, Grandpa Samuels struck at the top of her spine where the head flares down into the neck and there is a little stalk of bone, with a hunting knife he had kept for many years. There was no sound, only the sudden sliding of the cord as it made a dip and hung loose in Marcy Samuels' limp hand. Then Grandpa heard the quick clap of the door hitting the wooden floor of the trap outside, and a faint crumpling sound as of a dress dropped to the floor when Mrs. Samuels' blowsy head fell limp on her breast. Through the window Grandpa Samuels saw the white rooster leap pertly back from the trap when the door came down, a little frightened. And then he let out a peal of crowings in the rain and went away.

Grandpa sat silent for a moment and then said to Mrs. Samuels, "You will never die any other way, Marcy Samuels, my son's wife, you are meant to be done away with like this. With a hunting knife."

And then he wheeled wildly away through the rooms of Marcy Samuels' house, feeling a madness all within him, being liberated, running free. He howled with laughter and rumbled like a runaway carriage through room and room, sometimes coughing in paroxysms. He rolled here and there in every room, destroying everything he could reach, he threw up pots and pans in the kitchen, was in the flour and sugar like a whirlwind, overturned chairs and ripped the upholstery in the living room until the stuffing flew in the air; and covered with straw and flour, white like a demented ghost, he flayed the bedroom wallpaper into hanging shreds; coughing and howling, he lashed and wrecked and razed until he thought he was bringing the very house down upon himself.

When Watson came home some minutes later to check on the success of his engine to trap the rooster and fully expecting to have to wring his neck, he saw at one look his house in such devastation that he thought a tornado had struck and demolished it inside, or that robbers had broken in. "Marcy! Marcy!" he called.

He found out why she did not call back when he discovered her by the window, cord in hand as though she had fallen asleep fishing.

"Papa! Papa!" he called.

But there was no calling back. In Grandpa's room Watson found the wheel chair with his father's wild dead body in it, his life stopped by some desperate struggle. There had obviously been a fierce spasm of coughing, for the big artery in his neck had burst and was still bubbling blood like a little red spring.

Then the neighbors all started coming in, having heard the uproar and gathered in the yard; and there was a dumbfoundedness in all their faces when they saw the ruins in Watson Samuels' house, and Watson Samuels standing there in the ruins unable to say a word to any of them to explain what had happened.

The Bath of Death

JOAQUÍN ARDERIUS

A Spanish exile now living in Mexico City, Joaquín Arderius was born in 1890 in Spain. After a nomadic existence which took him to France and all over Spain where he was a horse dealer, farmer, and glass factory worker, he published his first novel, in 1923. For the next five years he published a novel a year, including one he wrote in jail (for plotting against Primo de Rivera, the Spanish dictator). Since then he has written over a dozen books. The following story was written in Spain in the days of the Spanish Republic, a period of great fruitfulness in modern Spanish literature.

PASCUAL WAS IN no mood for cutting grapes. For that matter, he was none too concerned over his donkey Mora, who was nibbling at the almond tree which was the pride of the master of the hacienda.

He stood dawdling behind the other grape-pickers, then finally roused himself, and began tossing pebbles with intentionally poor aim at the donkey.

"Mora! Go on, beat it! you slut, you!"

Mora turned to her master, threw up her head in the sauciest manner, and continued her ravages on the almond tree. She knew her master too well to mind his threats. Besides, was he not equally guilty in the matter of grapes? Mora had watched him at his work, and of a truth, more grapes went into his paunch than into his saddle-bags.

But that was Pascual's way; on all his jobs he proved himself a most expensive farm-hand. On pay-days, for instance, the pay-master very often ran out of small change; but Pascual didn't mind, so long as he did the owing.

"What's the smallest you got there?" he would ask. "A peseta? —a duro? Let's have it; I'll bring you the change in a jiffy."

But he never came back. No one had ever known him to keep his word. It was really absurd, having him for a debtor.

Wherever he worked, there his donkey grazed, devastating every square foot of tilled ground in her path. You might think he had put her up to it, for no sooner was she tied to a post than she expertly snapped her halter, stiffened her tail, thrust her ears back, and frisked away to the freshest sprout or the tenderest bud.

As for drink, you couldn't move her with a derrick toward a plebeian trough—she was too good for that. So when the girls, with jugs on their hips, came tripping down to a spring, like as not they found the water muddied by Mora's snout and colored with her dung.

Nor was her master any less a rogue. Not only couldn't you get a full day's work out of him, but you could count yourself fortunate indeed if, during the wood-chopping season, he didn't sneak home with a load of brushwood, or, at threshing time, with a bundle of shucks. Everything he touched seemed to stick to his fingers.

And yet his greatest skill lay, not in his purloining fingers, but in his matchless tongue. He wheedled his salary out of you, plus interest; he wheedled tips for the most trivial errands; and for his Mora he would have any tidbit you had about.

And if you took it into your head to inspect the accomplishments of this hireling who was so clever with his tongue, in passing over the earth he was to have plowed, you discovered that his tongue was doing double service, and his hands none. That was Pascual, all over. The farmhands just thought him a bit of a fool, and let it go at that.

"Mora! Drat you!" For the twentieth time he addressed her, and for the twentieth time threw a stone at her, and missed. He stood there, apart from the others, eating his grapes and shaking his head disapprovingly at the beast, whose stout appetite was being appeased at the expense of the master of the hacienda.

The vintagers were pushing up the sun-tinted hill like a flock of ragged sheep. Their leader clambered up ahead, as if he had been hit by a sling-shot; and the rest, swaying heavily from side to side as they followed, looked like those domesticated animals which rear up on their hind legs to eat the figs their master tenders. With one accord, they abandoned their quadrupedal postures and stood upright, stretching and yawning, then dispersed in search of some shelter where they might eat the fruits of their sweat.

"Look Pascual!" Juan Reina shouted. "Look what your donkey's doing to the almond tree! Hit 'er with something. S'pose Uncle Clemente comes over the hill?"

"My arm's dead already from throwing things. She's the dumbest animal I ever had. She'll be the death of me, yet. Beat it, you!"

He stopped abruptly and burst out into a loud guffaw. He winked his left eye, then the right—grey eyes sparkling like two drops of mercury. Frenziedly he began scratching himself under the armpits, pawing and stamping like a puppet. He had the itch.

As he danced up and down, the whole crowd gathered around him as around the court jester of some ragamuffin king; and in the center, resplendent in his gaudy shirt and narrow, blue-striped pants, he cavorted about wildly, making the most grotesque gesticulations.

"Tell us the story of the salt pork in the pot."

"Say a mass!"

"Bray!"

"Imitate the town-crier!"

"Talk like Don Roque, the master of Fenilla."

They were all clamoring for him to show his tricks.

"Gimme a smoke, an' I'll do anythin' you want!" he answered in his shrill joice, jumbling his words, pawing, scratching his armpits, winking his tiny mercury eyes, and twitching his nostrils, all at the same time.

"Here!"

"Take mine!"

"Me first!"

"No, me!"

They were shouting, pushing each other out of the way to thrust their tobacco pouches at him.

"You're first!" he decided. "You've got the best tobacco. What'll it be?"

"Show us how Doña Rita, the schoolmarm, walks."

"Sure thing! But hand over the pouch, first. I gotta get paid, if I'm gonna perform."

Thus, on that red-gold hill, with his belly full of grapes, Pascual played the fool and got all the tobacco he needed for a week to come.

The moments of silence during his performance were punctuated by a monotonous *crunch, crunch*. It was Mora, still nibbling on the trunk of the almond tree, pride of the master of the hacienda.

When Pascual had done with his antics, his audience broke into little groups to seek shelter under trees, and opened their lunch-boxes. From above, the sun hurled firebolts at the earth, but the vintagers sat cool as cucumbers, jesting between mouthfuls of bread and ham.

Mora, lying beside her master, slept the deep sleep of the innocent. Pascual and his wife, Andrea, sat eating a vegetable salad, skewering chunks of bread with the points of their knives. Next to them was another couple, Josefa and Jeronimo.

This Andrea was a beauty. Her voice, her smile, the luminous eyes under her broad forehead, all revealed that serene, profoundly human wisdom to be found among peasants. She loved Pascual, and every act of her life, every wish of her being was directed toward his welfare. On market-days, when she went to town to sell her chickens and eggs, she always spent the proceeds in little gifts for him.

On holidays and Sundays Andrea saw to it that Pascual was without exception the most gaudily dressed man at the hermitage. She revelled in this superiority of her husband over the rest. Then, jestingly, she was fond of calling him, before the others, not "my Pascual," nor "my husband," but "my fool."

And you may be sure, she was just the kind of wife to sit him in the tub and scrub his back for him; and to load his dinner-plate and keep plying him throughout the evening with every manner of dainty. The house they lived in, they owned outright; and the many bushels of wheat which the fertile soil around the house yielded, these Andrea herself had sown and reaped.

When they went to town together, Pascual always chose the meandering paths that skirted the steep precipices, and with Andrea walking ahead, he would sit on Mora, his buttocks buried in a pile of sheepskins—he humming softly to himself, his pipe between his teeth; she plaiting a rope or singing as she ploughed through the thick dust.

To her he was no fool. She held her tongue, however, wishing to have him for herself alone, and never revealed his true character to anyone. She was convinced that her "fool" was the wisest man on earth; so she obeyed him implicitly. And if people laughed at him, it was just too bad about them. Watching him act, tell his stories, cut capers in the thick of the crowd, always raising shouts of hilarity about him, she pictured him as the spout of a fountain making a glorious spray with millions of drops of water. Yes, the greater fools, they, for laughing at her fool.

For his physical powers she knew only adoration. His nervous energy, the egoism animating his hasty, incoherent speech and gestures, all these raised the tide of passion in her. Often he would sit in her lap, murmuring nonsensical things in her ear and fixing his passionate glance on her, with his tongue clucking like a male partridge wooing its mate; and she would tremble with excitement, and her breasts would grow hard under her blouse.

"That's enough, silly!" she would protest; but Pascual, with the dexterity of a rustler branding a cow, would upset her and always have his way with her. His ardor, however, was so short-lived, that Andrea never knew complete satisfaction. But this she had imputed to her barren womb.

Indeed, Pascual was the archetype of egoism. He loved no one, and everything he could lay his hands on, he retained for himself. He was the king, and Andrea his slave.

And now, finally, after five years of marriage, Andrea was pregnant.

Pascual sat under a tree, eating his salad avidly, to finish it before anyone thought to share it with him.

"God, what heat!" Andrea remarked to Josefa, wiping her moist brow with her apron.

"Well, tomorrow at this time I'll be cooling my body at the seashore with him," Josefa replied, shrugging one shoulder at her husband Jeronimo.

"When are you going?" Andrea asked.

"At daybreak, when it's cool, God willing."

"You're lucky!" Andrea exclaimed.

"Why, aren't you going?"

"I'd love to, but him—" she broke off sadly, pointing to Pascual.

Pascual, however, had no mind for anything but his lunch; silent, insatiable, he went on eating strips of pimento and slices of tomato.

Andrea turned impulsively to her husband. "Don't you wish we were going? Come on, let's go this once."

Pascual raised his head, wiped the tomato seeds from his chin, looked at her indignantly, and said nothing.

Jeronimo nudged him with the tip of his sandal. "Don't be stubborn—go on, take her."

"Mind your own business!" Pascual snarled, like a dog disturbed over his bone.

"Well, if he won't go," Josefa urged, "you come with us."

"Don't you worry; if I decide to go, I'll go. When I get something into my head, it sticks there, especially now that I'm getting big."

"If I were that way," Josefa replied, "believe me, nobody would stop me from going."

Pascual glowered at her, and went on eating.

Andrea knew there was nothing to be gained by making a scene; he always had his own way. Occasionally, however, she could soften him with meekness, cajolery, and a few caresses.

Motioning to her friends to be quiet, she assumed the most agreeable expression she could muster, and leaned toward Pascual. Everyone went on eating in silence.

"Pascual," she wheedled in her softest tone, "let's go with Jeronimo and Josefa."

Pascual merely grunted, twitching like a hog in a tubful of maize who had just got a whack on the snout.

"Come on, let's go with them."

"I'll take you to the bullfight next Sunday." Pascual liked nothing better than a bullfight.

"Oh, Pascual, not a bullfight. You know it always makes me cry."

"All the better! Then you won't wet the bed nights."

"I wanna go to the beach! Take me there for a dip," she wheedled, tearfully. "I wanna go to the sea, darling."

" 'To the sea thou art going; I shall go there with thee,' " he mocked, singing a snatch from a popular song.

"You can't get out of it by joking. You're gonna take me!"

"Oh, go bathe in the sink!"

"No, I'm going to the sea! I'll get everything ready this afternoon. We can take a couple of rabbits from the hutch—and the big red cock, and some tomatoes."

"Nice grub for you and *it!*" he broke out in his high-pitched voice, pointing at her with a grotesque gesture.

"Take me for the baby's sake," she pleaded, laying her hands on herself.

"The kid won't like the water. Babies cry when they're wet."

"I wanna go. If I don't, I'll get upset, and something might happen to the child."

"Suits me! Then we won't have to feed 'im."

"And God only knows what'll happen to me!"

"Bosh! What could happen?—the brat wouldn't come out the right way? Then you'd spit it out, eh?"

Andrea gulped down great sobs, and tears trickled down on her apron.

Jeronimo was moved to indignation. "You're a dog! Just look at her, crying her eyes out! Listen, you fathead! don't you ever give a thought to anything but yourself and your own belly?"

Pascual had stopped eating and, with his nose in the air, was nervously scratching his head.

"I see it coming—I'll get sick as a dog," Andrea sighed, weeping into her apron.

"What's the sense in that?" Josefa remarked. "You might die from it. Believe me, when I got that way, Jeronimo did everything I wanted—every little thing! That's how all my children were born."

"Just keep it up," Jeronimo warned, "and one of these fine days, the devil will be draggin' you down to hell, sure as your name's Pascual."

"Don't joke, Jeronimo, please don't joke about such things!" exclaimed Pascual. For he had an overpowering fear of the devil.

"The moment your Andrea shuffles off into another world, the devil will come along and take you by the ear—and down the kitchen pipe you'll go!" Jeronimo continued, hoping to frighten him into consenting.

"Yeah, an' if she died, do you think I'd sta' aroun' twiddlin' my thumbs? No, sir! I'd take her down to the sea and bathe her, before I buried her; that's what I'd do. No, sir! I don' wan' no trouble with the other world!" Pascual spoke with all the sincerity of his soul.

"Every decent man around here is taking his wife to the baths this year. And I'm going with Jeronimo, ain't I? Now what's the matter with you?" Josefa interposed.

"He's doin' you a big favor, eh? Well, if I had a mistress the way he has, I'd take Andrea to the baths in a jiffy—and dance the fandango all the way down."

The mention of the mistress had a singular effect on the group: Josefa turned pale, Jeronimo red, and Andrea, toying with her apron-strings, fixed her husband with a glance as if to turn him to stone. There was a moment of embarrassed silence; but Pascual, unperturbed, filled his pipe.

He was right: Jeronimo had a mistress—and Josefa knew it and stood for it because there were certain economic advantages.

Macaria was a woman of fifty, the widow of an overseer. In men's eyes the slight measure of beauty she retained was undoubtedly enhanced by the knowledge of the acres of land and the plenteous head of cattle she owned. Having fallen in love

with Jeronimo, who was young, robust, and, in her dazed eyes,
handsome, she took him to her, and in exchange gave him financial aid.

For a week now, Macaria had been disporting at the beach
with Jeronimo. She would go in for a dip, and then call to
Jeronimo to warm up her fat body for her. And he, like a
masseur, would set to work rolling her over in the sand, and
thumping her with his immense hands, until the exercise had
roused in both an appetite for the ham that always comprised
their lunch. Then she would stuff him with food, and pull him
back on the sand for frolicking. This was Macaria.

Pascual suddenly broke the silence he had occasioned by
mention of the mistress. "Well, guess that's all I'll have. You'd
better run along home, now."

"You, too. It's getting late, and the children are all alone,"
Jeronimo reminded his wife.

The two women got up. "See you later," they both murmured;
and with their baskets under their arms, their heads bowed with
mortification, they disappeared over the hill.

Pascual and Jeronimo remained seated.

"What a double-crossin' bastard you turned out to be!" Jeronimo exclaimed, turning furiously on Pascual. "You'd trade
your soul to the devil if you could get somethin' to pin on
God and the whole outfit—you're just the type! What in hell's
got into you, shooting off your mouth in front of Josefa?"

"Shut up, you snake in the grass! With a wife to keep you
warm, an' somebody on the side to shell out money—say, you're
a fine one to be talkin'."

"I hope you get pimples on your tongue!" Jeronimo cursed
him, throwing a handful of sand at his back and breaking into
good-humored laughter.

"Why don't you try it on me? See if I mind, and over that
dame with all her dough, an' I'll let you tell Andrea any day in
the week. How about it?"

Pascual lay on his back, looking into the warm, sea-blue sky,
across which four black crows were flying.

Andrea could not sleep all night. Racked by the excruciating
pain inside her, she had to get out of bed every now and then.
In her chemise, by the light of a candle, she sat writhing on

the edge of a chair, until the pain had eased and she could return to bed. Between the intervals of the cramped pain that left her stiff and ashen and drenched with sweat, she felt her insides turning over in her.

And Pascual called sleepily, "Squeeze hard and force it out."

Andrea moaned, and he muttered, "Too well hooked is it? Well, we're in for a pleasant night."

The foetus remained intact, throbbing violently inside her.

When the crisis had passed, she drew the sheets about her, and lay in a pleasant stupor. While Pascual slept to the thunderous accompaniment of his snores, she turned over in her mind the question of the child: Would it all turn out well, or was she going to miscarry?

"God grant I may not lose it," she prayed. "Holy Virgin, I promise to wear the Franciscan garment if you watch over me. On my knees I'll go to the hermitage on a day of wind and snow. Holy Virgin, make Pascual take me to the sea, and ease my troubled mind, which is killing me and my baby. I want just one dip in the sea, just one."

Again a horrible feeling of nausea seized her, and again she got up and sat writhing in the chair. And when the pain left her, she lay down in peace. So it went, through the night.

When the sun rose, and its first rays had pierced her windows, she remembered to pray to the Holy Virgin again for the bath.

Suddenly Pascual woke, with the warm flood of light on his body, and cried out, "Say, why didn't you wake me? Before I turn aroun', it'll be noon already. Do you want me to lose a day's pay?"

"It doesn't matter. Even if you are late, you'll only lose a quarter of a day."

"Ain't that enough?"

They dressed quickly. Pascual, with half a loaf of bread and a slab of bacon wrapped in a newspaper, started out for the vineyard. As he opened the door to go, Andrea begged him again, "Please take me, Pascual, only for one little dip."

"We're going to the bullfight."

"Look at the awful condition I'm in. Don't leave me this way; it'll kill me. It hurts more and more each time."

"We're goin' to the bullfight!"

"If the animals were in my condition, you'd do everything

for them. If your donkey was like me, it would be a different matter!"

"How you talk!—as if one thing was the same as the other. What the animals give birth to is worth good money, and what you carry aroun' with you is good for nothin' but to eat us out of house and home, an' to bring worry."

Thereupon he strode out, unleashed Mora, and was off down the path. At some distance from the house he turned and yelled to Andrea, "Listen! Give the hogs a good feed so they won't be gruntin'."

Andrea watched him in the distance. She was sick at heart and weak in body, and her eyes were filling with tears. But she would bear this as she had borne everything in the past; for she had all the holy love of a mother for an egotistical, perverse, and conscienceless son.

After his day's work, Pascual kept up an idle chatter with his comrades, till the waning sun robbed him of his audience and left him nothing to do but to return home to his lamenting wife. As he went along, the crescent-moon cavorted on tip-toe through the sky in pace with his Mora.

Pascual was in no hurry. Sucking on his pipe and singing out of the corner of his mouth, he let his donkey graze. She ate the vegetables and corn in the little gardens by the knolls which bordered the path, crushed plants under her hooves, and from time to time became preoccupied with sucking her teats, while her tail flew sidewise and up and down with the vigor of a bobbin on a sewing machine.

They went on, and came to a little brook splashing its way down the hillside. Twisting in and out between the rosebays and the tamarisks, it crossed the path and continued along on the opposite side. He led the donkey into the stream, brought her to a halt, opened her mouth, had her rinse it, and then splashed water over her flanks and rump. She reveled in these ablutions, and her loose skin quivered with pleasure. Finally, he washed her nose and ears, ran her up on the bank, and proceeded on down the path. Suddenly he stopped, remembering he had a thirst, and retraced his footsteps. He crouched, cupped his hands, and sucked in the cool water. He wiped his hands on his blouse, and rejoined Mora.

The night was warm, and the moon shed its plentiful light

over all the land. In the air was a fragrance of ripe wheat and
fresh grass, of stalk and seed.

Serenely, contemplatively, Mora plodded on ahead of her
master. A rabbit leaped out from the corn into the middle of
the path, and crouched a moment in the sand. Pascual flung a
stone at it, and the creature scurried off, disappearing into a
patch of olive trees.

As they passed the peasants' cottages, dogs howled; in the
distance, a donkey brayed; and standing at a clothes-line un-
pinning her dry wash, a woman sang melodiously.

Now a shadow figure was bearing down on Pascual, raising
its arm and shouting. "Ain't you got no home?"

"That you, Celestino?" Pascual asked.

"Yeah. Say, gimme a light, eh? I've used up all my flint."

"Here, take it outta my pipe."

"Ain't much to get a light off'n."

"Well, don' use it all, neither."

"Say, you wouldn't give away even a stalk of wheat on Palm
Sunday!"

"Yeah? An' it's swell guys like you that come aroun' beg-
gin' off suckers like me. Come on, how about some tobacco?"

"Here y'are, tightwad!"

They separated, each going his own way. After a while Pascual left the road and, climbing on a slight rise, viewed his own
farmhouse in the distance. On the crest of a hill, with its sides
whitewashed, it looked like a pale phantom huddled in a cape,
keeping ghostlike watch from the dome of a palace.

"Andrea! Andrea! Are you deaf, Andrea?" Pascual cried, as
he entered the house.

Silence. He paused in the center of the kitchen, and listened.
No answer.

"Andrea! Where the hell are you?" Still no reply.

"Andrea! Andrea!" He lit a candle, "Andrea! Andrea!"

He went into the bedroom. There she lay on the bed, sound
asleep.

"Andrea! Andrea!"

A fly hissed, its wings caught by the candle-flame, and
dropped into the hot tallow.

"Andrea!"

He watched her, puzzled, scratched his head, and winked.

A beetle flew serenely in through the window, and brushed his cheek. He swung at it with his open palm, clumsily knocking the candle over with his other hand.

He could see her in the moonlight now, in deep repose.

"Andrea! Andrea! Andrea!" he called more softly, poking her shoulder. Still she did not answer. He shook her roughly by the arms. No response. He seized her by the ankles, lifted her legs, and dropped them back on the mattress. Andrea lay still, mute, stiff as a corpse.

"Maybe she's dead," he murmured, scratching his arm-pits. He looked at her blankly for a moment. Lying on the bed, dressed, she was like a confused bundle of clothing.

"She is dead!" he said at length, with some conviction. He thrust his head out of the window and stared at the moon.

"Frera," he thought to himself, "only two hours away. I've got plenty of time, plenty."

Then he turned back to the bed: "Andrea, my girl!" He coughed with embarrassment.

"Dead as a door-nail!" He coughed again.

"Got to bathe her, that's all there's to it. Can't bury her without that bath, or I'll have all the devils on my back. No, sir! Can't afford to fool around with those birds."

And light-hearted once more, he went to saddle Mora.

Across the frames for carrying the water-jugs, Pascual placed the wicker hurdle on which he dried his figs. With a piece of rope he managed to tie it securely around Mora's belly. Then, on top of the frame, he spread a fleecy sheepskin mat, providing a makeshift equestrian bed for his foolish wife, who had gone and died on him.

He carried the corpse of Andrea out, placed her face-down on the mat, and covered her with a sheet he had got from the trunk. The whole business was carried through with a serenity bordering on unconcern, as though he were taking a bundle of shucks to market. For what did not affect Pascual's own self was no very great matter to him.

He planned, now, to take her to the ocean and bathe her, so that, when his turn came to die, he might not be dragged below, where all the devils in Hell were sure to stamp on his prostrate body. Such was his code of ethics.

As he was about to start, he turned to the moon again and addressed it thus: "I don't like your face tonight, you double-crosser, you!"

He grimaced, calculating the moon's position, and finally decided "About eleven—eleven, more or less. I'll be back before sunrise, for certain."

He filled his pipe and lighted it. The smoke poured through his nostrils in two thin streams.

"Gee'-up, Mora!"

He did not have to tell Mora where to go; he just faced her in the proper direction, and in her ambling way she got there. The path to Frera was no exception; she knew every inch of the way, for at Frera Pascual used to buy fish and peddle them to the farmhouses in the district.

When they were almost half way to Frera, he skirted the foothills of the great chain of mountains whose peaks were outlined in soft curves against the sky. On they moved; Mora with the dead woman slung across her back, and Pascual behind, serving as the funeral cortege.

It was a gruesome spectacle: the pale-blue sky, empty and fathomless, the hunchbacked mountains, all grey under the moon, the moving blotches of the black beast, the ashen corpse and the man in his black hat, white shirt, and grey pants. The horizon was tinged with the mystery of death, the cold of snow, and the mist of all beginnings.

At each step Pascual looked up at the sky and, facing the moon, cried out, "Somethin' bad'll come out of a night like this. Somethin' bad! If nothin' happens, it'll be a miracle."

As he climbed higher, he felt his chest contracting, and from his soul came a deep sigh. Bit by bit, fear creeping into his heart. He stopped suddenly, and grasping Mora by the tail, pulled her up short.

His eyes encompassed a great circle as he scanned the horizons. He saw nothing but Mora and the dead woman, silhouetted against the mountains and the sky.

Pascual dared not continue on to Frera. In a quandary, he stood scratching his head, pawing the ground, and coughing. If only there were a pool nearby in which to bathe her! But the place was drier than chaff! Besides, come to think of it, he had to have salt water for her; and anyway, it was the Frera beach she had asked for. Well, so be it!

He filled his pipe again, lit it, puffed furiously on it, and slapping Mora on the rump, gave the command to proceed. They descended down the slope to a deep ravine, with walls of rock and sandy floor, through which a tiny stream wound its way. From both walls, rows of poplars and elms, sheaved in their leafy gowns, stood out straight over the ravine.

Mora sensed the need of speeding up her journey along this passage, for such was Pascual's wont here; and she broke into a trot. It was a dangerous spot, and several hair-raising stories were told of it. That deep torrent, flanked with stone, emptied into the sea near Frera. At the top, between the two walls, the sky looked like a river, and the moon a buoy.

At the moment the ravine was dimly illuminated, and the leaves were capped with whiteness. The floor exuded a fresh smell of brine, rosebay, and rosemary. In several places the stream split the path, so that Mora had to wade through while Pascual leaped over.

The screeching and hooting of night-birds broke the silence. Mora snorted, and her hooves went ringing down the canyon. Pascual's heart skipped a beat. The branches of an elm tree shook, and Pascual started back, terrified.

"What's that?" he cried, then recognized it for an owl, and moved on. He made as little noise as possible, but the donkey tramped on like a club beating on a skull. Pascual was panicky.

Few persons dared pass through at such an hour. The smugglers of Frera, by perpetrating murders there, had succeeded in giving the place a ghastly reputation.

Before Pascual's eyes, spectres in horrible postures passed, re-enacting the events which he knew had actually taken place here. He saw the fierce, violent faces of men committing crimes —livid faces, pale faces; eyes of fire, and eyes like pools of stagnant water. He saw a man fleeing, with another pursuing him, and heard cries. He was paralyzed with fear at the apparition of shepherdess, the same that had been found at dawn in this spot, being torn to pieces by two red dogs, while a tiger-colored one defended her from the attacks of a raven which was trying to claw out her eyes. Then there was re-enacted before his eyes the fight between two monsters, who in their attempt to rape a little girl, had ended with murdering her, to deny each other possession.

Pascual felt as if his feet were wrapped in cloth, so noise-lessly did he walk. But Mora scampered on heedlessly along the path.

After a few moments the phantoms fled, and he perceived again the rows of trees, the rosebays with their red brocades, and the black body of the beast, halved by the white mass of the dead woman, plowing through the sand, splashing through the water, like a cross of jet and mother-of-pearl pulled by a string of diamonds along an endless journey over ashes.

Someone was coughing! Yes, and close to his ear! He leaped back, cowering, seized two rocks in his fists, and carefully fol-lowed the donkey, prepared for an encounter with a shadow. But no phantoms appeared; only, from the rocky walls came low-throated laughter.

"Crack! crack! crack!" sounded Mora's beat along the path, as if her bones were breaking under the weight of her burden. Pascual's breath came now like the beating of a wounded eagle's wings.

The spectres again loomed up from behind rocks and came forth on tip-toe, skulking behind trees, their faces lit with grim expressions of mirth. Once again Pascual's eyes lit up in horror, and his fingers tightened on the rocks he held.

Pascual heard the cough again.

"Heavens!" he muttered. "This canyon is just a great big womb!—everything is alive here, even the rocks! Guess it must be the elms and poplars coughing!"

The mule began to pant.

"So!" thought Pascual. "It was Mora all the time! And I thought somebody was coughing!"

Now, in the distance, the strip of sky had dropped like a curtain to the earth. It was the sea! Pascual breathed freely again; it would soon be over.

"Gee'-up, Mora!" he exclaimed, while he intrepidly paused to fill his pipe, light it, and blow two streams of smoke from his nostrils.

Soon, they were out of the canyon and headed straight toward the beach, with its waters glistening under the moonlight.

Pascual laid the corpse out on the sand. Mora, thankful for the disburdening, browsed about for giblets.

About a kilometer away, the houses of the village of Frera were visible.

Pascual gazed at the body of Andrea resting in the sand, in her gaudy red dress and her blue kerchief. He stooped, undid her sandals—she wore no stockings—and pulled her dress up over her head, leaving her in her chemise. Then, with her gleaming in his arms like a mass of foam, he began to wade out into the sea. With the water to his knees, he stopped and looked at his wife. He felt an overpowering desire to possess her.

Dead? Why not? Did it matter? She had always been just as dead as she was now. And he had possessed her every day of their married life. Now he desired her more than ever; she was so still, so defenseless—all his. The greed in him rose as he advanced deeper into the water, the softer the bed. Here, with the water at his elbows? Farther, farther yet. He waded on, halted, and looked at her again.

His eager hands itched to rip off her chemise and throw it on the waters like the rent wing of a swan.

He stood staring down at the length of her, his nerves afire. A little farther on, the water would be taking her from his arms, and carrying her off. He advanced one foot, then the other, and prepared to launch her, when suddenly, out of the silence, came:

"Ay! ay! ay! ay!"—followed by resounding laughter.

Pascual abandoned the body to the waves, and fled ashore screaming like a madman.

"Don't be scared! I'm not dead! I wasn't dead before, either! Didn't you hear me cough in the canyon? I was afraid you'd find me out then. A mosquito got caught in my throat!" exclaimed Andrea, up to her waist in the water.

Pascual, who had fallen in the sand at the feet of Mora, cried in alarm:

"Don't come near me! Don't come near me!"

"But I'm as much alive as you, Pascual! Come on, let's take a dip. If you only knew how happy the kid is to be here in the water!"

"Don't come near me, Andrea! You're dead, and you know it! The devil himself is inside you, moving and blabbering at me. You can't fool me!"

"Come here! Don't be silly!"

"Only when the devil leaves you an' you're dead!"

"But I'm not dead! It was La Cana who put me up to this to save the baby—and me too. It's fatal to be this way and have a wish you can't fulfill—did you know that?"

"It's the devil makin' your tongue wag! He's aimin' to catch me, so he can put me in his cauldron to boil. Don't come near me! Just hurry up an' die, like a good girl! Go on, Andrea, die! An' be quick about it!"

"Come on Pascual, let's bathe together!" she exclaimed, beaming happily as she waded toward him. Playfully, she began to splash him.

Pascual, his eyes bulging, took one leap, seized her in his arms and brutally thrust her under the surface. She thrashed about a few moments, sending the water churning, then sank. A few bubbles rose to the surface, indicating her grave; and in a moment, the water resumed its peaceful wash.

"Jeronimo was right," Pascual muttered. "Guess if I'd waited a little longer before bathin' her, they'd sure of got me, those devils!"

Andrea's body rose slowly to the surface. She was dead enough now. He watched the waves a moment, as they cradled the corpse, then turned back to Mora. And together, they made their way home again.   (TRANSLATED BY ANGEL FLORES)

"And I Am Black, but O! My Soul Is White"

PEGGY BENNETT

Born in Hendersonville, North Carolina in 1925, Peggy Bennett attended the Florida State College for Women in Tallahassee. Then, after working for a year as a payroll clerk at Camp Gordon Johnson, Florida, she studied at Black Mountain College in North Carolina. She returned to her family's home in Florida to write a novel, The Varmints, *which was published by Alfred A. Knopf in 1947. Her short stories and poems have appeared in* Accent, Partisan Review, Harper's Bazaar,

Mademoiselle, New World Writing, *and* Harper's. *She is married, has two small daughters and is currently working on a novel in New York City.*

ONE OF THOSE unique local incidents that happen everywhere, something people of the locality look back upon uneasily. One of those peculiar incidents that are the infrequent heritage of any one township and affect all that one township's people like a bloody trainwreck or the collapse of a central water tower.

It belongs specifically to Tupelo. Like Chicago's great fire to Chicago, San Francisco's earthquake to San Francisco, this event belongs to Tupelo. (And inconsequentially to the whole world.) It happened about this time.

The sun had not shown its brilliant nakedness through the atmosphere for weeks. The sky was like a swamp full of muck. The smells of the earth were vile, violent and voluptuous. Smells of moist clods, chicken dung from the chickenyard, and rotting leaves. Odors were not changed, never left the humid air. The weather was unsanitary. On "Nigger Hill" and across the tracks in the varmint section the outhouses perfumed their parts of town.

The duets of cats upon the gateposts and elsewhere consumed the late hours with songs of passion so intense that their only logical conclusion seemed to be murder instead of savage mating.

The rank earth was continuously wet. Clothes would not dry on the clothesline. Hustlers became sluggards. Emotions in general became amphibious. Heads ached and hearts hung heavy. Minds seemed to mildew. It was a subtle psychological time of great flood. It made moist children wish vehemently for a time of great drought.

The boy Eddie was found in a cloven bank of a ditch, a gully, with his skull broken into by a heavy iron bar.

(The stimulation of working in the drugstore, of meeting all kinds of people day by day, of hearing about all kinds of experiences, had kept Mutt perpetually excited. It seemed that anything in the world could happen these days, might happen, and—Mutt fervently hoped, barbarian—would happen.)

When that morning Eddie was found lying face down in a

gully with a cracked skull, the news was brought into the drug-store like an irrepressible flame of powerful issue. Mutt was quite stunned. No sorrow or joy clutched him, no emotion but a bafflement as to how he should behave. O, he knew not to re-joice, but he understood that he should become pale and mournful and perhaps shed a tear. After the first squeak he made ("Eddie? Dead? No kidding!"), he suddenly realized the role he must play as Eddie's co-worker, so he went around grimacing surlily, as if Eddie's death angered him, and once he managed to squeeze out a tear.

All day people came and went with long drawn faces, spas-modic sentences of horror and grief, melodramatic vehement talk about lynching the murderer if ever he could be found (but no one, not even Eddie's own mother, could ever suggest the murderer; it was simply the ghost of woe's handiwork, the eerie sigh), and the town hugely enjoyed its sensations of awe and horror and fury. It gave the town a chance to unite in indignation and denunciation of a common enemy and in a headless aggressiveness. There was muffled thunder in their low quick conversations ("They found anything yet?" "No." "By golly, some sneaking son-of-a-bitch . . .") and a sense of exul-tation in righteousness and power (through strength of number, brute force). And so, does war bring spiritual greatness?

People had died before in Tupelo, and, furthermore, people had been born. On an average of once a week the news of some new death of a town ancient or former resident reached Tupelo at large. In the past month Henny Harmon, who was sitting on the front porch, had dropped off, dead. Old Sue Dun-can had et something that disagreed with her. Hiram Sneed finally died, he who had been living on half a kidney. To take their places, there were births, and there were also people who migrated to Tupelo and away, thin trickles of them.

But usually people lived with steady rhythms: the dream-ing plodders, to whom death was yet a stranger and every death a conundrum. Each death was a shock to the senses of these sleepwalkers, these dreaming plodders, because they were their senses, and death was commonly supposed to be a state of per-manent insensibility. Especially when the young died, a high school girl of leukemia, a tiny boy of diphtheria, especially then death was a curious blow. How should one take it? There is so much, it seems, to be lived.

So many people, suddenly rendered inutterably dear by the
abnormal finality of their absence, are dead. If only we could
take a vote to establish a heaven after death where all would
be known each to each, and each loved by all, then the world
would have meaning. Then people would think, "Ah what's the
use of all this earthly commotion, this brawling?"—and they
would throw away all weapons, psychological and whatnot, perhaps. What a fellowship there would be, on earth as well as in
heaven! The Christians are right, after all. Anyway, they're
far better off than we skeptics are.

Back in the drugstore, at the prescription counter far in the
back of the little building, Mutt listened to a haunted sailor
tell of death as he knew it. It seemed that he had to tell it, now
that he had a chance to purge himself of the dreadful secrecy
that had poisoned his spirit. It was Silas Markham, his fingers
fluttering over his eyes with the weary flutter of a bird coming
at last to safety out of the storm: "We had a kid, a greenhorn,
on board this last trip. O, God, if I never forget anything . . ."
And with this prayer breathed between blanched lips, Silas
rubbed his low wrinkled forehead with the back of a clenched
hand and squinted, his eyes shut tight. "Kid got caught in the
steam boiler, lost his head. The only way you kin git out of
that place is from the inside, the inside, you gotta unlatch that
panel from the inside. God, we had to listen to him. God. God.
O God."

After the sailor was gone, his face burning as if he had fever,
Mutt heard the prescription clerk, Martin Mooney, tell softly
how he remembered the First World War. He was a veteran. "I
remember I saw my brother git killed. I didn't think I'd ever git
over that. He screamed like a woman. I wished to hell it had
been me." But at once the silver-haired man brightened up, as
if this sober memorying had been a crime, a social crime. "Lord,
I remember how raw my belly got, just from climbing around
on them rocks."

Cepheus, the negro boy who worked for the jeweler across
the street, Cephus, perhaps more than a namesake of the
longdead Ethiopian king, stood around in the drugstore waiting for a prescription to be filled for the obese jeweler. His
dark pink-palmed hands were rammed deep into his pockets,

his air was vague and somber ("as if he didn't have good sense"), his profound thoughts seemed too profound, idiotically profound, and his expression was enigmatic, inscrutable.

Mutt, moving about, polishing the little round tabletops or sweeping the floor with a longhandled pushbroom, more than once looked up and found Cepheus' strange stupid stare fixed on him. But Mutt didn't care what that "nigger" was thinking as long as he didn't bother Mutt.

In fact, Mutt was hardly aware that such a person as Cepheus existed. And why did Cepheus exist? The inscrutable dusky boy, the anonymous darky?

Mutt worked hard all day. The funeral would be the next day, and all the stores would close at ten o'clock in the morning for the sad wild occasion.

Mutt left the drugstore at six-thirty that evening. A damp furry wind flew into his face. The clouds brooded in mass demonstration, thick over the magnolia trees and other trees and second-story housetops. There were dark lumps in the cloud and then lighter cloud surrounding the murky brown lumps, but nowhere did the evening sky show. The streets were like gorges, and the world seemed robbed of all its glorious hues: the terrestrial green had turned to gray.

And because he had a mind susceptible to dramatic fears, he imagined, he knew, he was as sure of it as of the fact that he was born, that someone was following him. He *knew* it. He once slung himself around savagely because he had even *felt* a hand or something, an object, hovering right over the nape of his neck. Finally he could bear it no more. Again he slung himself around with a spontaneous little bellow. There was no one there, nothing. Then he began to run.

He had left his bicycle home with a flat tire. Without it he felt oddly bound, so dependent had he become upon its easy wheeling movement and rollicking speed. He missed the superior velocity, just as a man accustomed to a typewriter must feel when he finds he must write a letter without one, or a woman accustomed to an electric stove when she must cook with kerosene. Thus we progress.

"Hey, Bud, pipe the pedestrian! Hey, Son, whyn't you git you a airyplane?"

"Haw haw haw, hi, Mac. Flivver's laid up. Damned if I don't

feel crippled. How about a lift to town? My laigs is all in, and I don't know as I could make it stumpin." How glad Mutt would have been if one of his automobiled acquaintances had hove in sight.

The streets were as deserted as streets on the moon. Mutt began to feel so alarmed that sweat rolled down the sides of his face. It was so strange, this savage mood of naked sickening fear. He was not usually so nervous. All those stories he had heard. Maybe he was sick. Yes, maybe he had fever. He was afraid to walk in the street for fear an automobile would come cruising around the corner and men of a ferocious otherworld kind of breed would leap out and seize him before he could cry out and carry him off to kill him and dump him into the sea. Or perhaps they would just strike him dead on the spot, as someone had apparently struck Eddie dead. That was it. His imagination was playing on that theme. Mutt began to wonder feverishly if he had made any archenemies. He was afraid to hover over the streets. He was also just as afraid to walk on the zigzagging sidewalks past deeply weeded lots and hyper-thyroid-like shrubs, past the lurking mouths of alleys. There were sporadic houses on either side of the streets, but their people were deep in their bosoms, and their yards were desolate of *human* beings.

He kept changing from the sidewalk trails to the street, to the sidewalk trail on the opposite side of the street, and then back to the street again, and finally to the initial trail. His vision took on a nightmarish quality. Time seemed leaden and still. He felt a premonition of death so vivid that he wanted to howl, "I don't want to die!" Gooseflesh chased up and down his spine with delicious coolness, icy fingers. He almost died of sheer fright. And back of it all, like a master of puppets, was the very strange and evasive illusion, faint and vague and persistent, something he had not fully realized even when he had first experienced it, something he probably would never be able to express for the simple reason that he would never realize fully what it was.

It was a twilight awareness of a strange gaze from enigmatic inscrutable and presumably stupid eyes. An awareness that lingered with him from some experience he could not remember save as a stare somehow inhumanly cold and knowing. If he had kept pulling on his imagery, on his memories, by some train of association he might have half-realized what it was. It was right on top of him, almost, in time locality. (That morning. Cepheus' eyes.)

He reached home almost delirious, nervous as a cat. But eventually the naked droplight shone into the crevices of his soul with unwinking electrical glare, and the nearness of such flesh-and-blood critters as the firm-seeming young Hilliard and the fearless-looking Old Man soothed him back to his usual state of enviable equanimity.

A curious relationship existed between Mutt and the young Hilliard. Mutt was poor in English grammar, literature, mathematics, general science, history, and all the remainder of his school subjects without exception. Hilliard, who was well beyond his age in all phases of school work except athletics, surpassingly skilled as a reader, a symbolist, an expressionist, helped Mutt with his homework. In return for which service Mutt, the year around, not just during school terms, helped Hilliard realize the peculiar kind of world Tupelo represented by sharing with Hilliard his experiences, by collecting all kinds of gossip to tell Hilliard, by chaperoning Hilliard whenever Hilliard felt a need to come to town. Because Mutt was loyal to his little brother, feeling an honest sentiment of love for him, and because Hilliard pitied Mutt, who was such a blind, deaf, and dumb little oaf, they made a beautiful harmony together, never fussing or fighting. And their self-discipline grew stronger, and a quality of tolerance in their souls also grew.

Night came with an epic quality, lasted until morning, and then fled stealthily, taking all its peculiar manias with it so that when the light came it overran the land, and only the shadows remained as debris of that terrible and silent battle between darkness and light, that savage massacre. The skies cleared the next morning, all golden and fine, and the vault of heaven was a virile blue, and like all blue, a symbol of mystery.

The funeral was one of the largest the town ever saw, cars on cars all lined up and following each other bumper to bumper in a long serpentine figure through the town.

People cried (it is not certain why they cried) and ate the cake of melancholy in general, and made it one of the most intellectual of all funerals, so full of conjecture. Mutt went and suffered in his new shoes, which were a sight too stiff and small. His pinched white face moved the Methodist Minister to put his kindly hand on the boy's tense shoulder. "Son," he said sympathetically, "all things, in the long run, happen for the best."

"I got a blister on my heel where my shoe slides up and down," explained Mutt appealingly, his suffering mind on one track. The funeral ran its course, and everyone suffered. The Minister reminded everyone of the good in the boy, something that had been so submerged before this time, and people were remorseful who were not usually remorseful (except at funerals in the presence of a dead being's stunned and wretched relatives). Each held out as the center of his small universe, but sorrowed therein nevertheless.

After the Minister's soulcleansing solution was delivered and the last dramatics dramatized, people broke away from the cemetery and babbled together with renewed energy. Mrs. Busybody maintained that she distinctly remembered that blah had blah-blah and bosh, and she personally had blah. Old Sage So-and-So remembered that at such and such a time he had remarked this and that, and it had never been known to fail, not in his lifetime. Everyone had his conjecture, and his resolution mitigated somewhat the sting, the sore, of not-knowing. But the mystery was fomented all right. Since there *was* a solution to this riddle, why could it not be found?

"I'm doing everything a man possibly can," said the licentious old Sheriff in a mild huff, and he bit savagely on his plug of tobacco. Official duties irritated him no end.

Three nights later George Sorenson, known to his teen-age friends as El Slicko or Giorgio or even Georgia (because of his dandified appearance, his obsession with glittering jewelry and bright silk ties) was murdered in his own backyard. Knifed. It was preposterous.

A peculiar fact about these incidents. None was ever published by any newspaper abroad, outside the county, outside of the little mimeographed Friday sheet of the Tupelo Times, in fact. If one of the murders had happened in one of the colossi of the North, in Boston, for example, it would have stood a fair chance of becoming nationally and even internationally known. And both of them together, the victims being youths sacrificed

to the passion of some fiend, would have constituted a headline
scream, perhaps. It would depend on the issues of the times.

Now the town was armed with its knowledge, and subse-
quently every stranger was suspect, and every theretofore harmless lunatic, and, because the murderer had shown considerable
insight into the lives and habits of the two teen-age boys who
were unfortunate enough to be victims, every man, woman, or
child in town was suspect. Men warily eyed one another.

Boys were quizzed by groups of hawkeyed citizens to find
out who had offended them and why and what had been done
about it. But it was a futile gesture, fusillades fired into the
ocean wave. (Who would ever know what, if anything, had
been hit? So fruitless it seemed, so baffling and banal where
an iron truth and profundity should have lain. Men kept thinking that the answer must be obvious, on the ends of their noses,
but it seemed that only mirrors were there on the tips of their
noses, and when they seemed to have discovered a clue they
bumped into themselves. Must start all over again.)

The Old Man arranged to come after Mutt when the drugstore closed on Saturday night, for that night was Saturday
night, and the fiend might become unleashed again, might it
not? Groups of armed men patrolled the streets. Teen-age boys
observed a curfew by order of the mayor, could not be out
after 7:30 unless accompanied by a grown man. All stores
would close at 8:30 that Saturday night.

A man was coming down by train from Washington, an-
nounced the Sheriff proudly, a smile of triumph on his haggard
old face. His duty was done.

The Old Man, stopping by the jewelry store to leave his
"good" watch for repair, almost collided with an industrious
young colored boy, who was dusting the counter. "Hey," said
the Old Man in mild surprise, "almost stepped on you, didn't
I?" Cepheus just looked at him noncommittally and then resumed his energetic dusting, his tongue fat and pink caught
between his open lips, his brown forehead puckered by his
effort. The Old Man stepped on back to where the jeweler sat in
an easy chair, philosophically looking on.

"I don't think an ape could be as stupid as that black boy of
mine," remarked the jeweler in greeting, in even, fatalistic tones.
The jeweler knew himself to be the cream of wisdom all

wrapped up in his one fat body. "Awful about our boys, isn't it?" he continued. "Wouldn't be a bit surprised if one of these nigger monkeys isn't on the deal end."

The Old Man, who had worked with negroes and learned to love them in general and some of them a great deal, grunted tolerantly and gave the jeweler the little paper parcel in which he had wrapped his watch. "Fix this for me, will you?" he said briskly. "I think the mainspring is broken."

All afternoon people wore a mute expectancy that gave their lives immediate values they had forgotten. Suddenly life itself was dignified, and even food tasted more delicious than before. That most obvious human heritage, the body, was suddenly rescued from the shades, the background of the obvious, and sharply focused as something not so certain after all. The moral code, "Thou shalt not kill," had been violated. The outcome of this affair would determine whether or not "Thou shalt not kill" was a command or a bluff, and the people were determined that it should remain inviolate. Justice must be done, or people would literally and figuratively perish. Justice was a form of that "vision" without which "the people perish." (Justice is so often an elusive theme, its profile taking different shapes dependent on the position in which you are standing. You must keep moving, rotating around Justice, to get any accuracy of impression. But now, in Tupelo, Justice became quite one-dimensioned for the time.) Every person seemed intent only that the murderer be found and killed for his heinous behavior, the only disagreement being on how he should be disposed of, and every person seemed content to let the future take care of that, as it could not be definitely imagined that a human being was involved. It was a maniac, they thought, and a maniac was not wholly responsible.

Saturday night came and went in a terrorized town, a town terrorized by its own imaginations. The night was unfathomably quiet and still. People came and went, knocking at one another's doorways to inquire, and frightening each other to death. The sky was like the vault of a tomb, the color of ink, and the little patrols behaved like parties of grave-robbers. Night lasted a little short of eternity, and dawn came grey and cold through the streets like a resurrection, a true Easter morning, and the dazzling sun made fear hide and memories seem absurd. Oh, this mad, mad world! People came out on the streets and laughed now, a little nervously at first and then wildly and loudly, laughter that kept their sense of defeat from stifling them.

"Haw, haw, haw, Mamie, was that you that let out that screech when I tapped on the windersill? Lawd, I thought it was a wildcat you kept in there!"

"Don't you jaw me, you stinking hyena. I know you, sneaking around like that there on purpose to scare people. You ain't fooling me."

(It was as if an ignorant people, after living through a meteoric shower, had been waiting for some poor prophet's proclaimed "End of the World," and had lived through the heraldry and the time stipulated for the heralded event and found it all a fluke, a fraud. Only instead of hanging the poor prophet, who had slipped away, vanished, perhaps, they laughed harshly, jeered at one another.)

Sunday night came, and boys who had boasted of their fearlessness during the day became a little uneasy again, but Sunday night went as tranquilly as it had come. The town began to relax a little. "It's lak my William sez. 'Mama,' he sez, 'that murdrer ain't gonna show up around hyere zlongz we's yhere uh-waitin fer im. Eez gonna wait til we ain't watchin fer im. Eez smart. Ee knows tha ropes.' "

It was three weeks later that Mutt was going home at a time when darkness was diffusing itself throughout the area of light, and the little beads of streetlights had just popped on all down the line. It was late, but not too late: September light waned almost as soon as it had waxed clear and fat, it seemed. Mutt was thinking how he soon would be in school all day, and the thought itself was grueling. How glad he would be to be a man and free. Mutt pedaled along with slow doggedness, just as he would spin along through days at school. The mood possessed him quite utterly. O God, the crucifixions of youth.

At Siddons' lot, a big tangled square in the neighborhood, full of grapevines on tumbledown trellises and honeysuckle on rotting fences and Virginia creeper swelling up from the ground and ragweed vagrancy everywhere, plant monsters (shapes of brush that loomed up like weird moonmonsters in moonlight and sighed as if in league with the howling squealing denizens

of the wind), at Siddons' lot, which was already losing its innoc-
uous daylight meanings of botanical interest in the depravity of
deserted dusk, Mutt absentmindedly and in obedience to the
voice of his habit steered his bicycle into the diagonal trail. A
shortcut home.

The Old Man, who had worried a little about the tardy Mutt,
was standing at the opposite corner of the square lot, delib-
erating. If he, the Old Man, went down the back street, while
Mutt rode up the far street, that would be the heck of a merry-
go-round. On the other hand, if Mutt took yet another street,
and he might well already have done that, *that* would be the
heck of a note. The Old Man stood there, his weight on one leg,
his thumbs caught in his pants pockets, and thought hard, his
mind rapidly traveling a maze, going up one corridor and then
down another. On still another hand, the Old Man reflected, he
wasn't doing Mutt much good standing *here*.

At that moment, through a little valley in the brush, he
caught sight of a shadowy figure moving up near the other
mouth of the trail. He couldn't tell whether the figure was moving toward this corner of the lot or the opposite corner, but he
thought it might be Mutt or someone who might have seen
Mutt, so he watched and waited alertly. For an old man his
eyesight was pretty keen.

Exactly forty-four seconds later there was a wild barbaric
yell that reverberated in the air; it seemed that the air shook,
and the Old Man, with a thundering pulse, went running square
into the thicket where he had last seen movement. A strange
form came hurtling out of the thicket howling like mad. It
seemed to be headed straight for the Old Man, but it saw him
just in time and swerved and went beyond him in the general
direction of home. The Old Man put on his own brakes and then
turned to make a small survey. It was Mutt all right. It seemed
that the Old Man could see a bloody gash on Mutt's calf where
the pants-leg was rolled up so that it would not catch in the bicycle chain. He could be wrong about it of course. The Old
Man did not try to stop the youth, who was slowing down near
the end of the next block and bellowing to the first faint stars
in the soft purple of evening. He was certain to rouse the town.

Meanwhile the Old Man hastened into the brush, his little
eyes darting like the eyes of eagles, every sense alert. There was

something in that lot, or perhaps escaped beyond by now. As the Old Man got to the big pine tree where Mutt's bicycle lay on its side, one pedal spinning with a quiet steady hum in the air, the other pedal rammed deep in the black earth, he slowed down.

It seemed that instantaneously he heard a shot from beyond the lot, somewhere in the general direction of town. He broke into a run again and came out upon the dusty shell road.

Now he heard shouts and cries, and down the street he saw people running, forms like insects flitting across the road. He saw a car stop, then reverse its movement until it reached the street corner it had glided beyond, and then turn off, visible no more.

Finally the Old Man found the little hive, the hubbub, in Cooper's alley. Ernie Elwood Barton stood with a gun beside the body of the young negro, Cepheus, which lay limp and dusky in a little heap, looking very much like a bundle of rags.

Ernie was barking orders frenziedly, as if trying to vindicate himself for what would plague him like a crime whether it was just or no. Ernie would be always a frenzied kind of person, acting on freakish impulses. It was perfectly plain to the Old Man what had happened. Ernie had been sitting on the porch of his house across from Siddons' lot and had seen Mutt enter the lot, heard Mutt's devilhounding yell, and had seen Cepheus flying out with a strange hunted-animal stealth. Ernie had stood up; the gun he was holding and cleaning in his lap clattered to the floor. Cepheus saw Ernie with dazed catastrophic sight, displayed the face of a demon paralyzed by its own guilt, and darted off in an entirely different direction from the one which he had planned to take, the one which would take him into the labyrinth of "Nigger Hill," where no negro would betray him. (Every negro would lie soberly and blithely somehow. "Cepheus, that boy of Ben Swade's? No, we ain't seen him. We ain't seen him in a long time. No, suh! Sure habmt.") This was the pay-off. Why had Cepheus gone so far to make this final and fatal move against all that he knew. Even as he made this magnificent blunder he knew he was making it. From then on he was mentally paralyzed, a poor hopeless cripple. Why had he ruined himself with this futile gesture when he might have saved his hide so well?

In each of the three murders this moment had come upon him when a powerful impulse to fly into the face of disaster had swayed him to and fro like a leaf, but in the other two times his exultation in success had been stronger, he had taken care, had clung to reason. But between this third and final murder and the first two the water had flowed in catastrophic floods beneath the bridge. He lost the sense of beauty in savagery that had formerly been with him. He lost his feeling of superiority. He lost his self-control. His thoughts seemed to burst in his head, to dart wildly in all directions at once. It took him a long time to knit his nerves for this third murder; he had had to force himself, and finally, as he had suspected it would, it killed him.

Ernie chased the boy down as he might have chased some frantic wild hare caught through its own mistake, the decision made when in a moment of indecision it left the home ways as familiar to it as its own skin.

One look at the boy's dark skin was enough to decide the justice of the deed in the quick eyes of most excited "white" men (men burnt red in the face by the sun-blaze, men hairy and swart, men jaundiced and puffy, men of purplish pink pimples, men palely and pinkly tan). They knew that they *must* take the side of the impulsive Ernie. It was one of those race fights now, and only one side could win. That was the "white" man's side. The white man must always win. He can be benevolent, a benefactor, to "niggers" if it makes him feel good, but he can't "coddle" them, and he must always remember this: no matter what comes up, the "white" man must always win.

"Boy, that was a lucky shot," said Albert Kirvin, standing near-by.

Eventually even Mutt was brought up, still dazed and sobbing incontrollably. The Old Man started from his philosophic stupor, his preoccupation with his own confusion, when he saw the boy, and swung quietly over to Mutt's side. Someone had wrapped a man's handkerchief—and it was flecked with dirty dried mucous—around the boy's leg. The Old Man grabbed the leg to investigate, and it was explained to him by two or three excited gabby people that it was only a scratch, as the Old Man soon saw himself. A scratch made when Mutt leapt from his bicycle. The old dexterity had stood Mutt in good stead. O, we never know how many odd bits of knowledge will prove pertinent to our lives, and will sometimes be fatal by absence.

Someone had found the icepick the negro boy had hurled at Mutt. It had whizzed by him into a bush beside the pine tree. It was now a vicious looking weapon, the homely icepick with DRINK COCA-COLA sprawled in red letters on its handle.

"Jiminy Cripes" and "Good Lord of Moses" were simultaneous comments by two fervid young observers. Boys ganged around Mutt to soothe him and to ask him naked and abrupt questions, like "How did it feel?" One fellow shouted to another, "Say, Pete! Howdja like t'git gigged by this here thing?"

The group around the dead negro youth was somehow more somber, more dumbstricken. What did he symbolize, exactly? A kind of life in death? No one was sure, and everybody was afraid. Yet no one could speak his fear; it was too great for him to fathom. So far only "white" people were present, and the boy was unmistakably a negro. Yet somehow the boy looked "white," or human, or divine. Something about the poor little carcass with its mutilated head. At such a time not many of that distinct little group were thinking the cruel impossible "eye for an eye and tooth for a tooth" thoughts. The small remote elements of decency were, here and there, coming to the fore. What was there to think? How helpless men are.

But already a couple of small boys were whispering together over by Clancey's shed. In their excitement they took insidious pleasure in bloodchilling thoughts. "You reckon it could be a bunch of niggers like Murder, Inc.?" "Say, you know, you got something there. Jesus! You know I bet this ain't the only one!" Melodramatic smallboy thoughts.

The jeweler arrived by automobile, and when he saw the corpse he cursed softly in his selfpossessed manner. "My nigger, huh?" he said; as if he had owned that soul, and to give credit where credit is due, it is barely possible that he did in a way own that poor distorted soul. The jeweler stood with his hands hung on his fat hips and frowned and shook his head. Then he sauntered over to the most elegant group of young ladies present to pay his respects, for his soul was owned by the exquisite bodies of womanhood supreme. He flashed sparks to draw fire. This was his sublimest expression of himself. The limp body of a negro boy was a non-entity. This was a sophisticated man. He convulsed the ladies.

Then the Sheriff arrived with a tall well-made negro in faded jeans in tow. The Sheriff pushed the man ahead of him into the ever-swelling throng, still, strangely, not graced by negroes. This was the first negro (alive) present. A group of coarse women, on seeing the worn dark face, broke into ferocious jeers, and one spat in his direction. But in general the milling throng was quiet.

When the negro arrived at the side of the corpse, he broke into wild weeping, weeping like a woman's weeping, and began to speak in a high tenor garbled by sobs, a wild high pleading with "the Lord."

The white people standing around, some with haughty contempt-hued faces, began to grow uneasy and some to walk away as if they could not bear anymore of the hideous spectacle, and their hearts burned. A few of them bitterly blamed the negro race for their vague wretchedness, but some were merely heavyhearted and morose from lack of simple emotional response, from confusion.

The Old Man knew the negro man, who, in fact, had worked for him, was not a bad fellow at all. The Old Man stepped up close. The negro became aware of the Old Man's intent face, began to direct all his remarks to him imploringly.

It would have flattered some men to be singled out this way as the king bee, the chief justice, the possible savior of a terrible situation. It weighed on the Old Man like many, many tons of worry, but he held himself erect and listened almost gently, for his sympathy was keen.

By that time the negro ambulance had arrived for the dead boy, and the crowd was dispersed in large measure. The Old Man and the Sheriff were hearing an odd story in the meanwhile. The Sheriff, who had been known to lash the faces of his negro captives in perverted efforts to force confessions, sometimes leaving the scars of his watch-chain written on their faces, this same stupid and depraved Sheriff, this obscene man, was acting mean and threatening. He listened with an ugly leer, his lone long fang glistening yellowly against the cavern of his gawping mouth.

The Old Man saw his black looks and said quietly and in finality, "I wouldn't worry this man, Sheriff, if I was you. I know him. He's a good nigger."

And such was the Old Man's power over his fellow human beings (and such was his reputation in Tupelo) that the Sheriff detached himself from the negro and bothered him no more.

Benya Krik, the Gangster

ISAAK BABEL

Isaak Babel was born in 1894 in the Moldavanka district of Odessa, Russia, a part of town which was very corrupt, poor, and crime-ridden. The son of a business man, he began to write stories in French at the age of 15, in the manner of Guy de Maupassant. Years later Babel said that one of his great ambitions was to write a story as elegantly as his French master. After his college days, he went to St. Petersburg. He met Maxim Gorky there and became Gorky's disciple immediately. From 1917 to 1924, Babel was a soldier and a journalist. His first really serious stories appeared in 1924. His reputation as one of the great short story writers of modern times is based on the slim output of two volumes of short stories, Red Cavalry *and* Odessa Tales. *Since 1936 there has been no mention of Babel's name in any Soviet publication. He is believed to have died in a concentration camp.*

IN ODESSA

I WAS THE ONE to open the conversation.

"Reb Arye Leyb," I said to the old man, "let us talk about Benya Krik.[1] Let us talk about his meteoric beginning and his

[1] *This character was allegedly modeled on Misha Yaponchik, a notorious Odessa gangster. It is said that at one time he headed the Jewish self-defense organization in Odessa, that he fought with the Reds against the White troops and was executed by a firing squad.*—Ed.

terrible end. Three black shadows block the paths of my imagination. Here is one-eyed Froim Grach. The rusty steel of his deeds—can you compare it to the dazzling strength of the King? And here is Kolka Pakovsky. This man's simpleminded ferocity had in it all that is needed for domination. And is it possible that Haim Drong couldn't recognize the brilliance of the new star? How is it, then, that Benya Krik alone reached the top of the rope ladder, while all the others were left hanging below on the limp rungs?"

Reb Arye Leyb, sitting on the cemetery wall, kept still. Before us stretched the green peace of the graves. A man who thirsts for knowledge must be patient. A man who possesses knowledge should be dignified. That is why Arye Leyb remained silent, perched on the cemetery wall. At last he said:

"Why he, why not they, you want to know. Well, forget for a while that you've got spectacles on your nose and autumn in your soul. Stop raising hell at your desk and stammering in public. Imagine for a moment that you're a fellow who raises hell in public squares and stammers on paper. You're a tiger, a lion, a wildcat. You can spend the night with a Russian woman, and the Russian woman will be satisfied by you. You are twenty-five. If sky and earth had rings fastened to them, you would grab these rings and draw the sky down to the earth. And your papa is Mendel Krik, the teamster. What does such a father think about? He thinks about drinking a good glass vodka, about socking someone on the jaw, about his horses—and about nothing else. You want to live, and he makes you die twenty times a day. What would you have done if you'd been in Benya Krik's boots? You'd have done nothing. But he did something. That's why he's King, while you fig with your fist in your pocket.

"Benya, he went to Froim Grach, who then already looked at the world with one eye and was what he is today. He said to Froim: 'Take me on, Froim. I want to be cast upon your shore. The shore I'm cast upon will gain by it.'

"Grach asked him: 'Who are you? Where are you coming from? And what do you live by?'

" 'Try me, Froim,' answered Benya, 'and let's stop chewing the rag.'

" 'Let's,' said Grach. 'I'll try you!'

"And the gangsters held a session to put their minds to the subject of Benya Krik. I wasn't at that session. But it is said that they did hold it. The late Lyovka Byk was elder then.

" 'What's going on under this Benchik's hat?' asked the late Lyovka Byk.

"One-eyed Grach gave his opinion: 'Benya doesn't talk much, but there's a flavor to his words. He says little, and you wish he'd say more.'

" 'If that's so,' exclaimed the late Lyovka, 'then let's try him on Tartakovsky.'

" 'Let's try him on Tartakovsky,' the council decided, and all those who housed a conscience blushed when they heard this decision. Why did they blush? You'll find out if you go where I'll lead you.

"Among us, Tartakovsky had the nicknames Yid-and-a-Half or Nine Holdups. He was called Yid-and-a-Half, because no one Jew could contain so much insolence and so much money as Tartakovsky. He was taller than the tallest policemen in Odessa and he weighed more than the fatest Jewess. And he was nicknamed Nine Holdups because the firm of Lyovka Byk and Company had held up his place not ten or eight times, but exactly nine. It now fell to Benya's lot to hold up Yid-and-a-Half for the tenth time. When Froim passed this information on to him, Benya said 'Yes' and walked out, slamming the door. Why did he slam the door? You'll find out if you go where I'll lead you.

"Tartakovsky has the soul of a murderer, but he's one of ours. He came from among us. He is our own flesh and blood, as if one mother brought us into the world. Half Odessa was employed in his stores. And it was his own Moldavanka people who made trouble for him. Twice they kidnapped him for ransom, and once during a pogrom they staged his funeral, with a choir too. That was when the thugs from the Sloboda section were beating up the Jews on Bolshaya Arnautskaya Street. Tartakovsky ran away from them and came across a funeral procession with a choir.

" 'Who are they burying with a choir?' he asked.

"The passers-by told him it was Tartakovsky's funeral. The procession reached the Sloboda cemetery. Then our people took a machine-gun out of the coffin and made it hot for the

Sloboda thugs. But Yid-and-a-Half hadn't expected that. Yid-and-a-Half was scared to death. And who in his position wouldn't have been scared?

"The tenth holdup of a man who had been buried once already—that was really uncivil. Benya, who wasn't King then yet, understood it better than anyone else. But he had said 'Yes' to Grach, and the same day he wrote Tartakovsky a letter like all letters of that kind:

" 'Highly Esteemed Ruvin Ossipovich!

" 'Be so kind as to place under the rain-water barrel next Saturday . . .' and so on. 'Should you take it upon yourself to refuse, as you have recently done on several occasions, a grave disappointment in your family life awaits you.

Respectfully, one whom you know,
Benzion Krik.'

"Tartakovsky, no dawdler, wrote his answer without delay:

" 'Benya!

" 'If you were an idiot, I would have written to you as to an idiot. But I know that you are not, and God forbid that I should have to change my opinion. It looks as if you're making believe you're a child. Don't you know that there has been a bumper crop in Argentina and that we sit here and don't find one customer for our wheat? And upon my word, I'm tired of eating such bitter bread in my old age and having such a disagreeable time of it, after slaving all my life like the lowest teamster, and what do I have after a lifetime of hard labor? Ulcers, sores, aggravation, sleeplessness. Give up them fool ideas, Benya.

Your friend, much more than you imagine,
Ruvin Tartakovsky.'

"Yid-and-a-Half did his part. He wrote the letter. But the postoffice didn't deliver it. When he got no answer, Benya got mad. The next day he showed up in Tartakovsky's office with four friends. Four masked young men carrying revolvers barged into the room.

" 'Stick 'em up!' they said and began brandishing their guns.

" 'Calm down, Solomon,' Benya remarked to one who shouted louder than the others, 'don't get into this habit of being nervous when you're on the job,' and turning to the clerk who was white as death and yellow as clay, he asked him: 'Is Yid-and-a-Half at the plant?'

" 'The proprietor is not at the plant,' answered the ·clerk, whose name was Josif Muginstein and who was the bachelor son of Aunt Pessya,—she sold chickens on Seredinsky Square.

" 'Who is in charge here, then?' they asked the unhappy Muginstein.

" 'I am in charge here,' answered the clerk as green as green grass.

" 'Then with God's help, open the cashbox for us!' Benya ordered him, and so began an opera in three acts!

"Solomon, the nervous one, packed cash, securities, watches and jewelry into a suitcase; the late Josif stood facing him with lifted hands; in the meantime Benya was telling stories from the life of the Jewish people.

" 'If he makes believe he's a Rothschild,' Benya was saying, referring to Tartakovsky, 'then let him burn on a slow fire. Explain it to me, Muginstein, as to a friend: he gets a business letter from me; why couldn't he get into a trolley for five ko-pecks then, and ride up to my place and have a glass vodka with the family and a snack, taking potluck? What kept him from having a heart-to-heart talk with me? "Benya," he could have told me, "thus and thus, here is my bank balance, wait a couple of days, let me get my breath, give me a chance to turn around . . ." What would I have answered? Hog don't meet hog, but man meets man. Muginstein, do you get me?'

" 'I do,' answered Muginstein and told a lie, because it wasn't at all clear to him why Yid-and-a-Half, a respectable, substan-tial man, one of the leading citizens, should take a trolley to have a bite with the family of Mendel Krik, the teamster.

"Meanwhile misfortune was prowling around the house like a beggar at dawn. Misfortune burst into the office with a bang. And although this time it took the shape of a Jew by the name of Savka Butzis, it was as drunk as a water carrier.

" 'Haw-haw-haw!' shouted the Jew Savka. 'Beg your pardon, Benchik, I'm late,' and he stamped his feet and waved his arms. Then he fired a shot, and the bullet struck Muginstein in the stomach.

"Are words needed here? There was a man, the man is no

more. There lived an innocent bachelor, like a bird on a bough, and now he has perished, stupidly. Come a Jew who looked like a sailor and fired a shot, not at some bottle with a surprise in it, but at a living man. Are words needed here?

" 'Clear out!' shouted Benya, and was the last to go. But as he was running off, he took time to say to Butzis: 'I swear by my mother's grave, Savka, you'll lie beside him. . . .'

"Now tell me, young gentleman, you who cut coupons off other people's bonds, what would you have done if you'd been in Benya Krik's boots? You don't know how you would have acted. But he knew what to do. That's why he is King, while we two sit on the wall of the Second Jewish Cemetery and shade our faces from the sun with our palms.

"Aunt Pessya's unfortunate son did not die at once. An hour after he was brought to the hospital Benya appeared there. He summoned the doctor-in-charge and the nurse and, without taking his hands out of the pockets of his cream-colored pants, he said to them: 'I want to see the patient Josif Muginstein get well. Just in case, let me introduce myself: I'm Benzion Krik. Spare no expense. Camphor, air cushions, a private room— you must give him everything. If you don't, remember that no doctor, not even a doctor of philosophy, needs more than six feet of earth. . . .'

"Nevertheless Muginstein died the same night. And it was only then that Yid-and-a-Half let himself be heard all over Odessa.

" 'Where does the police begin,' he bellowed, 'and where does Benya end?'

" 'The police ends where Benya begins,' sensible people answered, but Tartakovsky wouldn't calm down and in the end this is what happened: a red automobile with a music box in it played the first march from the opera *Laugh, Pagliacci* in Seredinsky Square. In broad daylight the automobile raced up to the little house where Aunt Pessya lived.

"The automobile thundered, spat smoke, glittered brassily, spread a stench of gasoline, and played arias on its horn. A man leaped out of it and walked into the kitchen, where little Aunt Pessya was writhing on the earthen floor. Yid-and-a-Half sat on a chair, waving his arms.

" 'You gorilla!' he shouted when he caught sight of the visitor, 'you bandit, you, may the earth spit out your corpse! Nice fashion you've started, killing living men. . . .'

" 'Mosoo Tartakovsky,' Benya Krik said to him in a quiet voice, 'it's the second day now that I been mourning for the deceased as for my own brother. But I know that you don't give a damn for my young tears. And where, Mosoo Tartakovsky, in what strong box did you lock up shame? You had the gall to send the mother of our late Josif a miserable hundred bucks. My brain, let alone my hair, stood on end when I heard the news. . . .'

"Here Benya paused. He had on a chocolate jacket, cream-colored pants and raspberry boots.

" 'Ten grand, in a lump sum,' he roared, 'and a pension for the rest of her life, may she live a hundred and twenty years. If not, then let's leave this room, Mosoo Tartakovsky, and get into my car.'

"There was a row between the two. Yid-and-a-Half and Benya had words. I wasn't here when the argument took place. But those who were remember it. The two agreed on five thousand outright and a monthly payment of fifty roubles.

" 'Aunt Pessya,' Benya said then to the disheveled little woman who lay on the floor, 'if you need my life, you can have it, but everybody makes mistakes, even God. A terrible mistake has been made, Aunt Pessya. But wasn't it a mistake on God's part to settle the Jews in Russia, where they've had to suffer the tortures of hell? Would it be bad if the Jews lived in Switzerland, where they'd be surrounded by first-class lakes, mountain air and nothing but Frenchmen? Everybody makes mistakes, even God. Open your ears to what I'm saying, Aunt Pessya. You have five thousand in hand and fifty roubles a month till you die, may you live a hundred and twenty years. Josif will have a first-class funeral: six horses like six lions, two carriages for the wreaths, the choir from the Brody Synagogue, Minkovsky himself will sing at your late son's funeral.'

"The funeral took place the next morning. About this funeral ask the beggars who hang around the cemeteries. Ask the synagogue beadles about it, the kosher poultry men or the old women from the Second Poorhouse. Odessa never saw such a funeral, and the world will never see another like it. That day policemen put on cotton gloves. The synagogues were wide open, they were decorated with greenery and blazed with elecric lights. Black plumes swayed above the heads of the white horses that drew the hearse. Sixty choir boys walked in front of the procession. Boys they were, but they sang with the voices of women. Elders of the synagogue of the kosher poultry dealers led Aunt Pessya, one at either elbow. Behind them marched members of the Society of Jewish Salesmen, then came attorneys-at-law, physicians and trained midwifes. On one side of Aunt Pessya were poultry-women from the Old Market, on the other the milkmaids from the Bugayovka district, wrapped in orange shawls. They stamped their feet like gendarmes on a holiday parade, and their wide hips gave off the odor of the sea and of milk. The employees of Ruvin Tartakovsky brought up the rear. There were a hundred of them, or two hundred, or two thousand. They wore black jackets with silk lapels and new boots that squeaked like suckling-pigs in a sack.

"And now I shall speak as the Lord did on Mount Sinai out of the burning bush. Fill your ears with my words. It was with my own eyes that I beheld all I beheld, sitting here on the wall of the Second Jewish Cemetery, alongside of lisping Moiseyka and Shimshon, from the cemetery office. It was I who saw it, I, Arye Leyb, the proud Jew who is neighbor to the dead.

"The hearse drove up to the cemetery chapel. The coffin was placed on the steps. Aunt Pessya trembled like a little bird. The cantor climbed out of his carriage and started the funeral service. Sixty choir boys echoed him. At that moment a red motor car shot out from behind a bend on the road. It played *Laugh, Pagliacci,* and came to a halt. The people were as quiet as the dead. The trees were silent, and the choir boys, and the beggars. Four men climbed out from under the red roof, and walking slowly, carried to the hearse a wreath of roses the like of which was never seen before. And when the service was over, four men placed their steel shoulders under the coffin and, with eyes blazing and chests thrust forward, marched in the ranks of the Society of Jewish Salesmen.

"In front walked Benya Krik, who had not yet been called King by anyone. He was the first to approach the grave. He stepped on the mound of earth and stretched out his arm.

"Kofman, of the burial brotherhood, ran up to him.

" 'What do you want to do, young man?' Kofman asked Benya.

" 'I want to make a speech,' answered Benya Krik.

"And he made a speech. It was heard by all who wanted to hear. It was heard by me, Arye Leyb, and by lisping Moiseyka, who was perched on the wall beside me.

" 'Gentlemen and ladies,' said Benya Krik, 'gentlemen and ladies,' he said, and the sun stood above his head like a sentry with a rifle. 'You have come here to pay your last respects to an honest toiler who perished for two cents. In my own name and in the name of all those who aren't present here, I thank you. Gentlemen and ladies, what did our dear Josif get out of life? A couple trifles. What was his occupation? He counted other people's money. What did he perish for? He perished for the whole working class. There are people already doomed to death, and there are people who haven't begun to live. And it just happened that a bullet that was flying at a doomed breast pierced that of Josif, who did not get anything out of life but a couple trifles. There are people who know how to drink vodka, and there are those who don't know how to drink it, but drink all the same. The result is that the first get pleasure from both joy and grief, while the second suffer for all those who drink vodka without knowing how. That is why, gentlemen and ladies, after we have said a prayer for our poor Josif, I will ask you to accompany to his grave Savely Butzis, unknown to you, but already deceased. . . .'

"After he made this speech, Benya Krik stepped down from the mound. The people, the trees, the cemetery beggars were all silent. Two grave-diggers carried an unpainted coffin to a near-by grave. The cantor, stammering, finished the prayers. Benya threw the first shovelful of earth into Josif's grave and walked over to Savka's. All the lawyers and the ladies with brooches followed him like sheep. He made the cantor chant the complete service over Savka, and the sixty choir boys joined in. Savka had never dreamed of such a service—believe the word of Arye Leyb, an old oldster.

"They say that on that day Yid-and-a-Half decided to retire from business. I wasn't there when he made that decision. But that neither the cantor nor the choir nor the burial brotherhood asked to be paid—that I saw with Arye Leyb's eyes. Arye Leyb is my name. And I could see nothing more, because the people, after walking slowly away from Savka's grave, began to run as from a house on fire. They rushed away in carriages, in carts and on foot. And only the four who had come in the red car drove off in it. The music box played its march; the car shook and was off.

" 'A King,' said lisping Moiseyka, looking after the automobile, the same Moiseyka who edges me off the best seat on the wall.

"Now you know everything. You know who was the first to utter the word, 'King!' It was Moiseyka. You know why he didn't apply that name either to one-eyed Grach or to ferocious Kolka. You know everything. But what good does it do you, if you still have spectacles on your nose and autumn in your soul? . . . "

A FATHER

Froim Grach had at one time been a married man. That was long ago; twenty years had passed since then. His wife had borne a daughter to Froim at the time, and had died in childbirth. They named the girl Bassya. Her maternal grandmother lived in Tulchin, a money-grubbing, purblind, wretched small town. The old woman had no love for her son-in-law. She used to say to him: "Froim is a teamster, and he has raven-black horses, but Froim's soul is blacker than his horses."

The old woman had no love for her son-in-law and took the newborn child to bring up herself. She and the girl lived together for twenty years, and then the old woman died. Thereupon Baska came back to her father. Here is how it all happened:

On Wednesday, the fifth day of the month, Froim Grach had been carting wheat from the elevators of the Dreyfus Company to the port, for the steamer "Caledonia." By evening he had finished work and driven off for home. On turning off from Prohorovskaya Street he met Ivan Pyatirubel, the blacksmith.

"Greetings, Grach," said Ivan Pyatirubel. "Some woman or other is banging away at the door of your place. . . ."

Grach drove on, and caught sight of a woman of gigantic stature in his courtyard. She had enormous flanks and cheeks the color of red brick.

"Papa dear," said the woman in a deafening bass, "I'm bored as hell already. I been waiting for you all day. Grandma died in Tulchin, you ought to know."

Grach, who was standing up in his dray, stared at his daughter, his eyes popping out.

"Don't be getting in the way of the horses!" he shouted in desperation. "Take the bridle off the shaft-horse—what do you want to do, hurt my horses?"

Grach stood up in the cart brandishing his whip. Baska took the shaft-horse by the bridle and led the horses off to the stable. She unharnessed them and went to busy herself in the kitchen. The girl hung her father's foot-clouts on a line, scrubbed the sooty teakettle with sand, and started warming up a beef stew in a cast-iron pot.

"You've got such filth here, I can't stand it, papa dear," said she, and threw out of the window the musty sheepskins strewn over the floor. "But I'll get rid of that filth," Baska shouted, and set her father's supper on the table.

The old man took a swig of vodka out of an enamel teapot and polished off the beef stew, a beef stew as fragrant as a happy childhood. Then he picked up his whip and went to sit outside his gate. Baska followed him there. She had put on men's half-boots, an orange dress, and a hat adorned with dangling birds; and now she seated herself on a bench. The evening sauntered past the bench, the sunset's glowing eye dropped into the sea beyond Peresyp Suburb, and the sky was red, as red as a red-letter day on a calendar. All the shops had already shut down on Dalnitzkaya Street, and the holdup men were riding by on their way to Gluhaya Street, heading for Ioska Samuelson's bawdyhouse. They rode along in lacquered carriages, as vivid as hummingbirds, in their gay jackets. Their eyes were bulging; each had one foot extended toward the footboard, and each clutched in an outstretched hand of steel a monstrous bouquet wrapped in tissue paper. Their lacquered light carriages moved slowly along; there was but one fare seated in each carriage, and the drivers, erect on their high boxes, wore bowknots, like ushers at a wedding. Old Jewish women in their kerchiefs listlessly followed the flow of this customary procession with their eyes; they were indifferent to everything, the old Jewish women;

the sons of shopkeepers and shipowners were the only ones
who envied these kings of the Moldavanka district.

Solomonchik Kaplun, the son of a grocer, and Monya Artil-
lerist, the son of a smuggler, were among those who averted
their eyes from other people's splendor. The two of them
walked past Baska, swaying like girls who had come to know
love; they whispered awhile together and launched into a panto-
mime, their arms demonstrating how they would hug Baska, if
she wanted it. And lo, Baska did want it, right off, inasmuch
as she was but a simple girl from Tulchin, from a money-grubbing, purblind, wretched small town. She weighed a hundred
and eighty pounds, and then some; she had lived all her life
among such small fry as Podolian middlemen, bookpeddlers
and petty contractors in the timber business, and had never
seen such people as Solomonchik Kaplun. Therefore, on be-
holding him, she started scraping the ground with her stout
feet shod in men's half-boots, and said to her father:

"Papa dear," said she in a thunderous voice, "take a look
at that little gent: he's got little feet like a little doll; I could
simply hug such little feet to death. . . ."

"Oho, Mr. Grach," an old Jew sitting alongside whispered
then, an old Jew by the name of Golubchik, "I see that your
little one wants to be put out to grass. . . ."

"This trouble I've got to have on my head yet," Froim answered Golubchik, toyed awhile with his whip, then went home
to bed and fell peacefully asleep, because he hadn't believed the
old man, and he turned out to be wholly mistaken. The one
who wasn't mistaken was Golubchik. Golubchik earned a living by matchmaking on our street; of nights he read the Psalms
over the well-to-do dead, and about life he knew all there was
to know. Froim Grach was the mistaken one. The one who
wasn't mistaken was Golubchik.

And, as a matter of fact, from that day on Baska passed all
her evenings outside the gate. She sat on the bench and sewed
away at her trousseau. Pregnant women sat alongside her;
mounds of linen crept over her widespread mighty knees; the
pregnant women swelled up with all manner of tidbits, even as
the udder of a cow at pasture swells with the rosy milk of
spring, and meanwhile their husbands, one by one, would come
home from work. The husbands of the shrewish wives wrung

out their beards under the faucet, after which they yielded their place to hunchbacked crones. The crones bathed fat infants in troughs; they slapped the glowing buttocks of their grandsons and wrapped them up in their worn skirts.

And thus did Baska from Tulchin behold the life of Moldavanka, our generous mother—a life chock-full of suckling infants, drying rags, and nuptial nights filled with suburban chic and soldierly tirelessness. A desire seized the girl for the same sort of life for herself, but soon she learned that the daughter of one-eyed Grach could not reckon on a decent match. Thereupon she ceased calling her father "papa dear."

"You redheaded thief!" she would yell at him of evenings. "Come eat your supper, you redheaded thief. . . ."

And this went on until Baska had finished sewing six nightgowns and six pairs of lace-trimmed panties for herself. Having finished sewing on the lace, she started crying in a high voice, not at all like her own, and said through her tears to the imperturbable Grach:

"Every girl," said she to him, "has her own interest in life, and I am the only one who lives like a night watchman looking after someone else's warehouse. Either you'll do something for me, papa dear, or I'll put an end to my life. . . ."

Grach heard his daughter out. The next day he put on his long sailcloth cloak and set out to call on Kaplun, the grocer, on Privoznaya Square.

Hanging over Kaplun's shop was a gold-lettered sign; it was the foremost shop on Privoznaya Square. Within was the smell of many seas and splendid lives we know nothing of. A boy was sprinkling the cool depths of the shop with a watering can as he sang, a song fit only for grownups to sing. Solomonchik, the proprietor's son, stood behind the counter; ranged upon the counter were olives that had come from Greece, olive oil from Marseille, raisins from Lisbon, coffee in the bean, Philippe & Canot sardines and Cayenne pepper. Kaplun was sunning himself on a glass-enclosed porch, as he put away a watermelon, a red watermelon with black seeds, almond-shaped like the eyes of sly Chinese women. Kaplun's belly was resting on a table in the sun—and the sun couldn't do a thing with it. But just then the grocer caught sight of Grach in his sailcloth cloak and he turned pale.

"Good day, Mosoo Grach," said he, and moved away from the table. "Golubchik warned me you were coming round, and I've got a pound of tea all ready for you, something special, I tell you. . . ."

And he began to talk about this new sort of tea, brought to Odessa on Dutch ships. Grach listened to him patiently, but after a while cut him short, inasmuch as he was only a simple man with no tricks about him.

"I am only a simple man with no tricks about me," said Froim. "I spend my time with my horses, and I stick to my business. I am giving new underwear along with Baska and a couple of old coppers, and I'm there for Baska to look to and if that's not enough for anybody, in a fire he should burn. . . ."

"Why burn?" Kaplun countered hurriedly, and stroked the teamster's hand. "There's no need for such words, Mosoo Grach, because we know you for a man who can help another man, and then too, you can hurt a man, and as for your not being no holy rabbi from Cracow, why, I didn't stand under the wedding canopy with no niece of Moses Montefiore neither, but . . . but we've got a Madam Kaplun on our hands, a very grand lady, and the Lord God Himself couldn't get to know what she wants. . . ."

"Well, I know," Grach, dreadfully calm, cut the grocer short. "I know that Solomonchik wants Baska, but that Madam Kaplun don't want me. . . ."

"Yes, I want you," Madam Kaplun, who had been eavesdropping at the door, shouted at this point, and she came into the sun parlor, all ablaze, with bosom heaving. "I want you, Grach, like a man wants death, I want you like a bride wants boils on her head. Don't you forget that our grandfather, *olav hasholom,* was by groceries, my papa dear, *olav hasholom,* was by groceries, and that we should stick to our line. . . ."

"So stick to your line," Grach answered the blazing Madam Kaplun and went on home.

There Baska was waiting for him, all dressed up in her orange dress, but the old man, without so much as a look at her, spread a sheepskin coat under a cart, lay down, and slept until such time as Baska's mighty arm thrust him out from under the cart.

"You redheaded thief," said the girl in a whisper that did

not sound at all like her usual whisper, "why do I have to stand for your trucker's manners, and why are you keeping as quiet as a tree stump, you redheaded thief?"

"Baska," Grach spoke with a dreadful calm, "Solomonchik wants you, but Madam Kaplun, she don't want me. What they're looking for there is a grocer."

And, straightening out the sheepskin coat, the old man crawled in under his cart again, while Baska vanished from the courtyard.

All this happened on a Sabbath, a day of rest. The sunset's purple eye, searching the earth, stumbled upon Grach that evening, snoring under his dray. The impetuous ray flamed reproach at the sleeper and led him out onto Dalnitzkaya Street, which sent forth dust and glitter like green rye in the wind. Tartars were walking up Dalnitzkaya Street—Tartars and Turks with their mullahs. They were returning from their pilgrimage to Mecca, returning home to their Orenburg steppes and to the Transcaucasia. A steamer had carried them to Odessa, and they were on their way from the port to the inn of Lyubka Schneeweiss, nicknamed Lyubka the Cossack. Striped, stiff robes rigidly encased the Tartars who flooded the pavement with the bronze sweat of the desert. White towels were wound about their fezzes, denoting men who had bowed before the dust of the Prophet. The pilgrims reached the corner; they turned toward Lyubka's yard, but could not pass through, because a crowd had collected at the gate. Lyubka Schneeweiss, a huge purse hanging at her side, was beating up a drunken peasant and shoving him toward the middle of the street. With one hand clenched into a fist she was pounding his face as if it were a tambourine, while with the other she held him up to keep him from slumping. Little streams of blood trickled from the peasant's mouth and ears. At first he was pensive and eyed Lyubka as if she were an utter stranger, then he fell on the cobbles and went to sleep, whereupon Lyubka gave him a shove with her foot and went back to her place. Yevzel, the veteran who worked for her as watchman, shut the gate behind her and waved his hand to Froim Grach, who was passing by.

"Greetings, Grach," said he. "If there's anything in the world you want to see, just drop in at our place—you'll find something to laugh at. . . ."

And the watchman led Grach toward the wall near which
the pilgrims who had arrived the evening before were sitting.
An old Turk in a green turban, an old Turk, green and light as
a leaf, was lying on the grass. He was beaded with pearls of
sweat, breathed with difficulty, and kept rolling his eyes.

"There," said Yevzel, and straightened the medal on his
threadbare jacket, "there is a drama from life for you—out of
the opera, *The Sick Turk*. He's about to kick the bucket, the
little old man, but you mustn't call a doctor for him, because he
who kicks the bucket on his way home from the god Moham-
med, is, they think, the luckiest and richest of men—Halvash,"
Yevzel shouted to the dying man, and went off into peals of
laughter, "here comes the doctor to treat you. . . ."

The Turk gave the watchman a look of childlike fear and
hatred and turned his head away. Thereupon Yevzel, satisfied
with himself, led Grach to the opposite side of the yard, to the
cellar where the winehop was. In the winehop lamps were already lit and music was playing. Old Jews with dirty beards were
playing Rumanian and Jewish airs. Mendel Krik was at a table,
drinking wine out of a green glass and telling how his own sons
had maimed him—Benya, the elder son, and Lyovka, the
younger. He was bawling out his story in a hoarse and frightful
voice, exposing his worn-down teeth and letting everybody feel
the wounds on his belly. Zaddiks from Volhynia with porcelain
faces were standing behind his chair and listening in a trance
to the unheard-of boasting of Mendel Krik. They were aston-
ished at everything they heard, and Grach despised them for it.

"The old windbag," he muttered his opinion of Mendel, and
ordered wine for himself.

Then Froim called out to the proprietress, Lyubka the Cossack, to come over to him. She was standing near the doorway
swearing foully and drinking vodka.

"Talk!" she yelled at Froim, and crossed her eyes in her
fury.

"Madam Lyubka," Froim said, and made her sit down beside him, "you are a smart woman, and I have come to you like
to my own mother. I am depending on you, Madam Lyubka—
first on God, then on you. . . ."

"Talk!" yelled Luybka and after making a dash across the

cellar, came back to her place.

And Grach said:

"The German colonists are having a bumper wheat crop, and in Constantinople groceries are going for a song. You pay three roubles a pood [1] for black olives but here they bring thirty kopecks a pound. . . . The grocers are having it good now, Madam Lyubka, the grocers are raking it in, and if a man was to handle them right, why, a man could strike it rich. But I've been left all alone in my work; the late Lyova Byk is dead now, I can't turn anywhere to find help, and so I'm all alone—as alone as God in heaven. . . ."

"Benya Krik," said Lyubka then. "Benya Krik . . . You tried him on Tartakovsky; what is wrong with Benya Krik?"

"Benya Krik?" Grach repeated, filled with amazement. "And he's single, no?"

"He's single," said Lyubka. "Get him and Baska hitched, give him money, make him a somebody."

"Benya Krik," the old man repeated like an echo, like a distant echo. "I never thought of him. . . ."

He stood up, muttering and stammering; Lyubka dashed ahead and Froim hobbled in her wake. They stepped out into the yard and went up to the second floor, to the quarters of the women whom Lyubka kept for her guests.

"Our bridegroom is with Katyusha," Lyubka told Grach. "Wait for me in the hall," and she made her way into the room at the other end, where Benya Krik was lying with a woman by the name of Katyusha.

"Enough slobbering," said the proprietress to the young man. "First you've got to get yourself fixed, Benchik, and after that you can go ahead and slobber. Froim Grach is looking for you. He's looking for a man to do a job and can't find anybody. . . ."

And she told him everything she knew about Baska and the affairs of the one-eyed Grach.

"I'll think it over," Benya answered her, covering Katyusha's bare legs with a sheet. "I'll think it over; tell the old man he should wait for me. . . ."

"Wait for him," Lyubka told Grach, who had remained in the hallway. "Wait for him; he'll think it over."

[1] One pood equals thirty-six pounds.

The proprietress moved up a chair for Froim, and he sank into an inordinate spell of waiting. He waited patiently, like a peasant cooling his heels in some government office. Behind the wall Katyusha was alternately groaning and going off into peals of laughter. The old man dozed for two hours near Katyusha's locked door, two hours and maybe even more. Evening had long since turned to night, the sky had gone black, and the Milky Way had known its measure of gold, glitter and coolness. Lyubka's wineshop was closed by now, the drunks were strewn over the yard like broken furniture, and the old mullah in the green turban had died toward midnight. Later music had come from the sea, trumpets and French horns from British ships; the music had come from the sea and had ceased, but Katyusha, the thoroughgoing Katyusha, was still stoking her gaudy, her ruddy Russian paradise for Benya Krik. She moaned on the other side of the wall and went off into peals of laughter; old Froim sat on at her door without stirring; he waited until one in the morning and then knocked.

"Man," said he, "are you making fun of me, maybe?"

Thereupon at long last, Benya, opened the door of Katyusha's room.

"Mosoo Grach," said he, abashed, and all aglow, covering his nakedness with a sheet, "when we're young we think that women are the goods; but after all they're no more than straw that is set on fire by nothing at all. . . ."

And, having dressed, he tidied Katyusha's bed, fluffed up her pillows, and went out into the street with the old man. Strolling along, they came to the Russian cemetery and there, beside the cemetery, Benya Krik and one-eyed Grach, the celebrated holdup man, came to an understanding. They agreed that Baska would bring her future husband three thousand roubles as dowry, two blooded horses, and a pearl necklace. They also agreed that Kaplun would have to pay two thousand roubles to Benya, Baska's groom. Kaplun was guilty of family pride . . . Kaplun from Privoznaya Square had got rich on Constantinople olives, he had shown no pity on Baska's first love, and therefore Benya Krik decided to take upon himself the matter of collecting two thousand roubles from Kaplun.

"I'll take that upon myself, papa dear," said he to his prospective father-in-law. "God will help us, and we'll square accounts with all grocers."

This was said at daybreak, when night had already passed . . . and it is at this point that a new story begins, the story of the fall of the house of Kaplun, the tale of its slow ruin, of incendiarism and gunfire in the night. And all this—the fate of the proud Kaplun and the fate of the girl Baska—was decided on the night when her father and her sudden bridegroom strolled past the Russian cemetery. The lads were dragging their girls behind the cemetery enclosures, and resounding kisses floated over the gravestones.

THE KING

When the wedding ceremony was over, the rabbi sank into an armchair; then, rising and going outside, he viewed the tables arrayed all down the courtyard. There were so many of them that those right at the end even poked out into Hospital Street. Velvet-spread, they wound their way down the yard like so many serpents with variegated patches on their bellies; and they sang full-throatedly, those patches of velvet, orange and red.

The living quarters had been turned into kitchens. A sultry flame beat through the soot-swathed doorways, a flame drunken and puffy-lipped. The faces of the old crones broiled in its smoky rays; old women's tremulous chins and beslobbered bosoms. Sweat with the pinkness of fresh blood, sweat as pink as the slaver of a mad dog, streamed this way and that over those mounds of exorbitant and sweetly pungent flesh. Not counting the washers-up, three cooks were preparing the wedding feast; and supreme over all the cooks and washers-up reigned the octogenarian Reisl, tiny and humpbacked, as patina'd with tradition as a scroll of the Torah.

Before the feast began, a young man unknown to the guests made his way into the yard. Wanted a word with Benya Krik. Led Benya Krik unobtrusively aside.

"Listen here, King," said the young man. "A word in your ear. I'm from Aunt Hannah in Kostetzkaya Street."

"Right," said Benya Krik, alias the King. "Out with it."

"Aunt Hannah told me to tell you that there's a new police

captain down at the station house."

"Knew that much day before yesterday," said Benya Krik. "Go on."

"The captain's gone and gathered the whole lot together and made a speech."

"New brooms," said Benya Krik. "He's planning a raid. Go on."

"Suppose you know, King, when the raid will be."

"It's scheduled for tomorrow."

"For today, King."

"Who said so, boy?"

"Aunt Hannah. You know Aunt Hannah?"

"I do. Go on."

"The captain, I say, assembled all his men and made a speech. We must settle Benya Krik's hash, he said, seeing that where there's an emperor there's no room for a king. Today, when Krik's sister's getting married and they'll all be together, is just the day. We can nab the lot."

"Go on."

"Well, the dicks began to get cold feet. If we raid 'em today, they said, on a day when Krik is celebrating, he'll see red, and then blood will flow. So the captain said, Duty before everything."

"Right. Off you go," said the King.

"What shall I tell Aunt Hannah?"

"Tell her: Benya knows all about the raid."

And so the young man departed. After him went three of Benya's pals. Said they'd be back in half an hour. And so they were. That's all.

Not according to their years did the wedding guests take their seats. Foolish old age is no less pitiable than timorous youth. Nor according to their wealth. Heavy purses are lined with tears.

In the place of honor sat the bride and groom. Today was their day. In the next place sat Sender Eichbaum, father-in-law of the King. Such was his right. One should know the story of Sender Eichbaum, for it is no ordinary story.

How had Benya Krik, gangster and king of gangsters, become Eichbaum's son-in-law? Become son-in-law of a man who owned sixty milch-kine, all save one? The answer lay in a holdup. About a year before, Benya had written Eichbaum a letter.

"Mosoo Eichbaum," he had written, "have the goodness to deposit, tomorrow morning, in the entrance to No. 17, Sofievskaya Street, the sum of twenty thousand roubles. If you fail to comply with this request, something unheard-of will happen to you, and you will be the talk of all Odessa. Yours respectfully, Benya the King."

Three letters, each one more to the point than that preceding, had remained unanswered. Then Benya took steps. They came in the night, nine of them, bearing long poles in their hands. The poles were wrapped about with pitch-dipped tow. Nine flaming stars flared in Eichbaum's cattle-yard. Benya beat the locks from the door of the cowshed and began to lead the cows out one by one. Each was received by a lad with a knife. He could overturn the cow with one blow of the fist and plunge his knife into the vaccine heart. On the blood-flooded ground the torches bloomed like roses of fire. Shots rang out. With these shots Benya scared away the dairymaids who had come hurrying to the cowshed. After him the other bandits began firing in the air. (If you don't fire in the air you may kill someone.) And now, when the sixth cow had fallen, mooing her death-moo, at the feet of the King, into the graveyard in his underclothes galloped Eichbaum, asking:

"What good will this do you, Benya?"

"If I don't have my money, Mosoo Eichbaum, you won't have your cows. It's as simple as that."

"Come indoors, Benya."

And indoors they came to terms. The slaughtered cows were divided fairly between them, and Eichbaum was guaranteed the integrity of his possessions, even receiving a written pledge with affixed seal. But the wonder came later.

During the raid, on that dreadful night when cows bellowed as they were slaughtered and calves slipped and slithered in the blood of their dams, when the torch-flames danced like black maidens and the milkmaids lunged back in horror from the muzzles of amiable Brownings—on that dread night there ran out into the yard, wearing nought save her low-cut shift, Tzilya, the daughter of old man Eichbaum. And the victory of the King was turned to defeat.

Two days later, without warning, Benya returned to Eichbaum all the money he had taken from him; and then one evening he paid the old man a social call. He wore an orange suit; beneath his cuff gleamed a bracelet set with diamonds; he walked into the room, bowed politely, and asked Eichbaum for his daughter's hand. The old man had a slight stroke, but recovered. He was good for another twenty years.

"Listen, Eichbaum," said the King. "When you die I will bury you in the First Jewish Cemetery, right by the entrance. I will raise you, Eichbaum, a monument of pink marble. I will make you an Elder of the Brody Synagogue. I will give up my own business and enter yours as a partner. Two hundred cows we will have, Eichbaum. I will kill all the other dairy farmers. No thief shall walk the street you live in. I will build you a villa where the tramline ends. Remember, Eichbaum, you were no rabbi in your young days. People have forged wills, but why talk about it? And the King shall be your son-in-law; no snotnose, but the King."

And Benya Krik had his way; for he was passionate, and passion rules the universe. The newlyweds spent three months on the fat lands of Bessarabia, three months flooded with grapes, rich food and the sweat of love's encounters. Then Benya returned to Odessa to marry off his sister Deborah, a virgin of forty summers who suffered from goiter. And now, having told the story of Sender Eichbaum, let us return to the marriage of Deborah Krik, sister of the King.

At the wedding feast they served up turkey, roast chicken, goose, stuffed-fish, fish-soup in which lakes of lemon gleamed nacrously. Over the heads of defunct geese, flowers swayed like luxuriant plumages. But does the foamy surge of the Odessa sea cast roast chicken on the shore?

All that is noblest in our smuggled goods, everything for which the land is famed from end to end, did, on that starry, that deep-blue night, its entrancing and disruptive work. Wines not from these parts warmed stomachs, made legs ache sweetly, bemused brains, evoked belches that rang out sonorous as trumpets summoning to battle. The negro cook from the "Plutarch," that had put in three days before from Port Said, bore unseen through the customs barrier fat-bellied jars of Jamaica rum, oily Madeira, cigars from the plantations of Pierpont Morgan and oranges from the environs of Jerusalem. This is what the foaming surge of the Odessa sea bears to the shore; this is what sometimes comes the way of Odessa beggars at Jewish weddings. Jamaica rum came their way at the wedding of Deborah Krik; and so, having gulped their fill like infidel swine, the Jewish beggars began to beat the ground deafeningly with their crutches. Eichbaum, his waistcoat unbuttoned, scanned with puckered eyes the tumultuous gathering, hiccoughing lovingly the while. The orchestra played a fanfare. It was just like a divisional parade: a fanfare—nothing but. The gangsters, sitting in compact rows, were at first excessively embarrassed by the presence of outsiders; later they loosened up. Lyova Katzap cracked a bottle of vodka on the head of his beloved; Monya the Gunner fired a shot in the air. The rejoicings reached their pitch when, in accordance with the custom of older times the guests began bestowing their wedding presents. *Shammesim* leaped on a table and there, to the stormy wailing of the fanfare, sang out how many roubles had been presented, how many silver spoons. And now the friends of the King showed what blue blood meant, and the chivalry, not yet extinct, of the Moldavanka district. On the silver trays, with ineffably nonchalant movements of the hand, they cast gold coins, rings and threaded coral.

Aristocrats of the Moldavanka, they were tightly encased in raspberry waistcoats; russet jackets clasped their shoulders, and on their fleshy feet the azure leather cracked. Rising to their full height and thrusting out their bellies, the bandits clapped in time with the music; with the traditional cry of "Bitter, bitter!" called on the married couple to kiss, and showered the bride with blossoms; and she, Deborah of forty summers, sister of Benya Krik, disfigured by her illness, with her swollen crop and her eyes bulging from their orbits, sat on a pile of cushions side by side with the feeble youth, now mute with misery, whom Eichbaum's money had purchased.

The bestowal of gifts was drawing to a close, the *shammesim* were growing hoarse and croaky, and the double bass was at cross purposes with the fiddle. Over the courtyard there suddenly spread a faint smell of burning.

"Benya," said Papa Krik, famed among his fellow truck drivers as a bully, "Benya, d'you know what I think? I think our chimbley's on fire."

"Papa," said Benya to his inebriated parent, "eat and drink, and don't let such trifles bother you."

And Papa Krik followed the filial advice. Drink and eat he did. But the smoke-cloud grew more and more pungent. Here and there the edges of the sky were turning pink, and now there shot up, narrow as a swordblade, a tongue of flame. The guests, half rising from their seats, began to sniff the air, and the womenfolk gave little squeaks of fear. The gangsters eyed one another. And only Benya Krik, aware of nothing, was disconsolate.

"The celebration's going all to pieces," he cried, filled with despair. "Good friends, I beg you, eat and drink!"

But now there appeared in the courtyard the same young man as had come earlier in the evening.

"King," he said, "I'd like a word in your ear."

"Out with it, then," said the King. "I've always a spare ear for a spare word."

"King," said the unknown young man, and giggled. "It's really comical: the police station's burning like a candle!"

The shopkeepers were silent. The gangsters grinned. The sexagenarian Manka, ancestress of the suburban bandits, placed two fingers in her mouth and whistled so piercingly that her neighbors jerked away in fright.

"You're not on the job, Manka," observed Benya. "More sang-frwa!"

The young man who had brought these astounding tidings was still doubled up with laughter. He was giggling like a schoolgirl.

"They came out of the station, forty of them," he related, vigorously moving his jaws, "all set for the raid; and they hadn't gone fifty yards when the whole place was on fire. Why don't you folks drop round and watch it burn?"

But Benya forbade his guests to go and view the conflagration. He set out himself with two comrades. The station was in a proper blaze. Policemen, their buttocks waggling, were rushing up smoky staircases and hurling boxes out of windows. The prisoners, unguarded, were running off. The firemen were filled with zeal, but no water flowed when the nearest tap was turned. The police captain—the broom that was to have swept clean—was standing on the opposite pavement; the ends of his moustache curled into his mouth, and he was biting them. Motionless the new broom stood there.

As he passed the captain, Benya gave him a military salute. "Good health, Your Excellency," he said, deeply sympathetic. "What do you say to this stroke of bad luck? A regular act of God!"

He stared hard at the burning edifice and slowly shook his head.

"Ai-ai-ai!" he went.

When Benya got back home the little lamps in the courtyard were flickering out and dawn was beginning to touch the sky. The guests had departed and the musicians were dozing, leaning their heads on their double basses. Deborah alone was not thinking of sleep. With both hands she was urging her fainthearted husband towards the door of their nuptial chamber, glaring at him carnivorously, like a cat that, holding a mouse in her jaws, tests it lightly with her teeth.

(TRANSLATED BY AVRAHM YARMOLINSKY)

The Eye

J. F. POWERS

Born in 1917 in Jacksonville, Illinois, J. F. Powers was educated at Quincy College Academy (now called Notre Dame of Quincy) in Illinois. He attended Northwestern University but has no degree. In 1948 he received a Guggenheim Fellowship in Creative Writing, and a grant from the National Institute of Arts and Letters. Mr. Powers' short stories have appeared in many magazines and he has had one book published, Prince of Darkness and Other Stories *(1947). He gave writing courses at Marquette University in Milwaukee for two years, but he is now devoting all his time to writing. He was married in 1946 and he has two young daughters.*

ALL THEM THAT dropped in at Bullen's last night was talking about the terrible accident that almost happened to Clara Beck —that's Clyde Bullen's best girl. I am in complete charge of the pool tables and cigar counter, including the punchboards, but I am not at my regular spot in front, on account of Clyde has got a hot game of rotation going at the new table, and I am the only one he will leave chalk his cue. While I chalk it and collect for games and rack the balls I am hearing from everybody how Clara got pulled out of the river by Sleep Bailey.

He is not one of the boys, Sleep, but just a nigger that's deef and lives over in jigtown and plays the piano for dances at the Louisiana Social Parlor. They say he can't hear nothing but music. Spends the day loafing and fishing. He's fishing—is the story—when he seed Clara in the river below the Ludlow road bridge, and he swum out and saved her. Had to knock her out to do it, she put up such a fight. Anyways he saved her from drownding. That was the story everybody was telling.

Clyde has got the idee of taking up a collection for Sleep, as it was a brave deed he done and he don't have nothing to his name but a tub of fishing worms. On the other hand, he don't need nothing, being a nigger, not needing nothing. But Clara is Clyde's girl and it is Clyde's idee and so it is going over pretty big as most of the boys is trying to stay in with Clyde and the rest is owing him money and can't help themselves. I chipped in two bits myself.

Clyde is just fixing to shoot when Skeeter Bird comes in and says, "Little cold for swimming, ain't it, Clyde?"

It upsets Clyde and he has to line up the thirteen ball again. I remember it is the thirteen 'cause they ain't nobody round here that's got the eye Clyde has got for them big balls and that thirteen is his special favor-ite, says it's lucky—it and the nine. I tell you this on account of Clyde misses his shot. Looked to me and anybody else that knowed Clyde's game that what Skeeter said upset his aim.

"What's eating you?" Clyde says to Skeeter, plenty riled. I can see he don't feel so bad about the thirteen getting away as he might of, as he has left it sewed up for Ace Haskins, that claims he once took a game from the great Ralph Greenleaf. "You got something to say?" Clyde says.

"No," Skeeter says, "only—"

"Only what?" Clyde wants to know.

"Only that Bailey nigger got hisself scratched up nice, Clyde."

"So I am taking up a little collection for him," Clyde says. "Pass the plate to Brother Bird, boys."

But Skeeter, he don't move a finger, just says, "Clara got banged up some, too, Clyde. Nigger must of socked her good."

None of us knowed what Skeeter was getting at, except maybe Clyde, that once took a course in mind reading, but we don't like it. And Clyde, I can tell, don't like it. The cue stick is shaking a little in his hand like he wants to use it on Skeeter and he don't shoot right away. He straightens up and says, "Well, he hadda keep her from strangling him while he was rescuing her, didn't he? It was for her own good."

"Yeah, guess so," Skeeter says. "But they both looked like they been in a mean scrap."

"That so?" Clyde says. "Was you there?"

"No, but I heard," Skeeter says.

"You heard," Clyde says. He gets ready to drop the fifteen.

"Yeah," Skeeter says. "You know, Clyde, that Bailey nigger is a funny nigger."

"How's that?" Clyde says, watching Skeeter close. "What's wrong with him?" Clyde holds up his shot and looks right at Skeeter. "Come on, out with it."

"Oh, I don't know as they's a lot wrong with him," Skeeter says. "I guess he's all right. Lazy damn nigger is all. Won't keep a job—just wants to play on the piano and fish."

"Never would of rescued Clara if he didn't," Clyde says. "And besides what kind of job you holding down?"

Now that gets Skeeter where it hurts on account of he don't work hisself, unless you call selling rubbers work or peddling art studies work. Yeah, that's what he calls them. Art studies. Shows a girl that ain't got no clothes on, except maybe her garters, and down below it says "Pensive" or "Evening in Paris." Skeeter sells them to artists, he says—he'll tell you that to your face—but he's always got a few left over for the boys at Bullen's.

Well, Skeeter goes on up front and starts in to study the slot machines. He don't never play them, just studies them. Somebody said he's writing a book about how to beat them, but I don't think he's got the mind for it, is my opinion.

Clyde is halfway into the next game when Skeeter comes back again. He has some of the boys with him now.

"All right, all right," Clyde says, stopping his game.

"You tell him, Skeeter," the boys says.

"Yeah, Skeeter, you tell me," Clyde says.

"Oh," Skeeter says, "it's just something some of them is saying, Clyde, is all."

"Who's saying?" Clyde says. "Who's saying what?"

"Some of them," Skeeter says, "over at the Arcade."

The Arcade, in case you don't know, is the other poolhall in town. Bullen's and the Arcade don't mix, and I guess Skeeter is about the only one that shows up regular in both places, on account of he's got customers in both places. I'd personally like to keep Skeeter out of Bullen's, but Clyde buys a lot of art studies off him and I can't say nothing.

After a spell of thinking Clyde says to Skeeter, "Spill it."

"May not be a word of truth to it, Clyde," Skeeter says. "You know how folks talk. And all I know is what I hear. Course I knowed a long time that Bailey nigger is a damn funny nigger. Nobody never did find out where he come from—St. Louis, Chicago, New York, for all anybody knowed. And if he's stone deef how can he hear to play the piano?"

"Damn the nigger," Clyde says. "What is they saying, them Arcade bastards!"

"Oh, not all of them is saying it, Clyde. Just some of them is saying it. Red Hynes, that tends bar at the El Paso, and them. Saying maybe the nigger didn't get them scratches on his face for nothing. Saying maybe he was trying something funny. That's a damn funny nigger, Clyde, I don't care what you say. And when you get right down to it, Clyde, kind of stuck up like. Anyways some of them at the Arcade is saying maybe the nigger throwed Clara in the river and then fished her out just to cover up. Niggers is awful good at covering up, Clyde."

Clyde don't say nothing to this, but I can tell he is thinking plenty and getting mad at what he's thinking—plenty. It's real quiet at Bullen's now.

"Maybe," Clyde says, "maybe they is saying what he was covering up from?"

"Yeah, Clyde," Skeeter says. "Matter of fact, they is. Yeah, some of them is saying maybe the nigger *raped* her!"

Bang! Clyde cracks the table with his cue stick. It takes a piece of pearl inlay right out of the apron board of the good, new table. Nobody says nothing. Clyde just stares at all the chalk dust he raised.

Then Skeeter says, "Raped her first, rescued her later, is what they is saying."

"What you going to do, Clyde?" Banjo Wheeler says.

"Clyde is thinking!" I say. "Leave him think!" But personally I never seed Clyde take that long just to think.

"Move," Clyde says.

The boys give Clyde plenty of room. He goes over to the rack and tips a little talcum in his hands. The boys is all watching him good. Then Clyde spits. I am right by the cuspidor and can see Clyde's spit floating on the water inside. Nobody says nothing. Clyde's spit is going around in the water and I am listening to hear what he is going to do. He takes the chalk out of my hand. He still don't say nothing. It is the first time he ever chalks his cue with me around to do it.

Then he says, "What kind of nigger is this Bailey nigger, Roy?"

Roy—that's me.

"Oh, just a no-good nigger, Clyde," I said. "Plays the piano at the Louisiana Social Parlor—*some* social parlor, Clyde—is about all I know, or anybody. Fishes quite a bit—just a lazy, funny, no-good nigger . . ."

"But he ain't no *bad* nigger, Roy?"

"Naw, he ain't *that*, Clyde," I say. "We ain't got none of them kind left in town."

"Well," Clyde says, "just so's he ain't no *bad* nigger."

Then, not saying no more, Clyde shoots and makes the ten ball in the side pocket. I don't have to tell you the boys is all pretty disappointed in Clyde. I have to admit I never knowed no other white man but Clyde to act like that. But maybe Clyde has his reasons, I say to myself, and wait.

Well, sir, that was right before the news come from the hospital. Ace is friendly with a nurse there is how we come to get it. He calls her on the phone to find out how Clara is. She is unconscious and ain't able to talk yet, but that ain't what makes all hell break loose at Bullen's. It's—un-mis-tak-able ev-i-dence of preg-nan-cy!

Get it? Means she was knocked up. Whoa! I don't have to tell you how that hits the boys at Bullen's. Some said they admired Clyde for not flying off the handle in the first place and some said they didn't, but all of them said they had let their good natures run away with their better judgments. They was right.

I goes to Ace, that's holding the kitty we took up for the nigger, and gets my quarter back. I have a little trouble at first as some of the boys has got there in front of me and collected more than they put in—or else Ace is holding out.

All this time Clyde is in the washroom. I try to hurry him up, but he don't hurry none. Soon as he unlocks the door and comes out we all give him the news.

I got to say this is the first time I ever seed Clyde act the way he do now. I hate to say it, but—I will. Clyde, he don't act much like a man. No, he don't, not a bit. He just reaches his cue down and hands it to me.

"Chalk it," he says. "Chalk it," is all he says. Damn if I don't almost hand it back to him.

I chalk his cue. But the boys, they can't stand no more.

Ace says he is going to call the hospital again.

"Damn it, Clyde," Banjo says. "We got to do something. Else they ain't going to be no white woman safe in the streets. What they going to think of you at the Arcade? I can hear Red Hynes and them laughing."

That is the way the boys is all feeling at Bullen's, and they say so. I am waiting with the rest for Clyde to hurry up and do something, or else explain hisself. But he just goes on, like nothing is the matter, and starts up a new game. It's awful quiet. Clyde gets the nine ball on the break. It hung on the lip of the pocket like it didn't want to, but it did.

"You sure like that old nine ball, Clyde," I say, trying to make Clyde feel easy and maybe come to his senses. I rack the nine for him. My hand is wet and hot and the yellow nine feels like butter to me.

"Must be the color of the nine is what he like," Banjo says.

Whew! I thought that would be all for Banjo, but no sir, Clyde goes right on with the game, like it's a compliment.

A couple of guys is whistling soft at what Banjo got away with. Me, I guess Clyde feels sorry for Banjo, on account of they is both fighters. Clyde was a contender for the state heavy title three years back, fighting under the name of Big Boy Bullen, weighing in at two thirty-three. Poor old Banjo is a broken-down carnival bum, and when he's drinking too heavy, like last night and every night, he forgets how old and beat up he is and don't know no better than to run against Clyde, that's a former contender and was rated in *Collyer's Eye*. Banjo never was no better than a welter when he was fighting and don't tip more than a hundred fifty-five right now. What with the drink and quail he don't amount to much no more.

And then Ace comes back from calling up the hospital and says, "No change; Clara's still unconscious."

"Combination," Clyde says. "Twelve ball in the corner pocket."

That's all Clyde has got to say. We all want to do something, but Banjo wants to do it the worst and he says, "No change, still unconscious. Knocked out and knocked up—by a nigger! Combination—twelve ball in the corner pocket!"

"Dummy up!" Clyde says. He slugs the table again and ruins a cube of chalk. He don't even look at Banjo or none of us. I take the whisk broom and brush the chalk away the best I could, without asking Clyde to move.

"Thanks," Clyde says, still not seeing nobody.

I feel kind of funny on account of Clyde never says thanks for nothing before. I wonder is it the old Clyde or is he feeling sick. Then, so help me, Clyde runs the table, thirteen balls. Ace don't even get a shot that game.

But, like you guessed, the boys won't hold still for it no more and is all waiting for Clyde to do something. And Clyde don't have to be no mind reader to know it. He gets a peculiar look in his eye that I seed once or twice before and goes over to Banjo—to—guess what?—to shake his hand. Yes sir, Clyde has got his hand out and is smiling—smiling at Banjo that said what he said.

Banjo just stands there with a dumb look on his face, not knowing what Clyde is all about, and they shake.

"So I'm yella, huh, Banjo?" That's what Clyde says to Banjo.

I don't know if Banjo means to do it, or can't help it, but he burps right in Clyde's face.

Boom! Clyde hits Banjo twice in the chin and mouth quick

and drops him like a handkerchief. Banjo is all over the floor and his mouth is hanging open like a spring is busted and blood is leaking out the one side and he has got some bridgework loose.

"Hand me the nine, Roy," Clyde says to me. I get the nine ball and give it to Clyde. He shoves it way into Banjo's mouth that is hanging open and bleeding good.

Then Clyde lets him have one more across the jaw and you can hear the nine ball rattle inside Banjo's mouth.

Clyde says, "Now some of you boys been itching for action all night. Well, I'm here to tell you I'm just the boy to hand it out. Tonight I just feel like stringing me up a black nigger by the light of the silvery moon! Let's get gaiting!"

Now that was the old Clyde for you. A couple of guys reaches fast for cue sticks, but I am in charge of them and the tables, and I say, "Lay off them cue sticks! Get some two by fours outside!"

So we leaves old Banjo sucking on the nine ball and piles into all the cars we can get and heads down for the Louisiana Social Parlor. I am sitting next to Clyde in his car.

On the way Ace tells us when he called the hospital the second time he got connected with some doctor fella. Ace said this doctor was sore on account of Ace's girl, that's the nurse, give out information about Clara that she wasn't supposed to. But the doctor said as long as we all knowed so much about the case already he thought we ought to know it was of some month's standing, Clara's condition. Ace said he could tell from the way the doctor was saying it over and over that he was worried about what we was planning to do to the coon. Ace's girl must of copped out to him. But Ace said he thanked the doc kindly for his trouble and hung up and wouldn't give his right name when the doc wanted to know. We all knowed about the doctor all right—only one of them young intern fellas from Memphis or some place—and as for the some months' standing part we all knowed in our own minds what nigger bucks is like and him maybe burning with strong drink on top of it. Ace said he hoped the nurse wouldn't go and lose her job on account of the favor she done for us.

The only thing we seed when we gets to the Louisiana is one old coon by the name of Old Ivy. He is locking up. We asks him about Sleep Bailey, but Old Ivy is playing dumb and all he says is, "Suh? Suh?" like he don't know what we mean.

"Turn on them there lights," we says, "so's we can see."

Old Ivy turns them on.

"Where's the crowd," we says, "that's always around?"

"Done went," Old Ivy says.

"So they's done went," Skeeter says. "Well, if they's trying to steal that piano-playing nigger away they won't get very far."

"No, they won't get very far with that," Clyde says. "Hey, just seeing all them bottles is got me feeling kind of dry-like."

So we gets Old Ivy to put all the liquor on the bar and us boys refreshes ourselfs. Skeeter tells Old Ivy to put some beer out for chasers.

Old Ivy says they is fresh out of cold beer.

"It don't have to be cold," Skeeter says. "We ain't proud."

Old Ivy drags all the bottled beer out on the bar with the other. Then he goes back into the kitchen behind the bar and we don't see him no more for a little.

"Hey, old nigger," Skeeter says. "Don't try and sneak out the back way."

"No, suh," Old Ivy says.

"Hey, Old Ivy," Clyde says. "You got something to eat back there?"

"Suh?" He just gives us that old *suh*. "Suh?"

"You heard him," Skeeter says.

"No, suh," Old Ivy says, and we seed him in the service window.

"Guess maybe he's deef," Skeeter says. "You old coon, I hope you ain't blind!" And Skeeter grabs a bottle of beer and lams it at Old Ivy's head. Old Ivy ducks and the big end of the bottle sticks in the wall and don't break. It is just beaverboard, the wall.

All us boys gets the same idee and we starts heaving the beer bottles through the window where Old Ivy was standing, but ain't no more.

"Hit the nigger baby!"

"Nigger in the fence!"

We keeps this up until we done run out of bottles, all except Skeeter that's been saving one. "Hey, wait," he says. "It's all right now, Grampaw. Come on, old boy, you can come out now."

But Old Ivy don't show hisself. I am wondering if he got hit on a rebound.

"Damn it, boy," Skeeter says. "Bring us some food. Or you want us to come back in there?"

"Suh?" It's that old *suh* again. "Yes, suh," Old Ivy says in the kitchen, but we don't see him.

Then we do. And Skeeter, he lets go the last bottle with all he's got. It hits Old Ivy right in the head. That was a mean thing Skeeter done, I think, but then I see it's only the cook's hat Old Ivy's got in his hand that got hit. He was holding it up like his head is inside, but it ain't.

The boys all laughs when they seed what Old Ivy done to fool Skeeter.

"Like in war when you fool the enemy," Clyde says.

"That's a smart nigger," I say.

"So that's a smart nigger, huh?" Skeeter says. "I'll take and show you what I do to smart niggers that gets smart with me!"

"Cut it out," Clyde says. "Leave him alone. He ain't hurting nothing. You just leave that old coon be." That is Clyde for you, always sticking up for somebody, even a nigger.

Clyde and me goes into the next room looking for a place to heave, as Clyde has got to. It is awful dark, but pretty soon our eyes gets used to it, and we can see some tables and chairs and a juke box and some beer signs on the walls. It must be where they do their dancing. I am just standing there ready to hold Clyde's head, as he is easing hisself, when I begins to hear a piano like a radio is on low. I can just barely pick it out, a couple a notes at a time, sad music, blues music, nigger music.

It ain't no radio. It is a piano on the other side of the room. I am ready to go and look into it when Clyde says, "It ain't nothing." Ain't nothing! Sometimes I can't understand Clyde for the life of me. But I already got my own idee about the piano.

About then Skeeter and Ace comes in the room yelling for Clyde in the dark, saying the boys out front is moving on to the next place. We hear a hell of a racket out by the bar, like they broke the mirror, and then it's pretty still and we know they is almost all left.

Skeeter gives us one more yell and Ace says, "Hey, Clyde, you fall in?" They is about to leave when Skeeter, I guess it is, hears the piano just like we been hearing it. All this time Clyde has got his hand over my mouth like he don't want me to say we is there.

Skeeter calls Old Ivy and says he should turn on the lights, and when Old Ivy starts that *suh* business again Skeeter lays one on him that I can hear in the dark.

So Old Ivy turns on the lights, a lot of creepy greens, reds, and blues. Then Clyde and me both seed what I already guessed —it's the Bailey nigger playing the piano—and Skeeter and Ace seed it is him and we all seed each other.

And right then, damn if the nigger don't start in to sing a song. Like he didn't know what was what! Like he didn't know what we come for! That's what I call a foxy nigger.

Skeeter yells at him to stop singing and to come away from the piano. He stops singing, but he don't move. So we all goes over to the piano.

"What's your name, nigger?" Skeeter says.

"Bailey," Sleep says, reading Skeeter's lips.

Old Ivy comes over and he is saying a lot of stuff like, "That boy's just a borned fool. Just seem like he got to put his foot in it some kind of way."

Sleep hits a couple a notes light on the piano that sounds nice and pretty.

"You know what we come for?" Skeeter says.

Sleep hits them same two notes again, nice and pretty, and shakes his head.

"Sure you don't know, boy?" Clyde says.

Sleep is just about to play them notes again when Skeeter hits him across the paws with a fungo bat. Then Sleep says, "I spect you after on account of that Miss Beck I fish out of the river."

"That's right," Skeeter says. "You spect right."

"You know what they is saying uptown, Sleep?" I say.

"I heard," Sleep says.

"They is saying," I say, "you raped Clara and throwed her in the river to cover up."

"That's just a lie," Sleep says.

"Who says it's a lie?" Clyde says.

"That's just a white-folks lie," Sleep says. "It's God's truth."

"How you going to prove it?" Clyde says.

"Yeah," I say. "How you going to prove it?"

"How you going to prove it to them, son?" Old Ivy says.

"Here, ain't I?" Sleep says.

"Yeah, you's here all right, nigger," Skeeter says, "but don't you wish you wasn't!"

"If I'm here I guess I got no call to be scared," Sleep says. "Don't it prove nothing if I'm here, if I didn't run away? Don't that prove nothing?"

"Naw," Skeeter says. "It don't prove nothing. It's just a smart nigger trick."

"Wait till Miss Beck come to and talk," Sleep says. "I ain't scared."

"No," Old Ivy says, "you ain't scared. He sure ain't scared a bit, is he, Mr. Bullen? That's a good sign he ain't done nothing bad, ain't it, Mr. Bullen?"

"Well," Clyde says. "I don't know about that. . . ."

Skeeter says, "You sure you feel all right, Clyde?"

"What you mean you don't know, Clyde?" Ace says. "Clara is knocked up and this is the bastard done it!"

"Who the hell else, Clyde?" I say. I wonder is Clyde dreaming or what.

"He ain't a bad boy like that, Mr. Bullen," Old Ivy says, working on Clyde.

"I tell you what," Clyde says.

"Aw, stop it, Clyde," Skeeter and Ace both says. "We got enough!"

"Shut up!" Clyde says and he says it like he mean it.

"Listen to what Mr. Bullen got to say," Old Ivy says.

"This is the way I seed it," Clyde says. "This ain't no open-and-shut case of rape—leastways not yet it ain't. Now the law—"

Skeeter cuts in and says, "Well, Clyde, I'll see you the first of the week." He acts like he is going to leave.

"Come back here," Clyde says. "You ain't going to tell no mob nothing till I got this Bailey boy locked up safe in the county jail waiting judgment."

"O.K., Clyde," Skeeter says. "That's different. I thought you was going to let him get away."

"Hell, no!" Clyde says. "We got to see justice did, ain't we?"

"Sure do, Clyde," Skeeter says.

Ace says, "He'll be nice and safe in jail in case we got to take up anything with him."

I knowed what they mean and so do Old Ivy. He says, "Better let him go right now, Mr. Bullen. Let him run for it. This other way they just going to bust in the jailhouse and take him out and hang him to a tree."

"The way I seed it," Clyde says, "this case has got to be handled according to the law. I don't want this boy's blood on my hands. If he ain't to blame, I mean."

"That's just what he ain't, Mr. Bullen," Old Ivy says. "But it ain't going to do no good to put him in that old jailhouse."

"We'll see about that," Clyde says.

"Oh, sure. Hell, yes!" Skeeter says. "We don't want to take the law in our own hands. That ain't our way, huh, Ace?"

"Cut it out," Clyde says.

"Maybe Miss Beck feel all right in the morning, son, and it going to be all right for you," Old Ivy says to Sleep. The old coon is crying.

So we takes Sleep in Clyde's car to the county jail. We makes him get down on the floor so's we can put our feet on him and guard him better. He starts to act up once on the way, but Skeeter persuades him with the fungo bat in the right place, *conk,* and he is pretty quiet then.

Right after we get him behind bars it happens.

Like I say, Clyde is acting mighty peculiar all night, but now he blows his top for real. That's what he does all right—plumb blows it. It is all over in a second. He swings three times— one, two, three—and Skeeter and Ace is out cold as Christmas, and I am holding this fat eye. Beats me! And I don't mind telling you I laid down quick with Skeeter and Ace, like I was out, till Clyde went away. Now you figure it out.

But I ain't preferring no charges on Clyde. Not me, that's his best friend, even if he did give me this eye, and Skeeter ain't, that needs Bullen's for his business, or Ace.

What happens to who? To the jig that said he pulled Clara out of the river?

You know that big old slippery elm by the Crossing? That's the one. But that ain't how I got the eye.

The Morning Watch

JAMES AGEE

James Agee wrote the scenarios of The African Queen *(with John Huston); Stephen Crane's* The Bride Comes To Yellow Sky; *and the widely-acclaimed documentary film,* The Quiet One. *Mr. Agee was born in Knoxville, Tennessee in 1909. After his graduation from Harvard College, where he edited the* Harvard Advocate, *he joined* Fortune Magazine. *While on an assignment for* Fortune, *he collected material for his long, lyrical work of prose,* Let Us Now Praise Famous Men, *published in 1941. The book—text by Agee, photographs by Walker Evans—is a study of conditions under which Alabama tenant farmers manage to exist. Mr. Agee has also written verse; his collection,* Permit Me Voyage, *was published by Yale University Press as part of its "Younger Poets" series. In 1939 he joined* Time Magazine *and five years later he became the movie reviewer for* The Nation. *He left both magazines in 1948 to devote his time to prose and film writing. He died in 1955 of a heart attack.*

I

> *My soul fleeth unto the Lord*
> *before the morning watch: I say,*
> *before the morning watch.*
> > —PSALM CXXX

IN HIDDEN VAINGLORY he had vowed that he would stay awake straight through the night, for he had wondered, and not without scorn, how they, grown men, could give way to sleep in this night of all the nights in their life, leaving Him without one friend in His worst hour; but some while before midnight, still unaware that he was so much as drowsy, he had fallen asleep;

and now this listening sleep was broken and instantly Richard lay sharp awake, aware of his failure and of the night.

Too late: already it was time: now it was the deepest hour of the deepest night. Already while he slept, with wrathful torches and with swords and staves they had broken among the branches of the Garden; Judas, gliding, had stretched against that clear Face his serpent's smile; Peter in loyal rage had struck off the dazed servant's ear and He in quiet had healed him: and without struggle had yielded Himself into their hands. Could ye not watch with me one hour? No Lord, his humbled soul replied: not even one: and three times, silently, gazing straight upward into the darkness, he struck his breast while tears of contrition, of humility and of a hunger to be worthy, solaced his eyes, and awakened his heart. O yes it was an hour more deep by far than the Agony and Bloody Sweat: no longer alone, unsure; resolved, and taken. That was already fully begun which could come only to one ending. By now He stood peaceful before Pilate, the one calm and silence amid all that tumult of malice and scorn and guile and hatred and beating of unhabitual light through all the sleepless night of spring; while in the dark porchway, even at this moment, the servant girl persistently enquired of Peter and he in fury and in terror denied his Lord: now the bitter terrible weeping and now, saluting this mortal morning, the cock's triumphal and reproaching cry. A deep, deep hour. Soon now the sentence and the torment, the scourging, the mocking robe, the wreathed, wretched Crown: King of the Jews.

O God, he silently prayed, in solemn and festal exaltation: make me to know Thy suffering this day. O make me to know Thy dear Son's suffering this day.

Within Thy Wounds hide me.

Suffer me not to be separated from Thee.

From the Malicious Enemy defend me.

By a habit of their own, meanwhile, his hands searched and tested along the undersheet, and now they told him that this time he had wet the bed so little that by morning nobody would know. He let out a long thankful breath and looked down along his bed.

All he could see at first throughout the long room was a kind of gelatin glimmer at the alcoved windows, and the aisled ends

of the iron cots at right angles to his own: but when the foot
which had awakened him lifted from the yielding board and it
creaked again he saw in his mind's eye, large and close, the
coarse-ribbed shambling stocking, flecked with lint, and knew
that Father Whitman must be very tired; for to judge by the
hissing sound, his feet scarcely left the floor. He wondered
whether Father Whitman was sleeping at all, tonight.

Father Whitman touched a foot and whispered: "Quarter of
four."

"Okay Fathuh," Hobe Gillum said in his clear hard voice.

"Quiet," Father Whitman said sharply.

"Okay Fathuh," Hobe whispered.

Now that the priest came nearer as silently as he could between the ends of the cots, Richard could see the tall ghostly
moving of his white habit.

Father Whitman stopped at Jimmy Toole's cot, touched his
foot, and whispered: "Quarter of four." Jimmy mumbled
something in a light sad rapid voice and stuck his head under
his pillow.

Father Whitman stepped between the cots and touched his
shoulder. "Quarter of four," he whispered more loudly.

"Cut it out," Jimmy whined in his sleep.

Richard heard Hobe's knees hit the floor.

Father Whitman shook Jimmy's shoulder. "Quarter of——"

"*Quit* it you *God damn*—" Jimmy snarled, wrenching aside
the pillow; then, with servile Irish charm: "Aw sure Father, I
din know it was *you* Father."

At the far end of the dormitory there was a wild stifled
snicker.

"Time to get up," Father Whitman whispered.

The snickering became happier and happier. Father Whitman spoke more loudly into the darkness: "Now cut that out
fast or you'll be sorry you ever started it."

The snickering persisted as if uncontrollably, but now it was
blunted in a pillow. Father Whitman ignored it. "Better get
straight out of bed," he told Jimmy. "You'll go back to sleep."

Hobe was buttoning his shirt.

Without a word Jimmy rolled out of bed onto his knees and
buried his head in his arms.

Now that Father Whitman came toward him, Richard shut

his eyes. When he knew he was about to be touched he opened his eyes and whispered, "All right Father." He saw the stopped hand and, much nearer and larger than he had expected, the beaten, enduring horse face; he became aware of his deceitfulness and was ashamed of it.

"All right," Father Whitman said. Bet he says quarter of four, Richard thought. "Quarter of four," Father Whitman said.

"Yes Father."

"Put your shoes on down stairs," he whispered, and turned away. "Put your shoes on downstairs," he told Hobe, "and don't let Jimmy go to sleep again."

"Okay Fathuh," Hobe said, gallusing himself into his overalls.

"And don't you dawdle when you're done," Father Whitman told him. "You kids see to it you come right back here to bed."

"Yes suh Fathuh."

"Don't think I won't be watching for you."

"No suh Fathuh."

Richard knelt by his cot and sank his face in his hands. O God, he prayed, I thank Thee that I did not wet the bed this night—enough to get caught, he added carefully, remembering Thou God seest me; for Jesus' sake Amen.

He said swiftly to himself the prayer Father Weiler had taught them as enough when, for any good reason, you did not have time enough for more: I praise my God this day I give myself to God this day I ask God to help me this day Amen.

Gripping his hair and pressing the heels of his hands tightly against his closed eyes he tried as hard as he could to realize what was happening as he had in the moment of waking. But now he could realize only what a special night this was, what grave and holy hours these were. There seemed to be a strange stillness and power in the air as there always was on very special occasions and never at ordinary times; it made him feel dry, light of weight, very watchful, expectant and still, and it almost made his scalp tingle. It was something like the feeling of his birthday, and of Christmas, and of Easter, and it was still more like the feeling he now seldom and faintly recalled, during the morning just after he learned of his father's death, and during the day he was buried. But it was not really like any of these, or anything else, except itself. These were the hours of Our Lord's deepest Passion. For almost forty days now this feeling had grown and deepened, not without interruption, for he had not managed perfectly to keep either his public or his secret Lenten Rules; yet he had been sufficiently earnest and faithful, and sufficiently grieved in his failures, that the growth had been deeper and more cumulative and more rewarding than he had ever known before; and now he was coming into the heart of it, the holiest and most solemn of its shrines, with heart and soul prepared and eager. Already it was no longer Maundy Thursday, the birthday of the Eucharist; that sorrowfully jubilant magnificence was turned under the world; already the world was brought a few hours forward into the most gravely majestic of all days, Good Friday; already the wheel was so turned that high upon darkened heaven white Easter dazzled, suspended, the crown of the year, like the already trembling start of an avalanche. Easter was very soon now, so soon, with his throat brimming with its hymns and his soul ardent for release and celebration, that it was difficult to be patient; yet his faith and absorption were such that at the same time he came into this day as sorrowing and careful as if Christ had never been crucified before, and could never rise from the dead. Yet now that he desired to retrieve his waking awareness he could not, but only knelt, sad, trying to taste the peculiar quality of the night and to distinguish it from other auras of momentousness, until, realizing how he had misled himself, he gripped his hair and pressed his eyeballs the more tightly, repeating in his heart: Jesus our Lord is crucified. Jesus our Lord is crucified. He saw the Head.

Thrown with fury, a shoe struck the wall next Jimmy's bed: the noise broke upon Richard with sickening fright. Then Hobe's voice:

"All right some mothuf - - - - - sonofabitch is agoana git the livin s - - t beat outn him if I find out who throwed that!"

"Shet yer God damn mouf," said a coldly intense, deeper voice at the far end of the dormitory.

"Yeah fer Chrise sakes *shut up*," said another voice, as several neutral voices said "Shut up."

In the rigid silence Richard and Jimmy dressed quickly

while Hobe waited. Carrying their shoes they stole barefoot on
tiptoe from the room and along the hall and past the iron cot
which had been set up by the stairhead for this one night for
Father Whitman. They could just make out how he lay there
in the dark in his long white habit, giving off a current of silent
and ominous power because they could not be sure as they
passed whether he was asleep or aware of them; the clacking
of his tin clock filled the pine stairwell with its flagrant loud-
ness. They tried hard not to creak the stairs. The pit of Richard's stomach still felt as it did when, without being too mad or
too desperate to care, he knew it was impossible not to fight.
By trying hard he was able to restore whole to his mind the
thorn-crowned image of his Lord, but now it was not as he
had seen it in prayer beside his cot but was very little different
from a pious painting he knew: the eyes rolled up in a way that
seemed affected, and in his cold sickness the image meant little
to him. It was not until they came onto the back porch that the
open night put them once more at their ease.

"Sonofabitchin mothuf - - - - - bastud," Hobe said. "At
shoe bettah be gone by mawning or *some* bastudly cocks-
- - - - - 's agoana be sorry."

"Aw shut up Hobie," Jimmy said. "This ain't no time to
talk like that."

"Hell do *I* keer," Hobe said. "*I* hain't been to Confession
yet."

But he started on down the steps without saying anything
more.

"What happened?" Richard asked.

"Jis trine wake up Jimmy," Hobe said. "God All Mighty
Christ, can't even wake nobody up in this friggin School—"

Richard followed them down the steps. He was glad he had
learned hardly even to think of saying anything. If Jimmy told
Hobie to shut up and quit cussing Hobie would take it off of
him, they were buddies; but by now he knew enough to
keep *his* mouth shut. He felt uneasy, though, because he was
glad he had not sworn. That was like being thankful you were
not as other men and that was one of the worst sins of all; the
Pharisee.

He had forgotten all about the shoes he carried and now
that unexpectedly, for the first time this year, he felt the ground

against the bare soles of his feet it was as if, fumbling among clothes in a dark closet, he had put his hand on living flesh. Even though the ground in this schoolyard was skimmed with dusty gravel, its aliveness soared through him like a sob and lifted his eyes in wonder upon the night. There was no moon and what few stars were out, they were made faint by a kind of smiling universal milky silence, not fog, or even the lightest kind of mist, but as if the whole air and sky were one mild supernal breath. Downhill in the Chapel a line of small windows meekly smoldered, dark orange; he followed his companions and saw that they too were carrying their shoes. When they came to the lawn beyond their building they left the gravel; the ground, with its scarce new grass, felt like a fish. There was a thick oak near the center of the lawn and Hobe and Jimmy, as they passed, stung it several times expertly with gravel. It had not occurred to Richard to pick up gravel and now he was glad, for he was sure he would have missed as often as hit.

II

The night smelled like new milk; the air which exhaled upon them when they opened the side door of the Chapel was as numb and remote as the air of a cave. Without knowing it they hesitated, subdued by the stagnant darkness and its smell of waxed pine and spent incense. Across the unlighted nave the open door of the Lady Chapel brimmed with shaken light; but just at their left, through the door to the vestry, came a friendlier and more mundane light, a delicious smell, and the tired grinding of the voice they most admired in the world. When he became aware of their hesitation beside this partly closed door, George Fitzgerald spoke to them with a formality as unaccustomed and gentle as if a dead body lay in the room behind him and they came in, silent and shy. By the loud hurrying little clock it was still only four minutes to four. They squatted on their bare heels against the wall and looked on, their six eyes emphatic in the sleepless light.

The inward wall of this long corridor was hung solid with cassocks and they were of all lengths from a size almost big enough for the giant sad boy they all called Undertaker, to the

all but baby size of Dillon Prince. At first Richard wondered
where all the cottas were; in the laundry for Easter, he realized.
The room was so weakly lighted by candlestubs that at the far
end it was hardly possible to distinguish the red cassocks from
the black. Just within the surer light, his jaw and his shoulders
sloping more heavily even than usual with fatigue and with his
low posture, Willard Rivenburg sat on a folding-chair which
gave out dangerous splintering noises whenever he stirred. It
was he who was talking, aimlessly, quietly, almost in his sleep;
and Richard could see that George and Lee Allen answered him
only so often as courtesy required, never turning their attention
from their work. Not only were they Prefects; it was also believed by some of the older people that they alone among the
boys now at the School, might have a Vocation. They were in
their last year now and it was generally understood that they
were both praying hard for this to be made clear to them before
they graduated. It was their privilege, tonight, to trim and
change the candles and to remove and replace the withering
flowers, and now white-girdled, incongruous in red cassocks,
they stood wearily beside a soup plate, replying gravely in
short words while, their eyes bright with the lateness of the
hour and fixed in the profound attentiveness of great scientists,
they revolved candlestubs between thumb and forefinger, just
above a flame, and watched the meltings add themselves to the
already considerable cone of wax and tallow which they had
developed on the plate. The shining melt spilled roundly, ram-
bling and congealing; wherever it ridged, they smoothed it delicately with their fingertips. From the apex of this rounded
cone sprang three long fiery wicks.

Because they were to be up all night these two had been forgiven the fast and had supplied themselves against possible
hunger. But neither had yet eaten or drunk, nor did either privately intend to unless, as seemed unlikely, he became too faint
or two sleepy to attend properly to his share of the work. Their
coffee frothed so noisily over its can of Sterno rather because
this enhanced their feeling of privilege and maturity; Willard
was drinking some while he talked although, Richard reflected,
it was long after midnight, when the fast began. He had also
practically finished off a box of Fig Newtons.

The coffee was so strong that it empurpled the wall of the

cup, and its smell was almost as enviably masculine as that of white lightning. The three younger boys kept respectfully quiet and looked on, eagerly and sleepily. They watched now the lapped purple rings in the slanted cup, now the shining of the living wax and its satin look where it had slowed and had been smoothed, now the strong loose smoky flame and the hypnotized faces which leaned above it, and now the reckless primitive profile and the slash-lined blue-black cheek of the great athlete Willard Rivenburg, whom they had never seen in quite such quiet intimacy. Nobody knew for sure just how old Willard was, but he looked as many men can only at thirty or so, and then only if they have been through a war, or years of the hardest kind of work. Richard tried to imagine why he was here tonight. He was fairly sure it was not for any kind of religious reason: Willard had been confirmed, and made his Confession and his Communion, but it was obviously just as a matter of course; when he took his turn serving Mass or swinging the Censer or carrying the Crucifix he was never exactly irreverent yet he always looked as if secretly he might be chewing tobacco; it looked as odd and out of place, somehow, as watching a horse dressed up in cassock and cotta and doing these things. He never even crossed himself at a hard time in a game, the way some of the others did. No, he wouldn't be here because he felt pious. It might be because everybody and everything on the place was thinking about just these things that were happening, and moving around them; a kind of shadow and stillness came over everything during Holy Week and it might be that Willard felt this and was made uneasy by it. But mainly it must be just that he was much too grownup to be able to stand all the silly rules, and tame hours, and good behavior, that were expected of living in a school; he must be even gladder than the little boys were to grab at any chance to break out of that routine, especially anything that would give him an excuse for staying up so long after hours. And yet, Richard reflected, Willard needed and took an awful lot of sleep, dropping off in dull classrooms or wherever he had to sit still, except for eating, as easily as a colored man or a dog. But maybe all that sleep was why he was able to be awake now, though as a matter of fact he wasn't really more than half awake, not nearly as wide awake as Richard felt. But then probably he had been up all night, and probably it wasn't for the first time in his life either.

In some way which it did not occur to him to think about or try to understand, Richard felt a warm rich comforting kind of pride in him and sense of glory as he watched him, as much, in a far quieter and even happier way, as when he watched his almost magical ability in sports; and he began to feel a sense of honor and privilege in having this surprising chance to be so near him and to watch him so closely, to really see him. For normally, when Willard was not playing or practising or sleeping or eating, he was kidding with somebody, in a loudly reckless, crazy way which was a pleasure to see because everything Willard did was a pleasure to see, but was impossible to see through; but now he wasn't kidding at all, only talking quietly and steadily like a grown man, among others whom he treated as grown men. He was finishing up about his grandfather who had come over from Switzerland to settle way back on the Mountain and who had never bothered to learn much English, and he was saying the few words and phrases of German he himself knew, and Richard was deeply impressed in realizing that Willard, who always seemed to him to know about as little as anyone could, except as an athlete and captain of genius and a powerful and experienced man, actually knew words in a foreign language. He himself was accustomed to feel a good deal of complacency because with Father Fish's help he had learned several hundred words of French, but now he felt ashamed of himself, and resolved to learn German, which seemed to him a much more virile language.

He was watching with shy and particular interest the hump between Willard's heavy shoulders, which he had often wondered about but never yet had the chance to examine so privately. It was almost as if Willard were slightly hunchbacked, the low way he always carried his head and sloped his shoulders and the way this hump bulged out just below the base of his neck; yet if he were deformed, he could not have such ability and strength. It must be a very greatly developed muscle, Richard realized, yet it was a funny place to have a muscle; he felt there now on his own body and there wasn't even the beginning of a muscle there; just bone. Could it be bone? But that would be a deformity; and on Willard, more than any other thing, it was what made him unique among others, and marked his all but superhuman powers. Whenever he had done anything physically creditable Richard carried his head low, let his mouth hang open, and tried to hump his back, scarcely knowing of it any more; and so, though it was not generally realized, did many other boys in this school.

"Hey you," Lee said, and startled, they looked: one minute past four. Richard felt a spasm of shame: could ye not watch with me one hour? Besides, they were keeping somebody over his time. *"Jesus!"* Hobe Gillum said, and they stood up quickly. Both of the boys in cassocks ducked in shocked acknowledgment of the Name and Willard's dark face brightened with his satanic parody of falsetto laughter. Lee Allen said with unusually kind gravity: "I sure would hate to have to report anyone for cussn right in Chapel, and on Good Friday too." Hobe's eyes turned Indian, with pride towards Willard, in defiance towards Lee. "Aw forget about it Lee," George Fitzgerald said, "he just wasn't thinking." "I don't want to report you or nobody else," Lee said. "You just watch your mouth, Hobie." "He didn't mean anything," Richard said; and even before everyone looked at him and said nothing, he was miserable. "Better put your shoes on you kids," George said, and with relief Richard sank his hot face over his shoelaces. They felt contempt for him, he was sure, and he felt contempt for himself. Willard thought better of Hobe for cussing than of him for standing up for him, and so did he. Lee jumped on Hobie because Willard's cackling about it bothered him and he couldn't jump on Willard. If it hadn't been Good Friday and Richard had spoken up like that he knew that somebody would have said coldly, "Well look who's talking." Keep your mouth shut, he kept whispering within himself intensely. Just keep your fool mouth shut. And as they left the room he tried to exorcise the feelings of injustice, self-pity and pain by crossing himself quickly and surreptitiously. Fine time to go worrying about your*self,* he sneered at himself.

The nave replied to their timid noises with the threatening resonance of a drumhead. Not even the sanctuary lamps were lighted, but the night at the windows made just discernible the effigies and the paintings and the crucifix, no longer purple veiled but choked in black, and the naked ravagement of the

High Altar. The tabernacle gawped like a dead jaw. By this ruthless flaying and deracination only the skeleton of the Church remained; it seemed at once the more sacred in dishonor, and as brutally secular as a boxcar. To cross its axis without the habitual genuflection felt as uneasy as to swim across a sudden unimaginable depth, and as Richard turned and bowed before the central devastation he realized: nothing there. Nothing at all; and with the breath of the Outer Darkness upon his soul, remembered the words: And the Veil of the Temple was rent in twain.

But here in peace and victory before the adoration of all creatures past and breathing and uncreated, shrined and enthroned, starred round with unabating light and with the stars of all the fields of spring as well, exiled there yet abides throughout this night the soul and substance of the everliving God Who shall, within these few hours now, be restored to His High Altar and there devoured, leaving His whole Church desecrate and unconsoled until the hour of His glorious Resurrection from the Dead. Tied in its white veil, stifled, a huge masked Head, a thinly clouded Sun, the monstrance stood from the top of the tabernacle and broke at its center a dense tissue of flowers and light: candles it seemed by thousands, spear-high and merely tall, and short, and guttering, each an abiding upright fiery piercing and, crisp and wearying, withering, dying, the frugal harvest of the dawn of the year: from faint orchards the last apple blossoms, still tenderly raveling their slow-borne blizzard; branches of mild-starred dogwood and of the hairy wild azalea, pink and white, from the mulled gray woods, and little fistfuls of those breathless violets which break the floor of winter, even the rare mayapple, the twinleaf, whose bloom stays just a day; and, of the first shivering domestic flowers, cold jonquils, crowds of them, greenish with chill or butter yellow or flaming gold, and clear narcissus, reaching, bowing, staring, fainting in vases and jars of metal and glass and clay and in drinking glasses and mason jars and in small and large tin cans, all these each in their kind and sufferance bore witness before God while they might. Few of these early flowers have strong fragrance, or any, yet the heat and the brightness and the fragrance brought forth by the burning wax and tallow and by the heat in the closed room, all one wall of dizzying dazzle, were

such that it was at first almost as difficult to breathe the freighted
air as to breathe water, and this air was enriched the more by
the devotions of those who knelt subsumed within the trembling light; and at the instant of stepping into this hot and
fragrant gold, going upon one knee and gazing upon the blind
rondure of the monstrance and the thousand-pointed blossoming of fire and flower, his heart was lifted up and turned vague
and shy as the words broke within him, upon each other, God:
Death; so that the two were one. Death: Dead, the word pre-
vailed; and before him, still beyond all other stillness, he saw as
freshly as six years before his father's prostrate head and,
through the efforts to hide it, the mortal blue dent in the impatient chin. He remembered within this instant how for the first
time he had been convinced, and how eternally convincing it
had been, when he saw how through that first full minute of
looking his father had neither stirred nor spoken, and how the
powerful right hand had lain half open against the exact
center of his body; the cloth of his coat was not moved by any
breathing and it was as if the hand were only a magically expert
imitation of a hand, a hand of wax and, now looking again at
the head, lips, and a face of wax, a dent of wax, a head of
wax immense upon this whole rich waxen air. Dead, the word
came again, and shutting his eyes he prayed swiftly for his
father the prayer of all his childhood, God bless daddy and
keep him close to Thee and may light perpetual shine upon
him, Amen; and casually, obliviously, as a trout into shadow,
the image and memory vanished. It is Our Lord's death today,
he said to himself, but at this moment he could see neither face,
that of his father, or that of his Lord; only the words returned,
God: Death.

No praying-benches were available at first, and they knelt
where they entered, the waxed floor brutal against their bones.
In the Name of the Father and of the Son and of the Holy
Ghost, Richard whispered rapidly to himself, moving his lips
and closing his eyes again. He crossed himself with care. There
was a sound of arising and departure and through his eyelashes
he saw Knox Peyton complete his genuflection and step un-
gainly between him and Jimmy, trying to subdue the reproach
and annoyance in his face. They stayed where they knelt, all

on their good manners before the one empty bench, and Richard heard the whispered "go on" several times before he realized that it was directed at him. Two worshipers glanced unhappily behind them, shut their eyes, and tucked their chins down, trying hard to pray. "I be damned if I will," Richard thought, and caught himself; he shut his eyes tightly and in despairing shame tucked his own chin down. "Go *on*," he heard. He decided that he ought to make a penance of it. Trying to look and to feel neither humble nor proud he crossed himself, got up, genuflected, tiptoed to the empty bench, genuflected, knelt, and crossed himself. Mr. Bradford closed his eyes, frowned, and deeply bowed his head. Home stretch, Richard said to himself, and quickly begged forgiveness for an irreverence which had not been premeditated but spontaneous. But wasn't it even worse to be so unaware of where you were that such a thought could occur spontaneously? Mr. Bradford completed his devotions and tiptoed towards the door, his eyes downcast. His effort to stay within himself was too successful; Richard heard him bump against one of the two boys, and his whispered accusing apology, and their feckless and ill-subdued reply. Deaconess Spenser, at the desk opposite his own, compressed her lips, crossed herself, got up, genuflected, and stepped behind him; he could hear the harsh whispered reprimand whistling through her false teeth. He looked carefully at his clasped hands, but he heard movement as the door was cleared and along the side of his eye Jimmy advanced and swiftly established himself at the newly empty bench and the Deaconess, her wattles a violent red and her mouth pulled in tight, returned to her own bench, genuflected, knelt, crossed herself, and sank her forehead into her hands. Behind him somebody else stood up and he heard the knee touch the floor and, knowing he ought not to, glanced back; it was Hog Eye Kelsey, one of the littler boys from his own dormitory; already Hobe was standing to replace him. Not Hog Eye, he told himself; he can't help it: Jeff.

Pay attention, he told himself. Mind your own business.

He looked at the veiled monstrance; the brightest threads of the veil sparkled like mica, gold-white on silver-white, and in one place a rigid shaft of metal radiance almost pierced the fabric. One azalea bloom strayed against it as if it were straining to be near it. Tiny threads sprang out of the flare of the blossom, the way small straight lines are drawn in a funny-paper to show music coming out of a horn. An apple-blossom fell. Looking at the tired sleepless flames of the candles, Richard felt as if he could almost hear them burning.

Soul of Christ sanctify me, he prayed silently; Body of Christ save me; but he was just saying it mechanically, and too fast. Slowly now, thinking carefully of each word, he began again.

Soul of Christ sanctify me: make me holy: absolve me from all spot of sin:

Body of Christ save me: save me: Thy Body which has already begun to suffer and die:

He braced his mind.

Blood of Christ inebriate me:

Carefully as he tried, he could not avoid it. Inebriate meant just plain drunken, or meant a drunken person, especially habitual drunkard, and as it was used here, it meant to make drunk, to intoxicate. And inebriety meant drunkenness and the habit of drunkenness. He had been fond of the word for a long time before he knew, or realized that he did not know, its meaning —which must of course be simply what the Blood of Christ might most naturally be expected to do: but what would that be, that sounded as nice as inebriate? During the past winter it had occurred to him to look it up in a dictionary. Since then the correct and disconcerting meanings had been indelible, and that part of the prayer had become thin ice. He could only get past it without irreverent or skeptical thoughts by saying it so fast or so shallowly that it was impossible to bear its meaning in mind, and that was no way to pray. He had asked Father Fish about it and Father Fish had shown him that it was possible to be amused by the word without feeling irreverent. He had said that some of these ancient prayers were rather extravagant in their way of putting things, and that there was no need to take them with absolute literalness. Although he had no way of being sure, Richard had a feeling that Father Fish had been as amused at him, as at the word; once again he wondered why, and stopped himself from wondering why because this was no time to. Don't take it literally, he told himself firmly; but the literal words remained and were even more firm: make drunk. Intoxicate. Good ole whiskey, he suddenly heard in his mind,

and he remembered how, drinking sodapop in Knoxville, boys
slightly more worldly than he would twist the bottle deep into
the mouth and cock it up vertically to drink, and taking it down,
breathless, would pat their stomachs or rub them in circles and
gasp, "Ahhh, good ole whisky!" But this wasn't even on whiskey. On blood. Jesus' blood, too. His uncle had once sneered,
"There is a pudding filled with blood," scornfully exploding the
first syllable of "pudding," and Richard had been both shocked
and amused, and he was shocked to find that he remembered it
with amusement now. Forgive us our trespasses, he whispered,
shutting his eyes tight. It was only a hymn, and so it was not as
bad to make fun of as some things were. But the blood was
"drawn from Emmanuel's veins," so that did make it pretty awful. And his uncle had said it with a kind of hatred which included much more than the hymn: all of religion, and everybody who was religious, even his own sister, Richard's mother,
and his Aunt Patty, and him, Richard, and his own sister. Forgive us our trespasses as we forgive those who trespass against
us, he prayed, and pushed the matter out of his mind. He does
like us all the same, he reflected, same as grandpa does. They
just don't like the Church.

Passion of Ch——

Water from the side of Christ wash me; and he felt that his
thoughts badly needed washing:

Passion of Christ strengthen me:

Within Thy Wounds hide me, he thought swiftly and with
great uneasiness, hugging the ground and the leaf coverage as
if beneath the skimming of a bird of prey: but try as he could,
the image plunged and took him. An older boy, the only one
Richard knew who also liked to read, had with great sophistica-
tion and delight explained to him what was meant in Shake-
speare's *Venus and Adonis*, by the words *he saw more wounds
than one*, and this had instantly become identical in his mind
with a rawly intimate glimpse he had had, three or four years
before, of Minnielee Henley when they were climbing a tree;
and now with these words *within Thy Wounds hide me* the
image fought in his mind with the image of those small but
deadly wounds in the body of Jesus, in which surely nobody
could hide, not even the one the spear made in His side. But
not there either, he insisted to himself; not even if He wasn't a

man. Yet there in his mind's eye, made all the worse by all the most insipid and effeminate, simpering faces of Jesus that he had ever seen in pictures, was this hideous image of a huge torn bleeding gulf at the supine crotch, into which an ant-swarm of the pious, millions of them, all pleading and rolling up their eyes, laden souls, by thousands meekly stealing, struggled to crowd themselves, and lose themselves, and drown, and dissolve.

It was the Devil, that was all. Just the Devil Himself, tempting him.

O good Jesus hear me, he prayed with deep self-loathing, almost aloud: and realized with gratitude that for once he had been able to say these words, which for months now had seemed to him fulsome and insincere, with complete desire and sincerity. You just have to mean it, he thought, for it to mean anything.

Suffer me not to be separated from Thee (a mortal sin is a sin that cuts us off from God):

From the Malicious Enemy defend me:

Of these closing lines he never felt doubt and now he repeated, with reverent emphasis and relish:

From the Malicious Enemy defend me:

In the hour of my death call me and bid me come to Thee:

That with Thy

No there was something really wrong about

He prayed, with fear and determination: That with Thy Saints I may praise Thee, forever and ever, Amen.

All the same it was wrong for people to ask to be saints, as flat as all that. Or even just to be *with* the saints, if that was what it meant. To just barely manage through God's infinite mercy to escape burning eternally in the everlasting fires of Hell ought to be just about as much as any good Catholic could pray for; and now Richard remembered still another prayer at which, when he was serving at Mass, he had for quite a while now been accustomed to keep silence or at most to make approximate sounds of the words, with his fingers crossed: where, in the General Confession, reviewing his iniquities, the penitent cries, "The remembrance of them is grievous unto us, the burden of them is intolerable." As a rule he was able to say "the remembrance of them is grievous unto us" with adequate sincerity; but it was seldom that he could feel, at the particular moment he felt required to feel, that "the burden of them is intolerable." It wasn't anywhere near intolerable, no matter how much it ought to be. At first he had been able to say it in the realization that it was intolerable to his soul, whether or not he in his mind and feelings was capable of feeling it just then, and that prayers are said by and for the soul, not the mind or the feelings; but in this he came to feel that he was mistaken: for it was, he noticed, only when he believed and felt deeply with his mind or his emotions that he was able to be aware that his soul, as such, existed. But that isn't true, he now thought with alarm. No matter what I think or feel, the soul is always there and always alive unless it has been killed by impenitence for mortal sin. The hardening of the heart towards God. I'm only trying to suit myself, he told himself; not my soul, and not God.

But how can you say things when you only ought to mean them and don't really mean them at all?

Have mercy upon us O God have mercy upon us, he found himself praying. These were the words of the Confession which followed "the burden of them is intolerable," and always, as now, he was able to mean them when he spoke them.

But not "that with Thy Saints I may praise Thee."

Now it occurred to Richard that perhaps this prayer had been written by a saint or by someone near sainthood, who was able to mean every extreme thing that was said; and he knew that anyone who could fully mean those things, and who could mean them every time they were said, was to be humbly respected. But in that case it was a prayer which was good only for saints and near saints to say, not for ordinary people, no matter how good they hoped to be. Nobody's got any business even hoping he can be a saint, he told himself.

God no!, he exclaimed to himself, for now suddenly it became vivid and shameful in his memory that he himself had for a while cherished, more secretly even than his lust, exactly this inordinate ambition. Good golly!, he whispered within his soul, feeling the back of his neck and then his cheeks go hot; and with a cold and marveling, compassionate contempt for the child he had so recently been, he lost himself in reflective remembrance, unaware that it was for the first time in his life.

It was hardly more than a year ago, when he was only eleven, that the image and meaning of Jesus and the power and meaning of the Sacraments and of the teachings of the Church, all embodied and set forth in formalities of language and of motion whose sober beauties were unique, and in music which at that time moved and satisfied him as no other music could, had first and, it had seemed, irreducibly, established upon all his heart and mind their quality, their comfort, their nobility, their sad and soaring weight; and, entering upon his desolation of loneliness, had made of suffering a springing garden, an Eden in which to walk, enjoying the cool of the evening. It had become a secret kind of good to be punished, especially if the punishment was exorbitant or unjust; better to be ignored by others, than accepted; better still to be humiliated, than ignored. He remembered how on mornings when he had waked up and found his bed dry, he had felt as much regret as relief. He had begun to take care to read in conspicuous places, where he would be most liable to interruption and contempt. He had pretended not to know lessons he had in fact prepared, in order that even such teachers as thought well of him, or thought "at least he's smart," or "he studies, anyway," might think ill of him. He had continued his solitary wanderings in the woods until it occurred to him that these excursions, for all their solitude and melancholy, were more pleasant than unpleasant; from then on he had put himself into the middle of crowds, especially on the drearier afternoons when even the hardiest boys stayed indoors and the restive, vindictive, bored, mob feelings were at their most sullen and light-triggered. The leaden melodies of the Lenten hymns had appealed to him as never before; lines in certain hymns seemed, during that time, to have been written especially for him. *Jesus, I my Cross have taken*, he would sing, already anticipating the lonely solace of tears concealed in public: *all to leave and follow Thee; destitute, despis'd, forsaken,* were words especially dear to him; *Thou from hence my All shalt be.* As he sang that he felt: nobody else wants me; and did his best to believe it, even of his mother. He remembered now that this kind of singing had satisfied him most at Stations of the Cross, on cold rainy nights. *Perish ev'ry fond ambition,* he would sing magnanimously; (no I *won't* become a naturalist; I'll never explore the sources of

the Amazon; I'll never even own a monkey, or be junior tennis
champion); *all I've thought or hoped or known;* then tears and
their subdual rewarded him: *Yet how rich is my condition*
(never to live at home again, never to be loved or even liked),
God and Heaven are still my own; and he saw crowned God
and Heaven shining and felt, in a humble kind of way, that he
literally owned them. Now remembering it he shook his head
almost as if in disbelief, but he knew it had been so. Everything.
He had done just about everything he could think of. He had
gone seldom to Father Fish's cottage, for friendliness was certain there, and often cookies and cocoa too, and he had found
that these luxuries meant most to him, in his desire to suffer for
religious advantage, only when they were indulged so rarely
that even while they were being enjoyed they enhanced the
bleakness of the rest of living. He even schemed to intensify his
always all but annihilating homesickness to the utmost possible,
asking permission of the Master of the Day the more often, that
it be the more curtly or impatiently or, at best, contemptuously
refused; watching his mother's cottage, the one place he was
almost never allowed to go, sometimes by the hour; sometimes
in ambush under dripping trees, relishing the fact that only he
knew of the miserableness of that watch; sometimes openly,
hanging against the fence, relishing the fact that she knew, and
others could see, and that even though she knew, she would try
to ignore him and stay out of his sight, and that when at last
she could ignore him no longer, she would hurt him by trying
to be stern with him as she told him to go away, and would
sharpen his unhappiness into agony by her idea of a sensible
explanation why this senseless cruelty had to be law. "Because
dear, mother thinks it's best for you not to be too near her,
all the more because you miss her so much." "Because your
father—isn't with us." "Because mother thinks you need to be
among other boys Richard. In charge of men." And worst of
all: "I know how hard it is now but I know that when you're
older you'll understand why I did it, and thank me for it."
Thank her! his heart sneered now, in bitter paroxysm. And for
a moment so brief that the realization did not stay with him, he
felt hatred and contempt for his mother, for her belief in sub-
missiveness and for her telling him, on certain infuriating occasions, that it is only through submitting bravely and cheerfully

to unhappiness that we can learn God's Will, and how most truly to be good. God's Will, he thought now: I bet it isn't just for people to be unhappy! Who wants to be *good*! *I* do, he answered himself. But not like that. I sure was crazy then, he thought, pleased that he was now able to recognize the fact. Just a crazy fool. The whole crazy thing had begun to fade away soon after Easter, with the good weather, and had vanished so completely during the free summer in Knoxville that he had forgotten the whole of it until just now: but all through that dreary winter and increasingly throughout that drizzling season of penitence, he realized now with incredulous and amused self-scorn, he had ever more miserly cherished and elaborated his wretchedness in every one of its sorry ramifications, as indispensable to the secret. the solution, he had through God's Grace discovered; and had managed easily to forgive himself those parts of his Lenten Rule which he meekly enjoyed in public, by inventing still other, harder rules which were private. His mother had tried uneasily to suggest to him that there might be a kind of vanity mixed up in his extreme piety—"not that you *mean* it, of course, dear"—against which he must be on his guard; but remembering the role of dismayed parents and scornful villagers in the early lives of many of the saints, he had answered her gently and patiently, with forbearance, that was the word, as befitted communication between creatures of two worlds so unbridgeably different. He had been tempted on more than one occasion to say to her, "Woman, what have I to do with thee? Mine hour is not yet come"; but he had suspected that this might be thought impudent or absurd or even blasphemous. Nor had he ever said aloud, when others jeered or tormented, "Father, forgive them, for they know not what they do"; but had often fortified himself with the silent words, "And He held His peace."

It had only gradually been borne upon him that he himself might aspire to actual sainthood; he had quickly realized that if that was to be his goal it was necessary, starting young, he might already be too late, to perform in private for God's eyes alone and in public that others might see, and be edified, and remember, and revere him, a long and consistent series of remarkable spiritual feats. Let your light so shine before men that they may see your good works and glorify your Father, Which is in

Heaven. But meditating what these might be, he had realized that there in truth he did run the danger of sinning through Pride, as those people do who look hungry when they fast; whereas his own ambitions were prompted (or so it seemed) by true religious feeling and by nothing else. These ambitions had crystallized during the late weeks of Lent, into a desire to do for Jesus as much as Jesus was doing for him and for all souls. He had experimented with extra fasting, but it was not possible to carry this far, since it was virtually impossible to be excused from meals without the sin of lying, and almost as difficult, he found, to sit at the table without eating, or eating little enough to give the fast any dignity or meaning. So he had chosen self-mortification instead. He had gone into the woods and eaten worms, but this had disgusted him, and he had been even worse disgusted when, on one occasion, he had come near tasting his own excrement. It had suddenly struck him as very doubtful indeed that Jesus would ever have done any such thing, and he had thrown the twig deep into the bushes and had carefully buried the filth. Efforts to scourge himself had been moderately painful but not sufficiently effective to outweigh the sense of bashfulness, even of ridiculousness, which he felt over the clumsiness of the attempt, in relation to the severity of the intention. So he had been reduced, mainly, to keeping very bitter vigil over his thoughts and his language and over his sensuous actions upon himself, and to finding out times and places in which it would be possible to kneel, for much longer than it was comfortable to kneel, without danger of getting caught at it. (He had been as frightened, once, by such an interruption, as if he had been surprised in a sexual act.) It was during one of these protracted and uncomfortable sojourns on his knees that his mind, uneasily strained between its own wanderings and efforts at disciplined meditation, had become absorbed in grateful and overwhelmed imagination of Christ Crucified, and had without warning brought to its surface the possibility of his own crucifixion. He had been wondering with all of a sincere heart how ever he might do enough for the Son of God Who had done so much for him when suddenly, supplanting Christ's image, he saw his own body nailed to the Cross and, in the same image, himself looked down from the Cross and felt his weight upon the nails, and the splintered wood against the whole length of his scourged back; and stoically, with infinite love and forgiveness, gazed downward into the eyes of Richard, and of Roman soldiers, and of jeering Jews, and of many people whom Richard had known. It was a solemn and rewarding moment; but almost within the next breath he recognized that he had no such cause or right as Jesus to die upon the Cross: and turning his head, saw Christ's head higher beside his own and a third head, lower, cursing; and knew that he was, instead, the Penitent Thief.

But it was of course out of the question that in a deep country part of Middle Tennessee, in nineteen twenty-three, he could actually manage to have himself nailed to a Cross; and although (if he should have the courage) he could undoubtedly nail his own feet, and even one hand (if someone else would steady the nail), his right hand would still hang free, and it would look pretty foolish beside a real Crucifixion. With any proper humility he would be content merely to be tied up, as the thieves usually were, and to hang during the three hours of Good Friday that Jesus hung on the Cross. Even that would mean a good deal, if only in token; the widow's mite, only it seemed rather more than the widow had managed; and he realized that many others besides himself would be moved, and impressed, and very likely improved, by the good example. It would be impossible of course to get a Cross without removing the image of Jesus from it, that big life-size one out in the vestibule, and that would be irreverent even if it were allowed. Or someone might make one for him but he doubted it. He might make one for himself if he could sneak into Manual Training Shop and get enough private time, only everybody knew he wasn't any good with his hands and simple as a Cross must be to make, they would just laugh at any that he would be likely to make. One of the school's gridiron bedsteads would be convenient for tying to, and very likely even more uncomfortable to hang against than a Cross, but he was forced to doubt, as with the nail-holding and the Cross, that he could manage the whole tying-up by himself, and as he thought of asking someone else to help him, he felt extraordinarily shy. As he singled over each of the few whom in any degree he trusted, or on whose affection he could at all depend, he became sure that there was not one who would co-operate in this, or even really understand about it. It would be necessary instead to anger and deceive people he disliked into doing it: but that, he felt, was both unlikely and sinful. If he got them mad they would do what they wanted to him, not what he wanted them to do, and he could not imagine how to suggest to them that the one thing he didn't want was to be stripped of his garments (except for a loincloth) and tied to a bedstead for three hours. And even if he should manage to, he would be tricking them into a sin, and that would be a sin of itself. It was easier just to imagine it as something already done, and as soon as he forgot about the problems of getting it done it was better, too.

There he hung, the iron bars and edged slats of the bed acutely painful against flesh and bone alike; but he made no complaint. Rather, his eyes were fixed steadfastly upon the expiring eyes of his crucified Lord, and his own suffering was as naught. There was a steady murmuring of scorn, pity, regard and amazement beneath him, and now and again a familiar face and voice was lifted, pleading with him or commanding him to come down. Father McPhetridge, the Prior, his wide red face reared up and told him that this was the most outrageous thing that had ever been done by a boy in this School and that he was to stop it immediately and come down and take his punishment like a man. He replied, gently and calmly, his voice all the more effective because of its quietness after all that indignant roaring, that "punishment" (he smiled at the word in his suffering) would have to come at its own good time; he would descend (with their help) promptly at three o'clock and not before; and would give himself up to his punishers without making a struggle. Scourge me, he said; paddle me with the one with holes in it; put me on bounds all the rest of the year; expel me even; there is nothing you can do that won't be to the greater glory of God and so I forgive you. The Prior, abashed, withdrew; Richard saw his whispering among the other monks and the teachers and his face was redder than ever, and their whispering eyes were on him. The football coach Braden Bennett, who had so often sneered at his music lessons; his face was changed, now: though with a scornful wonder, men see her sore oppressed. He looked straight back into those bullying eyes, with such quiet fortitude and forgiveness that the scorn and the wonder deepened, the wonder even more than the scorn. His mother pled with him to come down; she was even crying; and he was awfully sorry for her; but he shook his head slowly and, smiling gently, told her: "No, Mother, I deeply repent for making you cry, and feel so badly, but mine hour is not yet come." She collapsed with sobbing and the women of the place crowded around her; they took her arms and helped her as she walked away, all bent over. Some day you'll understand, he told her within himself, and you'll thank me for it; and he knew the happiness that comes only of returning evil with good. Willard Rivenburg's deep dark jaw hung open and Richard could overhear his whisper, to Bennett, "Jesus that kid's got guts." George Fitzgerald, scarcely able to contain his tears, held up a sponge soaked in vinegar, which Richard forgivingly refused; and Hobe Gillum and Jimmy Toole and Parmo Gallatin and Keg Head Hodges and the others looked at him, glum but respectful; even if it was no more than politeness, he realized, he would never be last again, when they chose up sides. Through the half-open Chapel door he could still hear the voice of the Three Hour Sermon, Father Ogle's voice, and he realized that the service had no more than an hour, at the outside, to go; but the voice sounded half-hearted and sailed hollowly around the almost empty Church; nearly everyone in the community was gathered here in the vestibule, and there were some even from nearby towns, and suddenly a photographer climbed onto the sandstone font and aimed at him and flashed a bulb. STRANGE RITES AT MOUNTAIN SCHOOL, he read: and, as blood broke scalding upon his nape, sank his face into his hands and prayed, in despair, *O God forgive me! forgive me if you can stand to!*

For, musing upon his past vanities with affectionate scorn or even as with a scornful wonder, the scorn, the living vanity, of one who has put away childish things, and dwelling upon them in remembrance, he had dwelt once more within them (within Thy Wounds hide me), ensnaring himself afresh. For these later imaginations were not wholly remembrance; some were newly his, and only now, even in the very hour of Christ's own passion, he had yet again seduced his soul. If others, if any other in the world, should know those absurd imaginations of his heart: by his dread and horror in the mere thought, he knew his contemptible silliness. But God of course knew, and

Christ Himself, even now when the Son was suffering and the Father, grieving that He might not take the Cup from Him, was hovering in love and sorrow, yes, engulfed, enchanted in woe though they were, They knew very clearly though, it now occurred to him, his secret was safe with Them. In insupportable self-loathing he squeezed his eyes so tightly shut that they ached, and dug his chin as tightly against his throat as it would lock and in blind vertigo, scarcely knowing his action, struck himself heavily upon his breastbone, groaning within his soul, *the burden of them is intolerable.* With the second blow he realized, in gratitude and in a new flowering of vainglory, that he had been surprised into contrition so true and so deep that beside it every moment of contrition he had ever known before seemed trivial, even false, and for an instant he questioned the validity of every Absolution he had ever been granted. Yet almost before this question could take form, and even while his fist was preparing its third assault against his inordinate heart, this new doubt was supplanted by a recognition that his action was conspicuous and that it must seem to others as affected, as much put on for outward show, as he himself, observing others, had come to feel that various mannerisms in prayer must be. Bringing his fist against his breast in circumspection he opened his eyes, raised his head a little, and without turning his head, glanced narrowly around him through his eyelashes.

Nobody seemed to have noticed anything out of the ordinary although he could not, of course, be sure of those who knelt behind him. He bowed his head again, twisting it a little to the right, lowered his right shoulder and drew it back a little, and observed from nearly closed eyes. He still could not see those who knelt directly behind him but so far as he could see, nobody seemed to have noticed him; then he caught Hobe Gillum's coppery eye, and blushed. He readjusted his head and shoulder and watched Claude Gray, who knelt a little ahead of him and to the right. Claude's head was flung far back and was so twisted in adoration that the point of his left jaw, bright gold in the candlelight, was the most conspicuous and almost the highest part of it. What was more, it was clear that he was praying, not to the Blessed Sacrament, but to the small, shrouded statue of the Blessed Virgin above the lavabo table;

and noticing now for the first time that a little cup of violets stood on the plaster ledge at her feet, Richard was sure who had searched them out among the wet dead leaves to honor that place. He looked at Claude again, particularly at the tilted curly back of the head and at the abandoned angle of the brightened jaw, and thought, He may really mean it, he may not even know it but I bet he does, I bet he knows it makes a picture and I bet he got it from some picture of some saint or other. But if he did really mean it, and no longer knew he was doing it, then it was not fair to blame him. He was probably thinking about his mother. It seemed a long time ago he had lost his mother to keep on making so much fuss about it but maybe he took things harder than most people. Richard suddenly felt deeply ashamed of himself in case Claude really was grieving and praying for his dead mother, and he began to feel pity for her and for Claude as well, but then he remembered Claude's voice, which sounded more girlish than a girl's even though it had changed, reciting to him the Litany of the Blessed Virgin in impassioned sugary tones; O most clement O most holy O most sweet Virgin Mary; something of that sort and a lot more besides. He had felt uneasy about the whole thing and at the instant that Claude brought such juicy emphasis to the words *mosst sweett*, with such meticulousness about both t's and pronouncing *most* like *moused*, Richard had decided that he definitely disliked the whole prayer; and looking at Claude now, he disliked it even more thoroughly, and he decided that even if Claude was genuine now in his praying, he did not trust that kind of praying. He remembered his mother's gossiping about Claude once, his desire that the School should put lace borders on the cottas and his special attentions to the Blessed Virgin, and saying impatiently, "Well what I can't see is, why doesn't he just—go on over to Rome!"

But now remembering the scorn and impatience which had been in her voice, and still watching Claude, with the long hair of the back of his head like a shabby chrysanthemum, tilted above the weak neck, he felt that Claude was pitiful, and that it was careless and cruel to think of him contemptuously, and as shameful to be watching him in this way, so unaware that he was being watched, or that he might look in the least silly, so defenseless, as it would be to peer at him through a keyhole. How do *I* know, he thought; he's probably praying all right, and even if he isn't I've got no right to look at him like this and——

With this, something he could not quite remember, which seemed to be prodding at the edges of his thought, came abruptly clear. He remembered that he had started looking at Claude, and speculating with mistrust about the quality of his praying, because he himself had done something, without affectation, which might easily be misunderstood to be affected. He could not quite understand it but he was in some ignoble way trying to put off onto Claude something that was wrong with himself, or even worse, was assuming that Claude was doing wrongly what he knew he himself had not done wrongly; and worse even than that, he had so wandered and so lost himself in speculating about the weakness of another that he had degraded and lost his own moment of contrition, and had forgotten the very sin for which he was contrite, in committing still another sin of much the same kind. But now, although he could see the first sin, and the moment of contrition, and the second sin, quite clearly, they formed something more like a picture than a feeling, and there were too many things in the picture for him to look at any one of them really closely. He felt shame and a sort of astonishment. He wondered whether he would ever learn, from committing one sin, how not to commit another of the same sort even in the very moment of repenting it; and he felt that it was strange, and terrible, that repentance so deep and real as he knew that his had been, could be so fleeting. He felt deeply sorry and was filled with self-dislike as he saw what he had done, but he knew that the feeling was of a much shallower kind than that in which, without foreseeing it, he had struck his breast so hard. He thought of Jesus suffering on the Cross, but that deep and truest contrition was not restored; he looked again at Claude's unpromising head, and felt a mysterious sadness, which he could not quite understand, for whatever was imperfect and incompetent: Claude; poor little Dillon Prince, with his square-bobbed tow hair and his pink lashless eyes, forever crying or just over crying or just about to cry; a hen, with a wry neck which could never be straightened, standing as if shyly to herself in one corner of the chicken run, with one wing hunched; his own imper-

fect and incontinent mind and spirit; and again of Jesus upon
the Cross, suffering and dying that all such imperfections might
be made whole, yes, even the poor darn hen; and tears came
into his eyes, which he relished, but he knew they had nothing
to do with the deep contrition he was trying to recapture. Ye
who do truly and earnestly repent you of your sins, he whispered almost aloud, and are in love and charity with your neighbors, draw near with faith and take this Holy Sacrament to
your comfort, and make your humble confession to Almighty
God, devoutly kneeling.

His heart opened. Almighty and everlasting God, he prayed,
Maker of all things, Judge of all men (and he saw as in a
wheeling rondure the shining of all things, the shadows of all
men), we acknowledge and bewail our manifold sins and
wickednesses (and they manifolded themselves upon the air
between earth and heaven like falling leaves and falling snow)
which we from time to time (and over and over, morning and
noon and waking in the night) most grievously have committed
in thought (the wandering mind, the lascivious image which
even now flashed before him), word (the words of obscenity
and of cursing) and deed (the shame and the violence of the
hands) against Thy Divine Majesty (flung upward like so
many arrows and so much filth against the dying Son upon His
Cross and the invincible Father upon His Throne), provoking
most justly Thy wrath and indignation against us (he bowed
his head deeply, with eyes closed, and the entire sky hardened into one spear driving downwards upon his bowed neck,
yet Christ upon His Cross merely looked into his eyes without
either wrath or indignation). We are heartily sorry for these
our misdoings. The remembrance of them is grievous unto
us (O yes it is surely grievous), the burden of them is (God,
forgive me, forgive me, make them intolerable, intolerable),
the burden of them is intolerable (it is, Lord, Lord God I want
it to be), is intolerable. Have mercy upon us most merciful
Father have mercy upon us (and he pressed his clasped hands
tightly against his forehead), for Thy Son Our Lord Jesus
Christ's sake forgive us all that is past (is past), and grant
that we may ever hereafter serve Thee and please Thee in newness of life, to the honor and glory of Thy Name, Amen.

That we may ever hereafter. Ever hereafter. Serve Thee

and please Thee. Serve Thee and please Thee in newness of
life. Forgive us all that is past. All. Past. Ever hereafter, in
newness of life. Serve Thee, and please Thee. To the honor
and glory of Thy Name.

He was as peaceful and light almost, as if he had just received Absolution. Keeping his eyes thinly closed, tilting his
head quietly back, he could see the tender light of the candles
against his eyelids, and he became aware once again of the
strong fragrance of all the flowers. Dying, he whispered to himself. Soon now. For me and for all sinners. O sacred Head. He
heard on his rose-mild blindness the infinitesimal flickering of
the clock like those tiniest of thorns which cannot be taken out
of the skin by thousands, by crown of piercing thorn. Opening
his eyes just enough to see, looking through their rainbow
flickering of little sharpness, sharp flames on the dark, thorn
flames in thousands, each a thorn, a little sword, a tongue of
fire, standing from pentecostal waxen foreheads; go ye unto
all the world, a briar-patch of blessed fires, burning, just audibly
crackling; no; the clock. Now pale flowers, round, in thousands, stared flatly among the thousands of sharp flames, as
white and lonely on the humming gloom as organstops, gazed
at too fixedly during a stupefying sermon, round and bright as
wafers, consecrated Hosts, in the tiny burning and prickling
of Time. He did not quite conceive of Time except as a power
of measure upon the darkness, yet opened his eyes now and
saw that it was almost twenty-five, twenty-three and a half, past
four. The clock stood on the lowest step of the Altar. Its leather
case was inlaid with silver wire almost as fine as hair, which
outlined intricate flowers and leaves. It was his mother's, and
it had been borrowed for use in the Lady Chapel, as it always
was for this Thursday watch, because it was the most nearly
silent clock on the place. Now that he looked at it he heard it
the more clearly, a sound more avid and delicate than that of
a kitten at its saucer, and now that he heard nothing else he
saw nothing else except the face of the clock, hard, handless,
staring white out of a shadow of trembling gold, like the great
Host in a monstrance; and when once again he saw the hands,
and the numbers, they showed that only two minutes of his
watch remained. Could ye not watch with me one hour? Now
he remembered the images and emotions into which he had

awakened, so acutely, that they were almost his again; but now in some way they had hardened, they stayed at some distance from him, and he began to realize that during this entire half-hour his mind had been wandering: there had been scarcely one moment of prayer or of realization. Hell of a saint I'd make, he said to himself; and added with cold and level weary self-disgust to the tally of the sins he must soon confess, I swore in Lady Chapel in the presence of the Blessed Sacrament. God be merciful unto me a sinner, he whispered in his mind, crossing himself.

Now for the first time he realized that his knees were very sore. The small of his back ached. When he moved, bending his back, shifting his knees, everything whirled hazily for a moment, then, with a kind of sliding or shunting like the falling into plumb of a weighted curtain, came clear and stayed still. I guess that was nearly fainting, he thought, with satisfaction. He searched the deep grooves in his knees along the edge of the board and re-established them exactly as they had been, and bore down on them to make them hurt the more, and he found that it hurt still more to keep his back completely straight and still, than to move it at all. The pain made him feel strong and reverent, and smiling he whispered silently to Jesus, "It's nothing to what You're doing." Our Father Who are in Heaven, he began; he knew now that he would stay another watch through.

Now it was half past four, but nobody moved. Nobody wants to be the first, he thought. No they're all praying, he told himself. I'm the only one noticed what time it is. Behind him he heard a sound of stealthy entering and of knees coming quietly to the floor. Now somebody will give up their place, he thought. It ought to be me.

Claude tilted his head to the other side and now Richard noticed the translucent lavender beads in his hands. He heard somebody stir and stand wearily up and he knew by the rustling starch that it was the Deaconess. She was in when I came. Been an hour. Maybe more. Quit keeping tabs, he told himself sharply. None of your business. There was the sound of her going away and the sound of another entering. Pray, he told himself. I ought to give my place. It was nearly thirty-three

minutes after. We beseech Thee O Lord pour Thy Grace into
our hearts, that——

The sacristy door opened and there was Lee Allen. He
looked more grave and tired than before and he avoided Richard's eyes with an aloofness which abashed him. That as we
have known the Incarnation of Thy Son Jesus Christ through
the message of an Angel: Lee came silently to the middle and
genuflected; then from where he stood, shifting the extinguish-
ing cone in exact rhythm, he put out seven shrunken candles
to the left and seven to the right. He genuflected again, and
leaned the tall snuffer into the corner, and returned, and genuflected; then strode to the Altar in a quiet and mastering way,
reached delicately among the interlocked flowers, and up-
rooted with each hand a smoking seven-branched candlestick.
He genuflected once again and tiptoed out, shutting the door
to softly with one shoe. Smoke crinkled from each dark candle
as he went. There seemed to be scarcely fewer candles than before, there were so many. There would be others to change,
five on each side; the rest were still tall enough. Through the
message of an Angel, so by His Cross and Passion: he heard
behind him the prudent raising of a window, and for the first
time realized how suffocatingly hot it was, and that he was
sweating. The sacristy door opened and there was George
Fitzgerald. His eyes were softer and brighter with tiredness
than before and his face was white and bright red in patches.
He met Richard's eyes quietly and impersonally. He came to
the middle and genuflected, and Richard could see that he was
looking at all the flowers before he moved. Some still had
strength and some were dying, and now he took two vases of
those which were dying, unmeshing them with great care from
among the others, and genuflected, and tiptoed out, shutting
the door to softly with his shoe. Petals flaked away as he went.
The living air touched the back of Richard's neck; now it even
cooled his forehead; and now, rank on rank, the flames of the
candles acknowledged the invading night; more petals fell.
Upon the fragrance of fire and wax and fresh and dying flowers
there stole the purity of water from a spring. Snaffling it desperately in an inept hand, somebody sneezed. Claude tilted
his head back the first way and started his beads all over again.
Richard heard the sound of bare feet withdrawing and knew

that it must be Hobe and Jimmy. I haven't even said my prayers, he realized. I'm going to stay, he told himself. Give up your
place, he told himself. You got no business hogging it. As
much business as: you got no business thinking that either: as
Claude with his head on one side and those beads. Give up
your place. Come back. Kneel on the floor. The same person
sneezed, more violently but better stifled. Claude, straightening his head, laid his beads down carefully, got up, stepped to
the middle, genuflected, turned, looking like St. Sebastian,
and went to the rear of the Chapel. Richard heard his careful
sliding-shut of the window; the flames stood straight; Claude
returned, and again began his beads at the beginning. Soul of
Christ sanctify me, Richard began aimlessly; the sacristy door
opened and there was Lee Allen.

Richard shut his eyes. O God forgive me that I can't do it
right, he prayed. O God help me do it better now. Make me to
love Thee and to know Thy suffering this day. For Jesus' sake
Amen. He crossed himself meticulously and got to his feet; he
was dizzy and for a moment his knees hurt very badly. He
stepped out of the desk, genuflected, and turned, and all of a
sudden he knew he would have to go out at least for a minute
or two, he was much too tired to stay. When he turned to
genuflect again at the door, Lee was lighting the second of the
tall new candles.

The darkness was cool and stale. From where he stood beside
the door of the Lady Chapel, looking back across the nave, he
saw the spaced badges of blacker darkness where the Stations
of the Cross hung veiled. Tall at his right shoulder, a Madonna
stood, a blind black monolith. He walked silently towards the
middle of the transept, and now he could see the white stops
and keys of the organ. He stood at the center, facing the
stripped Altar; sure that it ought not to be done, but in an
obstinate and loyal reverence, he put down one knee and then
both knees before the desolate shrine: until His coming again.

He bent his head deep toward the floor and heard his voice
whisper slowly and fearfully within him the words which he
suspected, only a priest may utter without blasphemy: For in
the night in which He was betrayed:

His skin crawled.

This is the night in which He is betrayed.

He felt the floor, bitter against his knees, and whispered aloud, "This is the night in which He is betrayed"; and with the whispering it no longer was, and he whispered within himself, He took bread, and brake it, and gave it unto His disciples, saying, Take, eat, this is my Body which is given for you; do this in remembrance of me.

He saw, and was himself, grown and vested, genuflecting, raising the consecrated Host, again genuflecting, while a bowed kneeling boy, who was also himself, shook the three bells.

Likewise after supper He took the cup, and when He had given thanks he blessed it, and gave it unto His disciples, saying, Drink ye all of this, for this is my Blood of the New Testament, which is shed for you and for many for the remission of sins. Do this as oft as ye shall drink it, in remembrance of me.

And with the words For this is my Blood of the New Testament, he knelt so deep in burden of blood that no priestly image entered him, and whispered again, Which is shed for you, and for many, for the remission of sins. And slowly one by one, while his hands lifted, the words stood up within his silence,

O Thou Lord God my Saviour: ("my Saviour," he whispered):

Look down on this Thy child.

Lord bless (he tried); O Lord lift up (he tried); O Lord forgive Thy child.

He could just see the empty Altar. There were no more words.

Do this as oft as ye shall drink it, in remembrance of me.

No more.

"Look down on this Thy child," he whispered aloud.

Now his knees hurt very badly.

"For Jesus' sake Amen," he whispered, crossing his breastbone with his thumb. He stood up.

If he went into the vestry they would say, What you doing up? They would tell him to get on back to bed. Not mean about it because of the night it was but they would tell him all the same. Because it was the rule. Or maybe they wouldn't but if they did and he didn't go on back to bed it would be even

worse than if they hadn't seen him. "I told him Father," he
heard Lee Allen say in his serious hollow voice. "That's right
Father," George Fitzgerald said, nodding soberly. And that
was always worse when somebody had told you; Prefects.
"What did you stay out for then?" "I dunno Father." "Course
you know. Why did you stay out? Why did all of you stay out,
Toole? You heard me tell you all to come straight back to bed."
Where were they? He was suddenly scared. If they had gone
back it would be even worse for him if he didn't go back too.
"Where's Richard?" "I dunno Father." "Course you know,
you all went together. Where is he?" "Honest Father *I* dunno.
Last I seen him he was still in Lady Chapel." That ought to
make it all right. Still in Lady Chapel. He was late but it was
because he was praying. Can't whip anybody for that. "You
know what the rule is." No. He'd say that to him, not them,
him, at Council Meeting; they'd come back in time. "You
know what I told you: come right on back to bed." "But I was
staying a second watch Father. Ask Lee. Ask George if I
wasn't." "I don't care what you were doing I told you to come
straight back to bed and you didn't do any such thing. Now
what have you got to say for yourself?" Or no, maybe he
would look embarrassed and just mutter something about You
see to it you do what you're told, and not punish him. Or no
he would maybe look mad when he heard that about he second
watch and say, "And you've got the nerve to use *that* for an
excuse?" And yet the year before he had stayed a second watch
and there had not been any trouble. But that year nobody had
told him to come right on back to bed. That was the year three
of the boys had never even showed up for the watch they signed
for but went over to Lost Cove and got some whiskey.

If they'd gone on back he was in trouble already.

Breathing light, and the breathing shaken by his heart, with
the greatest possible stealth he approached the vestry door
and, stiffening beside the frame like an Indian scout, spied
slopewise between the door and the jamb. George was carefully arranging wild azaleas in a Karo bucket. Lee was not
there. Hobe squatted against the wall; Richard could see only
his cheek, brown-orange in the light of the fiery mount of
wax, which had grown much larger. Willard hung out all over

the folding-chair; the quietly snoring head lay back and the blue chin was the highest part of it. Jimmy sat on the floor between his thighs; he looked very sleepy. Lee Allen came quickly out of the back passage at the far end and he seemed to look straight at Richard and Richard flinched away and froze, but it was clear by Lee's voice that he had not actually seen him. "Ought to wake up Burgy and send these kids to bed," he said. "They aren't doing any harm," George said. "*I* don't keer," Lee said, "but I don't want to get in no trouble either, you know what they told us." George said nothing for a little while and then he said, "Me neither," and after a while he said, "I don't want you to get in trouble, count of me, Lee. You send them out if you want to. Don't let me hinder you." After thinking, Lee said. "Nobody hindern me." After a little he said, "Where's Sockertees?" which was one of Richard's nicknames, and Richard felt his breathing go thin. And Hobe said, exactly as Richard had fore-heard him, "Last I seen him he was still in Lady Chapel." "Well he ain't there now," Lee said. "Probly went on back to bed," George said. "No," he reflected, "We'd a heard him go out." "Crazy kid," Lee said. Richard tried to be sure whether this was said in affection or dislike, but so far as he could see it was neither, just an indifferent statement of fact. Dislike would almost have been better; and now he knew that he could not go in, right after Lee's saying that, and that although he felt very lonely, and suddenly wanted very much to be in there with them where no fuss was being made about not going to bed, he wanted still more not to be anywhere near them or anywhere near anybody. Crazy kid: crazy kid; yet he could not go away, for they might say more about him. He could hear George saying, "Oh, he's a good kid" or even just "Oh, he's all right," and it made everything much better, he could almost have gone in; but George didn't say anything of the kind, or anything at all, he just seemed to accept it as a fact everybody knew; and after a little Lee said, "I got to thin out them candles some if they're goana last through"; and George did not answer, and Lee said, "I thought there was a whole box more of them," and George said, "Not that I know of": and Lee did not answer, and George said, "If you thin out the candles some, maybe it'll give the flowers a chance, anyhow. I sure do hate to see dead flowers"; and suddenly, frightened because he was spying, Richard shrank as small against the wall as he could, for someone had come out of the Lady Chapel and now he could make out that it was Claude and realized thankfully, He sleeps in St. Joseph's, he'll go out the front. And sure enough Claude came to the middle as if to bow or genuflect and stood there a moment and then tossed his head upward to one side in a peculiar, saucy way, and turned his back on the Altar and walked back up the middle aisle and through the vestibule door; and after a moment Richard could hear the outside door; and then nothing; and after his breathing was quiet again, he crossed the transept without pausing to bow, and went back into the Lady Chapel.

The prayer-desks were all taken; he knelt at the rear on the bare floor and crossed himself, and closed his eyes, and bowed his head. Lord make my mind not to wander, he prayed, successfully driving from his mind Claude's impudent head. This is the last chance, he told himself. By leaning a little he could just see the clock. Already it was nearly quarter of. He felt fury against himself and subdued it, for it was evil. God be merciful unto me a sinner, he prayed, shutting his eyes again.

He waited carefully with his eyes closed but nothing came to him except his emptiness of soul and the pain of his knees and of his back. Hail Mary, he whispered to himself, and went through the prayer twice. He repeated five more Hail Marys rather rapidly and then three very slowly, trying to allow each word its full weight, and still there was nothing, not even through the words Pray for us sinners now and in the hour of our death. What's wrong with me, he wondered. He kept his eyes shut. Perhaps exactly because he had given his knees a rest, they now hurt worse than ever. Or it was because they were now on the flat floor, instead of braced against the edge of a board. The grooves where they had been against the board hurt badly, the bones just below the kneecaps hurt even worse. And within another minute or so, the small of his back ached worse than it had before. He bent over a little, and though that hurt his back in a new way, it also gave it a sort of rest. He let himself slacken down so that his buttocks sat on his heels, and that at least changed the pressure on the bones of his knees. He leaned forward so that his chest almost rested against his knees, and that helped his back. It'll just look like at Adoration, he reflected; and was ashamed of his hypocrisy. All the same, he thought, if it'll help me pray. Hail Mary, he prayed again. But still there was nothing. His heart was empty and his mind was idle, and he could not forget his discomfort.

He opened his eyes and looked around for a kneeling-pad and he saw one, skated against the baseboard, ahead of him and across the Chapel. He would have to get up and go in front of Julian to get it, and Julian was not using one. He hasn't been kneeling as long as I have, he reflected. What of it. He'll think I came in late. Just now. What of it. But the more he thought about it the more clearly he decided he would not go over and get the pad. If I can't say my prayers right, he told himself, why anyhow I can do this. He felt proudly and calmly vindictive against himself. Closely attentive to everything he was doing, he raised himself straight onto his knees and he straightened his spine so that his knees and the small of his back should hurt as much as possible, and he put the heels of his hands together, the fingers extended, edge to edge, tips touching, and the right thumb crossed over the left, as he had been taught when he was learning to be an acolyte. Ordinarily this strange and careful position of the hands embarassed him, for it seemed sissy. Only a few of the servers kept to it; most of them, like Richard, simply folded their hands, and so did most of the priests; but now it seemed no more sissy than being on your knees in the first place. It was just the right way to hold your hands to pray, that was all. For all the aching in his knees and his back he was now even more clearly aware of his hands in this unaccustomed position, the palps of the fingers touching so lightly and competently, the locked thumbs, the cleanly hollow of shaded light within the palms; his hands felt full of goodness and quiet and they made him think of pictures of Cathedrals.

He tried to breathe so quietly that he could not feel his chest go in and out or even any air moving in his nostrils, and he gazed studiously at the monstrance, visualizing through the veil the spangling sunlike gold and the white center, and upon that center Christ Crucified, Whom he saw first in metal and then in wood and then in flesh; but he began to wonder whether these efforts at visualization were not mere tricks and temptations of emptiness, for still he was empty of prayer and of feeling. Now that he forbade himself images and dwelt within the discipline of his body his knees and his back began to hurt worse than ever and he began to think with quiet and increasing amazement of young men, boys really, hardly older than he was, not much older than George anyway, who knelt like this on Chapel stone the whole night through in prayer and vigil, their weapons and armor blessed and waiting, soberly shining in the lambent gloom, before the Mass and the Communion and before the greatest moment of their lives when their King touched the flat of the sword to the shoulder and the young man stood up and was assisted in putting upon himself the whole armor of God and rode forth into the glittering meadows of daybreak for the first time a knight, a knight errant, seeking whatever wrong God might send him to set right, whatever tests of valor and chastity the huge world might hold in ambush for him. O but I can do better than this, he exclaimed to himself in self-contempt; and he thought with envy and reverence of the early time which had belonged to those shining young men, and he pressed down with all his strength and weight, first on one knee and then on the other, so that it was hard not to cry out, and he held his back still more rigidly upright, and he was pleased to find that now, by the way he held his hands out, even his arms ached, deep into the shoulders. But it's so little to do!, he thought, imagining the first living Crucifix; and he did his best to imagine one hand, against splintery wood, and the point of a spike against the center of the open hand, and a great hammer, and the spike being driven through, breaking a bone, tight into the wood so that the head was all buried in the flesh and the splintered bone, and then to be able to say, *Father forgive them for they knew not what they do*. And that's just one hand, he reminded himself. How about both hands. And both feet. Specially both feet crossed on each other and one spike through both insteps. How about when they raise up the Cross with you on it and drop it deep into the hole they dug for it! And imagining that moment he felt a tearing spasm of anguish in the center of each palm and with an instant dazzling of amazed delight, remembering pictures of great saints, shouted within himself, *I've got the Wounds!* and even as he caught himself opening his palms and his eyes to peer and see if this were so he realized that once again this night, and even more blasphemously and absurdly than before, he had sinned in the proud imagination of his heart. *O my God,* his heart moaned, *O my God! My God how can You forgive me!* I'll have to confess it, he realized. I can't. Not this. How can I confess *this!*

The thing he had most dreaded to confess before, an impure act which in its elaborateness had seemed merely the more exciting in the doing and which was so nearly unbearable to specify to another, and a priest at that, that he had gravely considered the risk to his soul of merely generalizing it: beside this new enormity—and twice over in one night, and both times in the Presence—beside this, that ugly and humiliating lustfulness seemed almost easy to tell of. But I'll tell it all the same, he told himself grimly. Because if I don't I'm in mortal sin. No I'll tell it because I did it and I hate to so much, and I don't care who it is I have to tell it to either, I won't dodge whoever it turns out to be and wait for another, not even if it's Father McPhetridge. I'll tell the whole thing just the way it happened—way I thought it happened, that is. I'll tell it all right. Because I've got to.

He looked proudly at the monstrance and felt strength and well-being stand up straight inside him, and self-esteem as well; for it began to occur to him that not many people would even know this for the terrible sin it was, or would feel a contrition so deep, or would have the courage truly and fully, in all of its awful shamefulness, to confess it: and again the strength and the self-esteem fell from him and he was aghast in the knowledge that still again in this pride and complacency he had sinned and must still again confess; and again that in recognizing this newest sin as swiftly as it arose, and in repenting it and determining to confess it as well, he had in a sense balanced the offense and restored his well-being and his self-esteem; and again in that there was evil, and again in the repenting of it there was good and evil as well, until it began to seem as if he were tempted into eternal wrong by rightness itself or even the mere desire for rightness and as if he were trapped between them, good and evil, as if they were mirrors laid face to face as he had often wished he could see mirrors, truly reflecting and extending each other forever upon the darkness their meeting, their facing, created, and he in the dark middle between them, and there was no true good and no true safety in any effort he might ever make to realize or repent a wrong but only a new temptation which his very soul itself seemed powerless to resist; for was not this sense of peace, of strength, of well-being, itself a sin? yet how else could a forgiven or forgivable soul possibly feel, or a soul in true contrition or self-punishment? I'm a fool to even try, he groaned to himself, and he felt contempt for every moment of well-being he could recall, which had come of the goodness of a thought or word or deed. *Everything* goes wrong, he realized. Everything anyone can ever do for himself goes wrong. Only His Mercy. That's what He died for. That's what He's dying for today. Only His Mercy can be any help. Nothing anyone can do but pray. O God, he prayed, be *merciful* unto *me*, a *sinner*. Let me not feel good when I am good. *If* I am good. Let me just try to be good, don't let me *feel* good. Don't let me even *know* if I'm good. Just let me try. And in this humility, aware that it was of a true and pure kind which was new to him, he felt a flash of relief, well-being, pride: and tightening his shut eyes, cried out in despair within himself, *There it is again! O God make it go away. Make it not mean anything. O God what I can't help, please forgive it.* He wanted to put himself down on his face on the floor. *"All my trust I put in Thee,"* he whispered aloud and, aware that he had whispered aloud, opened his eyes in the fear that he had been noticed. Nobody seemed to have noticed. Now Jimmy and Hobe were kneeling a little ahead of him. He found that he was drenched with sweat and as short of breath as if he had been running. He felt weak and quiet. The burden of them is intolerable. He could feel the words sincerely and quietly now yet at the same time they meant nothing to him. All my trust I put in Thee, he repeated silently. O let me not fail Thee.

Tonight.
This very night.
For in the night in which He was betrayed.

Now fragments of his first moment awake returned but now they were dry and tired like dead leaves, as dry and tired as he was. He tried to realize what it all meant. But all that he could realize was dry and tired like the tired dry fire of the candles.

He came into the world to be with us and save us, and this is what happened. This is what it all came to.

The light shineth in darkness and the darkness comprehended it not.

He came unto His own and His own received Him not.

So there He was just sitting there waiting. Just waiting to die.

Words stirred and stood up inside him which lifted his heart: But as many as received Him, to them gave He power to become the sons of God.

And the Word was made Flesh and dwelt among us:

He closed his eyes and bowed his head.

Flesh.

All for us.

All his suffering for all of us.

He remembered the terrible thing his uncle had said: "Well who *asked* him to die for me? *I* didn't. He needn't try and collect on the debt," he had said, "because there's no debt, far's I'm concerned." Nearly always when he thought of this Richard was shocked almost into awe of such blasphemy; and some few times when some priest or his mother was insisting what we all owe Jesus he had been tempted to wonder, wasn't it maybe really so, for it was a fact; Jesus had done it without anybody asking Him to: but now it seemed neither blasphemous nor persuasive but only empty and idle and cruel and as he thought of it he could see the man of whom it had been said, sitting very quietly on a stool or maybe a bench among the iron-breasted helmeted soldiers while they hit him and spat in his face and mocked him. Nobody could come near him or help him or even speak a word of love or thanks or comfort to him now. He could see him only as if he spied down on what was happening through a cellar window and it would be torture and death to dare to even try to get in, and no use could come of it, even if he did. The way, maybe, Peter had stayed. All of Peter's betraying and cowardliness was over and done with now. Nothing could ever wipe out for him what he had done. He wasn't even crying any more because he couldn't even cry any more. He was just hiding around on the outskirts, spying through the window. He was afraid to show himself and he couldn't stand to go away. He must wish he was dead.

Judas, by now, had he hanged himself? Richard couldn't remember for sure when. But if he hadn't yet, that was all there was left for him to do. That was all he was thinking about all the rest of this night, all that was left of his life. I want to die. O I want to be dead. I can't be dead soon enough to suit me. Judas didn't feel contrition, Father Weiler said, he felt remorse. Probably he couldn't cry like Peter. Just terrible cold remorse, as cold and bitter as the sound of the word. Remorse is very different from contrition; a deadly sin. A mortal sin is a sin that cuts us off from God. With remorse you don't feel sorry like contrition, you feel, well you just feel remorse, that's all.

These were just the dead hours. The hours between. They must be the worst hours of all for Jesus and for everyone who loved Him. No more doubt now. No more praying to God the Father, if this Cup can be taken from me: that's over long ago. It can't. That's all. No more judgment, standing trial, answering fool questions. He's already been sentenced to die. He belongs to the Law. Now just the time between. So tired. No sleep all this night. Waiting, getting Himself ready inside, while they mock and sneer and holler at him, and spit in his face, and crown him with thorns, and put the reed in his hand for a scepter, just waiting through the rest of the long night, just getting ready to die, while the night slowly turns into morning, and it's the last morning of all. To suffer so he will cry out, *My God, my God, why hast Thou forsaken me?* And then die. *It is finished.* And then die. And meekly bowing down His head, He gave up the ghost. And then (Richard could remember in advance) the stunned and strange peacefulness, throughout that afternoon and night and through all the next day, and the quiet, almost secret lighting of the tremendous candle in the beginning of the dusk of Holy Saturday, everything still going as if on tiptoe, and then in the first light of morning, the stillest and most wonderful moment of the year, the quietly spoken and simple Mass: "He is risen." And then the rich midmorning and the blinding blaze of Easter. *'Tis the Spring of Souls today, Christ hath burst His prison, and from three days' sleep in Death, like a Sun hath risen.*

But not yet. That is still not known though at the same time it *is* known. We are all in most solemn sorrow and grief and mourning. We know a secret far inside ourselves but we don't dare tell it, even to ourselves. We don't dare to quite believe it will ever really happen again until it really happens again. Until His coming again. For in the night in which He was betrayed. It has happened over nineteen hundred times now and yet it has never happened before. Not yet. And we don't know if it ever can. Never dreamed it could. Can.

Not yet. Now is just the dead time between and he is waiting. This is his last night and his last daybreak begins soon now. Before this day is over he will be dead.

My Jesus, he whispered, clasping his hands strongly; his throat contracted.

O Saviour of the World Who by Thy Cross and Precious Blood hast redee——

O you are dying my dear Lord for me, his soul whispered, wondering, weeping. For *me*, and I can't do anything for you. I can't even comfort you, or speak to you, or thank you. O my Lord Jesus I can thank you. I can think about you. I can try to know what it is you are going through for me. For me and for all sinners. I can know that every sin I do big or no matter how little is a thorn or a nail or the blow of the hammer or even just a fly that teases and hurts you in your blood, crawling and tickling and sipping and eating at you in the hot day on the Cross with you unable to brush him away or even to move, and every good thing, or true thankfulness or thought of love must make it anyway a little less terrible to suffer. My Lord I love Thee. My Lord I grieve for Thee. My dear Lord I adore Thee. My poor Lord I wish I could suffer for Thee. My Lord I thank Thee. Lord have mercy upon me. Christ have mercy upon me. Lord have mercy upon me.

He opened his eyes in quiet wonder. It was indeed to him the very day. Not just a day in remembrance, but the day. There stood His consecrated Body, veiled among fire and flowers, but also living, in the flesh, on this very morning, at this very moment, He was waiting; and He was now within His last hours.

He won't see the sun go down today.

He looked at all the lights, spearing, aspiring, among the dying flowers. Knobbled and fluted with their own spillings, the candles stood like sheaves; some, bent by the heat, bowed over like winter saplings. Almost all the flowers hung their exhausted faces. They were so shrunken and disheveled now that he could see clearly among them the many shapes and sizes of the vessels which held them, the professional vases and ewers and jars, and the tumblers and tin cans from the poor cabins out the Mountain. He could just hear the clock. Tonight, he whispered, watching that devastation. This night This minute. He leaned, and looked at the clock. It was one minute after five. Something troubled him which he had done or had left undone, some failure of the soul or default of the heart which he could not now quite remember or was it perhaps foresee; he was empty and idle, in some way he had failed. Yet he was also filled to overflowing with a reverent and marveling peace and thankfulness. My cup runneth over, something whispered within him, yet what he saw in his mind's eye was a dry chalice, an empty Grail. No more I could do, he reflected, if I stayed all night. No more. No use: and he continued merely to look without thought at the emblazoned ruin. "Goodbye," something whispered from incalculably deep within him. *O goodbye, goodbye,* his heart replied. A strange and happy sorrow filled him. *It is finished,* his soul whispered. He looked at the humbled backs ahead of him and prayed: The peace of God which passeth all understanding keep our hearts and minds in the knowledge and love of God, and of His Son Jesus Christ. And the blessing of God Almighty, the Father, the Son and the Holy Ghost, be amongst us and remain with us always.

He opened his eyes; and it was all as it was before. Of course it was. He was light and uneasy and at peace within. There was nothing to do or think or say.

He signed himself carefully with the Cross, got up, genuflected, and left the Chapel; just inside the north door, he took off his shoes. Hobe and Jimmy came up behind him and they took off their shoes too.

III

They walked down the sandstone steps into an air so different from the striving candles and the expiring flowers that they were stopped flat-footed on the gravel. Morning had not yet begun but the night was nearly over. The gravel took all the light there was in the perishing darkness and shed it upward, and in the darkness among the trees below the outbuildings a blossoming dogwood flawed like winter breath. In the untouchable silence such a wave of energy swept upward through their bare feet and their three bodies into the sky that they were shaken as if a ghost had touched them. Sharply and almost silently, Hobe laughed.

They looked at the last tired stars and at the dark windows of their dormitory and they wondered what their punishment would be.

"S - - t fahr," Hobe said. "Can't even pray, what the f - - - *kin* ye do!"

Maybe, Richard reflected, they wouldn't say anything. Couldn't be a better excuse than praying. In brainless exaltation he flexed the soles of his feet against the ground. What of it if they do.

Rustily, so far down back of them across the fields they could scarcely hear him, a rooster crowed.

"Let's get the rackets," Richard said.

They took it as naturally as if one of them had said it.

"They'd catch us sure," Jimmy said.

"Hell we keer," Hobe said. "Tan our asses anyhow, now."

Creakily, a little nearer, but very faint, a second rooster answered.

Might not, Richard thought; not *anyhow*. What if they do.

"Let's go to the Sand Cut," Hobe said.

"Freeze yer balls off," Jimmy said.

"Sun-up, time we git thur," Hobe said.

Proud, fierce behind the cook's house, the cry of a third rooster shining sprang, speared, vibrated as gaily and teasingly in the centers of their flesh as a jews-harp.

"Come on," Richard said, and started walking rapidly across the pale gravel.

He was surprised that he had spoken and the more surprised to hear them following. How they do it, he thought, stepping along not quite steadily in silent uneasy elation; all there is to it. He led them down past the cook's house.

Pride, he realized; a mortal sin. How do I confess that?

Through the veering wire net he saw, black in the faintness, how the big rooster darted his vigilant head and shuffled his plumage: in the silence before daylight a priest, vesting himself for Mass. Something heavy struck and the whole body splayed, and chuckled with terror; the coward's wives gabbled along their roost.

Richard felt as if he had been hit in the stomach.

I'm scared of both of them, he reflected, specially Hobe, and they know it whenever they want to.

And bigger than either of them, he forced himself to recognize.

Younger. Big for his age that's why I'm clumsy and soft.

Bigger all the same.

Maybe that makes up for the Pride, he thought, as they walked past the bruising foulness of the backhouse.

Privately, safe ahead of them, he struck his breast.

Nothing makes up for anything. Confess you thought it did.

He tried to imagine how to confess it. I have sinned the sin of Pride and some other sin I don't know the name of. I was proud because when I said let's go to the Sand Cut (and it wasn't even me that thought of it first) they came along just as if one of them had said it and all of a sudden I knew that all you have to do is say something and go ahead yourself without waiting and they'll do it. Then something happened that made me know I was scared of them and I admitted to myself I'm : yellow : and then I thought maybe because I made myself admit that, why then I wouldn't have to confess I was proud before. I thought it made up for it.

He tried to imagine the priests to whom he would confess this. Father McPhetridge, Father Whitman, Father Weiler, Father Ogle, Father Fish. Unless maybe if he got Father Fish but even if you tried to dodge and choose which was probably a sin why you couldn't ever tell for sure who you'd get. The others would just think he was crazy or something. Crazy kid. Or trying to get credit. And maybe he would be.

What you say in Confession they never tell because if they do they go straight to Hell. But whoever you confess to, he knows all the same. And if he knows you honestly are trying hard to be good he gives you credit afterwards too, that you sin if you try to get, he can't help himself. And if he thinks you're just trying to get credit why everytime he looks at you from then on you know what he thinks of you.

If he really thought you were, though, probably he wouldn't give you Absolution.

If you know it's a sin why you've got to confess it, no matter what he thinks.

The ferment of the hogpen, deepest of blacks and heaviest of oils, so stuffed and enriched their nostrils that as one they slowed against the fence and looked in. Small as the light was, on all its edges the chopped muck shone like coal. Jimmy slid his hand inside his overalls against his naked body; becoming aware of what he had done, he thoughtfully withdrew it. Straining to see into the darkness of the shed they could just discern the close-lying egglike forms of the hogs.

"Oink: oink," Hobe grunted, in a voice so deep that Richard was surprised.

Crooomphth, a sleeping hog replied.

They crossed the stile and struck into the woods, using their unhardened feet somewhat delicately along the familiar path. It was as thrilling cold and as vague and silent here as leaving a hot morning and stepping into a springhouse, and the smell of dead leaves and decaying wood and of the arising year was as keen as the coldness. A dogwood dilated ahead of them, each separate blossom enlarging like an eye, and swung behind, and deeply retired among the black trees ahead they could see the shining of others in the first light, triumphal and sad, lonesome as nebulae; likewise blind clumps of unawakened laurel; and now as the light became adequate they saw that the floor of the woods was still the leathery color of last year's leaves, meagerly stitched with green. In the deeper distances the woods were neutral as a photograph, as they had been all winter, but nearer by, the trunks of the trees were no longer black. Some were blackish, some were brownish, some were gray and gray green and silver brown and silver green and now the forms and varieties of bark, rugged, mosaic, deeply ribbed and satin sleek, knobbled like lepers and fluted like columns of a temple, became entirely distinct. Some of the twigs looked still as dark and fragile as the middle of winter, many were knobbled and pimpled and swollen as if they were about to break open and bleed, and many were the color of bronze and some were the color of blood; on some there were little buds like the nubbins of young deer and on others new leaves as neatly fledged as the feathering ought to be for the arrows Richard had never been able to make perfectly. They could see a long way into the woods as the morning cleared and everywhere underfoot this leather laid its flat musing waves and everywhere among the retreating trees strayed sober clouds of evergreen and mild clouds of blossom and the dreaming laurels, and everywhere, as deep into the stunned woods as they could see, layer above unwavering layer, the young leaves led like open shale; while, against their walking, apostolically, the trees turned. The path among these winding, dancing trees, new to them since late fall, was supple underfoot, the droning trees against which they laid or slapped their hands felt as alive as the flanks of horses, the air was all one listening joy. While they approached the clearing each held in mind a festival imagination of the plum tree, but it hung black, all crazed elbows, in the widened light. From somewhere, however, the fallen silvers of the ruined house it seemed, they were pursued by the chiding, familiar song of an ambushed bird whose kind they did not know; and at the far side of the clearing Richard stopped short and the others passed him: for here, abject against sharp bark, he found a locust shell, transparent silver breathed with gold, the whole back split, the hard claws, its only remaining strength, so clenched into the bark that it was only with great care and gentleness that he was able to detach the shell without destroying it.

It was as if air had been tightened into substance; only by touch and sight, not at all by weight, could he know he held it. He held it in his cupped hand and looked at the hunched, cloven back, turned it over with one fingertip and examined the brutally elaborate structure of the legs and the little talons. He tested: they could pierce a finger. He turned it again and held it near his eyes: the eyes looked into his. Yes even the eyes were there, blind silver globes which had so perfectly contained the living eyes: even the small rudimentary face in its convulsed and fierce expression, the face of a human embryo, he could remember the engraving in a book of his grandfather's, a paroxysm of armor, frowning, scowling, glaring, very serious, angry, remote, dead, a devil, older, stranger than devils, as early, ancient of days, primordial, as trilobites. Dinosaurs heaved and strove; a pterodactyl, cold-winged, skated on miasmic air, ferns sprang, to make coal in these very coves, more huge than the grandest chestnuts. Silurian, Mesozoic, Protozoic, Jurassic, all the planet one featureless and smoky marsh, Crowns, Thrones, Dominions, Principalities, Archaeozoic, through all ranks and kingdoms, to the central height, armed in the radiant cruelty of immortal patience, Ages and Angels marched clanging in his soul.

When did he come out? Just now? Just this spring? Or has he stayed all winter. And that would mean all fall and summer before.

I'd have seen him; last fall; last spring.

If he was there all the time and I didn't before, how come I saw him now?

All winter. All year. Or just since the first warm weather. Or just now before I found him.

That whole split back. Bet it doesn't hurt any worse than that to be crucified.

He crossed himself.

He sure did hold on hard.

He tried to imagine gripping hard enough that he broke his back wide open and pulled himself out of each leg and arm and finger and toe so cleanly and completely that the exact shape would be left intact.

With veneration, talon by talon, he re-established the shell in its grip against the rigid bark.

By the time he caught up with Hobe and Jimmy they were almost to the railroad track.

At the far end of the break in the woods along the far side of the track they saw the weathered oak tower and soon, walking more briskly along the ties, the relics of machinery and the dead cones of putty-colored sand and the wrinkled sandstone and, at length, the sullen water itself, untouched in all these cold months. There were black slits along the sides of the tower where planks had fallen during the winter. The water was motionless and almost black. The whole place, familiar as it was, was deadly still, and seemed not at all to welcome them. As they left the track to round the near end of

the Sand Cut there was a scuttling among the reddened brambles but although they went as fast as they could on their soft
feet and threw rocks where the brambles twitched with noise
they got no glimpse of whatever it was, and soon the scuttling
stopped.

Now that they had stopped walking and stood in the brightened silence of the open light the day began to look practical;
they realized how chilly the air still was, even here out of the
woods, and how bitter the water looked, and they no longer
felt like going in. But none of them was willing to admit this
frankly even to himself, and it was only after they stripped
that they became openly hesitant. They took care not to shiver
more visibly than they could help or to appear to dawdle,
either, but they did all dawdle, and they found that they were
looking at each other, in this unhabitual place and hesitant
quietness, with more interest than in the dormitory. Although
Jimmy was the smallest of the three in every other way, his
was much the biggest and during the winter he had grown
much more hair than Richard had realized up to now. Hobe
still didn't have much but then he was said to be part Indian
so of course he wouldn't, yet, and probably never would have
a lot. What he did have was dark, though, and showed up well
against his dark skin, whereas Richard's was so light and there
was so little of it that he realized it could probably not be seen
at all, farther away than his own eyes. He suspected, however,
that his was really the biggest, because it looked as if Jimmy
had at least half a hard-up. Jimmy looked comfortable in his
supremacy whether it was real or not (he certainly had more
hair, anyhow, there wasn't any getting around that) and seemed
to feel none of the embarrassment which Richard always felt
acutely if he was seen with even a little bit of a hard-up. He
turned partly away, though, in honor of Good Friday, and for
the same reason he and Richard glanced at each other with
even less candor than they would have at any other time, and
Richard the more uneasily crossed and uncrossed his hands
in front of himself. Only Hobe, of any boy Richard knew, never
concealed his own body or his interest in another, and even
now, Good Friday seemed to mean nothing to him. He looked
at them, and watched them look at him, with a coolness which
seemed almost amused. He urinated a few drops onto his belly

and rubbed it in with the palm of his hand, against cramps. He made no gesture of covering himself and grabbed his testicles with one hand only at the instant he grabbed his nose with the other to leap with a spangling splash into the water.

He bounced up with an incredulous strangling yell and began a frenzied dogpaddle and both of them knew the water must be even colder than they had thought, and that there was no longer any chance of holding back. Jimmy went in feet first; Richard dove. The iron water distended enormously just beneath him and for an instant, knowing the brutal shock and the pain to which he had now inescapably committed himself, he felt the fatal exhilaration of a falling dream and had just time to dedicate within himself *for Thee!*, in a silent shout as deafening bright as a smiting of cymbals; then plunged into the smashing cold. Still crying *for Thee* within his ringing head, he slanted his hands to dive as deep as he could go and, though his eyes were open, could see nothing of the steep sandstone along which his hands guided him, but only the stifled effulgence of light above. It was so much colder than he had been able to imagine that in the first moment he had felt almost unconscious, but the diver's reflex had locked his breath and now that he searched from ledge to ledge downward along the much colder bottom there sprang throughout his flesh such an ardent and serene energy that he was aware of the entire surface of his body as if it were fire, and every muscle seemed to feel its own exact shape and weight, and he wished that he need never come up and lay against the deepest trench of the bottom, his belly foundering in ooze, his eyes shut, staying his hands on rocks. He lifted his face free of the ooze and cautiously opened his eyes; he could feel, more clearly than be sure he saw, the light which enlarged above him. He turned his head and looked up sidelong; there it was, a pure, heavy slab of still light which by imperceptible degrees shaded downward into most deadly darkness. His chest and his head began to knock, it became harder with every pulse to hold onto the rocks. O Lord let me suffer with Thee this day, he prayed, his lungs about to burst; and took hold more firmly. You got no right, his own voice silently told him, you got no right. No right; but still he fought off his need for air, filling his cheeks with the exhausted air from his lungs and taking it down again in the smallest possible gulps. His head was beating and ringing so fiercely that he could scarcely hear the fragments of his own efforts to dedicate and to reprove himself but blindly, with the last of his strength, held himself down. Then he knew that he had stayed down too long; too deep; he could not possibly reach the air in time. Good. That's fine. *For Thee!* he groaned. *No right! Get out!,* he shouted silently. But even before he could command it or fully decide to command it his body was working for him; his feet braced against a ledge, his knees bent, and he leapt upward through the brightening water with more strength than he had realized he had left although the water seemed interminably tall above him and he knew still that he would never reach the surface in time and cried out to himself, *I didn't have the nerve!* and, *Anyhow I tried,* meaning at once that he had tried to stay down too long as an act of devotion and that he had tried to save himself from the deadliest of sins; and broke the surface in time, head back, gasping, feebly treading water, watching the streaming bruise-colored clamorous and silent whirling of the world and taking in air so deeply that his lungs felt as if they were tearing; and soon the world became stable and all of the coloring and discoloration cleared and stood up strongly through the top of the woods across the tracks and he could realize that except for the remote voices of the two boys and the still more remote voice of a bird the world itself was delicately silent and all the noise was within his own head and was rapidly dying: all that he saw still twitched with his pulse and out of the woods, beating like a heart, the sun stood up.

His teeth still ached at their roots and although he clenched them to keep them from chattering his chin trembled like a rabbit's nose and his breath came out shakily in many small pieces as of glass or ice. From its surface down to about his waist, the water seemed surprisingly warm, but from waist to knees it was grimly cold, and his stony feet trod a mortal bleakness of cold and dark to which he was thankfully sure now that he would never go down again. Yet except for his feet, which no longer seemed to belong to him, his body still blazed with pleasure in its existence, and it was no longer urgent and rigid but almost sleepy. He slid his slick hands along his ribs and his sides and found that in his sex he was as tightly shrunken as if he were a baby. I could have died, he realized almost casually. *Here I am!* his enchanted body sang. I could be dead right now, he reflected in sleepy awe. *Here I am!* Now that he had his breath and was quiet he no longer tried to control the rattling of his teeth but hung standing in the water, his head so turned from the others that they might not see the silent unexpected tears and, drowsily trying to make himself aware of the suffering to which at this moment Jesus was submitting Himself, crying for tenderness and thankful wonder, gazed steadily into the beating sun.

But staying still so long, coldness at length overcame him, and after swimming as fast as he could twice up and down the length of the quarry, he stumbled out.

He had all but forgotten them; they were already drying themselves with their shirts. Hobe's body was purplish; Jimmy looked as if he had been caught in a blue net.

"What you trine to do?" Hobe asked. "Drownd yourself?"

"I was just swimming under water."

"I was damn near ready to dive in after you," Jimmy said, "when you come up."

"We began to think you was drownded," Hobe said.

"No, I was all right," Richard said. He reached for his shirt. *"Heyy!"* he shouted.

Steering, serenely, his sutured brow, the sum of those several thrusting curves which seemed not of themselves to exert strength but merely to drink and send backward through them the energies of the guiding head they guided, a snake more splendid than Richard had ever seen before was just achieving a sandstone ledge and the first heat of the risen sun. In every wheaten scale and in all his barbaric patterning he was new and clear as gems, so gallant and sporting against the dun, he dazzled, and seeing him, Richard was acutely aware how sensitive, proud and tired he must be in his whole body, for it was clear that he had just struggled out of his old skin and was with his first return of strength venturing his new one. His style and brightness, his princely elegance, the coldness of his eye and the knifelike coldness and sweetness of his continuously altering line, his cold pride in his new magnificence, were not at the first in the least dismayed, not even by Richard's shout; only the little tongue, to Richard's almost worshiping delight and awe, sped like a thready horn of smoke, the eye seemed to meet Richard's and become colder and still more haughty, and the vitality of his elegance advanced him still further along the stone: so that for a few seconds Richard saw perfected before him, royally dangerous and to be adored and to be feared, all that is alien in nature and in beauty: and stood becharmed. But as the others ran up, within an instant so swift that it was impossible to see just what transpired among those curves of liquid paroxysm, with a chilly rasping against stone which excited Richard as nothing he had ever heard before had excited him, drawing a stripe of coldness down his spine, the snake reversed direction and slipped rapidly between the ankles of briars and beneath fallen leaves, his brilliance a constant betrayal. The others were shouting and Jimmy shoved a stick under the snake and flipped him so expertly that for a couple of seconds he sailed on the air in a convulsion of escape, a fluid hieroglyph, and landed on open rock in a humiliating flash of ivory belly before he righted himself and with oily fleetness made once more for the bushes. But now Hobe reared up a rock so heavy he could lift it only clumsily, high above his reeling head; and Richard, standing just behind him, felt himself reach towards the rock to pull it backwards out of his hands. But even as his own hand lifted forward he became aware of Jimmy's astounded eye on him, and thus became aware of what he was doing and caught himself, realizing that they would never understand why he did it, that they would be angry with him and rightly so and might even be mad enough to jump on him; and becoming thus aware, became aware also that it was not only his habit of gentleness to animals which made him want to spare the snake, but something new in him which he could not understand, about which he was profoundly uneasy. These several kinds of awareness came over him with terrible speed and transfixed him into the slowness of a dream, so that the fraction of a second froze the high rock, the incredulous bystander, the bemused hand, and seemed to last almost interminably, while he strove to stay his hand and to set it free. But it was after all only an instant, and before he could bring himself out of this hesitation, Hobe brought the rock crashing down against rock and against one arc of the veering snake which, angled like a broken whip, continued uselessly to thrust

energy through its ruptured body, its eyes terrible, its tongue
so busy that its speed made the shadow of a blossom. Jimmy
hurried up with his stick and beat at its head but the head
was still alert to dodge under his blows. Richard felt for a moment as if he had just finished retching. Then he picked up a
small rock and yelling *Get out of the way,* squatted beside
the snake and pounded at its head. The head lashed about his
fist like summer lightning as he pounded and in the darkness
of his violence the question darted, over and over, *is he poison? is he poison?* but he cared only for one thing, to put as
quick an end as he could to all this terrible, ruined, futile
writhing and unkillable defiance, and at length he struck and
dazed, and struck and missed, and struck and broke the head
which nevertheless lifted senilely, the tongue flittering and the
one remaining eye entering his own eye like a needle; and
again, and the head lay smashed and shifting among its debris;
and again, and it was flattened against the stone, though still
the body, even out beyond the earlier wound, lashed, lay resting, trembled, lashed.

As he watched this trembling twitching, desperately wishing that he could so crush the snake that it would never move
again, he realized that it would not die until sundown, and
even as he realized this he heard Hobe say it and became
aware, through something quiet in Hobe's voice and through
Jimmy's shyness, that they respected him; that in putting his
bare hand within range of that clever head and in killing so
recklessly and with such brutality, he had lost their contempt
and could belong among them if he wanted to. He looked
coldly at his trembling hand: bloody at the knuckles and laced
with slime, which seemed to itch and to burn as it dried, it
still held the rock.

"Better warsh that stuff off," Hobe said. "Git in your blood:
boy!"

He still squatted, looking at his hand and wondering. In
their good opinion, and in the rugged feeling of the hand itself
and its ferocious moisture, he began to feel that he had
been brave in a way he had never been brave before and he
wanted the hand to clear gradually and naturally, the way
the smudge clears from the forehead on Ash Wednesday. He
could not be sure, in its pristine skin, what kind of snake this

was, and the head was wrecked beyond any hope of determining whether it had the coffin shape, or venomous fangs. But it was not a rattler, nor was it likely a copperhead, nor was it striped like a moccasin, so that he had to doubt whether, after all, it had been poisonous. If it had not been poisonous he had not been brave; and if it had not been poisonous he was sorry he had killed it or even been fool enough to yell so the others would see it and so automatically kill it, for he had for a long while been fascinated by snakes and had felt that the harmless ones ought to be let alone, as few people let them alone. He was aware that Hobe had spoken and that he had given no kind of answer, and this made him uneasy. He wanted very much to taste the slime; but they were watching. He turned up the rock and looked at it: the slime and breakage of the snake caught the whitening sunlight like mica. He slammed the rock into the middle of the water (just about where I dove in, he realized upon reflection) and clambered cautiously down to the edge and thrust his hand into the cold water and up to the elbow, beating quietly in the brilliant cold, and watched it in the water; the veins stood out on his forearm almost like a man. He decided that he would only submerge his hand, not wash it, no matter what Hobe advised. But Hobe said nothing.

They dressed thoughtfully and they had very little to say; now that they were on their way back there wasn't much to think about except the trouble which waited for them. There would have been trouble even if they had come straight back from Chapel, for they had outstayed the watch they had signed for by a long time. But they began to realize now that it would not have been as bad as it was bound to be now; maybe they'd even have been let off. If they had gotten back to bed at any time before daylight it wouldn't have been as bad as it would be now. If they had come in just while the sun was rising it would have been bad but not as bad as this. Now it was broad daylight and brighter every minute, and with every minute longer now that they stayed away they were in for worse trouble. They might be kept on bounds, they might have to pull stumps or clean out the pit of the backhouse, they might be whipped, they might even not be let go on the Easter Monday picnic and they had planned to go clear to Wet Cave which had never yet been fully explored, and find new passages and if possible, a new and secret entrance. There was no telling what, for the worst of it was that they had gone against a strict rule so conspicuously on Good Friday, and by taking advantage of a religious event, and there was no way of imagining how much more serious an offense this might seem to priests than to people. The train came down from Coal City and passed them while they dressed, making a great deal of happy and vigorous noise, but it only sharpened their realization that by now everybody was up and around and that certain people would be looking for them and watching for them already, so that they hardly even had the heart to look up at the blank baggage car and the empty coach and to wave at the engineer who saluted them.

Richard didn't even look up as the train passed, nor had the thought of punishment very clearly entered his mind; all the while he dressed, he watched the snake. From the break on back it lay belly up and the pallor of the belly, and the different structure of the scales, so well designed for crawling, were quietly sickening to see. He tried to see all that he could see without looking at the annihilated head, but his eyes kept flicking back to where it lay, mashed almost like soft metal against the rock, almost as flat and ragged as the toadfrogs and pennies they used to put on the tracks in Knoxville, after the streetcar ran over them. The snake moved very weakly now, but strongly enough that Richard could not doubt it would keep moving, and blindly experiencing the agony of death, straight on through the morning and the Three Hour Service and on through the afternoon until, at last, as the top rim of the sun sank out of sight, the tip of the tail would give one last quaver and the snake would lie still forever.

"Well come on," he was startled to hear Hobe's voice at his shoulder. He turned to go.

"Ain't you takin him?"

It had not occurred to Richard; now that it did, he certainly did not want him.

"No."

"Hell fahr, you kilt him didn you?"

"I don't want him."

Hobe and Jimmy glanced at each other. "Okay," Hobe said.

He took the snake carefully by the tail. The break in the body held firm; the head pulled loose from the rock like adhesive tape. He snapped him like a whip; now most of the head was lost.

"He'll bust in the middle," Jimmy said.

"Hell I keer," Hobe said. But he did not snap the snake again. Half a snake wouldn't be worth showing.

On the far side of the track they fell into single file for the woods path, Hobe ahead, swinging the limpid snake at the new leaves, then Jimmy, then Richard. Without consulting or imitation, all three had put their shoes on when they dressed; they walked rather quickly, and they did not talk.

In refusing the snake, Richard realized, he had lost a considerable portion of their esteem, though not all of it. He was still regarded as the hero of this occasion and he knew he was still one of them in a way he had never been before. He was still pleased to have been accepted and still pleased with his own courage, though he was sorry the snake had been killed, and unhappy and uneasy whenever he caught a glimpse of it ahead. He began to know how very hungry he was and with his hunger he remembered once again, with surprise and shame that he could have forgotten, what Day this was. It must be on past seven o'clock by now. He would not start carrying the Cross until nine. By now He would just be sitting on the stool or the bench in the garrison room, probably sort of like a locker room, while the soldiers paid Him no attention much but just hogged their breakfasts and maybe threw cornbread at Him, no it wouldn't be cornbread; He just sat there with nothing to eat or drink and some of the worst things were already over by now; He sat in the purple robe holding the reed and the blood was drying on His back from the scourges and the torn wounds were itching and the spit was drying on His face (like my hand is drying), not just spit but the nastiest kind of snot, too, if it happened here they'd spit tobacco juice, and down through the drying spit the blood ran from the Crown of Thorns; how did they push those thorns down around His forehead without hurting their hands? And here I am, he thought, suddenly remembering the absoluteness of emotions during the moments just after he woke up that morning. Here I am. He struck his breastbone and tried to imagine how it would feel to be scourged with a cat-o'-nine-tails with lead tips, and to wear a crown of thorns. Busy with twisted and uneven walking, he could not make it very clear to himself. He closed his eyes and almost immediately stumbled on a root. Jesus falls for the first time, he said to himself. God help me. God forgive me I didn't mean it. He kept his eyes open and took care how he walked.

The woods were full of ordinary sunlight now; the colors were no longer strange and the deep perspectives were no longer mysterious, but pleasant and casual. When they came to the clearing it was full of simple light and the bird was no longer singing. When they had come nearly to the other side of this warm open silence Richard hurried back to the tree on which he had left the locust shell, detached it gently, and with great care, scarcely looking at it, settled it into the breast-pocket of his shirt. They were not far into the woods when he caught up. His trotting and quick breathing, now that he slowed again to a walk, made him aware once more of his sharp hunger. It was going to be a long day without food, without, if he could help it, even rinsing his mouth out with water. I'll help it, he told himself, imagining water in his mouth. I'll not do that, anyhow. He thought again of the thorns, and the spittle, and the patience and courage, and of his maculate hand. The least I can do, he told himself. The *least* I can do! The day lifted ahead of him very long and hard, a huge un-shaded hill. The climbing of it would go on in the heavy sun without rest throughout this livelong day and forever so long as he might be alive and there at the top there was dying: His; his; so hard and so long. It won't be over till sundown, he said to himself. Such a terrible and cold heaviness distended in the pit of his stomach, and his knees became suddenly so weak, that for a few moments he had to lean against a tree, and found it difficult to breathe. He had never before known such heaviness or such cold, crushing sorrow *"Forgive!"* he whispered, barely able to bring the word out: *"Forgive! O God forgive!"* But the cold and enormous heaviness only increased, and the sadness now seemed more than his soul could endure.

After a little, however, he regained sufficient strength in his knees, and walked again, by now a good way behind the others. But the heaviness stayed, so that he felt as if he were carrying an all but impossible weight in the middle of his body.

By now they could see the first of the buildings through the lightleaved woods; and now the whole of the School stood up before them and the two boys ahead walked more slowly, wondering what lie, if any, might lighten their trouble. But they could not think of any that would do and when Richard over-took them, lingering unhappily at the stile, they were so far beyond hope that they didn't even bother to ask him whether he had any ideas.

Now that he was with them again, the heaviness was some-what less severe, and he began to wonder what had made him so deeply weak and unhappy, and what kind of trouble they would be in for; now he could clearly foresee Father Whit-man's hard sleepless eyes in his first look at them as they would come up from the woods, their hair spiky with incrimi-nating wetness; and much as he dreaded in advance the punish-ment, which would be a whipping for sure, he told himself, he dreaded even more the first meeting with these eyes, and the first words that would be spoken, though he suspected that these would be tempered to the day. He heard Jimmy say to Hobe that he better get rid of that snake, and he thought that he sure better; and he was neither surprised nor particularly troubled when, a few moments later, Hobe slung the snake in among the hogs. He stood with the other children at the fence and watched with interest while two of the hogs, with snarling squeals, scuffled over the snake, tore it apart at its middle wound and, while the two portions still tingled in the muck, gobbled them down. It occurred to him, with a lancing quailing of horror and pity, that the snake was still alive, and would stay alive in their bellies, however chewed, and mangled, and diffused by acids, until the end of the day; but now, re-membering the head, he told himself that the snake was so far gone by now that he must be a way beyond really feeling any-thing, ever any more (the phrase jumped at him): (Who had said that? His mother. "Daddy was terribly hurt so God has taken him up to Heaven to be with Him and he won't come back to us ever any more.") "Ever any more," he heard his quiet voice repeat within him; and within the next moment he ceased to think of the snake with much pain. When the boys turned from the sty he followed them towards the Main Building carrying, step by step with less difficulty, the diminishing weight in his soul and body, his right hand hanging with a feeling of subtle enlargement at his thigh, his left hand sustaining in exquisite protectiveness, the bodiless shell which rested against his heart.